# SHOWBIZ

Published by ECW PRESS
2120 Queen Street East, Suite 200, Toronto, Ontario, Canada M4E 1E2

LIBRARY AND ARCHIVES CANADA CATALOGUING IN PUBLICATION

Anderson, Jason, 1972-
Showbiz / Jason Anderson.

ISBN-10: 1-55022-714-9
ISBN-13: 978-1-55022-714-7

I. Title.

PS8601.N437S56 2005      C813'.6      C2005-904128-5

Editor: Jennifer Hale
Cover Design: David Gee
Text Design: Tania Craan
Production & Typesetting: Mary Bowness
Printed by: Marc Veilleux Imprimeur

This book is set in Futura and AGaramond.

The publication of *Showbiz* has been generously supported by the Canada Council, the Ontario Arts Council, the Ontario Media Development Corporation, and the Government of Canada through the Book Publishing Industry Development Program. Canadä

DISTRIBUTION
CANADA: Jaguar Book Group, 100 Armstrong Avenue, Georgetown, ON, L7G 5S4
UNITED STATES: Independent Publishers Group, 814 North Franklin Street, Chicago, Illinois 60610

PRINTED AND BOUND IN CANADA

ECW PRESS
ecwpress.com

JASON ANDERSON

# SHOWBIZ

ECW Press

*Two minutes to showtime. Ladies and gentlemen, Jimmy's hands are proud to host the pre-show jitters. Give them a big round. Don't be cheap.*

*He works the spaces in between thumbs and fingers. The skin there is scratchy, yet the palms are moist. He rocks on his heels, slightly. His thoughts get stuck in a cluster: cmoncmoncmonletsgoletsdothis. He hates to wait. He puts himself together, working down the checklist. The Boston bray and the hurried pace, the chewy elocution and the twenty-buck words, the hard "uhhrr" and "ahh" and the slight uptick at the end of the line that says, "You know I'm your pal, c'mon and loan me the money, I'm good for it." Jimmy juts his jaw as far forward as it'll go then brings it back to calibrate the position.*

*Jimmy knows he's nailed not just the president's voice but the way he presents words to the world, presents himself. What he conveys is the aura of old money, the kind that ages in oak barrels. It's the finesse that makes panties disappear so fast, they whistle in the wind. It's the priestly authority to change everything about the world where you live. And Jimmy mastered it without the benefit of a Yale education. When you've got what the critics call "an amazing ear for cadence" ("How to Wynn Friends and Influence People,"* Hancock's *magazine, Dec. 12, 1961) and "a nutty knack for mimicry" ("New in the clubs," Variety, Sept. 22, 1959), you don't need the Ivy League to be president. You don't even need a ballot box.*

*A gap between the curtains lets the light in. A long white rectangle falls on Jimmy's shoes. The shine seems a little much. Black shouldn't be so glossy, he thinks. Should be matte. He's not going out there to tap-dance. This act is classy, sophisticated — it's satirical. Glossy says razzmatazz, not dignified. He drives his thumb deeper into the meat of his palm. He thinks: fuggit, too late to fix. Maybe the jerk-off in the rafters will kept the spotlight off his feet.*

*He peers through the gap, being careful not to be seen. The folks in the front row are practically bouncing in their seats, already aching for a hit of his stuff. Where tonight? Chicago. Chicago has been good to Jimmy. It's his third time here this year. Chicago audiences are good and loud — he gets the kind of full-throated, deep-bellied laughs you hear from the well-fed. These aren't the desperate yelps from the cheap-suited jackals and sad-assed vampires Jimmy heard (if he was lucky) when he was plugging away in cellar dives. Nope, it's a big-city crowd tonight. They love their Cannon. The cities were all behind him, Chicago even more so. Jimmy's not supposed to know it (he was told strictly on the q.t. by a numbers guy) but Cannon had Vincent Delrocco to thank for the scale of the victory here. Delrocco's boys voted early, they voted often.*

*Cmoncmonletsdothis. Youmiserablecocksuckerhurrygetitoverwith-nownow. Still too much Jimmy inside. He squeezes those little bundles of tendons then fidgets with his tie. Steve — MC, bandleader, compère beyond compare — slides in from stage right. The crowd goes, is it him? Could it be? Nah, just some schmuck. They clap anyway. Steve's open-ing spiel is sugar-cane sweet and buttery smooth. Jimmy can always count on Steve to set him up right. When Jimmy plays with Danny, neither guy is inclined to be so generous. Jimmy's done with Danny now. Solo all the way.*

*It's only a few moments to go. Cannon's voice takes up more space in* the tight confines of Jimmy's skull. There's a yelp of residual Jimmy-ness before it's banished for the evening. It's a nothing thing, gone in an instant. Its supremacy now unchallenged, Cannon's voice gives Jimmy his body. The shoulders hunch, then draw him forward five, maybe ten degrees. The hands relax, the fingers tingling at the tips. As he readies himself for the big thumbs-up, Jimmy feels that juicy ripple of power run up and down his spine. The friendly twinge in his cock says bingo. Jimmy feels rightly presidential.

Jimmy hears the last of Steve's gold-plated spiel, which he crafted himself. "Number one recording artist in America!" "The toast of Las Vegas!" "Your comedy commander-in-chief!" Jimmy grabs the edge of the curtain, makes his space, and walks on through. He owns this night.

"Where any American can be BLAM!
The nation must be defended and BLAM!
The, ah, dawn of the next century BLAM!"

I listened to the looped litany of rhetoric and violence pouring out of the car stereo. I knew the voice — we all knew the voice. And like everyone in the room that night, I'd heard most of the words before in other, more reverent contexts. Now they'd been diced, scrambled, fried, and refried. The artist had strung together tiny excerpts of speeches by President Cannon then punctuated each fragment with the sound of a gunshot. Since the fragments were all roughly the same length, the shots created a steady beat — it was like a hip-hop track in which the rapper dodged a bullet after delivering every line. Thus was Cannon's familiar oratory style juxtaposed with the blunt aural signifier of his violent death — to wit, BLAM!. When I first heard it, I was impressed. After another two minutes, its value as entertainment had plummeted.

"The, ah, Ladies Home Auxiliary BLAM!
Students should ask not what they can do BLAM!
Millions of hungry children who miss BLAM!"

The car itself was a black 1962 Flavelle convertible, the same make and model as the car Cannon was killed in. The actual death car had a room of its own in the Smithsonian. This facsimile was parked in the centre of a white-walled gallery in Chelsea. The body of the car was spotted with bullet holes, several of them wet with what looked like blood. I thought: what kind of mileage do you get in a car with stigmata?

The convertible was surrounded by a cordon of yellow police tape and a wine-swilling throng of media professionals in black blazers and art scenesters in reconditioned clothes and battered sneakers. They talked through and over the racket blaring from the Flavelle's stereo. Valiant and determined as he'd been in life, their former leader sallied forth.

"The men of the 66th Congress BLAM!

We've got some entertainers who BLAM!

The fine, free-thinking people of BLAM!"

It was getting old. It all was. I had been standing around the gallery for half an hour, wallflowered once again by my friend Colin. He would do this to me sometimes — invite me somewhere promising free drinks and stimulating company, then leave me standing alone in a room full of sleekly dressed magazine folk who ignored me with the same efficiency in person as they did my phone calls and e-mails. Colin didn't inflict these woes upon me out of cruelty. His single-mindedness deprived him of tact. He would see someone he needed to cajole about some arcane aspect of the Cannon assassination and would forget about me. I would get our drinks and stake out a position in the room, shifting my weight from one foot to the other while his beverage grew warmer in my hand. I had the desperate air of a child that had been abandoned in a department store and was in the process of soiling himself.

That night, the site of my slow mortification was a media preview reception for *Cannon: A President and His Art*. This was not the exhibition itself — it was still in Los Angeles and wouldn't be in New York for another two months. As a result, the gallery only featured two pieces. The first was the car, a new installation work by Vito Acevedo. According to the pamphlet I struggled to read while holding a drink in each hand, it was called *Death Car: Cannon* (1998). I would have preferred something more like *The Antithesis of Parallax* or *The Icarus Kitchen* or *Untitled No. 19* or *It's Conceptual, You're Not Supposed To "Get" It.*

The second artwork was a nondescript photo collage by a Norwegian artist on the other side of the room. I fixated on a woman instead. I marveled at the delicacy of her features and the snugness of her sweater but it was her laugh that I noticed when I'd walked past her ten minutes earlier. The sound was musical and generous in spirit. She punctuated it with a shoulder shiver and a series of short breathy bursts. She was still talking to an olive-skinned man whose hair was short and spiky at the sides. I could tell that she enjoyed what he said though now I was too far away to hear her. There was only the ceaseless bombast of Cannon's death car rap, this weary monologue of perpetual assassination.

I was impatient for Colin's return. Whenever I accused him of neglecting me, Colin would say I wasn't taking advantage of the opportunity to network with editors and fellow writers who were far more prominent than I was. "These are the people who can make you," he told me once. "Give them a reason to."

That night in Chelsea, I had no such reason. I had only my envy for their style, confidence, and finesse. I had only the dying embers of the idiotic ambition that brought me to New York so that I could quietly fail. I didn't belong among their number. These people were actively conquering the world, whereas I'd used up all my resources getting out of Canada. I thought: no one sees me, no one at all. I thought: oh god, Nathan, could you cut the pity party for two minutes?

I looked around the room for my missing friend. Colin had been my ally since we were interns together at *Hancock's* magazine. His subsequent rise to prominence in the pages of *The Betsey* did not prevent him from consorting with me and I was pitifully grateful, despite his tactlessness. My gaze fell on Ms. Sweater again. She excitedly greeted another male companion. His hair was also short and spiky at the sides. I thought: maybe that haircut would work for me. I had been looking for ideas — for writing magazine stories, for making contacts, for getting noticed. So far the haircut was the only idea with promise.

"Connie and I would be very BLAM!

If a hunter wants to bag a bear BLAM!

The taxes faced by the average BLAM!"

I was getting a headache. I had finished my drink and was halfway through Colin's when I felt a flicker of nausea, too. Initially, I took it for a product of my anxiety. Then I noticed the stench of vomit wafting through the room. I'd been too busy watching Ms. Sweater to notice the commotion near the car. There was a man with his back to me, leaning over the side of the Flavelle. His shoulders were heaving as he retched onto the driver's seat.

"Germany is a country under BLAM!

The scourge of organized crime BLAM!"

A security guard with a gingery goatee came to the man's side and grabbed his elbow. The man tried to shake him off. I thought: this guy must be loaded. But he seemed perfectly sober when he resumed his standing position and carefully wiped his mouth with a handkerchief. The guard began to pull him away from the befouled installation piece. The art work was pungent. I saw people waving their hands in front of their faces and pinching their noses. Ms. Sweater put her hand over her mouth as if she might follow the man's example. I thought: I'll hold her hair back if she needs me to.

The man wrenched his arm away from the guard and leaned over the car again. I thought: he's not done. But instead of a further bout of reverse peristalsis, he reached out to punch the dashboard. Cannon's voice came to a halt.

"Wake up!" cried the man in a high nasal voice. "He lives among you! Wake up and see!"

I thought: maybe this is a performance-art thing. It was a good idea because the installation needed another dynamic element. But I couldn't understand what the vomit was supposed to represent, or why it had to smell so bad, or what the apocalyptic religious vibe was supposed to add to the experience.

People began to leave the gallery.

"Is this for real?" said a man behind me.

"It's some Cannon nut," said another man. "Some parties put anybody on the guest list."

A female gallery employee in wire-rimmed glasses blocked my view. "We need you to leave," she said as she hustled a group of us toward the door. "It's for your own safety."

"But I —"

"Please, sir, we don't know if it's an art terrorist or the real kind."

That was a good point, but I still resented her for being a killjoy. The mystery man was the hit of the evening. I was raised to believe in the right of free expression and the sanctity of copyrighted material but such was my sour mood, I enjoyed the despoiling of Acevedo's art work. It amazed me that Cannon's martyrdom — now thirty-five years in the past — continued to inspire so much pretentious crap. The art world needed more hecklers with nervous stomachs.

Nevertheless, I did appreciate the fresh air (or the Manhattan version of same) awaiting me outside. As the gallery crowd emptied out onto 23rd Street, I lost track of Ms. Sweater and found Colin instead. He was typically blasé.

"Show's over," he said. "I didn't even have time for a drink."

I let that comment slide. "Do you want to stick around to see what happens? It could be a good bit for *The Betsey*."

"I can't see how they'd be interested," he said. "Their office attracts his type every day. This one had the right idea, though. The inaccuracy of the car was profoundly irritating. The real death car had at least five holes. Everyone knows that." Colin hailed a cab. "I need that drink. I presume you do too."

"Anything to get that smell out of my head."

In the taxi, Colin called Ben, another friend from our *Hancock's* days. We told him to meet us at Dazzle Cuts in the East Village. Since Ben only lived half a block away, he was already waiting at a table when we arrived. Colin told him what happened at the gallery while I went to get drinks from the proprietor of Dazzle Cuts.

Phil was friendly but he never remembered my name. He grabbed two beers from the cooler and poured Colin his vodka tonic. He put the drinks in front of me and I paid him with a precious twenty.

"Cheers, sport."

"Do you want to give me a haircut, too?"

Phil looked pleased. "My first of the week!"

Dazzle Cuts had reached its peak of hipness two years before, when this converted barber shop was a haunt of the coolest New York bands, before it became populated by the suburban kids who'd read about it in the style bibles. When the punters moved onto the next spot, Dazzle Cuts was claimed by people in the neighborhood, like Ben and I. (Colin lived in Soho.) A marginal drop in bar prices reflected the new clientele.

There was a sign in the front window: "Haircuts Like Mom Used to Give You — $5." Originally, I'd misinterpreted the sign as irony. I did the same with the curled, faded pictures of well-coiffed male models on the walls — Troy with the gingery curls or Vance with the short back and sides — all evidence of the site's former life as a unisex salon. Phil was more bartender than barber but he deeply respected the scissory arts. During an outing with Colin and Ben the previous year, I asked Phil, "So can I still get a haircut?" He was beside himself. I don't think anyone had asked him for months. He told me — and this is nearly the only thing I'm good at, getting people to tell me things — his mother was a hairdresser. When he bought this place, he'd fully intended for it to retain some of its original function. "This was never meant to be a gimmick." One barber chair was intact. Drunks would spin around until they got too dizzy.

After delivering the drinks, I sat in the barber's chair and waited for Phil to bring the sheet. Ben called out to me from a few feet away. "Did you get a look at the puker?"

"Nope. He had his back to me."

"You should have interviewed him."

"He seemed preoccupied. Plus, Colin says there's no market for Cannon-nut stories."

"What about one on vomiting art critics?" asked Ben. "That could be a trend."

Phil came over with his scissors, clippers, and sheet. "So what are you looking for?"

"Make it short and spiky on the sides," I said.

Over at the table, Ben and Colin had begun one of their usual arguments. I tuned out while Phil fussed with the sheet.

I vaguely recognized the music on the stereo. It was Meat Locker, a British band big on rumbling bass lines, slackly paced drumming, and diatribes about market economics. It suited my mood.

"All set," said Phil. He lifted the scissors but was immediately called away by a newcomer at the bar. A Dazzle Cuts cut was a glacially slow process, which was another reason why Phil's chair didn't have many repeat customers. He constantly put down his scissors to serve drinks or talk up women, rarely making more than three consecutive snips.

I slipped my beer out from under the sheet, took a sip, then fussed with the sheet until it was straight and neat again. Bored by Meat Locker's drone, I zeroed in on Ben and Colin's conversation.

Ben hunched forward over the table. "It just goes on and on with you. You'll believe any wacko."

Colin shook his head. "I cannot see how you could accept the existence of a third participant and not give any credence to the possibility of a fourth or fifth. I have testimony from three different men representing at least two auxiliary teams. Cannon was targeted from multiple vantage points. That's elementary."

"That's paranoid bullshit."

"Fine, here are two pieces of information that have been repeatedly verified and that directly contravene the findings of the Miller Commission. One, that according to the extreme angle of the bullet that struck Cannon in his right shoulder, that shot had to have been fired from a position considerably higher than Cruz's on the second floor of the Hotel Atlantique.

"Two, the recording made by a policeman on the scene contains the noises of at least six distinct shots, more if you consider the possibility of a clustering pattern."

"Clustering pattern?" said Phil, once more at my side. "What are you guys talking about?"

"They're discussing the murder of the leader of the free world," I said.

"President McMurray is dead?" he asked.

"No, not him."

He assumed a grave expression. "Cannon."

Of course, the case was officially solved, but to hardly anyone's satisfaction. Colin was an expert at solving and un-solving it. A Chicago native who acted like a huffy New England prep — his accent was getting more and more complex — Colin landed a column in *The Betsey*, a glossy devoted to the history, legacy, and family scandals of President Theodore Ignatius Cannon (1921–63). The magazine took its name from Cannon's beloved yacht, reputed site of countless nautical bacchanals.

Colin investigated the conspiracy theories surrounding his

assassination on that fabled afternoon of August 26, 1963. Hence the nature of this conversation. Hence the nature of nearly every conversation with Colin. I'd already had plenty of Cannon this evening but there was always more to go around.

"I think the way President Cannon lived and the things he believed in were more important than how he died," said Ben with uncharacteristic earnestness.

"That's very sweet," said Colin patronizingly. "My point is, you have to be savvier about these matters if you call yourself a journalist."

Ben smirked. "Who said I was a journalist?"

Though Ben co-edited a small magazine about Asian-American pop culture with another Korean from Colorado, he had been developing a TV show for Network X, a channel that was devoted to the most extreme extremes in the world of extreme lifestyles. Having signed a confidentiality agreement, Ben could only say his show was about music. He had been back and forth to Los Angeles for meetings. His skin was developing a reddish-bronze hue, as if he'd been jogging on a beach somewhere, a serious breach of cool.

I tried to mollify matters with another joke. "Clearly Ben has no use for your petty facts and neither do I. They sully the work of real writers."

Colin glared at me over his G&T. "That attitude has gotten you far in this world."

It was a cheap shot. "Maybe it pays better to be a paranoid, self-satisfied crank."

"Why do I have so many mean drunks here tonight?" Phil slapped me on the head. "Settle down, sport."

Another Meat Locker song oozed out of the speakers. It sounded so lethargic, it could have been moving backwards. Phil left to attend to other matters. This haircut was going to take all night.

"Are either of you gonna have time for coffee tomorrow?" I asked.

"I should be around," said Colin.

"The same," said Ben. "What have you got going on?"

Nothing. My freelance career was a dust bowl. "It's slow," I said. "Agonizingly slow."

"You should try Daphne," said Colin, referring to *The Betsey*'s associate editor. "Pitch her some new pieces."

The mention of Daphne made me moony. I looked over to the bar. Phil was talking to a girl with a lip ring. I wondered if she was waiting for more cute friends. I thought: what the hell am I doing here? I thought: a haircut cannot solve my problems.

Phil returned with the girl in tow. "Thank you for your patience."

"Don't mention it." I tried hard to sound casual.

"I hope you don't mind that I brought a witness."

"Not at all. She'll come in handy for the lawsuit."

"I like your accent," she said to me. "Are you from upstate?"

"I'm from Canada?"

"Why'd you come here?"

"To be a writer?" Whenever my nerves ran high, I couldn't suppress my Canadian accent. Everything I said came out as both a question and an apology. This was a national curse.

"What do you write about?"

Her topaz stare made me gelatinous. I brought my beer out from under the sheet and knocked a clump of hair to the floor. Looking at this night (and all that comes after it) in retrospect, I realized my story about Jimmy began in this painfully protracted moment of deliberation. Of course, I didn't know that then. I was too busy trying to come up with something raw and true and astonishing. I was interrupted by three pieces of sensory input. First: the sight of someone dashing out the door and hoofing it south on Avenue A. Second: a hot sliver of pain near my right ear. Third: Phil shouting, "Agh, you little fucker!" directly into said ear.

I touched the slivery spot and felt something wet.

"Omigod," said the girl. "I'll get you some napkins."

I looked at my finger. The blood was purple in the bar's dim light. I thought: this is ridiculous — how can Phil even *see* my hair? By the time I looked up at the front window again, Phil was heading south, too. The offending scissors were still clutched in his hand. I hoped I wasn't witnessing the beginning of a killing spree.

"What the hell is this all about?" asked Ben.

The girl put a pad of napkins in my hand and took a look at my cheek. "Ah, it's just a nick, but you should press on it anyway."

"Good news," said Ben. "You still have both earlobes."

The room was buzzing with confusion. A minute later, Phil re-entered Dazzle Cuts. He stood by the bar, huffing slightly with his hands on his knees. "That little shit," he said to all inside.

"You shouldn't chase a guy like that," said the girl. "He could have a gun."

Phil waved dismissively. "I thought he got the cashbox, but it was only some CDs. Not even that — just cases."

"A criminal mastermind," said Colin.

I thought: maybe he didn't like Meat Locker. This could represent the evening's second act of art terrorism.

Phil noticed the wad of napkins. "Oh god, did I hurt you?"

"It's nothing."

He rushed to my side. "I'm so sorry, sport." I removed the napkins to show him the cut. "Shitshitshit. Never tell my mother I injured a client. She'll lecture me on how unprofessional I am."

Ben laughed. "Unprofessional? You cut hair in a bar, bro."

"Do you still want me to finish?" Phil's fretting was aggravating me. I suspected the girl found it cute. "I'll be real careful."

"Yeah, go ahead."

Phil went over to the sink and washed and dried the scissors before returning to his task. "You really are the best client I could hope for. You're so calm about this."

I wasn't calm. I just didn't want people to see me any other way.

I worked hard to be easygoing even though it felt completely unnatural. Sometimes I worried I had some kind of disorder. There were medications for people like me. I hoped to be able to afford them someday.

When the room settled down, no one but me even remembered what we were talking about and I was too irritated/upset/distracted/easygoing to re-introduce the subject of my ambitions. Phil and the girl talked about their brushes with violent crime. Ben and Colin discussed a story about Cannon's relationship with the Soviets in the previous month's issue of *The Betsey*. Meat Locker's leather-lunged singer droned on about the mechanization of human labour. I obsessed over the sting in my cheek. I knew my discomfort was worth several more beers, maybe even bourbon.

I pressed down hard on the cut long after the bleeding had stopped.

As I lay on my lumpy futon on Thursday morning, I was secure in the knowledge that no one expected me to be anywhere at any time. Nor did anyone expect me to do anything when I didn't get there. Manhattan was rapidly filling with people who had escaped the same soft, pillowy inertia that fixed me in place. These people showered and dressed, ate multivitamins, said their goodbyes to whomever they left behind (loving partners, indifferent cats, and/ or oversensitive ferns) in charmingly decorated domiciles and got down to whatever it was they got down to without sparing a thought for my well-being. They left me alone and would continue to leave me alone far into the foreseeable future. Their selfishness was absolute.

And so it was my misanthropy that drove me out of bed and into the bathroom. After I pissed, I looked in the mirror long enough to remember why there was a Band-aid there. I thought: they'll think I just learned how to shave.

The previous night, when Phil was out of earshot — I didn't want to make him feel any worse — I asked Ben if it looked like I had been in a fight. He thought about it carefully. "Not a real macho fight. More like one of those fights they used to have in music videos where everyone danced out their aggressions and grabbed each other's lapels all the time. More like a dance rumble. And no one goes to dance rumbles any more. It's just not done."

And that was still the state of me ten hours later. I fussed with the bandage but didn't put on a fresh one yet.

I went back into my bedroom and switched on the laptop, which was perched on a TV tray at the foot of the futon. There were twenty-one new e-mail messages on my computer. Eighteen of them concerned the length of my penis or hot wet teens. The first of the legitimate three was from Lance, my roommate. We'd been friends since high school in the suburbs of Toronto. Now he was another Canadian expat, on an architecture fellowship at Astor College. When he wasn't studying at school, he worked as a parking valet at a fancy Australian restaurant on West 57th. School was closer than home so he often crashed in the grad students' lounge before he made it back here. He had adapted to this transient lifestyle, keeping his toothbrush in a stainless steel case that he carried everywhere.

I could tell that he'd been home some time the night before because the kitchen was a catastrophe. I thought: bean casserole. I thought: maybe a fruit cobbler. Pots and dishes were piled on the stovetop, in the sink, and on the table. Whatever was left of the food — Lance never ate much — was packed neatly in Tupperware in the refrigerator, which also included two juice pitchers full of gazpacho.

This was not something I complained about. Other people have far less nutritionally conscious ways of coping with stress than Lance did. Even so, the quality of Lance's plates varied wildly. Whenever pressure mounted to complete a project, he became over-ambitious in the kitchen, working too quickly on dishes that needed more care. He cooked recklessly and constantly apologized for the results in Post-its: "Do NOT feel obligated to eat it."

I always ate it. It meant I didn't have to spend money I didn't

have in restaurants. I wasn't collecting rainwater or eating newspapers yet. There was still a cushion left from the sum I'd
inherited from a childless great aunt, a wonderful lady whose passing made it possible for me to move to New York nearly two years
before. I had also taken a big loan from my dad, which was fine
until he lost a heap of money on bad pharmaceutical stocks and
then got pushed out of the insurance company where he'd worked
for twenty-two years. I was afraid he'd ask for the money back.
There was nothing about it in the second e-mail of my day, a chipper, gossipy update on household activities from my mother.
Apparently, there was an unpopular new dog on our street.

The third message was from Colin. According to the time
stamp on the message, he'd already been hard at work since well
before 8:12 a.m. despite the lateness of our bloodied parting the
night before. He first asked if I'd cleaned the cut. "Could already
be infected," he wrote. "You should get tested for hepatitis." He
wanted to know if he should put in another word for me with
Daphne. Colin had already given me a big boost at *The Betsey* by
recommending me. The few Canadian magazine clippings and
tiny university newspaper awards that had gotten me the internship at *Hancock's* had done nothing else for me in New York. I
subsisted on scraps of work. I had managed to do three scraps for
*The Betsey*. The longest was about the fad for sharktooth necklaces
in the early 1950s. It wasn't so much a piece as an extended caption for a photograph of a young, handsome Cannon wearing a
sharktooth necklace on the deck of his yacht, the titular *Betsey*. I
was happy to get even these short pieces into *The Betsey*. Besides
earning me $1.25 a word (American), this was also the kind of
prestigious credit that would, in theory, make it easier for me to
pitch other New York glossies. So far, my accomplishments had
only made it marginally easier to pitch *The Betsey*.

Stories for *The Betsey* only had one subject. Its writers and editors were like a pack of sharks circling the same prey, all of them

only able to nibble at the meat lest they have nothing to play with. Though growing up in Canada gave me a sense of remove from the pervasive obsession with the martyred president, I still knew all the official highlights: civil war in Cuba; the Berlin armament crisis; "Third Way" geopolitics in Latin America, Africa, and Indochina; domestic unrest_over racial integration. The official mythology presented Cannon as a man of action, resolve, and honour. When he shuffled off this mortal (re)coil, he became the embodiment of his country's noblest ambitions. Even in Canada his image was everywhere — in newspapers and magazines, in coffee-table books and artworks, on TV specials.

Then there was the other Cannon — corrupt, amoral, opportunistic. To win the election, he colluded with industry oligarchs and crime bosses. Leftists attacked him for authorizing the overthrow of democratically elected governments. The white-rights faction peddled rumours about Cannon's not one but two illegitimate mixed-race daughters. (To be fair, those stories were later confirmed in a *Betsey* cover story — one of the girls capitalized on the publicity by running for the Arkansas state senate.) This Cannon lied, cheated, and humped with abandon.

*The Betsey* was founded by Cannon's son Peter to help further his dad's political aims. Thick with well-intentioned policy papers, the magazine burned through a significant portion of the Cannon family fortune before Peter was killed in a car accident while on a philanthropic mission in Nicaragua. In 1996, control ceded to his sister Rose Marie Cannon Foster. More determined to repair the financial damage than proffer any particular political agenda, she hired Winston Sharpe to turn the magazine around. Sharpe was a legend already. Wannabes like me copped their moves from paperback collections of his early investigative journalism. He had reshaped *Time/Life* after the merger, increased *Colliers'* readership by 30 per cent, and won a Pulitzer for *Taft: The Untold Story*. Sharpe realized that the reading public could handle a degree of ambiguity in terms of how Cannon's character and actions were presented. *The Betsey* became remarkably open-minded on the topic of Cannon. In the space of a few pages, it portrayed him as a sage and a reprobate, a social progressive and a tool of the military-industrial complex, a caring family man and a gonorrheal horndog. The strategy worked — *The Betsey* became the one-stop source of Cannon lore, trumping both the supermarket tabloids and competing highbrow glossies like *Colliers* and *Hancock's*. And no matter how much dirt was thrown at it, Cannon's image remained somehow sacrosanct to the majority of Americans. They believed in one kind of Cannon and the heretics believed in the other. Sharpe got both kinds of people to buy his magazine.

I was jealous of Colin for entering Sharpe's orbit as *The Betsey's* latest columnist — when I asked my friend to describe his boss, he called him "remarkably efficient." It was his highest compliment. Yet Colin shared his good fortune by boosting me to Daphne, Sharpe's second-in-command. She was a Foster by birth, a third cousin to Rose Marie. She had the air of a young woman determined to design challenges for herself, since the universe hadn't presented her with any great obstacles in the first place. Lord, how I pined. In a recent issue, there was a small photo of her and Sharpe at work in the office. Her hazel eyes had a stern yet thoughtful look as her pen hovered over a page of copy. I had clipped out the photo, feeling pathetic about the act from the moment I slipped my thumb into the scissor hole.

In my e-mail reply to Colin, I suggested a late afternoon drink. I planned to tell him about a *Betsey* pitch. Lance's cooking habits got me thinking about the kitchens in Cannon's White House. Colin could tell me how extensively the subject had already been plumbed. I was eager to increase my stature at *The Betsey*. I needed a major break. My Visiting Cultural Worker visa had expired along with my editorial assistant gig at *Hancock's*. I wasn't supposed to be in America at all. My only recourse was to find an editor who would consider me an Invaluable Cultural Asset in my Designated Field of Expertise before I came to the attention of the Department of Immigration, Naturalization, and Border Integrity. I broke into a sweat every time I spotted a capital letter.

All this worrying left me in need of a non-work distraction. I looked at the piles of the CDs I kept on the floor of my bedroom. Many were freebies sent by record companies for whom reviews on Web sites meant something. I sifted through them for titles I could easily unload at Matty's Music Mart, a place on Mulberry that paid fair prices. The selections had to be either sufficiently new or obscure so that the store wouldn't have thirty copies already, or else be such hot commodities that they could be re-sold pronto. I screwed up the timing sometimes. For example, I'd been hanging onto a rare early album by a mainstay at womyn's folk music festivals, thinking it would bring me a lucrative sale. Her cachet plummeted when the singer admitted she'd married a person with a penis. The second-hand stores were now clogged with her faux-lesbian songcraft.

I figured my new selections would fetch me beer money for a day or two, plus a few goodies from Matty's. I shut down the computer and headed to the shower, an act that marked the end of my last Jimmy-free morning. I would have savoured it a little longer had I known.

* * *

"Hey, Matty."

He didn't look up. He was sitting at the counter, his attention entirely focused on a crossword puzzle. He never said hello. When he did look up, it was usually to gaze at the consoling face of ageless country-music belle Evangeline Reynolds on the poster across from him. She was a popular figure for crushes among men of his generation and disposition.

In any case, Matty didn't look up so I took my CDs to the store's friendlier employee, J.C. He stood near the cash register, going through a stack of discs with a pricing gun. Mean, throbbing bass tones and clattery percussion emanated from his headphones.

I stood in front of him. "I have some discs to sell."

He nodded off-beat.

I put my CDs on the counter in front of him. "I'm gonna look around."

J.C. nodded again. It was almost as if he had heard what I said.

Slightly wheezy from my brisk walk through the April drizzle, I inhaled deeply. There was panoply of familiar store smells: the faint remnants of yesterday's after-hours cigarettes, the aroma of moist industrial carpet, the tomato-y tang of microwave pasta and takeout pizza. In every second-hand record store, you can count on finding the scent of middle-aged men who live alone (a combination of B.O. and burnt nutmeg) and a sharper whiff of cat piss. Then, of course, there was the mustiness that emanates from 500,000 LPs, which were the store's holdings according to the customized sandwich sign on the sidewalk. Individual records rarely smelled of anything. I remember a few that literally stank — a Captain Elephantiasis album drenched in Old Spice, a Room Service sleeve as rank as a vomitorium, a green-vinyl Edward Townes single that would've been quite valuable had the disc itself not stunk of skunk and boiled cauliflower. After touching it, I asked Matty if there was somewhere I could wash my hands. "This ain't a bus station," he said.

Matty's holdings were overwhelming; I had to be very strategic about my browsing lest I get caught in the store for the rest of the day and come out too poor for beer. I'd already investigated certain subgenres: Welsh punk rock, East German psychedelia, Polynesian reggae, outlaw country ballads. My most beloved find in the latter category was *Devil Woman with Angel Eyes* by Freddy

Capp and the Six Pack. The back sleeve portrayed the scantily clad devil woman about to be cornered by Capp's drooling posse in a hillbilly gangbang fantasy.

A few months before, I had also found the record that made me move to New York — I'd given away my last copy to my ex-girlfriend Linda. The band and the album were called Asphalt Diary. It was recorded in 1975 but I heard it in 1986, when I was thirteen. The singer, John J. Murphy, named himself after a park near Stuyvesant Town. He was a published poet and a committed junkie. Delivered over a musical backing at once elegant and abrasive, Murphy's lyrics put a romantic spin on New York street life — songs bustled with hippie burnouts, huckster con men, struggling immigrants, and girls half dead to the world. They often played CBGB's in the days before it opened a gift shop. I fantasized about life in the city Murphy portrayed in all its scum-encrusted glory. (It was cleaner by the time I got here.) I wrote despairing free verse about heroin addicts living in the Evergreen Hotel. I bought a brown leather jacket from the Salvation Army but was too shy to wear it outside my bedroom. I practised a scowl. I planned my escape from the genteel suburbia of Fairview, Ontario, a place without drama. I never wanted to live near a golf course again.

So far, so good with the escape. Except now I spent my days stalking the streets of New York feeling friendless and underemployed. I must've been feeling particularly starved for human voices that day because I started with Matty's spoken word and comedy section. This trove had already yielded treasures like Lenny Bruce's ace 1967 LP *Wisenheimer Deluxe* and an ultra-rare calypso record by Jack Hunter. One day when I had a little extra money to spend, I splurged on a double album bearing the imprimatur of early sixties skin rag *Boudoir*. The lady on the record cover promised to tell me "the things every man needs to know." I hadn't listened to it yet, saving it for a special occasion.

I found Jimmy's record when it slid out with its neighbour,

*Jasmine Woody: The Queen of Basin Street Burlesque*. Neither cover had — as I'd initially hoped — nudity. One did have a president. At first, I thought Jimmy's record must've been campaign songs. I had one already, a collection of perky, strident, hopeful numbers promising four more years with Dewey and victory for Lindbergh. Then I thought it was a compilation of speeches — I had often seen a late-night infomercial for a four-CD set of Cannon's "greatest oratorical achievements."

On the cover was a man in a dark suit and a blue tie to match his eyes. He was giving Cannon's signature double-thumbs-up gesture. He stood before a wooden desk and an American flag in the Oval Office, or rather what the Oval Office would look like with balsa-wood furniture, paper rugs, and cardboard walls. Despite the chintz, the picture closely resembled a famous photo that had been on the cover of *Look* in 1961. It was one of the most famous images of Cannon from his early days in office. The impostor here bore a definite resemblance to the president — sure, his hair was too dark, his chin too weak, and his features less attractive on the whole. But he had the body language right (the forward tilt, the raised shoulders) and smiled the same toothy, incandescent smile.

Across the top ran the title in the same florid and elegant script preferred by this nation's founders. It read: *A Square Peg in the Oval Office*. Underneath the man's shoes (matte black Oxfords, just like Cannon's) was a name: Jimmy Wynn. On the back was a list of titles (e.g., "Not on the Official Tour," "The African Ambassadors") and this note:

> This album is for fun. Laugh along with Jimmy Wynn and his gang The Capital Offence as they say some wacky things about some of the greatest people of our time. We hope that this record will be taken in the right spirit — no disrespect is intended. The very fact

that the folks we joke about are able to laugh with us and enjoy this record is a big reason why we admire them so. Jimmy is pleased to present the lighter side of life on Capitol Hill. "This country has given me so much in my life, it was time I gave something back," says our patriotic prankster. "I just hope America can make change — all I've got is a twenty."

*The Betsey* devoted countless column inches to the most minor and most tangential aspects of Cannon's life, from his preference for argyle socks to the Nielsen ratings of his favourite television shows. Yet I'd never seen any mention of Jimmy Wynn. This record smelled more like a lead for a story than it did skunk or cauliflower.

The $15 tag gave me pause. I took the record up to Matty. "Excuse me." He didn't bother looking up from his crossword. "Uh, can you go any lower on this one?"

He peered up from the paper. "What's that on your face? You get mugged?"

"No. I cut myself."

"Hmph." He took the record from my hands. He ran his hand over the sleeve. "Little scuffed." He slipped out the disc and had a look. "Barely played. You're lucky — a first pressing'll go for eighty-five bucks." Matty looked past me at Evangeline Reynolds as if asking for her confirmation on the price. "Fifteen."

"The sleeve's pretty rough."

"Sleeve's fine."

"This can't be so rare."

"You got that right. This was a number one record. Sold millions."

"So why's it so expensive?"

Matty stroked his whiskery chin. "Fair question. I remember going through piles of the thing when I worked at the record department in a big store on Lexington. Used to keep 'em at the cash register so I didn't have to run around. The same guy put out another record a few months later. This is the first one, I think. When is this? Sixty-one?" He scrutinized the fine print on the back cover. "Nah, '62. Mr. Jimmy Wynn. I used to see him on *The Manny Hudson Show*. Some people thought he was funny. Struck me as a square. Did Cannon's voice real well, though. Then, after that day . . ." Matty drifted off for a few moments then snapped back hard. "We took 'em off the shelves and never put 'em back."

"What happened to all those records?"

"Garbage," he growled. "People couldn't get rid of 'em fast enough. Every garage sale had one." He tapped his finger on the record's spine. "But seeing as folks did such a good job of making like Mr. Jimmy Wynn never existed, his records are almost rarities." He drew the disc closer to his chest and eyed me jealously. "I should be asking twenty."

"How about ten?"

"Eighteen."

"But the tag only says fifteen."

"That's a goddamn bargain!" he yelled. He looked sternly at me, then the record, then Evangeline's all-forgiving face. He shoved the record in my direction. "It's fifteen! Now get it out of my sight."

I went to the cash register before Matty tried to take the record back. I swallowed my pique over my failed negotiation and hoped that Jimmy Wynn was worth it.

I waited to play the record until after I had eaten a bowl of bean casserole. Lance had used too much savoury. I worried about him while I cleaned the kitchen.

I was very particular about how I listened to records. As objects, compact discs never had the same aura. I had gotten too many for free in the mail for even the ones that I bought to seem special. Records had a certain kind of appeal that the discs couldn't. It was archeological — on some level I believed that each time I bought a record from a shop or a milk crate on the street, I was rediscovering a past that had been suppressed or neglected. I hated it when a record I found was reissued on compact disc. Sure, the change in format made the recordings seem more permanent, but it wasn't the permanence those creators imagined. No, they dreamed of someone like me coming along in the hazy, distant future, someone who knew nothing of their lives yet was struck dumb by the product of their thimble's worth of hope and ambition. I proved that their work had lasted, regardless of whether it ever deserved to. Even if I tore the record off the turntable and smashed it against the radiator after enduring it for fifteen seconds, the gap between present and past was temporarily bridged. I treated every record — whether it was performed by a presidential impersonator, a briefly successful doo-wop group, or even a sad, drunk, middle-aged cowboy in a red codpiece — as an opportunity to fold time.

Thus did I pull the record from the sleeve, lower the stylus on *A Square Peg in the Oval Office*, and take up my position on the floor of the living room.

Here's some of what I heard.

The crackle of the record mixes with the low murmur of a studio audience. "Ah, testing, testing, one and, ah, two." The simulation of Cannon's voice is good enough to silence the audience — could it really be him? When they realize, no, it can't be, there's a ripple of relieved titters. "I'd like to, ah, welcome all of you listeners to a little something we've cooked up for your pleasure." The voice is smooth yet broadly Bostonian. There's less of Cannon's warmth — the charm is spiked with aggression, as if he's not so confident he'll be liked. "Connie? Connie, why don't you come over here and say hello to the nice folks?"

"Oh, honey, my hair's not ready." The woman's voice is not so close to the original — the words are too quick.

"It's a record album, Connie. They can't see your hair."

"But what about the photographers?"

"No photographers, either."

"Then how are they going to see me?"

"The listeners will just have to imagine you in all your, ah, glory."

"Well, I won't have anyone imagining my hair when it's in this state." Laughs from the crowd — this must have been recorded in a studio, somewhere with a stand of seats, tape on the floor, free coffee, and a sign that somebody holds up to elicit APPLAUSE APPLAUSE APPLAUSE. "And Theodore, I think your listeners would rather imagine you with your trousers on." Bigger laughs — no pants?!

"I would like to say that I am, ah, quite comfortable as I am. The listeners can imagine me however they like. So let's start the show."

The announcer bounds into the speakers. He punches the words JIMMY WYNN and THE CAPITAL OFFENCE like they owe him money. Snappy big-band jazz music underscores the audience's hoots and claps. I check the back cover to see if it listed the recording location. The 21st Street Theater. The producer is Isadore Berman. There's a big thank-you to Danny Pantero, the singer. I vaguely recognize the name of the woman credited with doing Connie's voice: Katie Perry. Wasn't she on a sitcom?

"Without futher ado," says the announcer, "here's your comedy commander-in-chief, JIMMY WYNN!"

The first bit. The president delivers a windy intro about a "very historic meeting" and "a spirit of togetherness." "I'm extremely pleased we could put aside the differences that have separated us in the past." The president sounds congenial, polished, focused.

"Daddy!" A grown-up woman with the cutesy-wootsy little-girl voice shatters the tone of formality.

"Yes, Rose Marie." Cannon's daughter — she would've been five in 1962. At the funeral, she tried to hug the casket.

"What are you doing with my dollies?" Laughs of surprise.

"Well, Rose Marie, I was very pleased to receive your invitation to the tea party. I thought I'd take this opportunity to meet our distinguished guests in a more casual circumstance and get what we call a feel for the room. Isn't that right, Senator Pooh Bear? Mr. Bear was telling me about some very interesting subsidies in his home state of North Palooka."

"Daddy, why did you put that ribbon on Tabby the Cat?"

"Tabby seemed a little underdressed for the occasion so I made her the Undersecretary of the Treasury. The position, ah, comes with a sash."

"And where's Miss Pretty?"

"I believe she was called to the phone. Knock on the closet and see if she's free."

"Oh, Daddy," the woman with the kiddie voice sounds awfully frustrated, "you don't know anything about playing with dollies."

Pres gets a tad huffy. "In the absence of a clear protocol, I believe that I have been getting along just fine with our guests. They seem very comfortable. What's that, Senator Bear? Why, of course, you can have more tea."

I like the sketch about the motorcade. There's the purr of an engine and the cheers of a distant crowd. The music is faint and martial.

Pres: "I really appreciate you fellows giving me a lift to work on my first day, Ben."

"Sir, it's customary for the new president to travel in a motorcade." Ben has the stiff manner of a veteran Washington lackey. He sounds like the Pres — did Jimmy Wynn do both voices? The back of the record lists The Capital Offence as two women and another man.

"I think you mean motor car."

"No, Mr. President, a motorcade."

"There's no need for fancy French words here, Ben. Hey, will you look at that? It's the Washington Monument. It seems, ah, a little grimy to me. Please remind me to prepare a presidential directive for polishing and maintenance."

"Yes, Mr. President." Sound of engine and crowds. I imagine a 1962 Flavelle convertible, then think: he probably had more than just the one car.

"I really am very moved to see all the people out to greet us. It's very fine to see so many patriotic Americans."

"Indeed, Mr. President."

"I do hate to keep them waiting like this. Surely we could get to the White House a little faster and get on with my speech."

"Mr. President, the speed of the motorcade is —"

Pres interrupts. "I see what the problem is, Ben. It's that black car in front of us. He can't be going more than fifteen miles an hour. And look behind us — he's got all of us backed up for a mile. Eddie?"

A new voice. "Yes, Mr. President."

"Could you, ah, lean on your horn there? I want to get that car to step on it."

"Yes, Mr. President." The two horn blasts are followed by the increasingly panicky voice of Ben.

"Sir, that car is carrying the Secretary of State."

"Dean's up there? He's driving like my grandmother. Eddie, give him another toot." Toot! "Oh, there's Dean. He's waving. Yes, yes, I see you, Dean. Hello, helllll-ooohh." He lays into the last word like he's Cannon doing an impression of goofball comic Sammy Mac.

"Mr. President, you don't understand. The —"

"It seems a shame that Dean's holding up all these other folks. They're probably waiting to get seats at the inauguration. Let's try waving them on."

"Mr. President, that won't be necessary."

He must've rolled down the window because the crowd gets louder. "Go around! Go around! Ah, everyone's just waving back. Yes, yes, I see you. Maybe this fellow on the motorcycle can get Dean's attention." There's a new engine rumble. "Hello there, citizen."

"Yes, Mr. President."

"Would you mind asking the fellows in that car if they can go a little faster? I have a speech to get to."

"Yes, Mr. President." The rumble recedes then returns.

"What did Dean say?"

"The driver says that he is unable to exceed fourteen miles per hour."

"That big car? Was it made in Mexico?"

Ben interrupts. "Mr. President, I'm trying to explain about the motorcade —"

"I can walk to the White House faster than this. Ben, please remind me to prepare a presidential directive so Dean gets an automobile with some decent horsepower. I cannot have the Secretary of State getting clocked by a kid in a soapbox racer. Excuse me, son?"

Motorcyclist: "Yes, Mr. President."

"Have you got an extra helmet?"

"Yes, Mr. President."

"I would be much obliged if you could take me on the back of your motorcycle up to the White House. These Washington drivers are completely intolerable." The sudden music and crowd noise almost obscure the punchline.

The rest of the first side is cute but not as funny. The president is portrayed variously as a loquacious schmoozer, a protocol-obsessed politician, and an overeager husband and father. He loves the perks of the presidential life but is frustrated by Washington's many pretensions. There are no references to the political manoeuvres or questionable alliances that brought Cannon to office, and certainly nothing specific about the controversies he created when he was there. There is no mention of race conflict or foreign wars. The only vaguely political sketch portrays the president preparing for a meeting with the "Attaché of African Affairs." The studio audience blows its collective gasket over his inability to pronounce "Zanbiba" or made-up politician names like "Tomumbatakko" and "Mobootay." When the attaché coaches him on the pronunciation of Prime Minister Ohweemoway, the president starts to sing "The Lion Sleeps Tonight." Pres gets chastised. Pres gets flustered. "I recommend that we cancel the official meeting and suggest a more casual event. I think it would be an absolutely terrific idea to come with me in Air Force One to Las Vegas. Danny Pantero's singing at the Sands tonight." There's a laugh of recognition in the audience.

"Mr. President, I have every confidence in your ability to conduct this meeting with the gravity it deserves. One last question:

can you tell me the name of the president of Kazatarana? You'll be
addressing him first."

There are chuckles in the audience. Pres rides out the pause, gets
more laughs. He gives an "ahhhh. . . ." Then: "Muuu . . . ba . . .
caaaahh . . . choo . . . Texas?" Big laughs.

The attaché sounds pissed. "Mr. President, these are very
important negotiations with the African leaders and . . . hold
on . . . I apologize, Mr. President. That's exactly correct. Mr.
Moobacachutaxsis it is."

Pres is triumphant. "How could I forget?"

I thought: yeah, how *could* I forget? Why hadn't I heard of
Jimmy Wynn before? It's not like he sucked outright. Though his
routine was family-friendly (no cusswords), the material was
snappy and appealing, probably much more so to the audience of
his day. And if he'd sold millions, he must've come to the attention
of Cannon. Cannon paid great attention to the media — he had
to have known. Was he flattered that another man would devote
so much care to emulating his voice and manner? Or did he feel
humiliated to be portrayed as a rube?

I listened to the record a second time. Some of the jokes were
still funny — a good sign. It took a professional to make a bit
sound fresh even when it was so clearly dated. Jimmy Wynn had
the knack, though I suspected I was only getting half the package.
I studied the stooped, dark-haired guy on the cover. His face said:
top of the world, Ma! Can you believe I got all this way? Maybe
his friendliness was a put-on. Was it a mask, as it must've been for
Cannon? When you assume another man's manner, do you inherit
everything else he carries?

The questions beget other questions. Finding out more about
Jimmy Wynn seemed like a good way to use up my day.

\* \* \*

I was late meeting Colin at the Corso, a sleepy café we liked in Chelsea. He was already at a table with his latte. "You're late." He eyed the bandage. "No more accidents on the way over, I trust."

"I was at the library doing some research."

"That bodes well. It sounds like you have something. On the phone you sounded like you'd discovered the cure for cancer growing in your roommate's casserole pan."

"I have a great story for *The Betsey*."

Colin raised an eyebrow. "That's good news. They need some decent features. Last month's story on the president's liver problems was impenetrably dull and it didn't need to be."

"This doesn't concern any of the president's vital organs except for maybe his larynx. Have you ever heard of Jimmy Wynn?"

"No."

"He was a comedian, a Cannon impersonator. He started out in an act with Danny Pantero, the singer. In '60, he began doing an impression of Cannon. People loved it. He had two Number One records in 1962. For a little while, he was the biggest-selling recording act in America."

"So why haven't I heard of him?"

"His career didn't survive New Orleans."

"The parasite died along with the host."

"That's not bad." I added the line to the notes in front of me. "Can I keep that? Anyway, I haven't done much research yet. I only found a few mentions of him after '63. Apparently, he toured with Lenny Bruce."

"What else do you know about him?"

"He was born in Detroit. Came to Vegas in '58 with Pantero. They wanted to be a big singing-comedy team, the next Jack Hunter and Sammy Mac. Wynn did impersonations. At some point, he created a whole revue about the president."

"Was it any good?"

"His impersonation was just about perfect. It still sounds good on record. I'm not sure how funny it is now, but everybody back then seemed to like it. When it comes to comedy, the majority rules."

"And what did the president think of this man's mode of flattery?"

"In one interview I found, Wynn said he had Cannon's blessing. There's a mention of a White House visit but I don't know when. Wynn makes himself out to be the official court jester."

Colin made a thoughtful "hmm" and held up a finger. "I have seen his name before, in connection with the Nevada Delegation."

"A political group?"

"No, purely social. It's a very controversial area of study. Cannon enjoyed visiting Las Vegas. The mobster Marco Delrocco would host parties for him in the Flamingo Hotel. All the top entertainers came through. They called themselves the Nevada Delegation."

"His own private Sin City. It must've been pretty wild."

Colin smiled slyly. "Caligula would have blushed. But we don't know exactly how wild. We know more than we ever cared to know about life below decks on *The Betsey* but this delegation's members have been extremely tight-lipped. When I get back to my office, I'll look up your Wynn in a few places. But that's good material so far. How do you see the story?"

"I haven't gotten all of this straight yet, but it's roughly this." I cracked my knuckles for theatrical effect. "Okay, so here's a young guy who's desperate to make it as an entertainer. He's at the very bottom rung of the ladder in Las Vegas. He's got a talent for voices and a passable resemblance to our glamorous new president. He tries it out onstage. At first, people are a little scared. They're thinking: hey, is this guy gonna take the piss out of our Cannon? They're still having their honeymoon. But no, Jimmy Wynn only takes very soft shots. He loves the president as much as everybody else does. The audience responds well and the routines get better and better. When it gets on an LP, it takes off like a rocket. Jimmy Wynn gets all the fame he could want plus a backstage pass to the White House. The trouble is, his fame is second-hand. When the president is shot by your two or four or eighteen gunmen imported in for the occasion from Cuba, Ghana, and the east side of Detroit . . ."

"There's no need to be facetious."

". . . anyway you slice it, he dies, too. No one wants to know about Jimmy Wynn because he reminds them of their shock, their pain, their whatever. What happened to him afterward, I don't know yet. Maybe he's still in show business. Maybe he collects shopping carts. Either way, the old parasite must have some stories about the good old days."

"You know he isn't dead?"

"I haven't found an obituary yet."

Colin chuckled. "Obituaries never prove anything. You know that."

I let that pass, not wanting to get into a digression about organs of disinformation. "Whatever. I just hope that Daphne doesn't want me to fit all of this into a photo caption. This could be a real feature opportunity."

"Why don't you do some more ground work? You could talk to someone who knew him."

"That occurred to me but I wasn't sure who to start with?"

"You could talk to Lenny Bruce?"

"How?"

"I've got his number somewhere. He calls me from time to time. He fancies himself a real expert on the assassination. His tips are worthless, but he may have something to say about your man."

"What is he, eight thousand years old? He must be pickled in morphine."

"Believe me, he's lucid, he's all too lucid. I'll call you later with his details." Colin saluted me with his latte. "I'm impressed, Nathan. You sound like you're onto something. I hope Jimmy Wynn doesn't mind being famous again."

I laughed. "Who wouldn't want a comeback?"

*Jimmy sits in the dressing room backstage at the Savoy. He waits for the end of the showgirl routine. It was some kind of mermaid thing. The girls left blue sequins on the floor. He pushes them around with his shoe.*

*Jimmy wrings his hands and thinks about the president. Like most people, his obsession was minted by that first TV debate. The TV people said Cannon's performance that night decided the election, but then, TV people would say that, wouldn't they? Jimmy was glued to the set that night, studying both men, breaking them down. Cannon's fellow candidate, Peter Barrow, was easier to nail. The military bearing, the regimented body language, the forced chumminess — it all reminded Jimmy of the impressions his pop would do of bigshots he'd met in the war. "C'mon, soldier, pull that shrapnel out of your ass! That ridge is ours for the taking!" The young senator from New Hampshire was harder to get. He didn't move or talk much like any other politician Jimmy had seen. He carried himself like he belonged on the Tropicana's big stage.*

*Cannon's voice radiated warmth even from the cheapest transistor radio. Jimmy had to smooth out his own edges. Onstage he projected too much aggression, too much raw need, too much cmonwhydontyoucmon. His early Cannon bits were so lousy, he couldn't blame Danny for not wanting them in the act. But he and Jimmy both knew they'd hit a ceiling without ever getting out of the basement. For once, politics couldn't make it worse.*

*Through the fall of '60, Jimmy would do a set without Danny about once a week. The parts of the act that were straight stand-up, they never stopped feeling thin. He struggled with the half-baked schtick that came in-between the impressions — he always would. The fear kept crawling up out of his throat. The losers out there in the dark smelled it on him — "Get this guy outta here!" "Learn to tell a joke, you dumb prick!" "Bring back the broads!"*

*What Jimmy wanted from Cannon was his aura. He'd learned the word from a call girl who tried to pass herself off as a fortune teller. She said it was what made special people special. "A magnetic force," she said, "that draws people in." He liked to roll the word around in his head, hoping its magic would rub off — auraauraauraaura. Jimmy knows he wasn't the only one who noticed Cannon's charisma. Women would do anything to be near him. Every guy in the country would've killed to get a little piece of whatever he had.*

*So when the mermaids went back into the sea and Jimmy took the stage that night, he knew he was doing something that everybody else wanted to: wear the man's skin. Even if what Jimmy did inside it was dumb or easy or cheap, it didn't matter. All those losers loved Jimmy for showing them it could be done.*

Built as a hotel in the twenties and retrofitted into a hospital in the eighties, the Bernard Johnson Residence for Seniors was a classy place to die. It wasn't where I expected a guy like Lenny Bruce to live out his last days. I would've imagined him in a fleabag firetrap where they cleaned the sheets twice a year, there was one IV bag per floor, the geezers all smelled like rotten cheese, and the nurses had fresh scars from the previous night's bar brawl.

Yet the middle-aged black woman at the information desk was scar-free and cheerful, at least until I asked where I could find Mr. Bruce's room.

"*Mister* Bruce?" she said, leaning hard on the appellation. "You *must* be new."

I signed a clipboard and she sent me to the third floor.

I didn't know much about Bruce's condition beyond Colin's claims about his lucidity. He'd sounded fine when I called. I asked him if I could meet him that afternoon. "Sure," he barked. "I'm not gonna live forever."

He might. He'd looked like a reheated cadaver for as long as I could remember. When I was growing up, he would constantly show up as a celebrity seat-filler on game shows or in commercials for old people (medical-alert bracelets, comformatic beds, country-style fruit compotes). He was somebody's dirty Jewish uncle, with a repertoire devoted to enlarged prostates, horny rabbis, and shiksas with hooters out to here.

But when I heard one of his early records, I was shocked to discover he used to be vicious. He went after the church, the police, the government, whites, blacks, men, women, straights, gays. Cops would bring Yiddish translators into the clubs to catch him out on the dirty words that weren't in English. By the late sixties, he was spending more time delivering his routines in court than in clubs. That left him burnt out and half dead. Then he traded in heroin and amphetamines for beet juice and vitamins. He wanted to entertain the nice people. The hipsters felt betrayed and told him so at every show. But Bruce persevered in creating a shtick with wider appeal. Gone were the cop-baiting commentaries. In came Good Time Lenny. He filled the Rainbow Room for months on end. He killed at Caesar's. He starred in cheeseball T&A comedies, hosted celebrity roasts, and cried on the laps of handicapped children on telethons.

I couldn't guess which of the two Bruces I was going to encounter. I hoped it would be the one with the weepy eyes and the incontinence jokes. The other one would bat me around like a cat toy before sending me off with nothing. I fought the urge to cut and run.

Inside Room 328 was a wrinkly faced man with a bald, blotchy head. He wore a bright orange sweater and Coke-bottle glasses. He was propped up in the bed, watching a women's beach volleyball game on a TV suspended from the ceiling.

I knocked on the open door but he didn't look my way. "Mr. Bruce, I'm Nathan —"

"Buddy, if you're here to stick your finger up my ass, I prefer not to be on a first-name basis. Makes it easier for me to believe I'm paying you."

"Uh," I said, already thrown off guard, "I'm not a nurse."

He pointed the remote at the TV. I turned and saw a deeply bronzed woman in a white bikini spike a volleyball.

"Like it?" asked Bruce. "Great sport. It's like a wet T-shirt contest but faster."

When Lenny Bruce smiled, his lips parted and I saw some of the shark he must have been thirty years before. Or maybe it was an angry squid I saw — the thick glasses made his eyes the size of coasters.

He finished the smile. "So who the fuck are you?"

"I write for *The Betsey*? We spoke on the phone?"

"The Cannon rag? You're like the souvenir program they give away at state funerals. Did you know that Martinez was a faggot working undercover for the feds? I've got it on good authority that he had a thing going on with a congressman. Ah, what was his name. . . ." Bruce snapped his fingers a few times.

"Do you mind if I ask you some questions?" I asked. "On the phone, you said you might have some time?" I could hear the accent creeping in.

He tipped the glasses down his nose and peered over the top. "Uh-huh. Ya see, I don't talk to the press for free — enough of you lousy shitstains have gotten rich off me already. There's a whole shelf full of books with my face on the cover and not one ever earned me a dime. I'm still paying the jerk who wrote the last one and that was supposed to be my autobiography. The hourly rate is five hundred dollars." He paused for a beat before stretching out his hand and waggling his fingers. "You with me here?"

I stammered something out. "Mr. Bruce, I . . . uh."

By this stage in my journalism career, I had done hundreds of interviews. I had developed certain techniques to overcome certain personal impediments. For one thing, I was shy with people I did not know. Encouraging them to talk about themselves made me feel like I knew them. I needed that feeble illusion. For another, I wanted to be liked. So if I could coax them with flattery, it was all the better. I still felt cheap when I needed to butter up a subject. I wanted to be more direct about getting what I wanted but I didn't know how. I wanted Winston Sharpe to teach me.

"Mr. Bruce, I just want to tell you how excited I am to meet you. I say that not as a journalist but a huge fan. *Huge* fan. You're a legend in this business, a comedy pioneer, a satirist, uh, supremacist. I've got all your records — *Lenny Bruce Raw, The Man Is Sick, Wisenheimer Deluxe, A Little Night Lenny*, the one with the big cocktail glass on the cover . . . all of them. Well, maybe not all of them, but certainly a lot of them. You've always been such a tremendous talent. Both before and after the, uh, time on the drugs in the sixties and everything. Then in, uh, *Cheerleader Fever* and *Vixen Patrol*. And you were always my favourite guest on *Match Game*, and . . ."

Bruce waggled his fingers some more, beckoning me to continue.

". . . and . . . *Bake Off?* The show where all the guests wore those tall chef's hats? You know it. Then there was the movie with the golfers. Again — amazing."

I thought: I am pathetic.

Lenny Bruce stared back. "That all you got?" He grunted. "Kid, that was the lousiest ass-licking I've ever had. Is this your first time? You're sweating harder than a Polack trying to read."

He turned to the TV. "Jesus, why do they always send me the retards? Don't I deserve professionals?" His hand flapped in my direction. "Vamoose, you little shit. Come back with the money and I'll be your best pal. Otherwise, feel free to fuck yourself."

I barely had the strength to lift my head, the humiliation was so great. But I could also be tenacious. When I saw Bruce aim the remote at the TV, I took my chance before the room filled with the sound of nubile flesh making contact with a volleyball.

"I want to find out about Jimmy Wynn."

One of his eyes twitched. "Who?"

"Jimmy Wynn? You did some shows with him in the sixties? He used to do an impersonation of President Cannon?"

Bruce slowly turned his head. "You a cop?"

"No."

A mean smirk temporarily lifted Bruce's sagging features. He folded his hands over his chest. "Jimmy Wynn, huh? Jeez. I can't believe I'm saying the words out loud." He scratched his chin. "You know what I could go for right now, *Betsey* boy? A chocolate pudding. Quitting junk gave me a real sweet tooth. Suddenly I was crazy for anything chocolate. I put on a hundred and fifty pounds in one year." He lifted his hands to mark the parameters of his long-gone belly. "Now they don't let me eat anything like that — screws up my glucose levels. But I know what I can handle better than they do." He leaned toward me. "If you and I are gonna chat about our mutual friend, there's a one-cup minimum. The cafeteria has a whole cooler full of pudding. It's the most beautiful thing."

I nodded. "I'd love to see it."

"Get me some water, too. My throat's drier than a nun's snatch."

The cafeteria was not quite as glorious as he'd described but I got what I needed. He was dozing when I returned. I knocked on the door and he perked up. "That's the ticket," he said.

I moved his bed tray up to his chest and handed him the cup and a plastic spoon. He peeled off the lid and took a whiff. "Oh, that's fantastic — you have no idea. I've got one taste bud still working and it lights up like a friggin' pinball game whenever it gets near this stuff. It's gonna give me a stroke. And you wouldn't believe the gas I get." He chuckled. "If you stick around, you won't have to imagine it."

I pulled a chair alongside the bed and took out my notebook and tape recorder.

"So what got you interested in our Jimmy? I don't hear his name much."

"I heard *A Square Peg*. I wondered how a guy who was so famous and so successful could disappear like he did. I don't even know if he's alive."

Bruce carefully dipped his spoon in the pudding, lifting only a tiny morsel to his lips. "Oh, he's alive. I would've heard about it if he'd kicked. Word gets around. It even gets in here. Not that I'm saying I have any clue where he is."

"And when did you first meet him?"

"Maybe '55? The dates are hazy. He was with Eddie Prefontaine at the El Morocco in New York. Eddie always had these boys around the club — he must've taken them fresh off the farm. Some of 'em wanted to be in showbiz, others just liked the attention of a refined gentleman. He gave them a leg up, if you know what I mean."

"Was this common in the business at the time?"

"It wasn't like the biz was run by some fruit syndicate, if that's what you're asking. Besides, Eddie was a classy guy. I was working the club for a few weeks. I remember one of Eddie's boys, a nervous kid, like he's ready to piss himself — even worse than you. He would ask me about performing. You know, like whaddya do if the audience does this, or how do you get this kind of reaction, or how do you use your hands. He'd try out some impressions on me. This turned out to be your guy, Jimmy Wynn." He laughed. "Jimmy Wynn. I can't even believe I'm saying it again. You know how theatre folks won't say Macbeth like they're worried they're gonna get the plague? Jimmy's name used to be like that. If a comic heard those words before his act, he was dead. If my heart stops any time in the next few minutes, you're gonna tell the nurse, right?"

"Depends on what else you've got to tell me about Wynn."

"Ack!" He clutched his chest with a theatrical gesture. "You're killing me!" He laughed his way into a coughing fit. "But seriously," he rasped, "the guy was bad news. Not always, though. Had some

promise. Him and Danny Pantero did a duo act in your less dis-
criminating Vegas lounges. Whenever I was in Vegas, I'd see them
hanging around Sinatra's pals, digging for crumbs. Sinatra acted
like he ran the place, like he was a real bigshot. There was no
shortage of guys ready to suck up to that prick. 'Hey, Frankie! You
sounded fantastic tonight! Whatta set! Can I lick your boots? You
say you like my girl? Here, bang her all night — anything for you,
Frank!' Anyway, Wynn and Pantero came up together. Then came
the Cannon thing, which was a stroke of genius. The president
was like a rock 'n' roll star. Chicks were throwing their panties on
the floor of Congress."

Though I was taping the interview, I frantically scribbled in
my notebook as a backup. I didn't want to lose this. Despite the
fact he'd barely troubled the dessert's surface, I hoped he wouldn't
run out of pudding.

"Wynn was a great Cannon, too. Real suave. Had the whole
thing down. I'd see him on *The Manny Hudson Show* or hear him
on the radio and I'd think, this kid has a licence to print money.
But he made a big mistake — he thought the folks who bought
the tickets and bought the records were crazy for Jimmy Wynn.
They didn't give a fuck about Jimmy Wynn."

"I saw a reference to a story that you got a laugh from mentioning Wynn in your act after the president was shot. What
happened that night?"

Bruce gravely pointed his spoon at me. "Yeah, that's a popular
story. That story, in fact, did more to keep that sad bastard's name
alive than anything he ever did. Here's what went down. I'm sitting in this club — the Blue Angel, I think — when I hear about
Cannon. I think, that's it. The whole country's going up in flames.
I think a civil war's right around the corner. You don't know what
it was like having him around. He made me proud to be an
American, I kid you not. He was stirring it up. People lost it when
New Orleans happened. Time stopped." He paused. I couldn't tell

if it was out of fatigue or for effect. "So anyways, I convince the manager to cancel the set that night — no one's gonna come out, anyway. And this guy says, 'You're right, Lenny, but I can't stay closed forever and I already paid you so you're going out there tomorrow. People are gonna need to blow off some steam.'

"So I spend the next day gobbling down every pill I've got — I don't want to think. Suddenly I'm not just a pissed-off Jew who says naughty words, I'm a spokesman on the state of the nation. I think, fuck that. Anyway, I come out on stage that night and the Blue Angel is packed. The energy in the room is weird. Some of 'em are trying to act cool, like what's going on isn't affecting them. But I can tell everyone's nervous about what I'm gonna say. Like, Lenny's gonna say something crazy, like someone should've taught the president to duck. And to be honest, I was planning to use some dumb crack about declaring open season on Congress — really stick it to the man. But I'm so high, I blank out completely. Nothing in there. So I walk the stage for a while. I walk and walk. I walk and walk. They're out there thinking, what the hell? Then I start shaking my head, like 'oh woe, oh woe.'" Bruce shook his head for me, too. "Finally, I say, 'Man.' I give it a long pause and then I say, 'That Jimmy Wynn is screwed.' And bang! The room goes off."

Bruce smiled a deeply satisfied smile. "The rest of the set, not so hot, but who needs that in the story?"

"So why did you do shows with Wynn?"

He took another smidgen of pudding. The sugar seemed to accelerate his speech and movements. His right eye twitched something fierce. "I would've brought a kiddie diddler on stage with me if I thought it would take some of the heat off. His agent Izzy Berman was always a good guy and I felt bad for him, always asking about this kid. I said, change the name at least. Jimmy thought: no, that's my thing. He didn't seem to have a clue what was going on. One night I turned to Jimmy and said, 'Man, my new record stiffed, no club in L.A. will book me, the pigs are busting my balls every chance they get. I just wish some wingnut would put me out of my misery — Jimmy, can you do me a favour and impersonate me in your act?' He'd get sore at that, but he was a good sport. He had to be — I was the only asshole who'd put him on stage. The other thing is that Jimmy Wynn was great as the president but he was still right fucking lousy as Jimmy Wynn. They'd eat him alive. But he was always talking about some great new bit that he was working into the set or some TV producer who was about to give him a shot. The comeback was always just around the corner. He wasn't done with showbiz, no way, even if showbiz was sure as shit done with him."

"He sounded hopeful."

"Absolutely friggin' delusional. Listen, I'm lying here with a colostomy bag that needs emptying, a dick that hasn't been hard since the last moon landing, and three bitch queen ex-wives who won't let me die in peace and I still wouldn't trade my life for Jimmy's."

"Wow."

"Yeah," he nodded. "I know."

"But what was his material like then? Was he doing characters?"

Bruce snorted. "I guess you could call 'em characters. They weren't famous people. The way his routine would go was this: he'd try a few straight jokes and screw them up completely. Then he'd do these little monologues as different 'types,' right? Jimmy would do the asshole dad and the hard-ass army sergeant and the racist cop and the hippie chick who won't put out until you read her pamphlet — shit like that. But the bits were just depressing." He pointed his finger at me for emphasis. "The second a comic wants to tell the audience the truth about anything, he's screwed. Jimmy thought the truth would set him free. But people don't want to hear that crap."

"What was the last you heard of him?"

"There was something about a show with Pantero around '80,

'81. There was some movie thing going on. You can understand why his name didn't get much discussion in my circles. He just depressed people."

"And did he ever talk about Cannon?"

"Not much. I'd ask him about it. They used to talk, ya know? Jimmy went to the White House. I never went to the White House. Well, not Cannon's White House. I went later. They had to hose down the place after I left."

"Really?"

He rolled his eyes. "No, kid. I'm jerking you around."

"Oh."

I read pity in his eyes. "Jeez, you really need someone to hold your hand. Anyhow, Jimmy always clammed up tight on the subject. He kept it to himself. I used to think I'd beat this big secret out of him someday but I bet he could take any crap I dished out."

A smirk crept across his lips. "Kid, let me ask you a question. Do you know what a horse is?"

He was setting me up for something. I thought: please don't show me your dick. "Sure," I said.

"Not a horse like the animal. I mean what sideshow and vaudeville types would call a horse. No? This was somebody whose act was about enduring unbelievable amounts of pain. They were like freaks of nature, they couldn't feel nothing. These were the guys who hung on crosses for hours or cut themselves with razors. There was one sorry prick who let folks beat the hell out of him. For a nickel, you could punch him in the face but it cost you a quarter to use the baseball bat. Sick shit, right? But if that's the only talent you've got, you make do. Well, that's what Jimmy Wynn was — a horse."

He winced. At first, I thought it was for effect again. Then he groaned.

"What is it?"

"Aah, I'm getting such a headache."

"Is it the sugar?"

"You a friggin' doctor?" He coughed.

The door opened. It was a nurse. "Lenny! What do you have on your tray?"

"Shit." He tried to hide the pudding by covering it with his hand. Realizing that it hardly obscured the cup at all, he tried another tactic by grabbing the cup and shook it angrily, spilling the remaining pudding over himself. "What am I, six years old? Can't I have a goddamn pudding?"

"You could have a heart attack. Then where would you be?"

"A better place than here, that's for sure." He searched for something on the other side of the bed. "Where's the control for this thing? I gotta lie down. Ah, here it is." He pushed a button. The top half of the bed rose sharply, pushing Bruce against the tray. "Dammit." He pushed the button again and he rose even higher. The nurse was trying hard not to look like she was enjoying this. "Nancy, get over here and fix this!"

Bruce was now sitting upright at ninety degrees, his face distorted with pain. "Oh, man," he muttered. Then he released a fart so loud, it rattled the bed.

Still standing in the doorway, Nancy laughed. Not a cruel laugh — more like that of someone who finds her cat halfway up a tree and unable to climb down. To my amazement, Bruce started to laugh, too. "Ah, I'm a mess. Get over here, Nance."

Nancy glided past me and corrected the bed's position.

I used this opportunity to make it to the doorway. "I have to be going now, Mr. Bruce. Thank you for your time."

"Yeah, yeah," he said, not looking over. "Just get outta here."

As I reached the hallway, I heard a shout. I poked my head in the room again.

"Do you wanna know who really killed President Cannon?"

The question caught me off guard. "Uh, sure."

"Hey, me too!" He waved me away.

5

I went deep into a Jimmy place and stayed there. Some of my weekend was spent transcribing my Lenny Bruce interview and deciding which quotes to use. I also studied the meagre amounts of Jimmy Wynn information on the Internet and made bids on his records on auction sites. The price for his second 1962 LP, *White House-Trained*, topped out at $2.50. There was also a 1965 LP called *Who Does This Guy Think He Is, Anyways?* up for grabs. The cover portrayed Jimmy Wynn in comical pieces of headgear: an Englishman's derby, a fireman's hat, a gumshoe's fedora, an Indian chief's headdress. Cannon was not represented in this pantheon. An online guide to comedy records had only this entry: "The washed-up Cannon impersonator's final platter is deservedly obscure. He barks his way through bits about an army sergeant who berates a soldier for losing his limbs and a cop too desperate to be cool to ever bust anyone. Marginally more fun than a Turkish prison." A ringing endorsement, then.

I went to the Strand bookstore and the library, looking for anything to do with Wynn, his time, or his art. I found various useful bits and pieces:

*Sick: Inside a Comedy Revolution* by Elliott List

There is a tiny entry on Wynn but I suspect the author deemed him too square to be sick. The book is more useful for describing the scene and the names of places Wynn might have played — the Zig Zag, the hungry i, the Latin Quarter, the Empire. List's history conjures up a late-night world of two-drink minimums, cackling audiences, and after-hours peccadilloes with skanky cocktail waitresses. There is some more information about Eddie Prefontaine, who died in 1986 of lung cancer. One comic calls the cluster of hopefuls at the El Morocco "Eddie's squeeze toys." Says another old timer, "Most of these kids didn't even know the meaning of the word queer — Eddie was just a guy who liked to give back rubs." The line made me think of hot oil. I put the book away.

*It's Crowded in Here* by Barry Beliveau

I looked for books about the art (and business) of adopting another person's voice and manner. There weren't many. Imitation may be the sincerest form of flattery but the trade secrets were seldom divulged. Even magicians were chattier.

One exception was this memoir by Beliveau, a Montreal-born impressionist who found fame in Vegas in the seventies. I remembered him as the host of a Canadian game show on which the daily grand prize was $50 and a case of split-pea soup. Though most of the book consists of inane showbiz gossip of use to no one — "Manny Hudson liked to relax by sketching portraits of his favourite guests in the guise of famous historical figures" — Beliveau makes one revealing comment about his craft.

"In a great impression," he writes, "the performer captures all the inflections, nuances, tics, and habits that we use to present ourselves to the world but usually don't even notice. They're the little things that make us who we are. More often than not, they have nothing to do with the physical details of our outward appearance. When I was first started out, I used to worry that I did not look anything like a particular celebrity. Eventually I realized that it didn't matter how that star dressed or styled his hair, or whether he was tall or short, skinny or fat — it didn't even matter if the he was a she! If I could talk the talk and walk the walk, then the audience saw whoever I wanted them to see."

*No, You're the Dummy: Ventriloquism through the Ages* by W.G. Cohn

I found the same point echoed in this book, which had a title I would have been proud to invent. It was about more than guys who stuck their hands up puppets' asses, though they got their due. Cohn's study of displaced voices stretches back to the Oracles of Delphi and the Witch of Endor. The author also explains how the ventriloquist's dummy is capable of an unlikely range of expressions. Besides working that creaky, creepy jaw, the ventriloquist might be able to make the dummy's eyes shift from left to right or get his eyebrows to rise and fall. When it is silent, the dummy appears to be a ridiculously primitive puppet capable of only the most rudimentary gestures. But when he's spewing saucy banter, the dummy's gestural range and complexity increases dramatically. Cohn attributes this phenomenon to the notion that just as the body produces a voice by physical means (diaphragm, larynx, tongue, lips), a voice can also create a body, at least in the eyes of a spectator. This "vocalic body" is what we witness, not the wooden bugger with the paint-bristle hair who tries to sing "The Camptown Ladies" while the other dude is drinking a glass of water.

This dummy psychoanalysis, oddly enough, helped shed some light on the only piece of video footage of Jimmy Wynn I had found, courtesy of a compilation tape of *The Manny Hudson Show*. I watched him on a grubby monitor in a New York library. He worked the studio audience from behind his podium, announcing his plans to rename Death Valley to something more cheerful, "like Sunny Glade, U.S.A. or the Delicious Desert." Even from this brief performance, I could understand how audiences saw him. By replicating his master's voice, he created a vocalic Cannon body. The words made Jimmy flesh. And lo it was pretty good.

*Was There Ever a Grief Like Ours?: A President and His Nation*
by Gore Hammerstein

My favourite Cannon hagiography. Hammerstein claimed Cannon spent the afternoon of November 18, 1962, "entertaining Jimmy Wynn, a Las Vegas comedian who did an impersonation of the president in his popular act." On December 12, there is a mention of a telephone conversation with Wynn. There was nothing anywhere in Hammerstein's book about Cannon attending a Nevada Delegation. Nor, for that matter, did Hammerstein mention whether Cannon had fathered two illegitimate mixed-race daughters or arranged kickbacks for the Chicago mob.

By Sunday afternoon, I had a pitch that was blinding in its magnificence. Angels would have wept at the sight. It was all there on the page — drama, farce, intrigue, tragedy. I had summarized the major details that could be gleaned from the sources so far, juiced them up with a few quotes from Bruce and mentioned promising leads like Danny Pantero. I firmly stated how our understanding of the president and the culture of his day would be rocked to their very foundations by these untold revelations — what did Jimmy and the president discuss? Did the comic become a confidant?

It hardly mattered that this foundation-rocking story was known to me only in bare fragments. What mattered was I believed in the integrity and the value of what I was about to write. And I quote: "Jimmy Wynn was the president's reflection in show business's funhouse mirror. He was the doppel-wisenheimer destroyed in the same moment America would be robbed of its greatest leader."

Ace.

However, my glowing pride in myself was temporary. Within an hour, these precious paragraphs — already the product of hours of spit, polish, and worry — would spoil at room temperature. They would become inane, incoherent, and needlessly hyperbolic. Any fool could see that I was faking it, that I wasn't any kind of writer, that I had no business in the same city as Winston Sharpe and the wastrel rock of Asphalt Diary. Angels would have gagged at the sight.

Then I worried that I didn't have an ending. What if I couldn't find Jimmy Wynn? Was there still a story without him? I hadn't a clue what his present circumstances were. Slow-motion suicide? Bitter alcoholic torpor? Decomposition? Dinner theatre? Before my confidence could completely deflate, I e-mailed the pitch to Daphne. She wouldn't see it until Monday morning, but I needed to be done with it.

Then I had my final surprise for the weekend: Lance arriving with groceries and three bottles of merlot. I relaxed and by relaxed, I mean ate and drank until I didn't care about comedians.

* * *

The phone woke me up. It was a long way to the living room.

"Hi, it's Nathan." My voice somehow wended its way up through the vino sludge in my throat. A vice tightened on my temples. Red wine headaches were the worst. Lance's ratatouille was bland so we overcompensated with the merlot.

"It's Daphne at *The Betsey*. I'm sorry if I'm calling too early."

My watch said 10:45 a.m. The last thing I remember was rifling through a stack of comedy records for Lance. We spent a long time with an LP by a raunchy black comic named Too Tanned. There was a long, almost nonsensical routine that started with a French girl being taught that fuck meant "to serve" and ended with a sailor saying, "Shit, if I knew if it was that kind of party, I'd have stuck my dick in the mashed potatoes." We played it a couple of times but still didn't get it.

"No, no," I sputtered. "This is just fine. I was already . . . reading the paper." I scanned the room in order to better place myself in the here and now. There was a dark puddle in the middle of the kitchen floor. Lance's bedroom door was open. I figured he was long gone, leaving me with the debris once again.

"I'm calling about your pitch. I've forwarded it to Winston. We're looking for a feature along these lines for our September issue. I think this one could work. Might you be available to come into the office and meet with us today? I know this is sudden but Winston's going to L.A. this afternoon."

"That's fine. I'll be here. There's nothing going on." I thought: don't say 'nothing,' you can't let her know there's 'nothing.' "I mean, I've got some things on the go but I can put them on hold." I thought: don't seem desperate, just eager. "I'd love to get on top of this, or on the case, or you know."

"Terrific. We'll talk more later."

"I'll stay right by the phone. I'll be here. Go ahead and call, I'll answer right away." I thought: just stop talking.

Despite the headache and the embarrassment, I had a keen feeling of triumph. *The Betsey* was on the hook. I only had to close the deal and I was one step further away from being destitute and deported.

When I went into the kitchen to make some coffee, I was faced with the extent of last night's cataclysm. The same casserole dish that I'd just scrubbed clean of five-bean casserole crud was now covered in a matter the consistency of tar. The frying pan and two rings on the stovetop were covered in a brown, greasy substance of unknown origin. There was a puddle of vinaigrette dressing in the centre of the floor and footprints all around. Streaks of vegetable juice had spilled off the counter and onto the floor. The remainder of ratatouille sat in Tupperware that I'd failed to cover or put in the fridge. I wrung out a cloth and bent down to wipe up the vinaigrette. When a hangover head rush nearly overwhelmed me, I decided to start with more vertically oriented tasks, like filling the sink with plates and dishes.

As I worked, I fantasized about life in the bosom of *The Betsey*. Winston Sharpe would groom me as his second. I would oblige him by cutting my hair and getting disciplined about my work. No more snidely worded record reviews for me — only Pulitzer contenders about foreign wars, terrorist conspiracies, and political corruption. At night, I would visit fast-breaking restaurants in the textile district with Daphne. I filled in the gaps in her backstory. Patrician East Coast household. Liberal arts degree from Ivy League institution. Published poem in friend's literary journal. First car a Saab. First boyfriend a law student. Flirts with veganism. Likes music by dead lady jazz singers.

If even two things turned out to be true, she was unlike any other woman on whom I'd seriously crushed. There was Candace, who I met in Grade 10 at a concert by Eight Ball. It took three years to escape the category of "really good friend," and then only briefly. Claire was a genuine French-from-France girl I met in a history class in first-year university. I was so beguiled by her accent, it took me two months to notice how dull she was. A few years later came Linda, the bassist in Now With Wings, an all-girl punk band whose record I'd reviewed (positively). We'd spend hours earnestly discussing identity politics, a term I no longer understand. We talked about living in New York and drank beer in bed. I loaned her my copy of *Asphalt Diary*. We lasted three months before she moved back in with her band's singer, who — as I would tell people with a mixture of heartbreak, hurt pride, and a raging hard-on — was the foxiest lesbian I'd ever seen. I couldn't compete.

I thought: maybe Daphne is one of those women who think men who do housework are sexy. Then I thought: if I were a woman, would I be one of those women?

The phone rang again. The dish splashed back into the sink. I darted toward the phone in the living room. My right foot went straight into the puddle of vinaigrette. Though Lance's dressing was not particularly oily, the liquid still defied traction. My foot shot out to the side, I came down on my left knee and the floor flew up to meet the left side of my face. That hurt. I don't remember how I made it the rest of the way.

"Yuh." I hoped what I said was a word.

"Nathan? It's Daphne again. Great news. Winston is excited about your story idea. He's going to Los Angeles in a few hours. Can you be here at 1 p.m.?"

"Wonn?"

"That's right. We'll see you at one. Bye for now."

"Bah."

I headed to the bathroom, curled up in the tub, and let the water stream over my head. It took ten minutes to feel sentient. My left cheekbone was puffy and purple. There was still a Band-aid sideburn on the right side of my face. No dance rumble had ever caused this much damage.

I walked the fifteen blocks to *The Betsey*'s office on lower Broadway with my head in a soupy fog. I'd managed to get myself halfway to presentable and stuffed my gourd with ibuprofen yet every step was a struggle. I tried to think of a good story to explain my state of disrepair because the truth made me sound like a guy who let bartenders cut his hair and lost fights with salads.

*The Betsey*'s offices occupied the top of a ten-storey building flanked by stone gargoyles. The gloomy façade had been a popular exterior for horror movies. The abyss of its darkened doors swallowed me up. Daphne met me at the reception desk. She wore a short black jacket and glasses embossed with the logo of an Italian designer. Her friendly demeanor contrasted with the building's sinister air and the frosty intellectual chic conveyed by her outfit. Though the receptionist visibly winced at the sight of my face, Daphne was too well-bred to be fazed.

"Let me take you to the boardroom. Winston's coming in a few minutes."

As I lumbered behind her, I glanced at the magazine covers on the walls. Alongside them were various examples of Cannon-related imagery — famous photographs as well as Irving Stella's paintings of his dogs and pop art silkscreens of the president's smiling mug.

There was the odor of earthy decay coming from the biggest office on the floor. Daphne told me the story during my first office visit. When Rose Marie inherited the magazine from her younger brother, she insisted that Peter would retain a vital if symbolic role at *The Betsey*. His office was just as he left it. The room had become another holy site in the Cannon folk religion. For one hour every Friday, visitors were allowed to leave flowers and other tributes at the office's threshold. Security guards removed any dangerous-looking wackos but a few — like that guy who liked to perform art criticism with the contents of his stomach — slipped through the net. Daphne saw one young man take out a whip and flagellate himself. Then there was the college student from Wisconsin who quietly left the office at the end of the appointed hour, pried open the elevator doors, and jumped down the shaft. The throbbing in my head compelled me to consider his example.

Daphne offered a chair to me near one end of the boardroom's vast table. As I sat down, I could tell that she was taking the opportunity to examine my features. "Do you want anything? Perhaps a cappuccino? Or water?"

I thought: a cold compress? Reconstructive surgery? "No, I'm fine."

She sat down across from me. "If you change your mind, let me know. As I was saying about the story, I think it will be very unique. We've done very little on how Cannon influenced the entertainers of his day. His connections to Las Vegas are also something we're eager to explore. Your timing is good, too — we're doing a Man and His Time special in September and we were looking for a strong pop-culture feature to add to the mix."

I nodded, being careful not to jostle my head too much. "That's how I see it."

"I'd never heard of Jimmy Wynn before you mentioned him."

"Oh no?" I said. "He'd been on my . . ." I made the mistake of striving for a tricky word. ". . . my . . . radar for a while." Trying to reassemble my thoughts was a losing battle. "He was the most famous man in America. Or second most. Famous."

An elegant man with slicked-back silver hair strode into the room. Daphne stood at attention. I stood too, immediately regretting the change in altitude as my field of vision speckled. When it cleared, I saw a beetle in Winston Sharpe's ear.

"Taki says Sony is in this thing all the way," he said. "Mmm-hmm. Yes. No, that's ludicrous. Where did you hear this?" He nodded at Daphne. I realized the beetle was a tiny black nodule. A thin grey wire connected it with a microphone clipped to his collar. "No, don't tell me. It's irrelevant." He gave me a curious expression when he saw my face but quickly recovered his poise. "Sometimes I worry that overexposure to the television business destroys brain tissue. All I need to know is how many board members will be at the restaurant tonight. And Sakamoto? Good. Good. Send the dossiers to my assistant."

Sharpe sat down, plucked the nodule from his ear and unclipped the mike. "Daphne, don't let me forget that here. Better yet." He beckoned over a young woman waiting in the doorway and placed the contraption in her hand. "Hold my calls, Alison. But not too tightly."

He stretched out a hand toward me. "Mr. Grant."

"This is Winston Sharpe," said Daphne, standing over his shoulder.

"He knows that," said Sharpe. "Mr. Grant, I have a teleconference in two minutes. Before you ask me any questions, let me have the opportunity to explain my interest." He stared at me with those blue-grey eyes that writers invariably described as "piercing" in magazine profiles that had headlines like "Sharpe Gets to the Point."

"I'm eleven years old. *The Manny Hudson Show* is a Sunday night tradition in my home. I watch the program with my mother and father. One night, Manny Hudson says he would like to introduce a very special guest. He piques my curiosity. The band plays 'Hail to the Chief' and a familiar man walks out on stage. I am excited because I believe that the man on television is the president of the United States. My parents start to laugh straight away. I do not know why. I think it is disrespectful. Then I notice that some aspects of the president's appearance are not right. He's too tall, his hair is too dark, his body is stiff. But when I hear his voice, I believe him. And when he uses the president's voice to say words the president would never say, I laugh, too. It hardly matters to me what he says."

His eyes continued to pierce. I thought: was Winston Sharpe this intense when he was eleven?

"I tell my father that instead of my next four allowances, I would like a copy of this man's long-playing record album. When I receive it, I learn all the parts by heart. I imagine tea parties with Senator Bear from North Palooka. I practise jokes about the traffic in Washington, D.C. I make up comical names for African diplomats. I want to be like the president, too. I see how this can transform me."

Sharpe interleaves his fingers and rests his hands on the table. "It was a childish obsession. After President Cannon was taken from us, I put away childish things. Before today, I had not thought about Jimmy Wynn for thirty-five years. The memory was too painful, too intimate. We live in a very different world now, but in so many ways, it is Teddy Cannon's world. He gave it to us. Jimmy

Wynn was one of the first men to understand what living in this world meant. I want you to regard him as its first true citizen."

Alison came back into the room, offering the tiny telephone back to her boss. Sharpe held a finger up to her to signal he needed one more moment. "I am aware of the articles you have done for this magazine. Daphne also forwarded the article that won some award for you back in Colorado."

I thought: that's Canada, not Colorado. I didn't interrupt him.

"While they show some promise, I am not entirely confident. I do, however, have a feeling." He pointed a long, talon-like finger to my nose. "I want you to answer this question honestly: are you up to this task?"

I consciously removed any "er," "uh," or "heh" from my answer and did not turn it into a question or an apology. "Yes, sir."

"Then I suggest you make good on this opportunity. I'll be keeping an eye on you." He rose to leave. "Daphne can sort out your travel itinerary."

"Travel?"

Sharpe left the room without another word.

My sense of triumph was undermined by my terror. I hadn't considered that the story might take me away from the comfort zone I was trying to protect. I liked doing telephone interviews. I liked languid afternoons of research at the New York Public Library. I liked waking up with a hangover in a familiar environment. Moreover, I couldn't tell Sharpe or Daphne about a serious impediment to any travel itinerary: the act of stepping on an airplane could get me tossed out of the country.

Daphne gave me a comforting smile. "I hope you caught all that. We can go back to my office and draw up a plan of attack."

I spoke as calmly as I could. "Could I get that water now?"

Danny Pantero does six nights a week in the Brigantine Showroom of the Empire Resort and Casino. I had already seen three in a row. I was enjoying the experience more than I would have thought possible, and that wasn't just because I was now the kind of person who could claim to have a regular table. Of course, it would've been swell to have caught Pantero's act when he was a young buck in the late fifties and early sixties, or in his splendiferous disco years in the seventies, or even when he was riding the first wave of nostalgia in the eighties. He was past the point of anachronism now. But he had arrived at a new order of m øagnificence. He was more like some kind of venerated holy relic, a material connection to a bygone age that otherwise existed only in myth. Plus, he knew how to put on a show.

Certain patterns had emerged in Pantero's shows. At first, they caused me to grow cynical about the moments I most enjoyed. Yet as I finished my second bottle of beer on Night No. 3, I began to understand how Pantero had weathered four decades filled with evenings just like this one.

Pantero's show was all action from the moment he came onstage. Wearing a white tuxedo and a red cape, he arrived on horseback. The animal appeared to be heavily drugged, but that was probably legal in Nevada. Not long after the introduction came a point in the show that I called the Pique. Pantero would get two lines into "Ain't That a Kick" before waving the band to an abrupt halt. "Hold on, guys," he said, shaking his head. "Hold on." There were mutters of confusion from musicians and audience members. "I couldn't go on with that. When we started the song, I heard two people out there say, 'Yeah!' The rest of the audience just sat there." He turned to us, the guilty culprits cowering in the dark. "Do you really want to hear the song?" I heard several people yell, "Oh yeah!" The rest of the audience assented with applause. Pantero still looked skeptical. "Really?" The cheers got lustier. "Well, now I believe you." Pantero smiled like some stern but kind country judge about to let us off the hook. "So let's do this!" He nodded to the band and the musicians picked up the song exactly where they left off. Pantero punctuated the song with an exuberant kick, as if to say, yes, we're gonna make it all the way to fourth gear!

After the fifth number ("Those Bedroom Eyes"), he began the March of Kisses. This involved planting one on each of the approximately forty women arrayed in the first and second rows of tables. He had a flawless instinct for knowing which women wanted to be kissed on the lips and which on the cheek. "Oh, mercy!" he would exclaim after the seventeenth or eighteenth woman. When he got an especially enthusiastic kiss from a lady in a married couple, Pantero would say to her partner, "Buddy, it's time you two went upstairs!" And the final woman in the March of Kisses got a little twirl. "There's a lot of love in this room," Pantero would say when he made it back to the stage. "I can tell we're going to have a good time tonight!"

And who will ever forget Elvis Time after seeing it once, or thrice? Halfway through the show Pantero would say, "We don't usually play this but we had a request from a gentleman in the audience." At the point he would point to a man at table C7. "He said that if we played his favourite song by Elvis Presley, he'd shake his pelvis for everyone. Isn't that right, sir?" So far, every single man I'd seen Pantero point out would laugh and nod. They couldn't have all made the same musical request. They could've figured Pantero had made a mistake and the request had come from a man at table B7. Or maybe when they bought their tickets for the show, they'd knowingly selected the most Elvis-appropriate seat in the Brigantine Showroom. Whatever the scenario, at some point during this interaction between performer and spectator they must have known that Pantero was lying. Pantero implicated an audience member in a calculated deception yet the man was invariably delighted rather than offended. To betray Pantero now by speaking up — by telling him, perhaps, that he thought Elvis liked to smear peanut butter on his privates and wiggle it at widows — would be like betraying show business herself.

That didn't happen tonight, either. Instead, Pantero launched into a thunderous rendition of "Blue Suede Shoes." Near the end of the song, Pantero said, "So we kept our end of the deal. Now let's see this gentleman show us his stuff!" The man at C7 would get up and do his best Presley leg twist. (The guy on the second night merely pivoted on his cane.) The audience squealed. "Wow, I think this fella's missed his true calling! He should be up here with me! Give him a big hand!" Pantero didn't let the band stop there. "We don't always get such a great audience," he told them, "so let's give 'em a little something extra." The number closed with "Viva Las Vegas." The song's breathless pace made the song sound like something the band hadn't played in a while. Yet as far as I could tell, they played it every night the same way — a little rushed. This time, I noticed the musicians were even playing the same mistakes I'd heard twice already. Not only was Pantero's show your proverbial well-oiled machine, it was a machine that disguised its own workings. I marveled at its ingenuity.

At no point did Pantero mention Jimmy Wynn, his partner for nearly five years. As the show barreled past Elvis Time toward the Gift of the Scarf, I reflected on the history of the partnership. I had gleaned many details from Danny Pantero's memoir, *The Boy Who Lived Down the Lane*, a remainder-bin perennial since its publication in 1989. Pantero wrote that Wynn was introduced to him by his brother, who had met the young comic when they were working at the Zig Zag in 1957. "Here was this skinny, awkward kid from Detroit who could turn himself into virtually anybody. I knew he would be incredibly valuable in my act. And I was right."

Wynn stays at the fringes of Pantero's life story, despite being "a crucial collaborator" and "one of my closest pals." The split in 1961 when Wynn went solo with the Cannon routine is mentioned in passing. In fact, much of the book is comprised of inspirational stories about kids Pantero helped through his horse ranch's "Trots for Tots" program.

Newspaper stories confirmed the two men were performing together even before Pantero, then only nineteen, had his first success with "The Girl Who Lives Down the Lane." The treacly smoocher reached No. 2 in the middle of 1959. That was also the year they began headlining the revue at the Midnight Room in the Overland Hotel. A review in *Variety* praised their "whip-smart combination of melodies and merriment" but criticized "material as stale as week-old cannoli." Though Pantero's hit gave the duo a boost, the reviewer implied that Midnight Room audiences had seen the likes of Danny and Jimmy many times before, i.e., the smooth singer and the zany comic. Ten years earlier, it had been Jack Hunter and Sammy Mac. Plenty of duos had recycled the schtick. However, the reviewer did make special note of Wynn's "nutty knack for mimicry."

In 1960 and '61 came short-run stints at lower-rung lounges. It was Wynn's Cannon impressions that revitalized the partnership in mid-'61 after months of workshopping it solo at the Savoy. It took them all the way up to the Sands. They broke up the partnership only when Wynn and Berman developed a full-fledged Cannon show at the end of the year. Luckily for Pantero, the split coincided with his second major hit, a moist towelette of a ballad called "Bring Your Love to Me." It went to No. 4 in 1962 — he didn't have another smash until "Forever in Your Eyes" in 1969, which he later recycled for a minor disco hit in 1977.

Unlike their idols Hunter and Mac, Wynn and Pantero didn't seem to hate each other after they broke up. There was no evidence of a feud. In his autobiography, Pantero seems to indicate (he's not big on facts and dates) that he played shows with Wynn as late as 1969. There were even shows scheduled for 1982 but they "fell through" for reasons he didn't specify. Pantero would surely have spared a few more lines if his old partner had died before the memoir was published in 1989.

I had come to Vegas because Pantero said he would give me more details. Pantero's publicist Sparkle (no last name was supplied or, come to think of it, necessary) originally scheduled my interview for Friday afternoon, the day after I arrived in Las Vegas. She gave me tickets to Pantero's show on Thursday night to help me "get a sense of Danny's artistry." When she called me on Friday, she told me Danny had to rest a sore throat and we'd have to reschedule for Saturday afternoon. She offered tickets again. On Saturday morning, Sparkle bumped the interview to after the show that night. "He likes to have a nice dinner after a big Saturday," she told me. "That's a very special show for Danny." I asked if I could see how special. As I sat at a table that wasn't C7, I had to agree — the show overflowed with specialness. It was sick with specialness.

I had spent my days checking out the archives at the University of Nevada. It had a fascinating trove of Wynn arcana — old advertisements and posters, photographs, press materials that hyped "a special audience with comedy's commander-in-chief." I had arranged a Sunday meeting with Steve DaVinci, his

MC and bandleader. I had looked up his number in the phone book, which was an accurate indication of my sleuthing abilities.

I ordered another beer and enjoyed Pantero's Surprisingly Moving Tribute to Our Troops. It was, again, surprisingly moving. His concern for U.S. soldiers stationed in Indochina and Panama seemed utterly genuine. So did Pantero's desire to bone an audience member during the sequence I called Saucy Banter with the Heavy-Set Lady Sitting to the Right of the Stage. My attention wandered after that.

As much as I was getting tired of waiting for Pantero to talk to me, I preferred it to the panic that accompanied my departure from New York. I had let Daphne book me a plane ticket. I considered other means of transportation but a train or a bus took the better part of a week. My major concern was that my Travel Identification Card — a measure introduced during last year's crackdown on airport security in the wake of the hijacking in Dallas — would alert officials to the fact I was no longer a Visiting Cultural Worker. Sure, I had an assignment, but it's not like I could ask Winston Sharpe to sponsor me before I proved myself.

I was determined to do that. My solution was elegant. I rubbed my TIC on my VCR until it had been demagnetized, then repeatedly scraped the strip with a house key. As for the numbers printed on the TIC, I used one of Lance's expensive pens to turn the threes into eights. I hoped my bush-league subterfuge would be enough because the TIC had been notoriously problematic since its introduction. Seeing as my passport was not from any of the countries on the official Territories of Concern list (e.g., Ghana, France, Syria, everywhere south of Mexico), I took a chance that it was all I needed.

At the airport check-in at LaGuardia, my card didn't scan at all. "I'm sorry, sir," said the nice lady from Trans-Con Air. "Let's try that again. Everything's a bit buggy today."

"Ah." I meant the expression to convey sympathy and under-standing.

"Let me just punch in your number." She compared the con-tents of the screen with my passport. "Hmm. Something tells me you are not Larissa Vestry of Fresno, California. There's something wrong with your card." She picked up the phone. "I'm going to have to sort this out with the call centre."

"There's never been a problem before. I've been back and forth between Toronto and New York all year. I'm an architecture stu-dent. At Astor College." I thought: don't volunteer more data than you have to.

"Yes, sir, but," she twisted the phone cord around her finger, "yes, I'll hold." She gave me a "hey, what can I do?" look.

"I really hope I don't miss this flight." My tone was measured, even sympathetic — I'd been practising it for hours. "It's my baby sister's wedding tomorrow."

We had a quiet moment. "A wedding in Las Vegas," she said, now more dreamy than flustered. She untwisted the cord and hung up the phone. "Oh, this is all such a hassle. You can go ahead. But I have to confiscate this card. Before your return flight, you have to go to the Department of Immigration, Naturalization, and Border Security in Las Vegas. They can issue you a new TIC."

"Thanks so, so much."

And that was it. I didn't even have to pull out my fail-safe about wishing that Father could've been alive to see me walk Sis down the aisle. Nor would I need the second half of my ticket. Theoretically, I could stay in Las Vegas forever. I had already begun to acclimate to the constant assault on my senses, from the infernal cacophony of the casino floors to the neon-lit ostentation of the hotels to the questionable freshness of a $1.99 shrimp cock-tail I ate not long after arriving.

A few years before, I'd come here with my parents and my brother Michael while en route to a hiking trip in Utah. I knew

that this time I wanted to stay away from the new end of town —
where the hotels either looked like space stations or the Taj Mahal
after a cocaine binge — and stick to the downtown strip, where
the action had been back in Wynn's heyday. Maybe he was here
right now. Though he wasn't in the phone book (I had to look),
he might have another identity. He could even be one of the
legions of fat losers who spent all day and night waddling between
the slots. Everything about this place seemed swollen.

Back onstage, Pantero worked hard to stay at fighting weight.
*"I've got two tickets to paradise,"* he bellowed. *"Pack your bags, we'll
leaving tonight — oh yeah!"* I thought: a-ha, the Just Gotta Rock
moment. That was when Pantero implored the band not to play
"another slow one." Pantero sensed that the crowd wanted something different on this night, something special. He knew they
were an open-minded bunch who liked all kinds of music. "Let's
show 'em how we blow the roof off this place!" That meant we
were coming up to the climax of the sequence. Looking like a
biker at a wedding, a tuxedoed man with a handlebar moustache
stepped forward from the bandstand and played a guitar solo.
Pantero cried, "Vance is on fire!"

He closed the set with a bravura "Bring Your Love to Me."
After the first chorus, he did the Gift of the Scarf. It was a less
elaborate gesture than the earlier March of Kisses, the mid-set
Bony Maronie Dance or the You Caught My Eye Confession.
Pantero walked up to a woman at one of the front tables (at this
performance it was just left of the centre), bent forward, and murmured into his microphone, "I couldn't help noticing how much
you seemed to enjoy the show tonight. I've got a little present."
He reached up and removed the red silk scarf from around his
neck. The woman beamed as he draped it around her shoulders.
He kissed her on the cheek (last night it was her lips) and sauntered back onstage as the band took the song to the bridge.

There was a man at the same table as the woman who had

received the Gift of the Scarf. I'd noticed him earlier in the show
— his lolling head and bark-like laughs suggested he was well and
truly loaded. He didn't appreciate the Gift of the Scarf. His wife
shushed him to no avail. He grabbed the offending article from
around her neck, scrunched it up angrily in his hands, and tossed
it onstage. Since he was giving some love to a table of biddies to
his left, Pantero didn't see it land. A wave of horror swept through
the audience as Pantero sauntered back to centre-stage and
stepped on the scarf. Like Lance's vinaigrette, the silk provided little traction and Pantero fell hard on his ass. The impact resounded
through the Brigantine Showroom's PA. The teen singing sensation of 1959 may have looked like a fit forty but he was a man of
almost sixty — the fall looked strong enough to shatter a tailbone.
Most of the band that noticed the disruption to the program
stopped playing immediately. The horn players continued for a
few more bars, mocking the fallen idol with brassy exuberance.

An awkward moment passed. Like everyone else in the room,
I was on the verge of crying out, of wailing to God in heaven for
allowing such a tragedy to happen. Then Pantero came to his
senses. He lifted the microphone to his lips. "Wow, I don't usually
get a chance to enjoy the view from here." There was a collective
burst of relieved laughter. He picked up the once-coveted scarf
and examined it on both sides. "Did I mark this Return to
Sender?" More laughter. Clutching Vance's hand, Pantero got
back on his feet. Without another moment's hesitation, he turned
to the band. "C'mon, guys, you're still on the clock. Meet me on
the top of the chorus." He swung up his arm, brought it down to
launch back into the song: *"Your eyes are all that I see / Your kisses
are as sweet as can be / I long to make you and I we / So bring all
your love to me!"*

"Now that's a helluva performer," said the man at C7 to his
companion as Pantero bowed to a standing ovation.

The audience was buzzing. I left the happy folks and headed to a small piano bar not far from the Brigantine Showroom. This was where I had arranged to meet Sparkle. She turned out to be a middle-aged blonde who, despite her name, had a greater affinity for pearls than diamonds. In any case, her expression was grave.

"Great show," I said. "He really pulled it out of the fire."

"I'm afraid we're going to have to reschedule. Mr. Pantero's doctor has to examine his injury."

I was surprised because he got through the encores without a hitch. "Is he badly hurt?"

"We don't know yet. We just don't know." She shook her head in despair. "This could have been even more serious. That man has been arrested." She was on the edge of tears. "We may still be able to do something tomorrow. Right now, I just don't know."

"That's totally fine. We'll talk tomorrow."

"Thanks for being so understanding." Sparkle clasped my arm. "Mr. Pantero sends his deepest, deepest regrets." She squeezed and was gone.

It had been an emotional night for all of us.

7

Steve DaVinci wanted to meet for lunch at Hinky's House of Waffles. "It's my little Sunday tradition," he told me on the phone. I expected Hinky's to be one of those joints that only the local characters knew about, which would make it the rare Las Vegas landmark that wasn't being prepped for detonation by a demolition crew — the newness of the city was relentless. I longed for some of New York's vintage filth and decrepitude.

I didn't get it from Hinky's. At the address DaVinci gave me was a gleaming low-rise development, built to accommodate bus-loads of suckers as they entered the city limits from the south. Only the façade of the original waffle house had remained — behind it was a hectic complex that contained a small casino, a cluster of factory outlet stores, several monstrous restaurants, and a bar called the Sportz Zone. The latter is where I found DaVinci, already halfway through a basket of chicken wings and a mug of coffee. He watched a highlight reel of the afternoon's European soccer matches on the big-screen TV. He was a heavyset man with a suspiciously dark head of hair. His lime-green golf shirt was two sizes too small. I was thankful a high collar spared me the sight of his bunched-up man cleavage.

"Mr. DaVinci?"

He grabbed a napkin to wipe his fingers before reaching out to me. "Steve, call me Steve. I hope you don't mind that I got some food already — no time for dinner last night. I had a helluva time." He pointed at my face. "Looks like you did too. You get the plate number on that truck?"

"What? Oh, no. I slipped in the shower."

He snickered. "I hope you had someone there to help you up!"

I sat down between him and the TV. He shifted his chair so he could continue to watch. "Ah, Juventus, you screwed me again. You watch soccer? Football?" He emphasized the "ooo" to make sure I knew what he meant.

"Not much."

"It's good stuff. I got interested in it a few years back when the sports books started taking action on it. They thought it was a good way to get some money off the limey, frog, and kraut tourists. Now I'm hooked. Did you know that more people watch the World Cup than the Super Bowl multiplied by the World Series?"

"Really?"

He smirked. "You interviewing me already?"

"No, why?"

"You keep saying things that sound like questions."

"I'm sorry. I'm Canadian."

"Ah. An ice coon."

I thought: did I just hear that?

He didn't let me answer. "I did a couple of years with Barry Beliveau. You know him?"

I thought: he thinks we all know each other.

"You mean the impressionist?" I stammered. "No. Not personally."

"Good guy," said DaVinci. "But cheap. Cheap, cheap, cheap." He licked some red sauce off his thumb as he repeated the word in a singsongy fashion. "So what are you drinking?"

"Coffee?"

"Just coffee? Lemme get Irina to Irish it up." He waved over a dark-eyed blonde with a Hinky's badge. "Hey, gorgeous. An Irish coffee for my friend here. What's your name again?"

"Nathan."

"Irina, say hello to Nathan."

"Halloh, Nay-tan," she said in a thick Russian accent. She handed me a menu.

"Irina's from Minsk. She's a minx from Minsk. She really lights up this place, don't she?"

"Stop, you."

DaVinci watched her go with a moony look. "Man, the girls in this town get sexier every year. This one's gonna give me another heart attack." He grabbed at his heart as his eyes rolled back in his head. "Oh, god, oh — errgk!" He fell forward until his forehead nearly touched his chicken bones. "What a way to go, right?! She'd have to crawl out from under me." He slapped me on the arm.

I added a timid "heh-heh." I pulled out my notebook and tape recorder.

"I get it. Just the facts, Steve." He took a slurp of his own coffee. "I didn't do it, officer, I swear! I was home all night — just ask your wife!" He slapped me on the arm again. "You're the bad cop, I can tell. Probably got a whole list of burning questions." He spoke in a squeaky voice. "So, Mr. DaVinci, how do you explain your success in show business?" He dropped down a few octaves. "Well, young man, I attribute my good fortune to hard work, determination, and a twelve-inch dong." He cracked up before returning to his natural voice. "Nah, I'm kidding. It's only eleven!"

I clearly had to take control over the conversation before he whipped it out and put it on the table. "I think I told you on the phone already that I'm writing a story about Jimmy Wynn."

"Pleased to hear it. The man was a great talent too soon forgotten."

"You don't mind saying his name out loud?"

He waved a paw at me. "Superstition is for shitheads and inbreds."

We shared a friendly round of snorts before I ventured on. "How did you meet him?"

"I was in the men's bathroom of the Las Vegas bus station and this young man turned to me and said, 'Hey, buddy, I'll blow you for five bucks, but if you gimme ten, I'll make you believe I'm Mitzy Harlow.'" He slapped his knee. "I kid, I kid. Truth be told, I was leading a little combo here that used to play the Fremont Hotel. 'Songs for Swinging Lovers a Specialty,' right? My agent knew Jimmy's agent, Izzy. Sometime in '61 Izzy calls me and says he needs a band for his guy Jimmy Wynn."

"Had you heard of him?"

"I'd heard the name. It was a real small town back then. But I wasn't too big on Danny Pantero so I didn't know their show. The only thing Izzy tells me is that the kid does impressions. I'm thinking this sounds a little bush league, but Izzy's offering decent green. So me and my boys go check him out. Jimmy was still with Pantero then and performing with Pantero's band but I could tell that he was ready to get something going on for himself. Second part of the show they were doing at the Sands, he does this bit about Cannon and the crowd's nuts for it. Absolutely out of their minds." DaVinci waves his hands in the air for emphasis. "I don't think I'd seen anybody as smooth as Jimmy. Real killer." He leans in. "The irony is I heard Pantero didn't even want the Cannon routines in the show. Really stole the spotlight. But you gotta give the people what they want."

"So you took the gig?"

"Oh, yeah. How could I not? The thing was taking off like a rocket."

"What was your role?"

"My role?" His voice went cold. "My role . . . I played Lady Macbeth. Are you asking what I did, what my little monkey act was like?"

His sudden sternness scared me. "Uh . . ."

He laughed and slapped me on the arm. "You shouldn't let me mess with you, kid. It's too easy. Anyway, my main gig was playing the vibes and keeping the band in time. Izzy also asked me to MC. I was the guy who introduced Jimmy every night. I did the whole spiel. 'Here he is, the toast of Las Vegas, lah-di-lah, get ready to laugh your ass off.' It wasn't so special until I had a real stroke of genius. You ever heard him called 'Your comedy commander-in-chief'? That was mine."

This was my only opportunity to flatter him. "Wow, that was really good."

He soaked it up. "Yeah, Izzy creamed in his pants when he heard it. Jimmy was like, 'Yeah, yeah, that's me.' A while later, he wanted me to say that he was the president of Funny. I told him, 'That's the same thing, only lousier.'"

Irina came back with my coffee. I could tell from the fumes coming off it that it was definitely Irish. I ordered a cheeseburger, too. DaVinci watched her ass intently as she crossed the room again.

"Did you disagree often?"

"Now you're my shrink, right? Vut can you tell me about your muzzar?" DaVinci put his finger under his nose to make a little moustache. I thought: is he confusing Hitler with Freud? "No, no, Jimmy and I were tight. We were best pals in those days. He wasn't an easy guy to get to know — he didn't like to talk about where he'd been, what he'd done. His ma was a little funny in the head so it didn't sound like any picnic growing up. Having Danny Pantero for your partner couldn't have been much fun, either. But we were on the road solid for two years. Town to town, doing the Cannon thing. The show just got better and better. Some of my guys would say, 'Steve, if I have to play "Hail to the Chief" one more time, I'll lose my freakin' mind.' But I had a ball. And Jimmy was a consummate professional. Not a loose cat, but real dedicated. Jimmy liked to say that what he was out to capture was not how the president talked or walked but his whole essence, you know? He called it the aura. Kind of a mystical thing."

"Did he often talk about that?"

"No time. It was all go-go-go. Get this — we did five straight nights at Carnegie Hall." DaVinci raises his hands and looks heavenward. "Carnegie Goddamn Hall. Can you believe that? And the chicks! I'd never gotten so much tail. Even my spic drummer was getting more than he could handle."

"Did Jimmy attract many women?"

"Our Jimmy wasn't so smooth when he was off the stage. His real coup was Katie Perry. You know her?"

"No."

"Jeez, you kids. You watch TV eighteen hours a day yet you learn nothing. She was this sweet little actress. Was on a big show at the time, *Daisy's School Days*. She played a college freshman, real girl-next-door type. Jimmy liked the Gidget type, you know? Young but not the kind of young that gets you thrown in jail." DaVinci chuckled. "Not in this state, anyway. But she was swift, too — a good actress. Jimmy used her on that first record."

"Was she in the Capital Offence?"

"There was no such thing. Jimmy did most of the voices. I did a few bits. Katie did Connie. Jimmy lucked out with her. It was all horseshoes until it turned to shit."

"And where were you when it turned to, uh, shit?"

"Kid, you're hilarious." His voice went squeaky again. "By shit, Mr. DaVinci, do you mean poo-poo?" He elbowed away the chicken bones and put his meaty arms on the table. "Let me tell you about shit. Shit is going from making a record that sells six million copies and doing a show that pulls in a thousand folks a night to becoming the punchline to a joke nobody likes."

He got silent for a long moment, as if he were saying a prayer for his long-gone friend and meal ticket. Then I noticed DaVinci's gaze was directed at the TV over my shoulder. "Dammit all to hell!" He thumped the table. "Man United's just lost me fifty bucks. I don't know why I bet on this sport. To be honest, it bores me to tears. Worse than baseball."

"Can you tell me about the day of Cannon's assassination?"

"Look at this limey fruit." I turned around long enough to see a player in red get mobbed by his teammates. "He gets one fluke goal every tenth game and everyone treats him like he's Jesus. I can't believe they paid ten million pounds for him."

"Mr. DaVinci."

"Steve," he said, still looking over my shoulder.

"Steve, can you tell me about what happened to Jimmy after Cannon's assassination?"

He looked me in the eye. "Now that was a bad day. No one ever had a day that bad. Write that down in your story." He looked at me long and hard. "What were you writing for again?"

"*The Betsey.*"

"That's run by the Cannons, isn't it?" He waved his empty coffee cup at Irina as she neared the table with my burger. "Would you be a Russian doll and fill me up?" He turned back to me. "I would like Jimmy to be remembered for something other than unhappy stories. He made a lot of people happy."

"I fully intend to do him proud." I still had no idea whether he was alive or dead — it unsettled me that DaVinci referred to him in the past tense.

He looked me dead in the eye like he'd never been more serious. I broke his stare and busied myself with condiments.

"August 1963," he intoned with uncharacteristic gravitas. "We're in town doing a stand at the Oasis. It's the afternoon before a show. Jimmy and I are going out to get something to eat for lunch. We walk into a restaurant — Wilbur's. Don't look for it, it's not there any more. There's usually this hostess at the front. Nobody's there. Hardly anybody in the restaurant, too. Looks like it might be closed. I remember I can hear a radio somewhere, probably in the kitchen. We wait for a little while. Then Jimmy calls out, 'Hey, is there anybody here? You've got customers waiting.' He turns to me and he goes, 'Check this out.' So he does the Cannon voice — perfect, like usual. 'Ah, excuse, excuse me, I would very much appreciate some of your attention. Connie and myself are famished.' These two waitresses with moist eyes come around the corner. They see Jimmy and they burst out crying. I'm like, what the hell is this? Then this guy walks up and says, 'Did you hear about the president in New Orleans?' Jimmy, still thinking there's some kinda gag going on, says, 'No, how does it go?' 'He's been shot. He's dead.'"

DaVinci drummed his fingers on the table. "Jimmy goes blank. I hustle him out of there and get back to the Oasis. The day just gets worse and worse. The whole town shuts down. The manager of the Oasis calls and says the show's off, probably indefinitely. Izzy's on the phone, losing his mind. Katie comes around but Jimmy's practically comatose. I've got problems, too."

"Did you talk to Jimmy much during this time?"

"He's not exactly talkative. One thing you gotta understand about Jimmy is that he was real, real comfortable as the president. It was natural to him. He'd slip in and out of it all the time. Cannon kinda filled him up. He was like two guys in one."

"How often did you see Jimmy after the show ended?"

"Not as much as I would've liked. I had a wife and a kid to support. The band and me, we land a spot backing up Jack Hunter at the Sahara. From what I heard, Jimmy was holed up in L.A. in some place near Venice Beach, doing some movie stuff when he wasn't going batshit crazy. What happened to Katie didn't help his state of mind."

"What?"

"You don't know shit about shit, do you, kid?" He folded his hands over his belly. "Like the brothers say, I gots to school ya."

He laughed. "A few months after the assassination, Katie and her sister die in a car crash. Jimmy really goes over the deep end. I try calling him. The one time I get through, he's a mumbling wreck. Izzy's pulling his hair out trying to take care of him but there's not much he can do. You know, this really eats at me some days. I should've taken better care of him, but my first responsibility was to my boys. I hear that he's out on the East Coast with some comic, I forget who."

"Lenny Bruce."

"That right?" DaVinci looked slightly impressed. "I used to like him. Before he got clean. Anyway, I run into Jimmy again in '69. He says he's doing some shows with Pantero. This is off the record but I never liked Pantero. He treated Jimmy like a punk. Danny wanted everybody to see how he's doing Jimmy this big favour by bringing him out onstage. He would've wheeled Jimmy out in a wheelchair if he could've. Jimmy just needed the money to get back on his feet. Once he got tired of being Pantero's charity case, he went back to L.A., got a new place, some ranch house outside L.A. He talked about getting into the music biz — the movies weren't enough for him. He was gonna call on me for my expertise." DaVinci laughed. "You don't know how bad he needed it. But I didn't hear from him. He wasn't the most reliable cat. Not quite right, you know. I'm talking mentally."

"Was that the last time you saw Jimmy?"

"I ran into him in Vegas again in '82. He was gonna do some more shows with Danny but they never happened. I think Pantero blew him off — same old story with that shitbag."

DaVinci loudly sucked on a morsel of chicken that he'd pulled from a cold bone.

"Do you know where Jimmy is now?"

"You got me. I've heard some crazy stories but I don't believe them. People say he lives in a nuthouse, that he's a wino, that he threw himself off a bridge and nobody'll ever find the body." His gaze shifted to my right again. "Ah, now I'm getting ass-raped by Real Madrid. I can't believe the day I'm having."

"One last thing I wanted to ask you about was the Nevada Delegation?"

"The Nevada what?"

"Delegation?"

"Is that like a state assembly thing?" He laughed. "You running for city council?"

"These were parties. For Cannon? At the Flamingo?"

"Right, right. People talk about that sometimes but there's nothing to it. I know Delrocco liked to play the big shot and Sinatra wanted to be the perfect little hostess, but that talk's a bunch of crap. All I know is that some Washington types would come into town every so often and have a good time. There was nothing weird about it. People got some real strange ideas about Cannon. The one time I met him, it was when we went to the White House. Jimmy got to know him a little but didn't talk about it. He loved being around him — he got real excited."

"Do you know what they talked about?"

"Jimmy was funny about it. He was discreet. I'd razz him about it sometimes, ask him when are we all gonna get to go sailing to Mexico on the president's yacht — or take the party down to Cuba, right? Jimmy didn't want to talk about Cannon but he wanted you to know they were tight. Then, after that day at the restaurant when we heard, when everybody heard, Jimmy got paranoid. I pressed him on it once — he had to know something. He looked at me real cold and said, 'They kill people who talk too much.'" DaVinci pointed a meaty digit at me. "You take that however you like."

DaVinci pushed himself away from the table. "Well, kid, it's been special. I gotta wrap this up." There was a flicker of something in his eyes. "I don't know what you're doing while you're in town, but you might be interested. You know about something called karaoke?"

I thought: uh-oh. "I've heard of it."

"I was the first to bring it here." He swelled with pride, which tested the fabric of his shirt even further. "Direct from Japan. I made a huge splash. I did my own bar with that. I ran the whole show — MC, producer, the works. I had to close that place a few years back, but I still do nights all over town. I do the Savoy on Fridays and Saturdays, Planet Hollywood on Tuesdays. I would appreciate it if you mentioned that in the article. Here's my card."

He pulled out a wallet bulging with slips of paper. He handed me a card that read: The Legendary Steve DaVinci, King of Karaoke. There was a cartoon of a dapper little man singing into an oversized microphone.

Irina deposited the bill on our table. DaVinci made no motion to pay. "I'd like you to have this." He slipped the card inside her shirt pocket, his fingers almost grazing her breast.

Irina sighed. "You already give me one, Mr. Steve."

"Then why don't you ever call me, gorgeous? I get so lonely."

"Ha," she said. Her expression was inscrutable.

DaVinci watched her ass as it crossed the restaurant along with the rest of her. "Damn . . . I never get tired of the sight."

I took a shuttle bus back downtown. Every block seemed to have
a construction site. Every time we passed a hole, I tried to imagine
the size of the one that Cannon's death left in Jimmy Wynn's life.

I returned to my hotel. It was on the new strip, a monstros-
ity named the Barbizon Bay. It was designed in a tropical South
Seas style, complete with wooden toucans. I was waiting for a
chance to explore my milieu more thoroughly, guessing that my
story might need the extra colour. I put that off for another time
and went to the Barbizon's utterly un-tropical business centre to
check my e-mail. It was the weekend so I didn't expect anything
from *The Betsey* people. When we'd spoken on Friday, Daphne
had expressed "confidence" in my ability to pull something
together in the short amount of time we had. Basically, I needed
results by the end of next week, the result in question being
Jimmy Wynn. Since this counted as my first missing-person case
ever, I wasn't sure how I was the right guy for the assignment.
But it was my story and I acted accordingly, making it sound as
if I'd have no trouble discovering Jimmy Wynn's whereabouts,
be it corporeal or ethereal. At the moment, I was more apt to
write stories about Las Vegas's bustling karaoke scene or recent

innovations in the field of Saucy Banter with Heavy-Set Ladies.

My brother wrote to say he'd had dinner with Mom and Dad the night before. Dad didn't ask for money but he was "looking old and worried." I didn't know what I could offer. I planned to call them when I had less on my mind, though this was hardly the town where you could expect sudden mental clarity. Billions of dollars were spent every second to prevent that terrible event from occurring.

There was a message from Colin marked urgent. "Call when you get this — v. important."

I rang him from upstairs.

"At long last," he said.

"I had a big interview this morning."

"Not as big as this."

"You discovered Cannon had a third nipple."

"Listen when I'm trying to tell you something."

"I'm sorry."

"Don't apologize, either. It's irritating. I have a lead for you. I heard from someone who was in, or at least very near, the Nevada Delegation. He's a former associate of Marco Delrocco."

I did not like where this was going. "The mobster?"

"He was a business partner of Mr. Delrocco. Conveniently for you, he lives in a suburb of Las Vegas and he's interested in talking about his experiences."

I imagined a guy with an icepick in one hand, a baseball bat in the other, and knives pointing out of the tips of his shoes. "I wouldn't know how to talk to him. I felt like I was out of my league talking to a karaoke host."

"This is simple. Listen to what he has to say. I would've done this over the phone but he prefers face-to-face."

"It's harder to shoot people over the phone."

"Nathan," Colin sounded exasperated. "The Delrocco crime family hasn't been an active force for twenty years. There've been countless books and articles on it already and to the best of my knowledge, none of those writers has suffered any form of reprisal."

"To the best of your knowledge."

"All you're doing is meeting someone who wants to tell you some stories."

"Like a fireside chat."

"His name is John Sifredi. Here's his number."

I wrote it down with a heavy feeling of dread.

"Listen, I wouldn't be giving you this lead if I didn't think, number one, he was harmless, and number two, it was crucial to your article."

"Fine, fine."

"And Ben wants to talk to you. Call him on his cell phone. He has a surprise."

If Ben's surprise was anything like Colin's, it could wait. That said, I was pleased that Colin had given me something I could use. Since this was a story for *The Betsey*, Cannon had to be front and centre of the story and this interview could clarify matters about a relationship between the president and entertainers like my Jimmy.

The phone rang. I expected Colin but it was Sparkle calling to cancel the meeting with Pantero that night. "There was some deep bruising." Pantero needed as much rest as possible and hoped I would honour him with my presence on Monday night. That was one of his nights off. Usually, he'd take his private jet to his horse ranch in Colorado or play a one-off date in another city but he was convalescing in town. We could meet at Lisette. I said that would be fine — the restaurant had an excellent reputation.

Wanting to make the best use of my night, I worked up the nerve to call John Sifredi. He had the mild, friendly voice of a professional, as in accountant, not hitman. He said he would be happy to meet that night. He lived in Sunrise Vista, a suburb in east Las Vegas. He gave me directions.

I had guns on my mind in the taxi ride out. Concealing a firearm was one of the rights I'd planned to take advantage of since coming to America. The only time I'd ever handled a firearm was when I went gopher hunting with my cousins in rural Manitoba. I shot five. The bullet clipped the last one near the top of its head. The lid of its skull flipped open and the animal began to jump head over heels again and again. Its cranium spilled its contents before the rest of him came to rest in a heap. That was how I imagined it would be for me if I was ever shot: the sudden exposure of a part I kept safe and hidden, then a furiously spastic bout of activity scattering my brain and viscera. It would all be over in a spray of goo.

John Sifredi's house did not look like the place where I was going to die. It had the healthiest lawn I saw in all of Vegas — it was a miracle of determination, precious water, and the most powerful chemicals ever devised by the hand of man. Situated in this verdant meadow was a bungalow the colour of terra cotta. As I stepped out of the cab, a sprightly looking elderly couple opened the door and waved.

"Mr. Grant?" He wore a checkered yellow shirt and a bright smile. The woman next to him was even happier to see me.

"Uh, yes. Mr. Sifredi?"

"John! John! Please call me John!" His handshake was confident but not crushing. "And this is Marla." The woman wore a kerchief around her neck. I politely clasped her hand as she beamed up at me.

My genial would-be murderers ushered me inside. The tidy living room was decorated with family photographs and knick-knacks from American tourist sites — Mt. Rushmore, the Cannon Space Center, Yellowstone National Park. Over the sofa was a blanket bearing a picture of a horse. On the coffee table was a green ashtray full of red potpourri.

"Can I get you something to drink?" asked John. "I like to have a little brandy on Sunday nights." The Italy in his voice had been almost entirely scrubbed away.

"Brandy would be terrific."

Marla went into the kitchen and came out holding a plate of biscotti. "If John had told me what you two were up to, I'd have insisted you come for dinner."

"I had dinner already, thanks. But whatever you had smells great."

"Lasagna. John's family recipe. You must let me put some in Tupperware before you go."

John put down two glasses of brandy near the potpourri and sat down on the horsey blanket. Marla put down the plate of biscotti and slipped coasters underneath the brandy glasses.

"Do you need anything else, bunny?" She wasn't talking to me but I was confident that I would get my own term of endearment real soon.

"Oh, no. This is wonderful. Just wonderful."

"I'll leave you to it then." Marla looked at me expectantly. "Mr. Grant, excuse me for asking, but would you like something for your cheek — some ice?"

I thought: oh no, it's getting worse. "No, I'm fine. It doesn't hurt at all."

"If you need anything let me know."

John pulled a case from his pocket and took out his glasses. "I'm so pleased you could see me, Mr. Grant."

"You can call me Nathan." I retrieved my notebook and tape recorder from my satchel.

"It's incredible how efficient that old grapevine can be. I've only recently begun to open up about those days. It was Marla's nephew Davis who encouraged me. He's in the Universal resort's marketing department. He says it's a great idea to get my name out there — spark some buzz for the book, as he says."

"You have a book?"

"Davis suggested I hire a ghost writer. But I've always been more comfortable taking care of things for myself. I enjoy spending afternoons in my office downstairs, pecking away on the keyboard. I very much admire your craft. It must take a great deal of self-discipline. There's nothing I admire more than self-discipline."

I had a nervous sip of brandy.

"And you write for *The Betsey*? Marla and I both think it's an excellent magazine. President Cannon had some zip, that's for sure. I understand you're writing a story about his visits to our fine city."

I thought: what did Colin tell him? "Yes, that's right." I tried to sound easygoing yet self-disciplined. "John."

"So you'd like to find out about the Nevada Delegation?"

His casual use of the term surprised me so much, I nearly choked on my brandy. "Is that what you called it?"

"I believe it was Mr. Sinatra who coined that one. He brought a sense of formality to some very informal times."

"I'm also writing about a comedian who he may have met there. Jimmy Wynn?"

"Very funny gentleman. He was a real favourite of Mr. Delrocco."

I tread carefully. "And this was Marco Delrocco?"

"Yes. I worked with Mr. Delrocco for thirteen years, from 1956 until his tragic passing in 1969."

"In what, uh, capacity did you work for him?" I had trouble seeing this chipper, white-haired fellow as an enforcer, but perhaps he was a maestro with piano wire.

"I did accounts for Mr. Delrocco. I also acted as a liaison with the wider business community." He smiled widely. "Oh, we had a grand old time. Las Vegas was a very different place then. You don't see any of that family spirit any more. Now the big casinos are just big businesses. They might as well take the change from your pockets with a vacuum cleaner!" I heard Marla's laugh in the kitchen. "Mr. Delrocco operated differently. He had a sense of decorum. Do you know what I mean?" He laughed. "Of course you do! You're a writer, you must know so many words. It's been very sad to see him painted with the same brush as his brother. Vincent liked to wield an iron fist, no question, but Marco was more accommodating. When he walked into any hotel in town — even a hotel in which we didn't have any investments — he always received a warm welcome."

"I see." I sensed the conversation needed some steering. "How did the Nevada Delegation come about?"

I reached for a biscotti and Sifredi leaned forward to pass me a napkin.

"It's my understanding that Mr. Delrocco had known President Cannon for some time. Cannon's father had a relationship with Vincent and it was Vincent who introduced Mr. Delrocco to the president — they were close in age and got along very well. Cannon would visit Mr. Delrocco in Las Vegas from time to time during the run-up to the election. Even though the meetings were social by nature, there were efforts to keep the candidate away from prying eyes — including my own! I was starstruck when it came to the President." Sifredi looked a little wistful. "Such a shame what happened. It was Frank Sinatra who first suggested having a special function for the president after he won the election. The Flamingo was a natural choice because it afforded the most privacy. The penthouse had its own elevator."

"Would you consider Sinatra the liaison between Mr. Delrocco and the entertainment community?"

"Frank liked to be the centre of attention. I hate to speak ill of the dead. Marla was just devastated after his plane crash. The whole town was. I hope you don't put this in your story, but he could be a little," he selected the word carefully, "overbearing. This was not Mr. Delrocco's approach at all."

"He didn't have to flaunt his power to prove he had it."

"That's it exactly. Exactly! Hold on, let me write that down." Sifredi pulled out a pad of paper from a side table and scrawled a note. "You phrase these things very well. Your parents must be proud. My parents didn't know what to make of me. I was one of those strange kids who just loved school. I loved numbers most of all. My father had worked for Vincent in Chicago and wasn't sure if I'd be useful. But Vincent recognized my talents and moved me out here to help his brother. Besides, I was never going to be one of them — my mother was Irish and the Delroccos were a traditional bunch." Sifredi shook his head. "Prejudice is a real scourge in society." His spirits seemed to lift again. "Then again, I had no taste for the muckier side of the business."

"Did the Nevada Delegation ever get mucky?"

"Nathan, I regret that I cannot be absolutely candid. Davis implored me to save some for the book. Another brandy?" Sifredi cheerfully poured another round. "Two's my limit, but you look like you've got a young constitution."

The next sip of brandy gave me the strength to forge ahead. "Did you know Jimmy Wynn personally?"

"Not well. Jimmy could be very shy in these circumstances. We were all awed by the president. It's natural that he was even more so. I'll never forget his jitters the first night he performed for the Delegation. I swear he was shaking like this." Sifredi did a funny little shimmy with his shoulders.

"When was this?"

"Sometime in 1961, I believe. Mr. Wynn impressed everyone that night. Mr. Sinatra wasn't very supportive of him in the early days. He thought it was disrespectful of the president. But after finally seeing him perform, he'd given Jimmy the all-clear to visit the Delegation at the Flamingo. And despite those jitters, he did not disappoint. I could tell President Cannon was just as pleased." Sifredi leaned forward again. "There was a terrific thing he used to do. He would finish his show with a kind of press conference, where he'd take questions from the audience. He'd answer them right off the top of his head! They were some of the funniest things I've ever heard. I wish I could remember some."

"What kind of relationship did he have with the president?"

"They were certainly . . . familiar." He let the word hang in the air while he took a sip of brandy. "I'm being very generous with the details — at this rate, there'll be nothing left for the book but a table of contents and my wrinkly face on the cover!" He tittered. "But I don't suppose Jimmy Wynn is of interest to many people. At least not until your story comes out." He composed himself, becoming stern again. "You seem like a smart young man so I presume you know about the tensions between the Delrocco brothers and Sam Amelio's associates in New York. Towards the end of 1962, there were some very ugly incidents. We were buffered from the harshest weather but tensions were high. Vincent's relationship with the president had soured for reasons you can certainly read about elsewhere. Vincent discouraged his brother from maintaining his association with Cannon. Mr. Delrocco hated to be pulled into this but family is family. And that was it for the Nevada Delegation."

He arched his eyebrows and waved his finger. "Now this is where your friend Jimmy Wynn comes in. Though we all had some sense that the '62 Christmas party was going to be the last one, we all did our best to keep spirits high. Jack Hunter was incredible that night, just incredible. After Jack's show, Mr. Delrocco told me that he had a very important meeting with Cannon and that he was not to be interrupted. It surprised me that this meeting also involved Mr. Wynn. I didn't dare ask Mr. Delrocco what that was all about, but it was certainly one of the things I recall about the final session."

"This was a long meeting?"

"As I recall." He laughed. "But I wasn't one to poke my nose around. Mr. Delrocco prized discretion above all else."

"Even self-discipline?"

Sifredi was very grave. "Even that."

"And that's why you've waited so long to talk."

"Well . . ." He peered over his shoulder at the kitchen, where I could hear Marla bustling about. I thought: has she been listening the whole time? Maybe Marla was wearing a wire. Sifredi cupped his hand around his mouth and leaned toward me. "It was in my best interest to outlast certain statutes. And certain individuals." He tapped me on the hand and smiled.

Sifredi offered to drive me back to my hotel. At the door, Marla handed me a Tupperware container of lasagna. "I so look forward to reading your story."

"Me, too."

She found that hilarious.

As we drove in his cherry red Cadillac, Sifredi pointed out the locations of restaurants and hotspots that were no longer there. "The city is so different now," he said with more than a little sadness in his voice. "I rarely come downtown. I prefer the place that exists in my noggin. That's the one going in the book."

Outside the Barbizon Bay, I wrote down his e-mail address — "It's so convenient for keeping in touch, I can hardly live without it" — and promised to send him and Marla's nephew Davis the names of publishers they could contact in New York. "What's this Winston Sharpe like?" he asked. "I think he's a terrific writer. Perhaps he can help me." Sifredi wanted to know when my article was coming out so he could capitalize on any attendant publicity.

Before I got out of the car, he grew serious once more. "I've never liked all the hearsay about the Nevada Delegation. Its purpose, you understand, was purely social. People had a good time. I would be disappointed if it were to be presented in a negative light." He turned steely. He gripped the steering wheel so tightly, his knuckles bulged. "I would be very disappointed," he said. His tone was as sharp as an icepick.

I felt his eyes fall on the bruise on my cheek. I really wanted to get out of that Cadillac.

"Well, then." He released the wheel and extended his hand in parting. He was a jolly grandpa again. "Enjoy the rest of your stay! If there's anything you want to clear up, feel free to call. I'll be beavering away on the book!" He wagged a finger at me. "That reminds me. Tell me what you think of this title: *The Heart of the Desert*."

"That's great." I thought: maintain self-discipline, you're almost inside. "Really great. I can't wait to read it."

"Me, too!" He laughed and slapped the steering wheel with delight at his impersonation of me.

After an exchange of heartfelt thank-yous, I walked briskly through the doors of the Barbizon Bay, cut a path through the lobby's tropical greenery, and went up to my room. I never wanted to come out again.

"*Did you hear about the president in New Orleans?*"

*Jimmy's instincts kick in. Though it only takes a tenth of a second, he's still slow off the mark. The gears are cold because it's early in the day. Plus, he just saw those waitresses crying. Sad people unnerve Jimmy. When his mother got like that, he shut down. Nothing seemed to work on her — not songs, not jokes — so he got quiet. What he liked was to be surrounded by noise and laughter. If he could have the audience onstage with him, flanking him on all sides, he would. Someday soon he'd test it to find out if it worked. It might look too weird. If it didn't, he would call them his cabinet. They could be local contest winners.*

*The president in New Orleans? Jimmy thinks Mardi Gras. Feathery costumes, coloured beads, Negroes with trumpets, and drinks called Hurricanes. Maybe something about Cannon in a parade. Cannon could get smashed and do something stupid, like pass out drunk or take his shirt off or make some speech about liberating the city from the French. Yeah, some confusion about the French. The Louisiana Purchase. Like he's trying to get something else out of the deal. 'I've had a series of meetings with President Napoleon and I've demanded that he . . .'" What? Cmoncmoncmon. He knows the Napoleon angle's not going to work — too intellectual. Strictly for the college tightasses.*

*The Louisiana Purchase might bear some fruit. Could be something closer to "I heard he's trying to sell it back to the French." But why would Cannon do that? Everybody likes New Orleans. Fun city, good crowds, real loose. Who wouldn't have a good time there? Only religious types and uptight squares and Cannon is neither. Unless something happened to him and the city turned on him somehow. "I heard he got cut off at the bar at Mardi Gras and he threatened to sell Louisiana back to the French." The French or the frogs? Selling it back to the frogs would work. The cutting-off part struck him as wrong, though. Cannon might look flushed after a few cocktails in the Flamingo but that wasn't public knowledge — discretion, discretion. Cannon isn't some good-time-Charlie with a lampshade on his head and his dick in his hand. Something about a costume then? Something happens to his costume. "I heard they lost his costume at Mardi Gras and now he's selling Louisiana back to the frogs." Nah, nah. Just getting fruity. Connie — take the shot at Connie. "I heard Connie wouldn't let him go to Mardi Gras so he's selling Louisiana back to the frogs." Makes no sense. "I heard Connie wouldn't let him go to Mardi Gras so he's selling her to the frogs." The combination of Connie and frogs was wrong — low-class. "He's selling her to the French." Better. Far from perfect, though.*

*By now, two seconds have passed and Jimmy knows he's run out of time to deliver his zinger. Fuck it, he thinks. I'm not on the clock.*

*"I don't know that one," Jimmy tells the guy in the restaurant. "How does it go?"*

9

As I lay in bed on Monday morning, I worried about my ability to maintain a low profile. Sure, I was a non-entity to the gamblers, goombahs, and grannies who constantly poured in and out of the city but I suspected that I had been noticed. I was digging through the past in a city that cared only about the next: the next roll, the next card, the next title round, the next hotel mega-complex to be shaped like the Leaning Tower of Pisa. Jimmy's city was gone.

My anxieties were compounded by the fact that I didn't know how to get out of this place — my return plane ticket sat on the desk, scorning me with its presence. By now, the Department of Immigration, Naturalization, and Border Security would have received my intentionally defective card. Being neither Latin American nor African, I was unlikely to garner serious attention but it wasn't wise to be on the wise in a country that didn't want me.

I spent the morning eating cold lasagna and transcribing interviews into my laptop. Colin wanted a copy of the Sifredi notes ASAP, wanting to know how my new data correlated with his research. He hoped another Delegation lead would surface. So far, my picture of Jimmy Wynn's Vegas life and rise to Cannon-spawned fame was filling in nicely. I was awaiting an important package from New York, too: Jimmy Wynn's files from Izzy Berman's office. Before I'd left, I'd contacted a woman in his old agency, which still handled theatrical clients. She said Berman was a pack rat and that there was a huge batch of files in the building's basement. I hoped that whatever she found would supply me with more stats, clippings, and contacts who could offer a few more let-me-tell-you-'bout-the-good-ol'-days quotes. I was looking to Pantero to give me a more intimate view, maybe some more about the nature of the relationship with Cannon — it sounded as if Jimmy and the president had shared a confidence. It could've been trivial or it could've been monumental — I needed to know more about it. The best-case scenario was that Pantero would deliver Jimmy himself. Maybe there'd be three of us dining on foie gras agnolotti at Lisette.

Even sweeter would've been a candlelit dinner with Ms. Daphne Foster. When I called *The Betsey*, the receptionist said she was in meetings all morning, but would I like her voicemail?

"Daphne, it's Nathan. Grant? I'm in Las Vegas. Things have been interesting. I've spoken to a few old-timers about our man. I'm getting closer to determining his whereabouts." I thought: why stop with this lie? "Danny Pantero has been very helpful. I should have this wrapped up in a day or two and then be on my way." I thought: how? By stagecoach? "You can call me in my room at the Barbizon Bay if you have any questions. You should have the number. I guess that's everything. Give my regards to Winston. To Mr. Sharpe. Ta-ta for now."

That was lame. I looked in the mirror, an act I'd been avoiding. At least my cheek didn't seem so purple. I'd also stopped using the Band-aids. There was a skinny red dash to mark the Dazzle Cuts incident.

I had to put some yardage between the phone and myself so I went downstairs for an early lunch. I checked at reception for my Berman package but there was nothing yet. Unsure of what to do with myself, I stood at the periphery of the casino floor and welcomed that moment of mental clarity. I thought: there must be somewhere I can buy a mantra.

I'd been too preoccupied in the past few days to pay much attention to my surroundings. For instance, I hadn't noticed that the Barbizon Bay's security guards wore pith helmets. That was an odd touch given the hotel's colonial-tropical theme. The suggestion of African exploration also clashed with the presence of a stuffed pheasant in the lobby.

There was nothing confusing about the casino. There were countless tables for craps, blackjack, roulette, and poker but the majority of the space was taken up by slot machines. They came in three major categories. The traditional slots had arms to pull and lights that flashed and were principally red, white, and blue in hue. They used familiar symbols like gold bars, dollar signs, cherries, and bells to inform players that they hadn't won squat. The next generation rejected the traditional iconography in favour of a more diverse range of motifs, like Gone Fishing, the Grand Ole Opry, the Super Bowl. The most new-fangled contraptions disregarded all of the slot conventions except for the lighted buttons. Here were machines that shimmered like galaxies, exhaled dry ice, and consoled losers in the voices of their most beloved sitcom actors. And all three kinds made sound. Every casino floor in town had its own ever-shifting symphony of dings, bings, bongs, whoops, whistles, sirens, canned laughter, cheering crowds, perky-voiced *try again*'s and coquettish *c'mon, big fella*'s. Then there were the layers of music — frenetic Eurohouse dance rhythms, marching bands with prominent tubas, classical filigrees, rustic country ballads, lascivious hard-rock guitar solos that dripped with oily sleaze. All of this sound swelled vertiginously without ever cresting.

Whereas the noise initially seemed impenetrable, I came to realize there was a myriad of routes. Whenever one path became overgrown with thickets, I tried another, moving deeper into its structure. The noise contained bulk and heft — it occupied the Barbizon Bay with more confidence than any of the human inhabitants. It was an aural sculpture of unfixed form. I wanted to write all that down.

Someone slapped me on the shoulder, knocking me out of my reverie. "About to hit the slots?"

I turned. It was my friend Ben. I hadn't seen him since that night at Dazzle Cuts. "You!" I gave him a manly hug with a thump on the back. I felt the wire that connected his headset mike to a device in his belt.

"Colin told me to call you. What are you doing here?"

"It's a Network X gig. I didn't want to say anything because I was afraid I'd jinx it. It was touch-and-go right until last week. Plus, there was a confidentiality agreement, but that doesn't matter now. You will be seeing me in action."

"What's the show about?"

"Them."

Ben pointed at a collection of pierced, tattooed, safety-pinned, and colorfully dyed young men in the lobby. Two of them were riding their skateboards around and between quivering hotel patrons. One was riding around and around in the revolving door with his buttocks pressed up against the glass. Another was relieving himself in a thicket of Barbizon greenery near the pheasant. Their actions were recorded by two different camera crews.

"They're trying to get kicked out of every hotel on the strip," said Ben. "The new strip, at least."

"Who the hell are they?"

"Don't you recognize them? It's Stink."

I scrutinized the face of the ass-glass-presser as he backed his way out of the lobby again. I recognized the mug of Von Hurley, the frontman of one of America's hottest punk-pop combos.

"Oh," I said with a sympathetic tone.

"They are complete fucking idiots," said Ben, smiling, "and

this is gonna be absolutely wicked TV." Ben cupped his hand around his mike. I was amazed he could communicate through the din. "What's that? Yeah. Yeah. So do you wanna clear 'em out now? Okay. Right. I'll be two secs." He shifted the mike away from his face. "We want them close to arrested but not hauled off to jail. It's a fine line. We call ahead to get clearance for the cameras but security doesn't know what we're gonna pull."

I pointed at the band member near the pheasant. "Won't he get thrown out if he takes a dump there?"

"Nah, John's not gonna do it for real. Or he hasn't yet." He spoke into the mike again. "What? Yeah? Okay, let's finish up." To me: "We're at the Universal. Call me there in a couple of hours. We've got a few more hotels to hit."

"When are you here until?"

"Wednesday morning. The band's doing a show tomorrow night, then we're driving back to L.A. When are you here until?"

"Depends."

"Come to the show tomorrow. We'll hang out. I need to talk to a regular person."

"And I'm regular."

He smirked. "You'll do fine."

Ben took off in the direction of the chaos. One camera crew shot over the shoulder of Stink's scrawny bassist — I think his name was Steve — as he tried to wrest his skateboard back from a pith-helmeted security guard who was the size of an entire NFL defensive line. The other shot Von, who appeared to be stuck in the revolving door and was fumbling to pull up his pants. John, the would-be defecator, was now chatting amiably with a girl in a Network X cap. Dirk, the guitarist, was already gone. Ben collected his cretins and waved them in the direction of the doors not containing Von. The singer soon freed himself and the carnival left town.

I felt stunned by my slots-fuelled cacophony/epiphany and the

Stink blitzkrieg. I sought a combination of sanctuary and nourishment. I found the Livingstone, a bar and restaurant set away from the casino floor. The title was another confusing nod to the dark continent but the interior was standard faux-British pub — there was one of these on every corner in Toronto. I was not only comfortable but intrigued: the sign outside had promised a noon-hour performance by a "sleight-of-hand artiste." I ate a BLT while a young man with slicked-back hair performed rudimentary card tricks and threw single playing cards at an oversized dartboard across the room. Six stuck into the board, two bounced out. I thought: that's a better average than I'd get.

I went back to the lobby to ask for the Berman file. While he checked for it, I surveyed the post-Stink scene. The greenery that had been subjected to pretend defecation and undisputed urination had been removed — the pheasant had merely been moved to another thicket of vegetation. The man returned to the desk with my package. I held onto it tightly as I rode the elevator upstairs.

Inside the box were two bulky manila envelopes. I removed the pages from the first one and put them in a pile on the bed. The first document was a one-pager hyping Danny and Jimmy's engagement at the Sands in 1961. Pantero was "the international singing sensation who's sweet on 'The Girl Who Lives Down the Lane'!" He was described as "a boy wonder!" — by '61, he had been in Vegas for four years and was still only twenty-one. Jimmy would've been five years older, though he was always second-billed. Pantero got three paragraphs of hyperbole while Wynn only had one line. "You'll be thrilled and amazed by Jimmy's impersonation of President Cannon — Jimmy's zany but respectful comedy stylings are the talk of the town!"

"Zany but respectful" — I wanted that on my tombstone.

The next intriguing item was a page-sized poster that portrayed a smiling Wynn in Cannon guise and an enlarged campaign button that read "Elect Jimmy Wynn." Like the cover of *A Square*

*Peg in the Oval Office*, it was styled after an already-famous piece of Cannon iconography, in this case an advertisement that had run in newspapers throughout 1960. The poster had a series of dates in various East Coast cities through the winter of '61–'62. "Las Vegas sensation Jimmy Wynn is on a campaign to spread hilarity from coast to coast," it stated. There was also a series of advertisements for *A Square Peg*. "The No. 1 most played record in Milwaukee!" "The Fastest Selling Record in America!" "Enjoy Jimmy Wynn's chart-busting phenomenon!" There was an alternate cover for the follow-up LP, *White House-Trained* — the picture portrayed Wynn poking through a doggy door at the front of the White House. That one was rejected. The approved, vaguely fascistic cover — Wynn, his fake Connie, and their two phony progeny enjoying a barbecue, each of them flanked by Secret Servicemen — did not capitalize on the title's pun.

Assorted press clippings and glossy 8 x 10 photos comprised the remainder of the first file. I had found many of the pieces already, but was happy to see a few substantive articles, like a profile in *Stage* from 1962 and two lengthy reports in *Billboard* the same year that summarized the history of the records, which boasted combined sales of nine million copies. I would read them more closely later.

The second file began with a note dated last Friday written by someone in the agency. "Mr. Grant," it read. "I regret to inform you that some materials are missing from this file. Several documents were for internal use only and have been withheld."

The statement of discretion was worrisome, though the package seemed plenty candid about Wynn's affairs. The next batch of material began with contracts from various booking agents and venues. More interesting were the production details on the recordings — where, when, who did what, and what they had for lunch.

The catastrophe of August 1963 was reflected in the documents that followed. There were unsent contracts for a three-week run in a New York theatre in October and a two-week engagement in Baltimore in November. Royalty statements from Rite Time Records indicated healthy sums were paid out to Berman all the way up to February 1964 before the numbers shrank to nearly nothing. I chalked the six-month lag time up to a sluggish account-ing department. Financial statements suggested that Berman had done something very clever. Evidently acting as Wynn's business manager, he had socked away a good chunk of Jimmy's earnings during the gravy years. The royalty rate on the records and the fees for Wynn's live performances were both surprisingly high. Knowing that the ride wouldn't last forever, Berman kept the money for him, basically enabling him to keep Wynn on a steady payroll long after 1963. To my amazement, the money continued to flow from Berman's office to Wynn until the early seventies.

As for Wynn's achievements in his post–Cannon assassination career, they were few in number. There was very little pertaining to the 1965 recording dates for *Who Does This Guy Think He Is, Anyways?* besides a letter from Rite Time Records explaining why the LP would not be stocked in most major department stores ("we are looking at more exclusive markets"). Of the 1967 shows with Lenny Bruce and 1969 shows with Pantero, there was just enough paperwork to confirm they happened.

There were several very useful pieces of information here. I now had a couple of addresses for Jimmy Wynn in California. One was in Los Angeles — it must've been the Venice Beach place. The other was in San Lupe, a suburb near San Bernardino. A change-of-address note for the San Lupe house was appended to the file in 1969. On the note, someone had written "Jimmy — Saddlecreek Ranch."

One of the final pieces of correspondence was a copy of a financial statement, sent in 1970 to the San Lupe address. Accord-ing to the statement, the funds were now payable to a Mr. James Saddlecreek. Maybe someone in Berman's office had mistakenly combined the names of Jimmy Wynn and the ranch where he apparently lived. Yet nowhere else did Wynn use the name "James" — the contracts were signed either J. or Jimmy. In the notes I was writing on the files, I wrote the name James Saddle-creek in block letters and underlined it three times. Underneath I wrote my three theories as to its origins.

1. Clerical error
2. Jimmy alias
3. Buddy who really owns the ranch house in San Lupe

I thought: a clue! I thought: hot damn! I felt like a hard-boiled P.I. on the verge of cracking a big case. Winston Sharpe would be proud. I thought of calling him then decided to wait until I could confirm one of my hypotheses.

I suddenly had the urge to do something manlier than rifling through decades-old paperwork so I packed up the files and headed back to the lobby for a pre-dinner drink. Danny Pantero would be no match for my awesome powers of deduction.

Once again, the wine girl took flight. My beautiful angel of booze soared high above the floor of the restaurant, swiftly ascending the strati of Napa Valley Cabernets, Australian Sauvignon Blancs, Ontario Icewines, and Super Tuscans. In her close-fitting turtleneck top, black tights, and tutu, she was a Dionysian Tinkerbell. She used rounded, palm-sized protrusions to guide herself to the top right corner of the wall, which was at least three stories high, forty feet across, and separated from the rest of the restaurant by an immense sheet of glass. The space was evidently refrigerated, which explained why our angel's dress was less revealing than that of the average Vegas waitress. The low temperature also resulted in a protrusion of the nipples that was perceptible only after rigorous study.

At the other end of her rope in a dimly lit space was the beefy man who facilitated her miraculous ascension, albeit with the help of a complex series of pulleys and hydraulics. My engineer brother Michael could've explained the mechanics if he was there but I don't think anyone in my bloodline had ever been to a place like Lisette. We were a salad-bar family.

A few moments later, the bottle she had snatched right out of the sky was being poured at our table. Vanessa, our server — who glided through the restaurant's lateral plane with the same finesse as her co-worker moved through its vertical one — splashed a thimble's worth in Danny Pantero's glass. He swished it around and tasted, pursing his lips as he did so. His expression went from pensive to perky and he nodded with enthusiasm. "Please." He gestured to my glass. Vanessa filled mine before giving Pantero his due share.

"This is from my favourite estate in Languedoc." Pantero's conversational voice was a touch higher in pitch than the one I heard during the performances. I suspected the sound system boosted his bass. "The vintner Marcel is a poet with his grapes."

It tasted oaky to me. Purple, too. Those terms seemed inadequate. "Wow, that's very nice."

Pantero gave me a smile of perfect magnanimity. He was in his element. In fact, Pantero's clothes combined the same tones of cream and cherry wood as the restaurant's interior — I suspected he chose the outfit for just this purpose. His colour-coordination enhanced the impression he gave of a king presiding over his court. I'd already seen several subjects come pay fealty. They didn't dare come near Pantero until he extended his hand or stood up to plant a kiss on a trembling wife or daughter. They mentioned seeing his show last year or last week and testified to its delights. Pantero always remembered the night they came. "That night was a *very* special performance," he would say.

At some point during these interactions, they would glance at me with wonder and confusion. Was I some misbegotten son who had failed to inherit the Pantero panache? An inner-city charity case who'd been subjected to terrible physical abuse? (Lisette's bright lighting was far from flattering.) Or had I been seated with Pantero by mistake and the great man was merely taking it in stride? I fought the inclination to shrink into my chair.

"Thanks again for meeting with me, Mr. Pantero."

"Please, you must call me Danny. I should be thanking you for waiting so long. It's been a wacky few days. That one little fall really threw me off. I want to say that it hurt my pride more than my derriere, but for once, that isn't true!" Like Sifredi's, Pantero's speaking voice only had the faintest speck of an Italian-American accent. Clearly, both men had adopted the local vernacular.

"How are you feeling?" I ventured.

"Oh, just fine." He laughed. "I'm particular about what I sit on but that's a wise practice in any circumstances."

"Words to live by."

"That's right." He sipped from his wine glass. "I hope you don't mind if I turn the tables for a moment and ask you some questions. As much as I enjoy doing interviews, they tend to be one-sided." He laughed heartily. "Even I get tired by the sound of my voice sometimes."

"That's hard to imagine, Mr. Pantero. I mean, Danny. Your voice is in great shape." I was already onto the flattery.

"It's the country air. I get out to my ranch as often as I can. I have a jet fuelled and ready to go whenever I want to get out to Colorado and see my beautiful Arabians. Do you ride Arabians?"

"What?"

I'd been distracted by my Tinkerbell. He turned toward her. "Quite something to behold. Is that the kind of lady who usually catches your eye?"

"The flying kind?"

Pantero laughed. "Not many of those around, not even in this town. No, I ask because I find that one of the best ways to get to know a man is to get a sense of his . . . let's call them his inclinations. In my opinion, Nate, love is the great motivator. Others may say wealth or power but I believe that those will only get you so far. Love is the strongest force we know. Now, I'm going to presume from your fascination with the marvelous creature over there that you're a traditional man who enjoys the company of women. I have plenty of good friends who prefer to stick to their own kind."

"No," I said, "I like women." I hoped I didn't sound defensive or homophobic. "I have gay friends," I added. "In New York. And in Canada." I stopped before I described the extent of these gay friends' gayness.

"Our line of work takes all kinds and that's a beautiful thing," said Pantero. "I pride myself on creating an accepting environment at all times. And if you prefer to accept the attention of an intelligent, elegant, desirable woman, who am I to stand in your way?" He tipped his glass in my direction. "But seriously, how do you like them? Blonde? Brunette? Redhead? The trademark of a fiery spirit."

I looked at Tinkerbell and thought of Linda the bassist, speaking earnestly about the evils of the International Monetary Fund while I stared at her bare breasts. "Brunette, maybe. I don't have any specific preferences."

"I think you like them long and lean, like those willowy French girls who stroll along the Champs Élysées, their scarves rippling in the wind. Magnifique, non?" He tipped his glass toward me again. "Or maybe you like them with a little more spark. You know, a little more grrrrr." He snarled and pawed at the air. "You like a woman you can hold onto." He thrust his hands into the space in front of his chest. His eyes gleamed.

I wasn't comfortable with where this was going. I was rescued by the arrival of Vanessa our server, who I immediately imagined strolling on the Champs Élysées. I thought: her breasts could be bigger and her nose thinner. I thought: she's not on the menu, or not officially.

"Are you ready to order, Mr. Pantero?"

"We are indeed. Nathan?"

Before entering the restaurant I had decided that I was not going to be meek about ordering. My confidence would send a message to Pantero that I was not to be trifled with, that I would assert myself however I saw fit. "Can I have the, uh, jumbo lump crab gratine to start? And the lamb rôti? With the crust of truffles?"

"Certainly."

She was a little thrown off when I didn't hand back the menu. I planned to steal it for Lance. "Can I hold onto this?"

Her face betrayed a split-second's worth of pique. "Of course."

"How's the monkfish bisque tonight?"

"Excellent."

"I'll have that. Bring two bowls — I'm sure my guest here would enjoy it. Then the foie gras terrine with pineapple and mache and the medallions of fallow deer. That'll be terrific." She began to move away when Pantero touched her arm. "Oh, yes. Nearly forgot. We'll both have lobster tails." He turned back to me. "Don't get the idea I eat like this every night. My dietician would murder me if she found out. But I say, after what happened to my poor keister, I deserve a night of indulgence. We'll keep this between us, won't we?"

I nodded solicitously, suppressing the urge to ask what made a deer fallow. I fished my tape recorder out of my satchel and set it on the table.

"You don't mess around, do you?"

"I don't want to waste your time, Mister . . . Danny."

"Before we get down to the nitty-gritty, tell me how someone of your generation got interested in Jimmy."

"As I understand it, he was just about as famous as a man could be in America." Pantero raised his eyebrows at that. He was a strong believer in his own fame. "I heard his records and thought they were very funny. What happened must have been hard to take — the death of the president affected him in ways that nobody else could have experienced. I knew it would be a good story for *The Betsey*."

Pantero looked grave. "I used to say that two people died that day but only one of them was in the ground. Not since Nero played his fiddle has an audience abandoned a performer so completely." He shook his head. "It was cruel, very cruel."

The ruefulness slid off his face and the magnanimity returned. "Have some more wine." He poured me a very generous portion then clinked my glass. "Drink up, my young friend. Tonight, we live!" He spontaneously exchanged toasts with the couple at the next table. "Good evening, my friends!" He continued to toast people all around the restaurant. I thought: Las Vegas, behold your regent.

I tried to get back on track. "I guess one of the things I'm realizing is that Jimmy is interesting for reasons other than his failure. I'm not sure what all of those reasons are, though he definitely understood the nature of the president's image and appeal better than most people of his time. His actual relationship with the president is another thing I'd love to know about."

Pantero broke in. "He was a marvelous entertainer and a very sensitive, intelligent man. I enjoyed working with him very much. We were like brothers, especially in the early days."

I switched on the tape recorder. "How did you first meet Jimmy?"

"It must've been 1957. I was a real pipsqueak then. Fresh from my father's bakery in Brooklyn, still smelling like cannoli. Barely eighteen and I thought I was a star already. I was desperate to get into the biz. My brother, he's working as a dishwasher in a club downtown called the Zig Zag. They had music and comedy there. All the acts played there on their way up. Me, I was happy just to hang around on the sidewalk, dreaming of bigger things. I was there one night to visit my brother and soak up the ambience when I was introduced me to an Irish kid from Detroit called Jimmy Wynn. This guy was a natural mimic. He didn't just do famous people either. He could be the manager at the Zig Zag or some guy he knew in the street or his pop's army buddies. His singing voice wasn't so good but he was great at others — Sammy Mac, Manny Hudson, the one and only Frank Sinatra — he could make it happen. I was looking for a guy like him for the act because I wanted to be just like Jack Hunter. You can imagine how thrilled I was when I got to know the man. He became a real patrone to me. Sammy was too silly for my tastes — all that bug-eyed nonsense — but comedy helped keep the spirit light. I thought that if you could put someone like Jack together with a guy who wasn't so wacky, who could support Jack instead of try-ing to score laughs all the time, then you'd have an unbeatable pair — two aces instead of a king and a joker."

Vanessa arrived with the bisque.

"Thank you so much," said Pantero. He turned back to me. "I had this worked out before I met Jimmy. He liked the sound of it and we decided to work on something together." He put a spoon-ful of bisque in his mouth. He closed his eyes, said, "Mmm," and raised his eyebrows. "I almost forgot to mention," he said, wiping his lip with his napkin, "the most important night I ever had in my life. It's 1956, I'm sixteen. Jack and Sammy were doing their final stand together at the Copacabana. There's no way I'm getting tickets. But my brother knows a kid who works in the kitchen. We meet him at the service entrance, he sneaks us through and ta-da!" Pantero shook his head, still disbelieving his good fortune. "Man, they were great. I cannot begin to describe how I felt. I knew with every fibre of my being that I belonged onstage. That was where the magic happened." He clinked my glass again. "To magic," he said.

"To magic." The wine was tasting better and better. I stole another glance at the acrobat.

"You can't take your eyes off her, you rascal. How old are you?"

"Twenty-five."

"The perfect age. By the time I was twenty-five, I had seven Top Ten hits."

He had inflated the number by five.

"You've got to work hard when you're young," he added. "You don't have all the time in the world, no matter what the song says."

"Which song?"

He crooned it for me: *"We have all . . . the time . . . in the wor-rrrld."* The other diners turned toward him. A few of them applauded. "Thank you," said Pantero, nodding. "Thank you all." He returned to his bisque.

"When did you and Jimmy come to Las Vegas?"

"We land here in 1958. The town's just beginning to take off. The next year I hit the top of the charts with a song called 'The Girl Who Lives Down the Lane.'" An elderly woman at the table behind Pantero gasped at the mention of the title. She put down her cutlery and looked at Pantero expectantly but he stayed focused on me. "The duo's going great. Sometimes Jimmy gets a little too off the wall, but I keep him in line."

"Was it early 1961 when Jimmy first began doing the Cannon impression?"

"That was a real stroke of genius. Here's what happened. I was watching TV and I see this Teddy Cannon and I think, wow, he's as smooth as any singer I've seen. The next day I tell Jimmy. He says, 'Hey, Danny, that's an incredible idea. It'll be perfect for the show.' And we're off."

I let Danny take the credit. "Was it the popularity of this routine that led to the engagement at the Sands?"

He finished his bisque. "I believe that would be placing too much emphasis on one part of a very finely balanced show. It's like with a great arrabbiata sauce. It wouldn't make any sense to say a great sauce is all in the salt or the spice. This, this . . . *entity* we called Danny and Jimmy was a balance of so many elements. Similarly, the material inspired by President Cannon was one of several crucial ingredients."

He paused. "Besides, not longer after the Sands engagement began, a song called 'Bring Your Love to Me' started climbing the charts." The elderly woman gasped again — her face was bright with expectation. This time, Pantero turned all the way around his seat and faced the senior. *"Your eyes are all that I see / Your kisses are as sweet as can be / I long to make you and I we / So bring all your love to me!"* The woman was ready to weep. Pantero briefly left the table to kiss her hand. "Enjoy your evening," he said to the rest of her table.

Pantero radiated a tremendous amount of good cheer and exuberance after this last impromptu performance. However, I'd seen enough of Pantero to feel suspicious. Were the awestruck diners ringers, paraded like the happy, healthy peasants that some Latin American dictator uses to trick a visiting dignitary? And what role did my Tinkerbell have in this plot? I watched her serenely fetch our next bottle, which Vanessa promptly brought to the table along with new glasses.

Pantero wanted to talk about entertainment next. Though I did my best to follow as I savoured my crab gratine, I was distracted not only by the breathtaking leaps of my Tinkerbell but the feeling that I'd already heard what Pantero was saying. In fact, I had read it in his memoir. He recited the part that laid out his theory about the performer's true goal: turning a spectator into a participant. He had a word for this new creation. Looking back on this part of the conversation now, I remember that the crab gratine was delicious.

". . . and the particispectator is the kind of person who, the next time he sees that neighbour or that co-worker at the water cooler, will say, 'You have to see this show. My wife and I had the most fun we've had in years.' Once you have that particispectator's allegiance, you have it forever."

"I see."

"It's important for you to have a clear understanding about my entertainment philosophy. It's something I work hard to promote to all my friends in Las Vegas." He laughed. "Someone told me that performers consider it kind of a milestone when they get the 'Danny speech.' Apparently I've given the speech to so many performers over the years that up-and-comers regard this as a real coming-of-age ceremony. You know you've arrived when you find me knocking on the dressing room door and sitting you down for a lecture. I hope they think I'm a little more fun than their teachers in school! But seriously, I like to do what I can for the new generation."

"Did you ever give Jimmy that speech?"

"Ah, we were kids then. We were just trying to keep our heads above water, maybe catch some of the tomatoes they were throwing so we could make some arrabbiata."

Vanessa cleared the plates and returned with the entrees. My lobster tail was placed a respectful distance from my lamb rôti. On Pantero's plate, the lobster and the deer medallions were a little friendlier. Pantero prided himself on bringing things together.

"What can you tell me about Jimmy's career after 1963?"

"What can I tell you?" Pantero ate half a medallion. "Oh, this is excellent. The sauce has a hint of maple syrup. It's very . . . foresty." He pointed his fork at me. "It seems a shame to ruin food this fine with a sad story. I don't mean to say it's all heartbreak. Jimmy was too talented not to shine when he got the chance. Our contact was more sporadic after our paths diverged. We were close, certainly, but it was a mad time for me. Tours, hit records, the movies."

I knew of Pantero's two movies. One of them had the word "Bongo" in the title.

"Jimmy was busy in L.A. I know his manager Izzy Berman tried very hard to get something else going on for him. You also have to understand how devastating it was for him to lose Katie Perry not long after Cannon. She was a real daisy, just like her character on TV. Bright, perky thing. Funny, too. We all worked together sometimes. She never had a chance to lose that shine like so many other girls do. But when it rained for Jimmy, it didn't just pour — it was a typhoon. Eventually, he came out from under that cloud and began working on some fresh character stuff. Very promising. I know he was doing some club stuff in Los Angeles. I believe that it's unfortunate he cut the record when he did. You know that record?"

"*Who Does This Guy . . .*"

". . . *Think He Is*, right, right. The thing with Jimmy is that the celebrity impressions were his real forte. The original characters, not so much."

"Something that Lenny Bruce told me . . ."

Pantero's hands froze, his knife and fork suspended in mid-cut. "I thought he was dead."

"No, not yet."

Pantero took a moment to digest this information before continuing. "I believe that what Lenny did was disgusting. It was psychological abuse putting Jimmy out in front of crowds like that."

"According to Bruce, he was the only one who'd put Jimmy onstage. He said people in the business treated Jimmy like he had a black cloud over his head."

Pantero grew flustered. "Lenny Bruce was like a cancer in this industry. For him to say that he helped Jimmy is outrageous — it's sick. And Jimmy always had a home here with me. I supported him in every way I could. That's why I asked him to tour with me when I hit the top again in '69 with 'Forever In Your Eyes' — you know the song."

Everyone did — it was a perennial favourite at weddings. I hated it. The disco version was even worse.

"I don't want to get too specific about Jimmy's issues but there was some chemical abuse — believe me, it's a real working hazard for anyone who spends time with Lenny Bruce. But I decide to give my friend another shot. The talent, the magic — it was all still there. We do some shows and they're terrific. But at some point in the tour, he thinks: hey, sorry, Danny, this isn't for me — I have my own life now. He's got some music things on the go, some movies. As always, we part as friends. I'm just happy knowing that I pulled him out of the hole that rat dug for him."

"And beyond '69?"

"These are very busy times. I get involved with the Las Vegas Entertainers Group. I know Jimmy got a place outside L.A., made a little recording studio there. I know he had some success in the music business and in the movies. A mutual friend knows this part of Jimmy's story better than I do. I'd rather put you two in touch than give you a bunch of wrong information. In any case, we come together again in 1982. Las Vegas was being revitalized. Another incredible time."

A distinguished old man in a cape interrupted us. "Danny! I just saw David on the television. How fantastic!"

Pantero beamed up at him. "It's amazing, I know. The kid can do anything. He's reinventing the whole art form."

When the man left, Pantero apologized for the intrusion. "I'm sure you know who that was."

"Uhh."

"Oh, Nate. It's Jerry Starr."

"The magician?"

Pantero looked around, as if checking to see if everyone else was as unimpressed with me. "*The magician*, the kid says." He laughed. "I hope I last in the memory banks a little longer."

My tape would later reveal four seconds of silence. They seemed longer at the time. Pantero began again. "The other interesting development around this time is the video cassette. Someone gets the idea to put together a set of my old TV appearances and advertise them. Big hit. We sell over a million of them. Because of that, there's a whole set of new fans for Danny and Jimmy. So I get in touch with Jimmy. He comes out here for some shows. The creative juices are flowing. We're like kids again. But Jimmy's luck being what it is, it didn't happen."

"Can you say why?"

We were interrupted again by Vanessa. With her was a man in white: Julian the chef. Pantero introduced me as "a very talented young reporter from New York." Julian and Pantero chatted like old pals.

I flipped the cassette in the recorder and started the other side. Pantero noticed. "Hey, Julian, watch what you say. The tape's rolling." They laughed. "Nathan, this man is the best chef in the continental United States. Get that down in your story." Julian gave Pantero what I interpreted as the Gallic version of the "aw, c'mon, don't" shrug.

When Julian left, I dropped my first depth charge. "Have you ever heard of James Saddlecreek?"

"Is that a place or a person?"

"A person."

"James Whatcreek?"

"Saddle."

Pantero chuckled. "Sounds like cowboys and Indians."

"He might be connected to Jimmy. It's been very difficult trying to pick up his trail after the sixties."

"You have to understand that Jimmy has been through a lot. I wish I could be completely honest with you but I respect the man's privacy. I hope that you go back to New York and write about how talented he was, how he was a kind and true friend, and how he continues to make a difference in many people's lives."

"So he's alive?"

Pantero's face betrayed a moment of surprise. "Sure he's alive. It's just that . . . sometimes people who are lost want to stay lost."

"Is there any way you can put us in touch?"

Now he looked almost conciliatory. "I wish I could. Every so often he reaches out with a phone call. Believe me, I do whatever I can. It's been four years since I last heard from him."

"Do you know anybody else who might still be in contact with him?"

"I can tell you're hot on this story, Nate. I hate to disappoint you." He reached over and patted my arm. "I mentioned this person I can get you in touch with. She might give you something more."

I tried out my last depth charge. "While I've been in town, I've talked to a few people about the Nevada Delegation."

He wiped his lips. "Hmm. You're a bright kid. Jimmy is lucky to have someone like you get interested."

"Did you attend these functions?"

"I can tell you I had a good time. I cannot tell you who I shared it with." He leaned forward. "Look, the whole country's been nuts for Cannon ever since he died. It never seems to end. But even a man like that deserved his privacy."

Vanessa came to clear our dishes and give us dessert menus. For all his talk of indulgence, Pantero had barely touched his meal. The lobster tail was completely intact.

"I apologize that I have not been entirely forthcoming. Discretion is very important to me. It's kind of the code I live by. Things go on here that people on the outside would misinterpret. Since Frankie passed on to his great reward, I like to think I've inherited some of his duties and responsibilities. I like to watch over this place. Some people like to call me the unofficial mayor. I don't take that lightly. It's a responsibility. And with that," he removed the napkin from his lap and put it on the table, "I must bid you bon soir. I must give my derriere its beauty rest — doctor's orders. I urge you to stay, have a dessert and a coffee — whatever you like."

"Who's this other person you were going to put me in touch with?"

"What day is today? Monday? Call Sparkle about that on Wednesday." He stood up and bowed to Vanessa, who had returned to the table. "As always, a pleasure."

"Thank you, Mr. Pantero."

"And give my regards to our butterfly Katerina." He nodded toward the glass enclosure. "My friend here is a big fan."

I blushed as I stood up to shake Pantero's hand.

"I know you're going to write an absolutely terrific article," he said. He simultaneously squeezed my hand and clasped my elbow.

He waved to the remaining diners on his way out. Several people applauded.

I asked Vanessa for a mint tea and a crème brûlée. I stopped my tape recorder and played back the last few seconds to make sure Pantero's voice was there. Satisfied with the technology, I put the recorder back in my satchel and put the satchel on the chair that Pantero had just vacated.

I was disappointed that Danny Pantero mostly talked about Danny Pantero. But he had confirmed several facts. The most important was that Wynn was alive. Another was Wynn's involvement with music and movies in California in the late sixties and seventies. I suspected that the trail he left in Los Angeles would lead to James Saddlecreek. Then again, Pantero didn't acknowledge any connection. Maybe his mutual friend would. I pondered these mysteries as I sipped my tea and ate tiny spoonfuls of my dessert.

The restaurant had emptied out. The sound system played old soul songs. The food and wine made me feel better than I should have. I thought of things I might say if Daphne were here. I would tell her about Vegas when the place was really something. That spirit was gone. There was a hole inside the city that couldn't be filled with money.

I realized I hadn't seen Pantero pay the bill. He left so suddenly that it hadn't occurred to me it never came to the table. I didn't recall Pantero saying anything to Vanessa about it. He passed on his regards to Katerina, wished me luck, and walked straight out. Perhaps he stopped at the front of the restaurant to pay. But he wouldn't have dealt with Vanessa because she was here with me while I ordered dessert. Surely someone would have caught him on the way out. He was the one with the money. I was obviously the charity case. It was impossible to believe a guy who looked like me (scruffy, nervous, recently assaulted) could have a titanium credit card. How much did this dinner cost? The cost of the wine alone would have wiped my bank account clean. Did Pantero run a tab or eat for free? Both seemed like reasonable perks for the mayor of the strip. Yet I couldn't take the risk of asking. I thought: damn you, Tinkerbell, you knew this would happen. I wanted to rise from my chair and make my getaway by soaring through a hole in the ceiling.

I had to make do with what I had. Vanessa was no longer nearby — we must have been her last table. I spotted her behind the big wall of glass, chatting with the now-earthbound Katerina. Her back was to me. I was gonna make a break for it. Swiftly and silently I rose from my chair. With a nimbleness that surprised me, I moved through the mostly empty restaurant. I went straight out the door without passing any other Lisette personnel. I thought: oh you're slick.

But as soon as I entered the arid Vegas night, I realized I had made a mistake. My satchel was still sitting on Pantero's chair. At first I thought: fuck it, just keep going. But I couldn't afford to lose the tape recorder — it would've meant sacrificing the Pantero interview and paying to replace the device itself. Plus, the satchel contained the menu I'd stolen for Lance. I thumped my head with the butt of my palm, inhaled sharply, and went back through the door.

With as much calm as I could muster, I strolled through the restaurant. I dodged the chairs with less finesse but at least I didn't knock anything over. When I reached Pantero's chair, I casually clutched the satchel's strap and turned back the way I came.

My composure was broken by a knock on the wall of glass. It was Vanessa and Katerina. They smiled at me. Vanessa even waved. She made no attempt to chase me down. Pantero must have taken care of things. I returned the women's attention with a tense smile and thought: I must seem like a whole other species to them.

11

"You should come see this." Ben's message on the voicemail from the night before was accompanied by the sound of honking cars and nearby laughter. "We're in front of the Pisa. The guys wanted to dress up like monsters and go scare people on the Strip. Von stripped naked, smeared himself with honey, and covered his body with prosciutto. Dirk pasted dog hair all over his face. He's biting people. Steve's going around shaking people's hands and handing out ten-dollar bills. John's idea was to wear a ski mask and a white T-shirt emblazoned with the words 'Molest Me.' John's clearly a kid with issues. What am I saying 'kid' for? He's practically forty. They're all pushing middle age. The record company dyed their hair, stuck some shorts on them, and hoped no one would notice. Anyway, I'm calling to tell you you're on the guest list for tomorrow's show and you better show up. You've got a plus one in case you pick up some hot Vegas skank. Believe me, I've seen weirder things this week. Call me at the Universal around noon. Tomorrow we're gonna go to a wedding chapel and see if they'll let Steve and Von get married."

I almost wished I could see that, but I wanted to get back to my research. I went down to the Barbizon's business centre and searched for Wynn's name in the online music and film databases. Jimmy Wynn was listed as a co-writer for a 1965 movie called *Village Idiot*. It appeared to be a vehicle for Bob Butler, an amiable comic actor remembered principally for starring on the sitcom, *Daddy's Little Princess*. The music database didn't turn up anything with Wynn's name.

James Saddlecreek was much more successful in both fields. He had a total of fourteen credits on movies made between 1970 and 1979. Several were for co-writing and there were a handful of acting appearances, his name typically ranking at the bottom of the cast list. The movies included *Fire Boulevard, Return of the She-Killer, Mutant!,* and *Corpse Nation*. I recognized some of the titles from a guide to American exploitation cinema that used to be my bathroom reading. I had even seen one of Saddlecreek's co-writes, *Born Wild*. I was seventeen. It was the second time I'd tried mushrooms — my friend Curt had brought a batch back from B.C. The movie had something to do with the rise and fall of a rock band in the late sixties — the bits I remembered were an orgy scene and an ultraviolent finale involving a group of albino African revolutionaries. The movie's bent for apocalypse suited my high.

Saddlecreek's movies were all produced by Mercury International Pictures, the same company that made *Village Idiot*. The company belonged to Hollywood's self-proclaimed king of schlock, Don Kirby. He was still making crap; in fact, the crap had made him respectable — film schools gave him honourary degrees.

Saddlecreek's musical cv was even more intriguing. He had acted as producer or songwriter on half a dozen records in the early seventies. Among his clients was Firefly, a Californian folk-rock group who had a breezy hit with "Special Kind of Mellow," a song about Sunday afternoons that was still played on lite-FM stations on Sunday afternoons. The band's record with Saddlecreek predated its success.

Again, I was shocked to see Saddlecreek's name on something

that was already dear to me. He was listed as producer on a record that I'd recently found at Matty's Music Mart. *This Morning Is For You* was the sole LP by Daisy, a sister act from a Californian desert town. Their father was convinced by some kind of divine vision that the girls would be global pop superstars. He pushed them to become musical prodigies, undaunted by the fact that the girls could barely sing or play. Their music was an ungainly, illogical mutation of old and new sounds — it was a pop record made by people who sounded like they'd never heard one before. Beleaguered by and possibly indifferent to their task, the girls constantly struggled to stay in tune and in time. In voices that quavered and stammered, they sang about teachers, puppies, and puppy love. Every so often, I'd hear a snatch of a melody from a half-remembered nursery rhyme or lullaby. This was true American folk art captured on vinyl for future generations to marvel at.

James Saddlecreek's attempt to marshal their non-talents and produce something recognizable as music seemed half-hearted at best. Some songs were built up through multitracking to approximate the popular music of the era. Other songs were left so bare, they might as well be demos. *This Morning Is For You* arrived in the marketplace in 1971. Despite their dad's divine vision, the sisters' record was a flop. It didn't go gold — it didn't even go wood. Yet over the next three decades, Daisy gained an inflated reputation. Underground tastemakers valorized the record's inspired incompetence and the many chance moments of beauty and grace. I'd heard a few songs on a college radio show in Toronto and I loved them like crazy. The one I found at Matty's was an original. It should've gone for five hundred dollars, but was so messed up with water damage, it could've belonged to a porpoise. I argued him down from twenty bucks to six. The vinyl was warped but it sounded fine on my turntable. With their awkward, aching sweetness, Daisy belonged in a country of their own.

The band was already on my mind because I'd planned to write about the CD reissue of *This Morning Is For You* — it had arrived in the mail shortly before I left New York. I could easily make an interview request to the indie record label that was putting it out. Apparently, one or two of the sisters still lived in California. Even if the Daisy women had little to say about Saddlecreek, I could peddle an interview to a music magazine. Winston Sharpe would be pleased to know I was so industrious.

This hearty helping of new data convinced me that Wynn's trail ran from Vegas to L.A. There would be people at Mercury who could tell me more about Wynn's foray into the movie business. There should be a way to get to Firefly or Daisy. I had leads galore. It was time to get out of Vegas.

I went back to my room and called Ben.

"I'm just heading out," he said. "We've got to find two wedding dresses."

"Hey, can I get a ride to Los Angeles tomorrow? My travel arrangements are kind of screwed up."

"Colin told me you were staying under the radar."

"I have no choice."

"Is your guy in L.A.?"

"Maybe."

"I'm happy to take you there. You can crash in my hotel room. We'll tell the guys you're my new lover. That would get them going. Two of them are closet cases, anyway. They're totally obsessed with anal. The VCR on the bus plays nothing but back-door love."

We agreed that Steve and Von's wedding night could be a hot one.

I hung up, inexplicably feeling like all was well with the world. I debated whether to inform Daphne of the next leg of my journey but decided to wait. I had already given her the impression that my Jimmy Wynn interview was in the bag. *The Betsey* need not be troubled with my fine details. The breaks had been rolling my way so far. It was only a matter of time before I found Jimmy.

I hadn't eaten anything so I went back down to the main concourse. The noise of the slots surged toward me as I walked to the Livingstone. The sign outside promised Jazz Magic! — a starburst anchored the exclamation mark. I ordered the soup and sandwich special and waited for my complimentary entertainment.

At 1 p.m., the lights came up on a small corner stage. A woman with long black hair and silver mascara played introductory trills on a Mamoru electronic keyboard while a man in a bright blue cloak plonked out a tricky series of notes on a stand-up bass. Anchoring the music was a cheerfully synthetic bossa nova rhythm courtesy of the Mamoru.

"Good afternoon. I'm Count Victor and this is Stina. We're here to tell you about a few of our favourite things. One is jazz." They took a few moments to trade a few flashy riffs. I nearly recognized the tune as a Sinatra song. As jazz players, they weren't half bad.

"The other," said Count Victor, "is magic." The music stopped dead as he pulled something from his pocket and hurled it on the floor. The little stage was suddenly obscured by red smoke. When it cleared, his bass was nowhere to be seen. He displayed his empty hands for the audience. An "oooh" was audible from a table of three old women in visors. I think I gasped as well. Then his right hand whipped back into the cloak as if he were a cowboy drawing a revolver. Instead of a six-gun, he pulled out a trumpet. "Ta-da!" cried Count Victor before he and his partner darted back into the tune where they left it.

"Neat," I said to no one in particular.

"Isn't it?" came the reply.

I turned and saw a young brunette at a table. She wore a crisp white shirt and a turquoise scarf. She returned my glance then directed her attention back to the stage.

I wasn't sure how to react to Jazz Magic!'s performance or to this woman's acknowledgement of my presence. "Neat" was hardly an impressive display of my well-honed critical acumen. Worse yet, I may have sounded ironic. I didn't mean to. I did believe that Jazz Magic!'s first number was neat. I could've used a more interesting word but "neat" seemed to cover it. How did she interpret my comment? I couldn't tell. Were we sharing a private joke at the expense of Jazz Magic!? Or was her appreciation of Jazz Magic! genuine?

These questions tumbled around in my head for the rest of the performance. Thankfully, the set lasted only twenty minutes, during which time they astonished the small but rapt audience with the re-materialization of the stand-up bass, the simulated destruction of a "priceless" soprano saxophone that "once belonged to the great Mo Parker," the levitation of a metronome, and several spirited renditions of jazz standards. "You've been enjoying Jazz Magic!," said Count Victor before releasing another smoke bomb. From somewhere in the mist, there was a lady's voice. "We'll be back after a short break," she said in a Swedish accent. When the smoke cleared, they were gone. I thought: are they taking a break in some kind of spirit dimension? I thought: should I say that out loud?

I turned my head toward the woman at the other table but stopped halfway between the stage and her. "Wow," I said, oh so casual. "That was something."

I didn't hear anything. I turned the rest of the way. For a moment, I thought she could've been Katerina, my Tinkerbell at Lisette. With her round face, brown eyes, and chic scarf, she had the look of a gamine in a French movie musical.

"I'm happy that I wandered in here," she said. "I couldn't stand the noise."

Her all-American voice didn't quite fit her Gallic appearance. The accent was untraceable, like that of a soap-opera actress.

I thought: think fast, don't lose her. "New in town?" That didn't seem half bad.

"I'm in town for a convention. It starts tomorrow but I came in for an early meeting."

I leaned my elbow on the back of my chair. I hoped my body didn't look as twisted as it felt. "What line of work are you in? If you don't mind me asking?" I thought: good, good. I thought: I hope she can't see my face clearly.

"I work for a company that sells medical equipment."

"Interesting."

"Not unless you work for a hospital."

I thought: go for the gag *now*. "Do you sell anything that uses lasers?"

She laughed. "Why is it that you guys always want to know about lasers?"

I tried to make the next line count. "Aliens. They might invade. We need protection."

I would describe her expression as indulgent. "Uh-huh."

The waitress delivered a bill to her table, upsetting our tentative connection.

"So . . . are you seeing some big shows while you're here? Danny Pantero, maybe?" I thought: I could tell her I know him.

"I hope to tonight. I want to explore more of Las Vegas, get a feel for the city."

"You should wash your hands after touching anything."

She laughed. Oh wow, it was a good laugh. "You're very funny. Is that what you do? You make women laugh?"

"I heard that a sense of humour is very attractive."

"It can be." She put some dollars down then pushed the tray to the edge of the table. "Are you staying for more?"

"I might. Please tell me, which did you like more: the jazz or the magic?"

"Magic more. I like music that's more aggressive."

"How about punk rock?"

She looked at me with some curiosity. "Sometimes."

I thought: she's definitely vibing on you. "Would you like to go see a band tonight? They're punk." I tried to avoid using their name, partly because it was vulgar, but also because the band wasn't very punk.

"What's the band?"

Damn. "Stink."

She laughed again. "Is that their name or how they sound?"

"Maybe both."

"Hmm. So you're going?"

"Yes. Would you like to join me?"

"It could be fun." She stood up from her table. She was a little shorter than I expected but still far, far above my league.

"I could meet you at nine." I failed to sound nonchalant. "Where do you want to meet?"

"Are you staying in this hotel?"

"Uh-huh."

"Why don't I just see you in the lobby?"

"Terrific."

She extended her hand. "I'm Danielle."

I rose and took it. Her skin felt impeccably moisturized. "Nathan."

"See you soon, Nathan."

I watched her leave the Livingstone. "Wow," I whispered to no one in particular. No one else answered this time.

The lights on the stage revealed Jazz Magic!. The sound of laser guns from the woman's keyboard triggered a waking dream of medical equipment of the future and the sexy women who sold it.

* * *

When I got to my room, there was a message from Daphne. I thought: all the ladies want my action. She said Winston was interested in my progress and I should call him today. She was asking when she could send out a photographer to shoot Jimmy Wynn. I decided to ignore that issue. I called the number that she gave me for Sharpe.

"Winston Sharpe's line."

"It's Nathan Grant? Mr. Sharpe asked me to call him?"

"Hold on, please." There was silence on the line. I thought: I can't believe I'm calling Winston Sharpe. I thought: I can't believe I have a date tonight and I'm calling Winston Sharpe.

"Mr. Grant, I apologize I have no time to talk."

"That's all right, I —"

"Let me say that Daphne has told me about your progress and I am very pleased. Your article will be vital in the issue. I believe the story of your comedian will reveal a side to the president that no one has seen before."

"Thank you so —"

"I expect for you to reveal whatever it was that passed between these two men. Keep digging until you know."

"Of course, I —"

"I must return to my meeting, Mr. Grant. Keep this number close by."

And that was it. He said he was very pleased. I can't describe the joy I felt.

The rest of my calls that afternoon went nearly as well. The publicist at Mercury said that Don Kirby would be available for an interview at his office on Thursday afternoon. A publicist at Firefly's record company forwarded my interview request to the band's manager — apparently, Firefly had their own theatre in Branson, Missouri. As for Daisy, the publicist at the label handling the reissue told me Rose, one of the sisters, was doing interviews at her café in Carloff, California. "It's worth the drive just to eat there." The offer was tempting.

The joy was gradually replaced by anxiety. I thought: Danielle won't show up, why would she show up? I frantically tried to

assemble an ensemble that would convey some mastery of the
adult world yet still be appropriate attire at a venue full of scruffy
fourteen-year-olds. I settled on black jeans and a black shirt with
a giant lizard embroidered on the front.

I was in the lobby by 8:52. She arrived at 9:03. She wore a jean
jacket over a violet dress. I felt a friendly tingle in my nether
regions.

We walked out of the hotel and onto the Strip.

"I don't think I asked you where you're from." I intentionally
delivered the question like a statement, contradicting the
Canadian habit.

"Chicago."

"You look very tanned for someone from Chicago."

"It must be from being by the pool this afternoon. I brown
really easily."

I wanted to talk more about her skin but didn't have any more
questions or statements.

"How about you? Where are you from?"

"New York?" I thought: oh shit, I hear question marks. "Well,
Canada first, but now New York? I'm a writer? I'm working on a
story?" I thought: stop, stop, *stop*.

"What's the story about?"

"A comedian?" I cleared my throat. "A comedian. He was
famous for his impression of President Cannon."

"Oh."

She looked more interested than she sounded. I told her an
abridged version of the Jimmy Wynn story as we walked toward the
Universal. It was the first time in many days that I'd tried to articu-
late it and it surprised me how much my new spiel deviated from
the original pitch. Though his Cannon connection was still the key
to the story (and would have to be if *The Betsey* were picking up my
hotel bill), I was more intrigued by Wynn's life beyond the nadir.
Whether he had to serve as punching bag for Lenny Bruce's fans or

a lowly opening act for Danny Pantero, he kept returning to the stage. His tenacity was as admirable as it was foolhardy. I didn't get into anything about the Nevada Delegation or Saddlecreek, though. I felt superstitious — maybe it was safer if she didn't know too much. I took enough of a risk by mentioning Jimmy Wynn by name. If there really was a hex, then I was killing this date.

It didn't seem like that was the case because she listened with evident interest. "I'm surprised I haven't heard more about him," she said.

"The real thing stood the test of time but the reasonable facsimile didn't stand a chance in a crowded marketplace."

She gave me a funny look, but swiftly resumed her smile.

We entered the Universal Concert Theatre just as Stink came onstage. We found a position at the back of the hall, at a safe distance from the teen frenzy already swelling. Von the singer wore a handyman's belt augmented with dildos and kitchen implements. He shook a few of them in the direction of the audience before taking the microphone and bellowing, "I am . . . *a fistful of love!*"

I cringed, momentarily feeling like I'd taken a first date to a porn flick.

Danielle stood at my left. She was more elegant than this scene would normally tolerate. Pierced boy-punks looked her way with longing, their girl companions with contempt. How old was she? Her bearing suggested that she had spent longer in the world of responsible adults than I had. I realized that I had asked her almost nothing about herself. I had gotten carried away with my Wynn talk. Now it was too loud for conversation. To compensate I offered to get drinks. At the concession, there was only pop and extreme energy drinks.

"Here." I had to yell to make myself heard. I extended a paper cup toward her. "I hope you're not allergic to ginseng. I think there's tiger balm in it, too."

"Thank you," she yelled back. She pointed at the band and yelled, "They're good."

I nodded. Actually, Stink were shit — rudimentary two-chord punk drunk on cheap bravado and trite innuendo. They complained about parents, politicians and "phony-assed" girls, struggling to make their bitching sound new. Yet, I didn't mind it at all. I was standing next to a beautiful woman in a city that promised the sky to one and all. I thought: bless you, Las Vegas, you lovable old whore.

The set eventually rumbled to a close. In the gap between the performance proper and the inevitable encore, the audience clapped and hollered. Danielle stood still. I longed to know what she was thinking.

I found out when she turned, put her hand on the back of my head, and kissed me hard. I was surprised. I thought: how'd this happen? I thought: *yes*. When the next song kicked in, the blare of the guitars nearly knocked me over. She moved her mouth to my ear. "Take me back to your hotel room."

I clutched her hand and led her out of the Universal. Fearing the moment would evaporate if I didn't hurry, I hailed a taxi. She kissed me again in the backseat. My mouth betrayed my nerves. When I came up for air, I asked, "Is it the sense of humour thing?"

"Sure."

I ignored her note of exasperation. I don't remember much of the trip between the taxi and my room. I was so giddy, I tripped over my feet. She found that funny, too. When I opened the door to my room, I saw that some of the Berman documents were still strewn over one side of the bed. I hastily collected them and tossed them on the desk. I thought: am I being presumptuous by neatening up the bed?

She slipped out of her jean jacket then pressed herself against me. I had the first of several excellent opportunities to assess her bust up close. The friendly tingle in my nether region was now a fire alarm. I thought: Las Vegas, I will never leave you.

"Turn off the light," she said.

And there was absolutely nothing ironic in the way that she fucked me.

* * *

I was woken by the sound of rustling pages. I opened my eyes. The light on the desk was on. My head was too full of sleep and happiness to understand why she was sitting there. Instead, I was thrilled at the sight of her nakedness, the very fact of her nakedness.

"Hey," I murmured.

She stopped still for a moment. Then she faced me. "I was looking for somewhere to write down my phone number."

"Are you leaving already?"

"Early meeting."

"Please stay."

"Only for a little while."

The second time I woke, it was the phone. When I picked it up, it was Ben. "The circus is leaving town in fifteen minutes," he said. He hung up.

Then I remembered I wasn't supposed to be alone. Or was I? I had no idea what the etiquette for this situation required. I didn't know how we'd left things — it had all happened so wonderfully fast and easy. I thought: maybe I should call her and tell her I had a good time. Maybe we could see each other again, later, in Los Angeles. Or when I got back to New York. Or something.

I looked on the desk for her phone number. It wasn't in plain view. Actually, nothing on the desk was as I expected. The pile of Berman pages was now an orderly stack. The laptop's lid was closed though I usually left it up. It was as if all my stuff had been examined. Then I noticed my notepad was missing.

I called the front desk.

"Hi, this is Nathan Grant in room 2046. Can you put me

through to another guest's room?"

"What name?"

"Danielle . . ." She hadn't told me the rest. "She's with the convention."

"Which convention, sir?"

"The one with the lasers. I mean, medical equipment?"

"I'm not aware of that convention, Mr. Grant."

"Can you look up Danielle? I have her, uh, purse. I need to return it." I thought: what about my wallet? Did she take it? And my kidneys? Did I still have two?

"If you would like to bring the purse to the front desk, we can try to return it."

"No, it's okay. Thanks for your help."

I grabbed my jeans from the floor and checked for my wallet. It was still there. Ben was waiting so I had to take inventory quickly. I could account for everything but the notepad. I had a fast shower and packed up my duffel bag with my clothes and laptop. The Berman files and my tape recorder went in my satchel. I dropped off my room key at the front desk and signed the bill that *The Betsey* was covering. Nobody asked about a lost purse.

Ben was waiting outside, the minivan already idling. "C'mon, c'mon," he said. "The band bus is already on the road. We have to keep the convoy together."

Another Network X crew member put my bags in the back and Ben hustled me into a seat. My head was spinning fast enough to produce centrifugal force. I did my best to pull a thought together.

"What's with you?" asked Ben. "You look totally fried."

"This is going to make me sound insane but I think someone seduced me in order to get information."

Ben looked at me in disbelief.

"Serious?"

I nodded.

"Man . . . that is *awesome*."

12

"So what's it like being pumped for information?"

I heard many variations on this joke during the first half of the van ride. Ben relayed my news to all of his crew members. Though I enjoyed the attention, it occurred to me that I may have endured something other than sexy espionage and the pettiest of petty thefts. She could have taken all of my Wynn findings rather than just a notepad of scribblings even I couldn't read. She could have lifted my wallet and used up the precious, life-giving remainder of funds available on my credit card, thereby ending this investigation. She could have drugged me and removed a much-treasured organ, like a kidney or a brain or a testicle. Or she could have cut my throat and left me for the housekeeper to find.

According to all prior indications, people have died for less. Colin often wrote about the witnesses of the assassination. These were the peripheral players who were cut from the main narrative. Ben Arnold was an auto parts dealer in Shreveport, Louisiana. He was one of several people who saw Martinez running toward the president's car. He also reported seeing two other suspicious men fleeing the scene — they wore the same silver sunglasses and yellow floral-patterned shirt worn by Martinez. He told police officers on the scene they might have been "decoys," deployed to seed confusion about the original location of Martinez or the number of assassins on the site. Arnold was killed in 1967 when his car drove off the road and hit a tree — there were no other cars on the road, nor were there any traces of alcohol or drugs found in his system.

Nathaniel Fontainebleu owned a sock factory on the outskirts of New Orleans. As a representative of a local small business association, he was to attend a private reception for President Cannon later that afternoon. A camera buff, he had his Super 8 camera rolling when the shots were fired. Fontainebleu's footage seems to indicate that the president repeatedly looked in Martinez's direction well before the gunman began his charge toward the car. The loving father of three young children, Fontainebleu committed suicide in 1968, leaving no note.

A housewife visiting from Houston, Annette Newton told a police officer that she saw a man unpacking a black duffel bag from a Cadillac with Louisiana plates in an alley off Decatur Street approximately thirty minutes before the assassination. Newton made it all the way to 1970 before being shot to death during a robbery at the bank where she worked. Co-workers claimed it was as if the thieves had specifically targeted her. One of the assailants had called for her by name.

So excuse me for being paranoid while I poked my nose into the life and times of a comedian who had one or more secret meetings with the president and knew things that he preferred to keep to himself.

As for Danielle, my hunch was that she was enlisted by Pantero to investigate my findings and send me a message. Since the method by which the message was delivered involved humping me silly, I did not understand it. There was the chance she was a woman who genuinely thought a sense of humour was the most attractive quality in a man and stole the pad as a memento, but the unlikelihood of that explanation depressed me.

"Ben," I said, adopting a serious expression, "don't joke about this. She could've done anything to me." I could not fight the urge to leer suggestively.

"I wish I could have a secret agent adventure." He leaned toward the woman driving the van. "Melissa, would you ever pump me for information?"

"Ask me again and it's sexual harassment."

"Oh." Ben sat back sheepishly. I couldn't tell if she was kidding, either. "Here," he said, "park in this lot."

The van rolled to a stop near the band's bus. The parking lot was otherwise empty.

I asked Ben why we stopped. We'd barely left Vegas. In fact, we seemed to drive eastward out of town, not westward to Los Angeles. It couldn't just be a matter of my anxiety and disorientation.

"We're doing a shoot," Ben said as he opened the van door. "Step lively."

Ben and the rest of the crew from Network X piled out of the van. Stink's yawning members milled at the side of their bus with their bleary young entourage. I doubted any of these people had seen this side of noon for a long time. The day was clear and bright, the desert air still chilly from the night before.

A Network Xer dropped a bag of gear next to me and bent over to rifle through it. "Where are we?"

He pointed to his right. Beyond the vehicles I could see an enormous wall of concrete, more pink than white, spanning the two walls of the canyon. The highway ran along the top of the wall before sloping down next to our parking lot. I walked across the highway and looked down. Hundreds of feet below was the Colorado River. I thought: hey, the Wilson Dam. I could hear the drone of the intake towers.

I walked back to the Network Xers and Stink kids, wondering how I'd ended up here of all places. One camera crew set off with the band toward a platform overlooking the dam while Ben conferred with the other crew. I caught Ben's attention. "Let me guess: you and Stink are shooting an educational film on America's greatest architectural wonders?"

"We're here for David Maher."

"The magician?"

"He prefers the term illusioneer. But yeah, him."

Ben indicated a space in the sky far above the dam. Shining like a crystal in the sun was a clear cube suspended from a construction crane parked next to the Wilson Dam visitor centre. I strained to see inside this dazzling space of white light. Eventually I could make out a man. He was shirtless and sitting cross-legged on the floor of the cube. The only other contents of the cube were a tank of water and a small mattress. I couldn't imagine a lonelier place.

"He's been there for twenty-nine days," said Ben. "He gets out tomorrow."

"What's he doing?"

"Starving, mostly."

I followed Ben and his crew toward a small group of people keeping vigil on another platform slightly up the slope. They sat in deck chairs and stared at the cube through binoculars. There was an assortment of coolers on the pavement around them. At the feet of one man was a cardboard sign that said: WE BELIEVE IN YOU DAVID.

"His fanbase," whispered Ben. "We outnumber them."

I heard a rumbling behind us. I saw a Network Xer dragging a barbecue across the highway and onto the lower platform.

"What's with the barbecue? Are you gonna smoke him out?"

"Maher hasn't eaten solid food in a month. We're gonna give him a little whiff of barbecue. Right now, we have to distract the fanbase."

Ben and his camera crew began to quiz the quintet of Maher admirers. "Why are you here today?" he asked a white-haired granny in a David Maher T-shirt. "What David is doing is beautiful. Every day we're told that our lives are not complete unless we have cars and riches and fancy things. By staying up there for thirty days, David is saying no. You can have nothing and still have everything."

Said the guy with the sign: "He reminds me personally that there's almost nothing we as people can't endure. We have the strength. We only have to look inside."

Ben posed his follow-up to the sign guy. "Do you think that what David's doing is at all insensitive toward the plight of people who are genuinely starving? Like, in Africa?"

"If people like that do not want to see the poetry in what's he's doing," he said, "that's their problem."

Meanwhile, two Stink-ers roughhoused at the edge of the platform — I hoped I would get to see one toss the other over the side. Clouds of smoke rose from the barbecue toward Maher's cube.

Ben's interview with the sign-guy was interrupted by the voice of Von through a bullhorn: "THE BURGERS ARE READY. COME AND GET 'EM. FREE BURGERS."

Von held the bullhorn in one hand and an oversized can of beer in the other. His bandmates chugged from their own cans. John lifted two middle fingers to the cube and laughed.

"Ah, not again," moaned the sign-guy. "Can't you people leave David alone?" he yelled.

Dirk was waving a pen in the air. It was a laser pointer. Sure enough, a red dot madly squiggled across David's face and scraggly beard. He didn't flinch. The illusioneer was as motionless as a stone Buddha.

"MR. MAHER," said Von, now flanked by two girls traveling with the band. "IF YOU ACT NOW, WE'RE OFFERING FREE LADIES. I REPEAT, LADIES FREE OF CHARGE."

The girls hiked up their T-shirts to reveal pale, tattooed, and generously sized young breasts. They leaned backwards and shook them obligingly in the cube's direction. The camera caught the action. I thought: they'll have to blur those for TV.

"THAT'S RIGHT," said Von. "FRESH TITTIES. COME AND GET 'EM."

The sign-guy stormed off toward the lower platform, with Ben and his camera crew in tow. I stayed at the minimum safe distance.

"It's horrible what they're doing," said the granny. "Horrible."

"Do people do this all the time?" I asked.

"I've seen them throw cans and cups. I've seen them throw food. Other people play their car stereos at night so he can't sleep. There was another man who tried to climb onto the cube. He could've killed David. We had him arrested."

"They should show more respect," said another woman in a deckchair.

Maher sat perfectly still. I couldn't imagine how much abuse he'd already endured over the preceding weeks.

"Why do you like what he's doing?" I asked the deckchair woman.

"Oh, I don't know," she said cheerfully. "It looks so dramatic, the cube there against the big sky. I saw David when he was buried up to his neck in New York Harbor. I was watching his live TV special when he was shot."

"He was shot?"

"With bullets," she said gravely.

Down at the lower platform, the sign-guy was shouting angrily at the Stink posse. He reached for the bullhorn but Von tucked it behind his back. John got in between them and screamed in the man's face. Ben's cameras caught the conflict from two different angles. A vehicle with a Wilson Dam logo pulled up and two men in police uniforms emerged. Their arrival did nothing to cool off the situation. John and the man continued to yell at each other, their faces only inches apart. With an almost casual air, the two

cops grabbed John, slammed him against the hood of the car,
cuffed him, and stuffed him in the backseat. Now the rest of the
Stink kids were yelling at the cops. Ben came forward with a conciliatory, "I'm the adult in charge, Officer" manner. It didn't do
anybody any good. The cops peeled away with John in the back.
The sign-guy gave a thumbs up to the police car and stomped
back up the slope toward me.

"Those little assholes," he muttered.

"At least they didn't take you away this time," said the granny.

"I've had it with these kids." He pointed up at David. "He's
trying to teach us something and they're too blind to see it.
They're the kind of people who jeered our Lord and Saviour when
he was up on the cross."

"PLEASE RETURN OUR DRUMMER." Von was now directing the
bullhorn at the fanbase. "HE MEANT YOU NO HARM." The Network
Xers were laughing but Ben looked worried as he dialed numbers
on his cell phone.

"Screw you!" screamed the sign-guy.

"Leave David alone!" screamed the granny.

Maher just sat there and suffered, as if that's all he'd done since
the beginning of time.

* * *

As John sat in a jail cell in nearby Wilsonville, Ben worked out the
situation with Network X and the record company's lawyers. The
sign-guy was going to press charges unless he got a considerable
payout. Ben was worried he may not be able to use the footage for
legal reasons. "I'm blurring out most of the faces anyway," he said.
"I guess I could just blur the whole dam."

The Stink kids and Network Xers hung around a restaurant in
the strip mall in Wilsonville. I left after lunch and went for a walk.
Last night's euphoria had continued to leak away. I saw dark forces

assembling against me. If they came at me again, the form they took would not be as luminous as Danielle.

I called Daphne from a phone booth. She picked up. "Thanks for checking in. Did you get my message?"

For once, her voice did not send me into paroxysms of delight. A night of fake seduction and a morning of doom had done a number on my libido. "I should have details for you soon. I'm on my way to Los Angeles." I sounded as confident as possible. "That's where Jimmy Wynn lives."

"You've found him?"

"Pretty much." Lying was so easy.

"Can you call the photographer and give him the contact information?"

"Why don't I call you when I've got my bearings?"

"All right, but we're short on time. Did Colin talk to you about the Nevada Delegation?"

"It was me who told him about it." While that wasn't precisely true, I was beginning to fancy myself an expert.

"Let me know what Wynn has to say about it. I was talking to Colin last night and we thought it might be a good idea to package the stories. Winston wants to go large."

I didn't like the sound of any of that, starting with Daphne talking to Colin outside office hours. "Is Colin writing about the Delegation?"

"He has some new information."

"But the Nevada Delegation is part of my story." I thought: that sounded like whining.

"You should talk to Colin and see what he has in mind." Daphne sounded firm rather than friendly. "I don't want overlap. And call me as soon as possible so we can deal with the photographer."

I promised and hung up. My mood darkened. Not only was Colin possibly targeting Daphne for acquisition, he wanted to claim the story, too. He had dozens of other stories to tell about Cannon and the assassination. He knew how badly I needed a major feature. I thought: I always knew he was a prick. I thought: don't jump to conclusions. I called Colin's number in New York — no answer.

My next call was to Sparkle. That too went to voicemail. I didn't ask her if the mayor of the Strip sent a beautiful woman to seduce and rob me. I merely informed her that when Pantero and I last spoke, he'd promised to pass on an important contact to me, a woman who could tell me more about Jimmy. I left Ben's cell phone number, which I'd given out to Daphne as well.

By the time I got back to the restaurant, word had spread that John would soon be sprung. Von was sitting at a table with one of the band's tattooed love slaves. He looked sullen and drunk. The girl looked bored and grouchy. He waved me over.

"Hey."

"What?"

"You wanna interview me?"

"Uh, no."

He squinted at me. "I thought you were a reporter."

"Yeah," I said, "but I'm not writing about you guys."

"What are you writing about then?"

I thought: keep the details vague. "President Cannon."

"Really?" His eyes temporarily widened. "He's amazing, man. He let the black kids go to school. Plus he got his bone smooched, like, eight times a day. I really admire him." He nodded. His movements were as sluggish as his voice was slurry. "Not like the guy we have now." He called out to Steve at the next table. "Hey, what's the president's name?"

Steve smirked. "President Douche Mist."

"Yeah," Von mumbled, "Captain Douche Mist."

We all had a good laugh at that. I thought: what will you morons do with the money you're making?

We were soon back on the road. The Network Xers in the van reminisced about the Wilson Dam adventure and the raunchy incidents at the wedding chapel the day before. Ben and his co-workers were pleased with what they had gotten on tape.

It was nearly 9 p.m. by the time we got to the Chateau Montpelier, an eight-storey, colonial-style hotel fabled for hosting rock-star bacchanals. Visions of chocolate-covered groupies should've been dancing in my head. For all I cared, it might as well have been a roadside motel in Iowa full of narcoleptic truckers.

Ben took me aside when we got out of the van. "Are you okay?"

"It's been a long day."

"At least you didn't spend it talking to lawyers. You're coming off a night of erotic adventure."

"You make it sound like a softcore movie."

"If you're interested in making another one, there's a party for the band at a bowling alley."

"I'm too bagged."

"There'll be strippers."

"At a bowling alley?"

"It's Los Angeles. They *invented* entertainment here."

I asked Ben to get a VCR for his room and walked to Sound and Vision on Alsada Boulevard. It was widely regarded as the coolest video store in the city. One former clerk had recently landed a three-picture deal with Paramount on the basis of a script about a cop with Tourette's syndrome. I loaded up on vintage Mercury product, fetching the tags for *Fire Boulevard*, *Born Wild*, *Corpse Nation*, and *Steel and Thunder*. I had a look around for a few more titles on my list before going to the counter.

"Do you have *Return of the She-Killer*?" I asked.

The clerk wore a Meat Locker T-shirt and thick-rimmed glasses. He looked at me with withering contempt. "Yes," he said, his tone thick with ennui, "but it's tripe."

On a day other than this one, I would have slunk away. Instead,

I wanted to drive my hand through his face. "Gimme it anyway."

Back at the hotel, I settled into a night of viewing. The movie database had listed James Saddlecreek among the bit players in *Fire Boulevard* (1972) and *Corpse Nation* (1975). I propped up the 8 x 10 glossy from the Berman file next to the TV and searched both movies for anyone bearing his features. *Fire Boulevard* starred Chip Harrelson, an actor who'd made it big on a sixties TV western before his career declined to the point where he'd work for Don Kirby. He played Griff McCoy, a quiet man in a small town who's pushed into the role of vigilante when drug-crazed hippies go on a spree of rape and murder, plunging the town into a state of topless barbarism. It was grim, sleazy stuff even when viewed on fast-forward. I didn't spot Wynn.

*Corpse Nation* had no hippies, only corpses. Set in the near future when all men's trousers would have single silver stripes down the sides, the story had to do with the dead being brought back to life by a wonder drug. Though the damage to their brains leaves them with little of their former intellectual capacity, they can be trained to do domestic chores. What the living don't know is that the apparent passivity of the dead is merely part of a sinister ruse. The lord of the reanimated dead is foiled by a fresh-faced couple who believe in the healing power of music. Again, Wynn wasn't among the corpses.

Saddlecreek had a writing credit rather than an acting one on *Born Wild* (1973). I watched it in case Wynn accidentally fell into the frame, just like those pesky boom mikes that kept dipping down into *Corpse Nation*. My mushroom-trip fave, *Born Wild* told the stormy saga of a psychedelic rock band called Gold Mind. I noticed the hand of Wynn in the character of the band's singer and raconteur, Green, who liked to entertain audiences with cryptic anecdotes and monologues in between the songs. The crowds enjoyed his words more than Gold Mind's music — Wynn was giving himself away. Green was the band's conscience by default

— he does not participate in the LSD-suffused orgy that escalates into a satanic ritual because he's too busy with the albino African radicals' scheme to blow up Mt. Rushmore. The final image of the presidential heads (as rendered in papier-mâché) blowing up over and over seemed less profound now that I wasn't high.

As for *Return of the She-Killer* (1976), it really was tripe.

It was nearly 2 a.m. but I pushed on. *Steel and Thunder* (1974) was next. I watched out for Jimmy. Here's some of what I saw:

The screen shows a road. We hurtle along it, the camera fixed on the front of a car or a motorbike. The yellow line that divides the highway is cracked up and faded. *STEEL AND THUNDER* blazes across the screen in blood-red, Mercury's house colour. A demonic blues song muscles out the silence. Jimmy Wynn's name is not among the opening credits. Cut to: side view of the road. Telephone poles, trees, brush, mailboxes, abandoned cars on blocks, other little roads that lead to who knows where. What are we looking for? Are we going somewhere?

Cut to: teenage boy landing hard on patch of gravel. A mean man says, "I've had it with you, boy." The boy's bleeding from a cut on his forehead. We get his POV up at an older man who fills the screen like a white-trash Colossus. "I'm gonna teach you a lesson you'll never forget." There's a switch in his hand. It comes down near the camera. It makes a splat and a crack when it lands. The boy screams, keeps screaming as the screen goes black. Next we get the kid running. "I'm not done with you!" says our Colossus. The kid's mouth is bloody, his teeth stained in Technicolor. There's a dirt bike leaning on the side of a shed. He gets on and takes off.

Cut to: the road we started on. We see a solitary rider. Big black helmet and leather suit, dark sunglasses — a rugged road Nazi. The kid swerves out onto the highway too fast. He doesn't have any control. The biker has to swerve to miss him. The kid panics, heads off the road. The biker keeps going long enough for us to wonder, "Is he gonna help the kid?" He slows down and turns around.

They meet. The kid stops sobbing long enough to tell the biker his woes. We know the hate in the boy's heart is sure to cause a mess of trouble, but the biker sees something of himself in the kid (not that he says so). The biker takes the kid to a roadhouse. There's a long line of Harleys outside. Inside, guys play pool, play cards, drink liquor out of shot glasses and stubby beer bottles. A too-pretty blonde dances in front of the jukebox. The song's another rockin' blues number. The biker tells the kid, "Hang back if there's trouble." The kid's needy look reads homoerotic. We get a look at the bartender — meaty guy with a handlebar moustache and a black cap. He's got his head down. The biker says, "Where's Mitch?" The bartender shrugs his shoulders. "Check the back."

It was the shrug that got me. I rewound the tape and watched it again. The bartender had raised his shoulders into the Cannon-patented position. I couldn't see his face.

The kid stays two feet behind the biker as he walks the length of the bar. There's another biker in an alcove. This one has dead eyes. He's the first to talk.

"Heard you got into a scrape."

"Nothing I can't handle." They talk about a package that was not delivered. The dead-eyed biker mentions a lawman. The live-eyed one says he's done with this business.

"You're not done unless I say so." The live-eyed one begins to walk out. The bartender and another rough dude block his way, their arms folded in front of their chests. The bartender gives the biker a menacing look. "Orders are orders, Rock."

The voice is wrong but the face is right. The bartender was in the shot for maybe two seconds before the camera tracked past him. I paused the tape and peered at the 8 x 10. I looked for the same features on the bartender's mug. It was hard to tell for certain. I let the video run.

Cut to: good-guy biker grabbing a pool cue. We see it smack into the side of the bartender's head. The cue splits in half, breaking too easily yet making a satisfying crunch. The other dude is reaching for a knife in his belt. The biker stabs him in the shoulder with the broken pool cue. Blood spurts. Man screams. Cut to: face of kid, his eyes wide with a mix of horror and amazement.

I rewound back to the point of contact between pool cue and head. I remember something. I feel like I've seen all of this already — not just the man playing the bartender but the whole scene. I didn't recognize the movie's title but I must have seen all this on late-night TV, long before I was looking for Jimmy.

I studied the face on the screen and found what I wanted. It was a rougher, hairier, paler Jimmy Wynn but a Jimmy Wynn all the same.

I thought: I found you, you old bastard . . . so now where are you?

13

"Mr. Kirby will see you soon, Mr. Grant. If you'd like to have a seat."

The receptionist at Mercury International Pictures had an oddly formal manner for a woman whose neck and arms were covered in tattoos. Inky strands of red, black, and purple curled and coiled to form rose petals, flaming hearts, buff-looking angels, and — on her right forearm — the words "sapere aude." I thought: I bet she'd like me if I could tell her what that meant in Latin. I wanted to know what was written on the other parts of her body. It must've hurt to get it all done. I stopped staring when she caught me.

I had been on the move since leaving the hotel, a task I was proud to accomplish by noon considering how long I spent watching movies the night before. When I was halfway through *Steel and Thunder* — it had crawled to within a few feet of not-that-bad before falling to pieces — Ben arrived, eager to tell me about the topless bowlers and Stink's many efforts at big-black-balls–related humour.

Ben was nearly as excited to hear Jimmy Wynn was James Saddlecreek. "That's your guy," he said when I held up the glossy next to the TV. "Not much of an actor."

"Doesn't matter — it's not much of a movie."

"But how exactly does this piece of information help you find him?"

He had a point. According to the movie database, Saddlecreek's meagre fame stopped at the end of the seventies. In fact, it was Jimmy Wynn who appeared on the radar most recently, reuniting with Pantero some time in the early eighties for the aborted shows.

So did it help me? I feared that I'd gotten way ahead of myself by heading to Los Angeles when there must've been more to dig up in Las Vegas. Maybe that was what Colin was doing, discovering more about what connected Wynn, Cannon, and the Nevada Delegation. I didn't have a clue what I was doing. I had never done any kind of investigation before. Whatever confidence I had in my instincts and abilities rested largely on a series of modest achievements in college journalism, the compliments of Winston Sharpe, and the fact that I had seen many TV shows in which people did this kind of thing — sleuthing, I mean. Saddlecreek seemed like a valid avenue of enquiry.

The Mercury office was located in a cluster of low-rise pearl-blue office buildings in Encino. It took me three buses to get there. Where Las Vegas had been a bruising extravaganza of noise and sensation, Los Angeles was merely taciturn to me. The tall palm trees looked like props, the sidewalks were always empty of people, the buildings ran out of ambition three storeys up, and the light had a hard, merciless quality that was unkind to my scuffed-up face. I was suspicious of the weather and bored by the landscape. I wanted New York. I lamented my lack of a better exit strategy than heading to the bus station and catching the next ride east.

As I waited for an audience with Kirby, I studied the movie posters on the walls. The predominant motif: heads and shoulders of characters superimposed over a gun, fire, or both at once. Those movies often had the word "maximum" in the title. Two posters featured women holding handguns straight out with both hands

— their breasts bulged between their elbows, the cleavage nearly touching their chins. The marketing for horror titles were more creative if not more tasteful. *Contagious*, a recent title about a killer virus, featured an overhead shot of a Petri dish filled with blood — the outline of a skull formed within the redness. *Drill Bit* showed a thick, blood-tipped power drill pointing straight up — for Mercury, this counted as subtle. At least the time had passed when they could stick a screaming coed in the background. *Headcase* had a man's face reflected in the broken pieces of the mirror. In the lower pieces, the mirror fragments that contained the sections of his mouth each suggested a different expression — a smile, a scream, a grimace, his teeth bared like an angry animal. I could see my own face reflected in the glass of the frame. I didn't look angry at all. I only looked bruised and wary.

The credits at the bottom of each poster began with "A Don Kirby Production." Kirby and his original partner Brian Winwood had founded Mercury International Pictures in 1959. To make their first movie, they had borrowed $50,000 from a consortium of pharmacists in order to shoot a drag-racing pic called *Wheels of Fire*. When the movie turned a profit, Mercury was in business. The company had made over one hundred and fifty movies since. The most famous of them were the hippie-filled youth-sploitation movies of the late sixties and early seventies. The home video boom in the eighties inspired a wave of erotic thrillers and ninja movies shot on the cheap in Latin America. Mercury made crud and a lot of it. Kirby himself gained a reputation for supporting young talent (he gave many major filmmakers their first chance to direct) and for maintaining tight fiscal control over his operation (he fired people if he believed they were profligate with staples).

The mini-studio's relationship with Jimmy Wynn began in early 1963. A paper in the Berman file indicated Wynn was contracted to write and star in a feature for Winwood. The movie was apparently about the comic misadventures of a man who is mistaken for the long-missing mayor of a New England town. It was eventually made in 1965 but not with Jimmy Wynn. It had been farmed out to Bob Butler, then a rising comic untainted by any association with dead presidents. Not having seen *Village Idiot*, I can only assume Butler did everyone proud with a heartwarming performance that was cruelly overlooked come Oscar time.

When I called to see about interviewing Kirby — Winwood died of a stroke in 1966 — I'd mentioned only Wynn's name. I had no idea if James Saddlecreek's identity was common knowledge in Los Angeles. I wanted to keep his name to myself for now.

"Mr. Grant?"

There was a young man in a black baseball cap standing next to the tattooed receptionist.

"I'm Don's assistant Rory. Don can see you now. He apologizes in advance for not having much time to talk. He's editing today."

I rose to attention and shook his hand. "What's he working on?"

"*Deadly Temptation 3: The Final Encounter.*"

"That's good," I said. "I had a lot of unanswered questions at the end of *Deadly Temptation 2.*"

Rory didn't smile. "Please follow me."

Rory led me through the requisite grid of cubicles and past glass-walled offices full of film and video equipment. Kirby's office was in the far corner of the space. The sign on the door said: IF YOU HAVE TIME TO READ THIS, WORK HARDER.

The room inside was cluttered. A Lifetime Achievement Award from the American Independent Film Association and an honourary doctorate from UCLA fought for space on the wall next to framed newspaper articles about Don Kirby and more Mercury posters. There was a mounted deer's head, too — a beige sports jacket hung from its sole antler. Kirby, still looking spry at the age of seventy-two, sat behind a large wooden desk, its surface covered in scripts, books, and an antique typewriter. He stood up to shake my hand but didn't come around the desk.

"Hello, Mr. Kirby. I'm Nathan Grant?"

"You tell me."

"I'm sorry. That wasn't a question. I'm from Canada?"

"I like making movies in Canada. A dollar goes a long way there. Plus you speak American and you're too polite to steal anything. Make a movie in Bulgaria and you've got to nail everything down."

I set up my tape recorder and sat down in the swivel chair opposite him. "Thank you for seeing me. I'm a big fan of your movies."

"You only say that because you haven't seen all of them," he said. I recognized his gruff yet amiable manner from his talk-show appearances and interviews. "And I don't know if I'll be of much use to you. You said you were writing something about Jimmy Wynn? The comedian?"

"I'm working on a profile of him for *The Betsey*. He wrote a movie for you, *Village Idiot?*"

"I don't recall if I ever met the man face-to-face. My old partner was the comedy man. I stuck with the sex and the violence."

"And the crab monsters," I said, pointing to a rubber model perched high on a bookshelf behind him.

Kirby leaned back in his chair and clasped his hands behind his head. "Crab monsters paid for my first swimming pool. Now if we got Jimmy Wynn to fight some crab monsters, he might've had a career in the movies. I ask you, where is he now?" I presumed this question was rhetorical because Kirby kept going. "That's not to say I had any big hopes for him. When my partner Brian told me he wanted to develop a movie around this kid who did impressions of the president, I thought, where's the movie in that? But then I heard he was selling millions of records, on tv all the time

— he had plenty of exposure we could capitalize on. Brian had a hunch so he signed him up and got a script out of him."

"You didn't meet Wynn?"

"I'd be surprised if Wynn ever set foot in our offices — we were in a place on LaBrea back then. That's a long way from Vegas. Plus, people were coming and going all the time so I can't remember all the faces."

"Why was he dropped from *Village Idiot?*"

"Why else? I didn't want to buy a ticket to a movie to see the dead president staring back at me. My wife would weep every time she saw Cannon's picture in a magazine — and she wasn't the only one. As a matter of fact, I was the first one in Hollywood brave enough to take on the Cannon assassination. I knew there was a movie in all the conspiracy talk. We did a picture called *The Pentagon Parallax* back in '74. You know it?"

I shook my head.

"That was a good one." He leaned forward over his desk. "Denny Robertson played a Secret Service guy who's guilt-ridden because the president got killed on his watch. Salma Saldana is the sexy Latin-American spy who falls in love with him. There's some hot stuff between them. We based the story on real facts, though we did have to change some details. We couldn't call the president Teddy Cannon, for instance — that seemed disrespectful, and distributors would never go for it. Some people carped about that, but hey, I don't make documentaries — a filmmaker needs poetic licence if he's gonna tell the truth."

I nodded. Kirby looked at my notepad then back to me. "Oh," I said. I wrote that down.

Kirby scratched his chin. "It would have been good to get Jimmy Wynn in for that picture. He would have been cheap. After what happened, Wynn was obviously not going to be starring in any picture of mine. But the script was already paid for so we gave it to Bob Butler. The picture did all right. It was always harder to make money on the comedies. Real touch and go. Kids at the drive-in aren't there to listen to guys talk about some cockamamie thing. They want to see some blood, some monsters, some cars, maybe some skin. They know what they like and I know what they like."

"I guess so." I chuckled along with Kirby. I thought: play your cards right. I cleared my throat and spoke. "I also heard that Jimmy Wynn was close to someone who worked on several Mercury films in the seventies."

"Is that right?"

"His name was James Saddlecreek?"

Kirby's posture stiffened. "Is that your question?"

"Excuse me?"

"Your question." His tone was acidic.

"I'm sorry if I —"

"Whether I *remember* James Saddlecreek. I don't know what you're playing at but I don't appreciate it."

My face felt hot. "I don't mean —"

"That name has caused nothing but grief around here. For forty years the major studios have benefited from the training people get working on my pictures. This was the film school of eight Oscar-winning directors — eight! And this is how they repay me, by painting Mercury as some kind of cesspool and trying to destroy my reputation. People have been very upset around here, very upset."

He looked ready to hit me. "I'm sorry I —"

"I hate to disparage the work of other filmmakers, especially someone who I once had the pleasure of working with, like Anthony Bowery." He spat out the syllables of the name. "He betrayed me by directing that pack of wanton fabrications and distortions. Sure, he changed the names, but he's lucky I haven't sued him for stealing my scenes. Don't you dare call it an homage. That's just fancy French word for 'I don't have an idea of my own so I'll take yours, screw it up, and everyone will call me a god-damn genius.' This whole situation's been an outrage, an absolute outrage." Kirby gripped the desk like he was ready to tear out a chunk and use it to bludgeon me.

I looked up at Kirby with pleading, fearful eyes. "Which movie?"

"Oh, c'mon, you little punk, don't play that."

Kirby gave me the exasperated look you give to a dog that peed on something expensive. "Mr. Kirby, I really don't know which movie."

He stabbed a finger in my direction. "I've directed twenty-nine features. I know acting. I've worked with the greatest. Don't think you can fool me."

There was a long moment of silence. "I really don't know."

Kirby scrutinized me for a moment. "Jesus, you look like you're about to cry. You said you were a reporter?"

"Yes." The words struggled to exit my mouth. "From *The Betsey*. In New York."

"Did that movie not play in New York? You'd make me a very happy man if you said it never did."

I didn't say anything.

"You don't have a clue, do you? What are we talking about here?"

"James Saddlecreek," I peeped.

"And you have no idea about James Saddlecreek's relationship with Mercury."

"I know about some of the movies he made here, like *Born Wild* and *Steel and Thunder* . . . and something about a she-killer."

"And you're telling me you don't know about *White Lines*."

"No."

Then a light flickered in a dark recess of my skull. It stayed on for just long enough for a connection to be made. The reason the scene with the bartender, the biker, and the broken pool cue in *Steel and Thunder* was familiar was because I had seen it before.

Except when I saw the scene, it wasn't in *Steel and Thunder*. In the other movie, the roadhouse was clearly a set on a soundstage, with crew members bustling around — a movie-within-a-movie thing. The bikers were actors stepping in and out of character as the scene was shot and re-shot. The actors were different, too — younger, better looking. What I saw was the shooting of the scene in *Steel and Thunder* being recreated. This other movie was *White Lines*.

"I think I remember." I sounded like an amnesiac about to reveal the killer in one of Mercury's crappy mystery movies. "*White Lines* was about James Saddlecreek?"

"Are you out on a day pass?" Kirby looked to the heavens and threw his hands up. "I cannot believe I'm having this conversation." He picked up his phone. "Tracy, have Rory escort out my guest." He looked at me again. "I see no point in continuing this interview. I'll be sure to call your magazine in New York and tell them how edifying this has been and how I was so impressed with your research skills. *The Betsey*, right? I'll get legal on the case. You write a word connecting James Saddlecreek or that goddamn movie about him to this studio and I will personally shoot you in the head."

"I'm so, so sorry," I stammered. "I had no idea."

"Damn right, you had no idea." He pounded on the desk with his fist. "Damn right." He pounded again. "I will personally," Kirby clutched his chest, "shoot . . ." He began to cough. "Urk."

"Mr. Kirby, are you all right?"

He slumped back into his seat. "Ack —"

Rory the assistant rushed through the door. "Oh no," he said.

Kirby made a sound like a hiccup, except louder and raspier.

"Is he having a heart attack?"

"Get a glass of water," he said, pointing at a pitcher on the coffee table behind me. "Mr. Kirby, where did you put your medication? Which pocket?"

"Urk —"

He feebly pointed toward the sports jacket hanging from the antler.

"Okay, they're in the jacket."

I thought: my incompetence just killed Don Kirby — I am the deadliest reporter of all time.

After fussing with an orange container of pills, Rory took the glass from my hand. Rory put the pill in Kirby's mouth and put the edge of the glass to his lip. "Swallow, Mr. Kirby. Just swallow."

He got it all down with an audible gulp. The tension in the room began to dissipate. People with concerned expressions were standing in the doorway, including Tracy the tattooed receptionist. I thought: that is some hot goth fox. I thought: you nearly killed a man, don't get distracted.

"Is he all right?" asked Tracy.

"He'll be fine," said Rory.

"Damn," I heard someone mutter from the back of the crowd. All but a few of the Mercury personnel dispersed.

Kirby sharply inhaled and exhaled. His eyes were red and watery.

"Fine," he gasped. "I'm fine."

He looked around the room until he found me. "You. Get out."

\* \* \*

I hadn't meant to cause any harm. Now I'd sparked a vendetta. I was terrified Kirby would really call *The Betsey*. I wasn't sure if he could sue over something that hadn't yet been written but a man like Don Kirby would have no shortage of determination.

I stood in the parking lot, trying to collect my thoughts and calm my own breath. No ambulance arrived while I was standing there so I surmised that what I had witnessed was not a life-threatening situation. For all I knew, it happened at every production meeting.

Some beefy guy I had seen in the office slapped me on the shoulder. "Nice work in there," he said. He got in his car before I could ask if his statement was ironic.

Wanting to put some distance between myself and the scene, I started walking away from the offices toward a shopping plaza about half a mile away. With each step I wished I knew how to cope. My investigation was a joke. I was so easily derailed. Colin was the real professional — had I been closer to my computer, I would have surrendered the rest of my research and transcriptions and let him decide what to do with the tale of Jimmy Wynn. That's what Daphne would've wanted.

But my self-pity break didn't last that long. Ten minutes later, I decided that my next course of action would be to find out about *White Lines* — I couldn't remember anything about it except for that one scene. I spied a Books and Books outlet in the shopping plaza up ahead. With its overstuffed chairs and cappuccino machine, the place promised some kind of comfort. Once I was inside, my nerves were soothed by the sight of the magazine rack. I thought: yes, I am a writer. I had worked hard. I had gone to school. I had overcome my shyness to interview men (and women) on the streets of Toronto about civic issues. I had interviewed British musicians too stoned to string together more than three words in a row. I was praised for my promise by instructors and editors. I had been accepted for a *Hancock's* internship, had thrived under its tutelage, and now had come west bearing the credentials of a major periodical. I had dined with Danny Pantero as recently as three nights before. I belonged to this world of long words and pretty pictures. And no vitriolic movie producer could get in the way of my mission. Or maybe he could.

I went to the film section of the bookstore and looked up *White Lines* in the latest paperback movie guides.

From *The 1998 Leonard Dent Movie Guide*:

> Energetic but derivative pic about actor and drug
> dealer in 1970s Hollywood involved in FBI sting.
> Director Anthony Bowery boasts flair for arresting
> visuals but lets storyline collapse into confusing
> series of sleazy vignettes. Based on true story.

The unnamed British critic in the *Big Mag Film Guide* was
more generous with the details:

> Former Mercury hack Anthony Bowery gets back
> at his old boss Don Kirby with this fictionalized
> story of Jacky Crowfoot, a part-time actor and
> small-time drug dealer who handles the dirty work
> for an exploitation-movie producer. Jacky also
> earns his keep by selling stories about the stars he
> supplies to a tacky tabloid reporter. When the FBI
> tries to use him as a pawn in a major Hollywood
> sting, Jacky's bizarre behaviour ensures that every-
> thing will fail to go according to plan. Bowery's
> recreation of seventies Hollywood and key scenes
> from classic Mercury exploitation titles are lovingly
> rendered. Yet *White Lines* is long on style and short
> on content. Bowery struggles to find the right
> tone, apparently unsure if this is a black comedy
> for movie-biz insiders or a bloody guns-and-drugs
> neo-noir.

Both books listed the year of the film's release as 1990. Upon
reading the reviews, I recalled the movie poster — a pair of gold
sunglasses and a pile of cash lying on a smudgy mirror.

Now I not only knew about a movie that starred James Saddle-creek but a movie that may have been *about* him. I wrote down the credits in my notebook (I had a fresh one in my satchel — take that, Danielle!) and went to the phone booth outside the store. Using my superior investigation skills, I found the name of Scott McCaffrey, the screenwriter listed in the Greater Los Angeles phone book. There were only three of them. I tried the listing in Santa Monica because it was in the richest area.

A man answered on the first ring. "Yeah," he said.

"Hi, is Scott McCaffrey home?"

"This is Scott."

"Is this the Scott McCaffrey who wrote *White Lines*?"

"How did you get this number?"

"Uh . . . it's in the phone book?"

"Oh. And why are you calling?"

"My name's Nathan Grant. I'm a journalist. I'm working on a story. I needed to ask you a few questions."

"If you want to set up an interview, you have to go through my publicist. You shouldn't be calling me out of the blue."

"I just need a few minutes."

"I'm on deadline here."

"So am I. Please. It'll just be a second."

I heard him sigh. "You're lucky I used to be a reporter."

I thought: oh yeah, I still got it! "I promise not to waste your time. I was very interested in *White Lines* because I was doing some research on James Saddlecreek for another article and —"

"Okay, first thing, *White Lines* is not about James Saddle-creek."

"All right, but —"

"The character was a composite of several people. One of those people may or may not have been James Saddlecreek."

"All right, then." I thought: don't get flustered, just ask the man a question. "How did you come to write the screenplay?"

"Anthony Bowery's production company optioned an article that I wrote for *L.A. Magazine*. That was the basis for the script. I was trying to get out of reporting and into screenwriting. They let me have first crack and liked what they read. You're probably aware of some of the other projects I'm working on."

"Uh, yes. I'm impressed. Very much so. If you don't mind summarizing the original article . . ."

McCaffrey sighed again. "This really is not a good time, bud."

"But can you tell me who the article was about?"

"The article was about a man named James Saddlecreek."

He had lost me. "But I thought you said the main character was a composite?"

"Someone else can tell you all the whys and wherefores that go into making a movie. It's Nathan? Okay, Nathan, do you know what life rights are?"

I thought: last rites?

He correctly took my silence for a no. "Let's say that for some reason, a movie company wants to make a movie based on your life story." He spoke as if he were trying to explain all this to a child or a monkey. "They don't want to have to change details like your name or where you're from or any of those things that make you who you are, all right? You can put restrictions on how your life is portrayed — you can't buy someone's life rights and then make a movie that portrays them as a necrophile rapist, for instance. So with *White Lines*, there was no way we were gonna buy up all the life rights we had to. In fact, the main problem was with Saddlecreek — no one could find him. I had a lot of stories about him but no direct contact. Without his life rights, there was no way we would be able to stick to the story as outlined in the original article. You can imagine the complexities involved if James Saddlecreek were to suddenly reappear and come asking for points. If I were a lawyer, I could explain more. I am not a lawyer. I am a writer. With a deadline. Capisce?"

"But you can confirm that *White Lines* is about James Saddle-creek?"

Another sigh. "No, I cannot."

"But the magazine article it's based on is about him?"

"That is correct. I'm sorry, that's all the time I have. Call my publicist, Janine Cooper, and she can set something else. Is this for a school project or something?"

"No," I said. "I'm a professional reporter."

When McCaffrey hung up, I knew he would not be offering me anything for my life rights. No one would. But I also knew that his original article would provide more pieces in the Jimmy puzzle. I called Ben for a ride to the central public library. Thankfully, he was close by and amenable to the request.

I bought a latte in the Books and Books café and sat near the window. Thirty minutes later, the Network X van pulled up. Ben was on the phone. He waved me over to his side of the van. "Here." He passed me the phone.

"Yes?"

"Nathan, it's Winston Sharpe. I just took a call from Don Kirby. He had some concerns about your methods and the ways in which you were representing *The Betsey*."

"I can explain."

"No need, Mr. Grant. I trust you have your reasons. I informed him as politely and directly as possible that we would not be swayed or coerced in any way. Any attempt at a legal injunction will be strongly rebuffed. As it so happens, I have an existing relationship with the Japanese concern that owns the controlling stake in Mercury International Pictures. Don Kirby was made aware of this fact."

I thought: jeez, this sounds like hardball. "Mr. Sharpe, I —"

"I wanted to tell you how impressed I am with what you have been able to accomplish in such a limited span of time. Daphne tells me you are very close to reaching our comedian."

I thought: don't argue. "Thanks so much, Mr. Sharpe."

"I regret that I am unable to discuss this further with you. I am in a meeting right now. I am eager to hear more."

"Thank you, sir."

Winston Sharpe terminated the call.

"Sir?" said Ben. "Are you his valet?"

But his attempt to belittle me with sarcasm was for naught — I felt invulnerable with Sharpe in my corner.

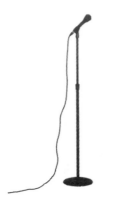

*All the parking spots along Vista Boulevard are taken. Ofallthefucken-things, he thinks. For a guy from Detroit, Jimmy really hates to drive. He'd been leaking a constant stream of cussing from the second he put the key in the lock back in San Lupe. Now he has to leave his truck three blocks away in a neighbourhood that's not even safe in daylight. He slams the door and starts the long walk to the set. Seething — he's seething. He needs to cover it with mellow.*

*Mercury uses a soundstage on Vista. No air conditioning means it takes two minutes for the actors to sweat through their makeup. Jimmy hates being inside. It's every lousy club he ever played packed into one dark, dank warehouse. Nothing but self-delusion, misery, and stupidity ever came out of a place like that.*

*The movie? The title just changed. Jimmy remembered it had "Revenge" in it. Or "Vengeance." The hero starts off as a mild-mannered type. He gets mixed up with a bad guy. Trouble brews. The hero's lady is raped, killed, or both. They haven't shot the scene yet. Jimmy doesn't want to be there when they do — that sort of thing always attracts a crowd and Kirby never has the class to close the set. When they were shooting* Born Wild, *the girls were freaked out by all the flunkies ready to ogle them while they stripped down for the orgy scene. Jimmy yelled at Kirby to clear them out. Kirby said, "It may be your sorry-assed script but it's my set, cowboy."*

*Anyway, the cops don't do anything after the lady gets it. The hero meets a real hardcase who teaches him how to kill — with a gun, with a knife, with his hands. The hero's a fast learner. Together they wipe out the bad guy's gang one by one, climbing all the way up the chain of command. Then the hero realizes the hardcase has another motive for helping him. Jimmy read the script but he can't remember the motive — hardly matters. The hardcase betrays the hero. After that, they fall down a flight of stairs together, then get up and keep fighting.*

*Jimmy squeezes the spaces between his thumbs and his fingers — too much tension. Not getting mellow enough, despite all the attempts at self-medication that had already taken place that morning. His walk feels a little too quick to look cool so he slows it right down. This is how James Saddlecreek walks — easy. Somewhere in the pockets of his leather is the powder. Not much, but enough to get put away for a long, long time. He's superstitious about carrying. He likes to be organized, to know just how much is needed before he drives in from San Lupe. He wishes he had some other reason to visit the set — one of the old reasons, like playing some dude or knocking some sense into a script — but this is what he did now: he's the bagman. Inside Jimmy's skull, his dad says: I knew you'd turn out to be a piece of shit.*

*Jimmy didn't know precisely who the coke was for but Kirby had to keep his actors happy. Kirby always barked about getting ripped off, always haggled about the price, but that wasn't the worst of it. Kirby mistook himself for hilarious. He thought James Saddlecreek was a cowboy because of his big black moustache and because his name sounded like a character in a Western and because sometimes he wore chaps just for the hell of it. Kirby said, "Saddle up, partner" and "Get along, li'l doggy" then he'd cackle his ass off. His flunkies would howl along like coyotes. Jimmy never intended for Saddlecreek to be a cowboy, just a tough dude. It's not like he wore a hat. He wasn't that kind of character. Jimmy knew what went into making a character. The* cowboy thing irritated the hell out of him. He thought about the different ways to kill Kirby — with a gun, with a knife, with his hands all the way around the asshole's throat. Jimmy knew that if he ever went down, he'd drag Kirby all the way.

The words inside Jimmy clumped up worse than ever. Hurry-upandputabulletinme.

Then Jimmy remembered. He had a new movie for Kirby. It couldn't miss. Jimmy had been working it over in his head all morning. He knew that the pills gave him too much confidence sometimes but this was it, the time was now. He was scared before. Now he was safe. They couldn't get to him now. He was off the map. And he was gonna use this opportunity to get it all out in the open, everything he'd heard, everything he'd learned. People were gonna know the real deal about the whole thing, top to bottom. And Jimmy Wynn was gonna play the lead role. That's right — Jimmy Wynn. He's back. Or soon. He'd be back soon.

Until Jimmy had all that ready to go, James Saddlecreek had his uses. He hits the entrance to the set. Joe the security guard waves him through. Kirby sees him and shouts through his bullhorn, "Howdy, partner! Be right with ya!" Jimmy clenches his fists, trying to cover the humiliation with more mellow, so much mellow. Then the new girl who never wears a bra asks Jimmy if he is carrying a little extra. Jimmy has to admit it — some parts of his day were a-ok. He wonders when the best time to tell Kirby about his movie was — before or after he got the stuff?

Probably after.

14

Ben took me to a Mexican place for lunch. It was cluttered but serene, with green roosters painted on the walls and tequila bottles for candleholders. Amid the plates of burritos and instrumental surf tunes on the stereo, a state of Californian inertia set in. I didn't want to budge. I savoured the respite from my Saddlecreek sores and my Jimmy (whirl)Wynn. I told him what happened at the Mercury office and Ben was again impressed: "You're a dangerous man."

Otherwise, Ben was nearly as tired as I was. He ignored two calls on his cell phone, an act that was uncharacteristic of him. He wanted to fill me in on the prospective arc for his Stink series. He saw a crisis percolating within the band, a power struggle between Von and Dirk, the sullen, largely non-communicative guitarist who wrote most of the songs. Dirk's girlfriend was egging him on to take a greater leadership role, despite Von's superior charisma. The bandmates' typical discourse of insults, pranks, and adolescent oneupmanship was turning genuinely nasty. Ben wasn't sure if anything too dramatic would happen at the two gigs in Los Angeles, slated to take place over the following two nights. Yet the band's upcoming recording sessions were shaping up to be eventful. Ben asked me if it was ethically sound for him to engineer scenarios that would encourage the conflict. He agreed when I told him it was not, but the gleam in his eye suggested that the demands of the medium were perverting his better instincts. "I have an obligation to entertain," he said, "and that means I have to make some scumbag moves."

I sipped my strawberry daiquiri with some trepidation.

After lunch Ben checked his messages. The first one stopped him dead. He passed me the phone. "You're getting some real interesting calls today."

The voice I heard was strained and tremulous, as if fragile from lack of use. "I'm calling for a Mr. Nathan Grant. My name is David Maher." He took a long, scratchy breath. "It has come to my attention that you are looking for Jimmy Wynn. I have some things to talk to you about." Another breath. "I would appreciate it if you could contact me as soon . . . as soon as possible. I am convalescing at the Devendra Center for the Medical Arts. Please try me at this number."

I wrote it down and passed back the phone.

"Weird," he said. "Who'd you give my number to?"

"Only *The Betsey*. And Danny Pantero's assistant. Maybe there's a Vegas connection." I remembered the skeletal figure in the bright white cube. "Do you think he knows I was at the dam yesterday?"

"Legally speaking, the incident never happened."

"Suits me fine. I'm not officially in this country, anyhow. I wonder what Maher wants."

"You should bring him a peace offering if you're feeling guilty. Maybe some barbecue. I bet he's hungry."

Ben took me back to Los Angeles proper and dropped me off at the library. Though I was put off by the sleek modernity of the building with its sharp corners of steel and glass and more of that unflattering light, I was reassured by some familiar library scents:

industrial cleaning products, old paper, and the B.O. particular to the underemployed or entirely homeless.

I checked my e-mail on a public computer. The interview request for the band Firefly came back negative-verging-on-fuck-off-forever. Firefly refused to say anything about James Saddlecreek because of outstanding money matters. The label that was reissuing the Daisy disc had sent out a mass e-mail alerting readers to a feature on the band in the new issue of *33RPM*, a British music mag. I planned to look for it the next time I passed a newsstand. And there was a new e-mail from Lance, who had been instructed not to reveal news of my travels to anyone. He let me know a man had called for me twice but refused to leave a message. I thought: stalker or fan?

I sat down with a hardbound volume of *L.A. Magazine* that contained McCaffrey's article. It was published in July 1988. The journalist never met the star of his piece, relying on declassified documents and interviews. McCaffrey lamented his inability to find Saddlecreek or any record of his demise. But judging from his opening description, the writer got a good handle on his subject. "With his handlebar moustache, long hair, and leather jacket, James Saddlecreek affected the look of the bikers who visited him at his dilapidated ranch house in San Lupe. Yet he lacked the bravado to really pull it off. People who knew him invariably referred to his nervous demeanor and eagerness to please. Movie producers took him for a small-timer but didn't mind him hanging around their sets or hearing of his cinematic ambitions as long as he had quality goods."

McCaffrey was unduly hard on Saddlecreek's oeuvre, saying it only amounted to "a few incomprehensible scripts and several godawful performances." But I was relieved there was no mention of Jimmy Wynn or *Village Idiot* — that secret was mine.

In general, the article made Saddlecreek out to be: a) a willing patsy, and b) nuts. After threatening him with incarceration, the

FBI outfitted him with bugs and let him loose on California's cocaine distribution business. The net eventually caught some low-level Peruvian cartel members, a set of dentists from Orange County trying out a new business venture, and half the cops in Santa Barbara County. Ironically, most of the movie folks implicated in the case weaseled their way out of indictments, though Don Kirby was condemned for exploiting his actors' drug problems in order to keep them in thrall to Mercury. In McCaffrey's piece, Kirby had no kind words for Saddlecreek, and the reporter noted that the producer had great difficulty controlling his temper. "I spend years helping out this dirtbag and in return he serves me up to the feds on a platter of lies and slander," he said. "This guy was like something you find underneath your shoe." And he said this well before *White Lines* brought him and his studio further ridicule. If I'd really wanted to kill Kirby, I would have mentioned McCaffrey, too.

According to the piece, Saddlecreek was to be relocated by the FBI in exchange for his efforts. But a source at the agency said that he disappeared before the FBI could fulfill its end of the deal. The article left the impression that no one was looking very hard for him — the source said that Saddlecreek had been "almost impossible" to deal with.

There was one very good reason why: Saddlecreek liked to ramble into the bugging equipment stashed around the room and on his person. McCaffrey included this example of Saddlecreek's soliloquies:

> Cowboy number one's got a problem with the deal, G-men, you guys think you know, you guys think, you guys think you've got a line on the situation here. No chance, daddio. You don't know James, not one bit. Nuh-huh-uh. Cowboy number one's gonna point his rocket straight at the moon

and show the world the true face. You know about the true face? I'll tell you about the true face. The true face is fire and light and heat. It's the divine oneness. Once you see its aura, you will know. You're gonna get it like a bullet in the neck. Stew on that, Hooverites. I ain't your punk. Not now, not ever.

McCaffrey claimed to have heard one of the tapes, describing the contents as a "smattering of paranoid ranting, hipster patois, celebrity impressions, song lyrics, and raunchy jokes." He quoted one of the latter:

So this Russian peasant's driving his cart next to the cemetery. Up on one of the graves, he sees this guy going at it with two naked broads. "Hey, comrade, is one not enough for you?" the peasant shouts. "Why don't you give me one?"

"To give you one!" the guy says. "Take my shovel and dig out as many as you like!"

"We had to listen to everything in case he said anything relevant to the investigation," said the FBI source. "I'm not sure if he understood there was an investigation. He treated us like his audience."

I thought: ah, Jimmy, you just couldn't resist the urge to spritz when you knew you had an audience. I was relieved to see how McCaffrey had done so much Saddlecreek research for me yet couldn't see Saddlecreek for what he was: a Vegas cured ham.

\* \* \*

Even as I trawled McCaffrey's piece for colour, data, and potential sources to tap, I couldn't get David Maher's frail voice out of my head. He sounded like he'd been calling from beyond the grave. I took the opportunity to find out more about him before getting back to him. It would be helpful to know his connection to Wynn. I went back to a public terminal and did a search for stories on the illusioneer. The official bio on his Web site caught my eye:

*The year is 1971. On a sleepy winter's morn in the city of Minneapolis, a child is born. All children are gifts to the world, but this one has a special blessing. He is destined to inspire wonder and amazement in everyone he meets. He will teach a troubled world to dream again. This child is David Maher.*

*A precocious boy, David developed an early interest in music, art, and performance. Though sociable with his friends, he could also be pensive, even secretive. At a friend's seventh birthday party, David met Dr. Presto, a man who would change his life. All of the children were mesmerized by the magician's disappointing coins and levitating rings, but David was the most curious of them all.*

*After the performance, he approached Dr. Presto with great trepidation. The magician was friendly but fearsomely tall. "I want to do that," he said.*

*Dr. Presto smiled kindly. "Would you like me to teach you how?"*
*The child nodded eagerly.*

*"Then you have to do two things for me. First, you have to ask your mommy and daddy for permission to come to my store once a week for lessons. But before I see you again, you have an even more important task." Dr. Presto handed David a tiny book. "You must teach yourself every magic trick in this book. You see, not everyone has what it takes be a magician. You must have discipline and determination. Do you know what those words mean?"*

*David shook his head.*
*"They mean you can never give up."*
*David spent hours in his bedroom struggling to master the tricks*

*in the little book. They had names like the Potato Chip Surprise, the Magnetic Hand, and the Jumping Rubber Band. As his fingers fumbled with nickels and playing cards, it was as if his hands were being guided by forces far beyond his understanding.*

*Wanting to make sure his tricks were perfect before presenting them to Dr. Presto, Maher practiced in front of friends, relatives, and his parents. His mother Bess was particularly amused with the stories he would tell to accompany the tricks. David claimed to have learned the Magnetic Hand "at the foot of a wise yoga." Finally, nearly a year after their first encounter, he was ready for Dr. Presto.*

*David could not believe his eyes when he saw the store — the dusty books and strange objects on every shelf made his imagination explode with colors as bright as fireworks in the night sky. David gathered up his courage. As he performed for Dr. Presto, his hands moved with a combination of fluid grace and cunning accuracy.*

*In David's last trick, he was to make a potato chip vanish into thin air. But the moment before the trick's completion, the chip slipped from his grasp and fell to the floor. David's confidence collapsed. He was so disappointed, he felt like he could cry.*

*Then Dr. Presto picked up the chip and handed it back to the boy. "Here," he said. "Now make me believe that dropping the chip was part of the illusion all along."*

*As David had read in Dr. Presto's little book, "Distraction is a magician's most important tool." David realized that by dropping the potato chip, he created a distraction. When he did the trick a second time, he dropped the chip intentionally. Using his imagination to improvise, David made the chip disappear somewhere between his hand and the floor. "Behold!" he cried. "The magical void!"*

*Dr. Presto was delighted. David knew then and there that he'd found his calling.*

I thought: behold the magical void? This was one weird seven-year-old.

The bio went on to say that Maher was only seventeen when his mother made arrangements with a long-time family friend — "legendary singer Danny Pantero" — for him to apprentice with some of Las Vegas's most famous magicians. One of them was Jerry Starr, the man in the cape who stopped by my table at Lisette. Maher was quite the golden boy.

When not serving his masters inside the theatres of Las Vegas, Maher performed for tourists outside. Drawing from both the elaborate illusions of his Vegas masters and the scrappier style of the street, he developed what he called "an illusion without illusion!" He dispensed with the term of magician altogether, preferring the term "illusioneer." The word reminded me of Pantero's spiel about the "particispectator." None of these entertainers could simply make do with words already in the English language.

His illusioneering soon took him to New York. Maher was submerged without any breathing apparatus off the edge of Ellis Island for two days. He was encased in cement up to his neck and hung over the side of the eighty-storey Parker Tower. He buried himself at the foot of the oldest tree in Central Park for three weeks. He also faked his death in less spectacular ways — during a live TV special, he was shot onstage ("with bullets," as the lady at the dam had said) and carried off by phony paramedics.

Each time he staggered back into the world, Maher's face bore "an expression that was exhausted yet full of peace." Sayeth Maher himself, "I want to teach people to live each day as fully and as beautifully as they can." His public pronouncements were littered with dimestore Zen.

I knew stuff about David Maher that the bio didn't mention. He seemed to cry in public at every opportunity. He burned many of those Vegas magicians when he revealed how their illusions worked on a TV special. He was currently dating a nineteen-year-old French pop star. He was the subject of a devastating parody on a popular sketch comedy show — the Maher-like character's catchphrase was "With the power of my mind, I compel you to remove your bra!" And Maher wore eyeliner all the time.

Feeling sufficiently armed with information (and a firm link between Maher and Pantero), I went to a phone in the library's lobby and called the number.

"Hello?" It was a woman's voice.

"Hi, I'm calling for David Maher."

"I'm sorry but he's asleep. He won't be well enough to speak for some time. Are you with the media?"

It only took me a beat to recognize the voice. "Sparkle?"

"Yes?"

"This is Nathan Grant. We met in Las Vegas last week. I came to talk to Danny Pantero?"

"Of course! I'm so happy to hear from you, Nathan. David's been looking forward to your call. Thanks so much for getting back to us."

"You work with David, too?"

"I do whatever I can for David. I've known him such a long time."

"Through Mr. Pantero?"

"He's been almost a father to David."

"How is David?"

"Very tired. You must've heard about what was happening at the Wilson Dam. He got excellent coverage. The people who came out to see him showed him a great deal of love and support and understanding. But there were others . . ." Her voice grew hard. "Some of these people would *throw* things."

"That's awful." I didn't ask her about barbecues or topless women.

"David is very sensitive. That's why any kind of further strain could be devastating. It's going to take him at least four weeks to get all of his strength back. The doctors say that he's in incredible shape for someone who went through what he just did. Were you hoping to interview him?"

"No. I mean, maybe. I'm not sure. He asked me to call him."

"I'm sorry, Nathan. You're absolutely right. He was quite insistent about reaching you."

"Do you know why?"

"I'd rather let him tell you."

"Should he really be talking to people? Does he have the strength?"

"David can do anything he puts his mind to. Can you come see us here tomorrow afternoon?"

"Sure."

"Call me when you arrive in the building and I'll escort you up. We have to be careful with the photographers. We have David on a private floor and they'll try anything to get up here."

Sparkle signed off cheerfully. I had a date with the future of magic.

* * *

My Wynn-fall for the day showed no signs of ceasing. I struggled to process all the fresh news about Jimmy and James, as well as the tantalizing connection with David Maher and the world of magic. The story was getting so crowded, I didn't know how much room would be left for the man Jimmy worked so hard to imitate but *The Betsey* would insist Cannon stay on the marquee.

Cannon was on my mind when I walked out to the street, which was clogged with rush-hour traffic. The din of engines, brakes, honks, and hip-hop on competing car stereos was nearly as monolithic as the slots at the Barbizon Bay. I looked around and thought: I hate this place.

It was then that I noticed the poster. In a kiosk in front of the library, I saw the familiar photo of President Cannon's smiling face, taken sometime during the 1960 campaign. Though the picture was

black and white, an artist had colourized it, covering sections of
the photo in blazing streaks of gold, red, and green. The result was
garish yet wildly vibrant.

I had seen the poster in New York, at the art show preview in
Chelsea with the death car and the art critic with the nervous stomach. This was the full exhibition, which had another week to run at
the Museum of Contemporary Art in Los Angeles before being
shipped to New York. It struck me as a good idea to see the show
now, in case any more Manhattanites harboured plans to defile its
contents. I followed the tourist-friendly signs to the MoCA, located
in the same shiny cluster of public buildings as the library.

Mounted to commemorate the 35th anniversary of Cannon's
death, the exhibition was named *Cannon: A President and His Art*.
The title was misleading, suggesting Cannon was a deft hand at
watercolours. In fact, the only artistic inclination he ever displayed was playing trumpet in his high school band. It had always
been up to other people to supply Cannon with His Art.

The MoCA was free on Thursday nights so I walked straight
in and up to the exhibition on the second floor. I was alone there
aside from a pair of middle-aged couples with cameras. The show
was featured in two large, bright rooms. The objects in the first
room were mostly innocuous. A lot were promotional items used
during Cannon's senatorial and presidential campaigns — party
rattles, paper hats, badges, pins, and Frisbees, all embossed with
the president's likeness or slogans like "Vote Cannon" or
"America's Hope." There was a lunchbox, too. One of the few
objects in the room not protected under glass, it sat on a pedestal.
I thought: hey, free lunchbox. But a little card on the pedestal
said: "DO NOT TOUCH OR ALARM WILL SOUND." I couldn't see the
telltale red laser beam.

Framed on the walls were pages from magazine profiles of the
First Family. A TV monitor screened the famous debates with Peter
Barrow, but the volume was so low, the high-flown rhetoric of the

candidates became two streams of indistinct mutterings. When I saw the sleeve of *A Square Peg in the Oval Office* mounted next to photos of Cannon posing with celebrities of his day, I felt both reaffirmed and unsettled. Someone else could have spied this curio and been inspired to investigate its origin. I hoped this quest was mine alone. Considering the sheer tonnage of presidential junk around, I suspected that Jimmy hadn't attracted much attention. Besides, there were many other parodic magazine covers and editorial cartoons on display. An example of the latter from the *New York Telegraph-Herald* portrayed him as a little boy in a wagon being pulled by his father toward some mobster types. Another had him replaced at the podium by a store mannequin. But these illustrations were the only sour notes sounded by the artifacts.

The feelings of good cheer and optimism inspired by the first room were quickly dashed by the second. According to the plaque on the first wall, these pieces were "contemporary works inspired by the president and created to provoke dialogue and debate about the enduring influence of the man and his ideals."

In a space on one wall were two speakers flanking a blown-up frame of Cannon from the film shot by Nathaniel Fontainebleu not long before the shots rang out. Vito Acevedo, evidently recycling his idea for the death car, had manipulated recordings of Cannon's voice to create previously unuttered slogans.

"We look to the youth of America . . . to bring a sense of achievement . . . to the youth of America."

"The eagle flies proudly . . . never flagging . . . in its defence . . . of the fine people of Evanston, Illinois."

"Connie knows . . . if I've ever been . . . less than completely honest."

"The integration of races . . . is impossible . . . in an age of limitless possibility."

"My dream . . . capital . . . the tears of widows . . . explained by our nation's top scientists."

Part of one wall was filled with sheets of butcher paper that had been taped together. Someone had written the names of Cannon, his intimates, his enemies, and other players in his saga, linking them with lines and circles. History was a net that trapped Cannon with everyone from Vincent Delrocco to Manny Hudson to dancer Lola Rivington to the martyred Latin-American leader Ruiz.

The most haunting artwork was a sculpture. Like the lunch-box, it seemed unusually unguarded. It sat on a waist-high wooden platform. Black plastic figurines kneeled around a child-sized white coffin. Inside was a larger plastic figure of Cannon. He looked much as he did in his real coffin, albeit miniaturized and with one almost imperceptible change: this Cannon wore Jesus sandals instead of his Oxfords. I thought: it can't be profound if I understand it. The tiny Cannon was protected for all eternity by the clear Plexiglas sheet that covered the top of the coffin. There was one last disturbing touch: the Plexiglas was disfigured by scratches, as if it had some animal had tried to claw its way in. Or out.

There was some more cheerful Cannon art — a large mural commemorated integration efforts in Mississippi — but the morbid stuff spoke the most powerfully. In the speakers of Acevedo's audio work, Cannon murmured to himself like a lonely, confused ghost. The room felt thick with death and art-world pretension, a combination that nearly brought me to my knees.

I carried that feeling of dread with me into the streets outside. I thought: did they have Jimmy in the right room? Maybe his record sleeve was better suited to the second gallery. I had a great idea: a performance artist could stake out one corner and charge visitors a quarter to punch him in the face. We could call the piece *Life After Cannon: Suicide for the Half-Assed*. Or were Jimmy Wynn's sufferings too minuscule to deserve any place in that exhibition? The march of history had pulverized him so completely.

It was all so depressing, I had to go get extremely drunk.

15

I thought: the last time I went to see Stink, I scored. But I didn't feel lucky. Back at the Chateau Montpelier, I tried calling Colin. I still hadn't found out what he was doing with the Delegation story. Though my leads were pulling me further away from Nevada, I knew I couldn't sacrifice that angle, by leaving it to him. His outgoing message said that he was out of town and would be checking in. I cheerfully requested that he return my call, keeping the suspicions out of my tone.

I headed out to the club with Ben and his crew. They had stuff to shoot before the show. I was in the back of the Network X van when Ben pointed out the back window.

"See that blue Thunderbolt sedan?"

I did.

"That's the third time I've spotted it since yesterday."

We stared out the window together. A sedan with tinted windows was about thirty feet back in the outside lane. Though the streets were busy, the Thunderbolt deftly navigated the traffic, maintaining a steady distance between us.

"You sure it's following us?"

"Pretty sure."

"Who is it?"

"Fans."

"Of you?"

"No, the band. Ever since news of the show hit the Internet forums, they've been all over us. They've been following every X truck in case it leads them to where they are."

"But it's no secret where the guys are tonight — they're doing a show at the Red Devil."

Ben nodded. "Good point."

We continued to stare at the Thunderbolt.

"Can they see us?" I asked.

"You mean the van. Sure they can see the van."

"No. Us. In the window."

"We're tinted, too."

Ben knocked on the window. "Hey," he said softly. "Identify yourselves or risk immediate termination." He cocked a finger at them and fired. "Pow."

The gesture confused me. Panic welled up inside me. "This isn't a game," I said.

"What?"

"This isn't a game. People have been killed, doing what I'm doing."

"And what the hell is that exactly?"

"Looking into, you know . . . stuff. To do with the president?"

Ben looked at me incredulously. "Are you a secret agent now? C'mon, Nate. You're trying to find some has-been comedian for a magazine sidebar."

"Who told you it was a sidebar?"

"Colin."

"When did you talk to Colin?"

"I don't know, maybe last night. He called me on the cell. He was wondering if we were still in Las Vegas because he was flying in to do some interviews."

My face felt hot. "He's trying to steal my story."

"What? He's not trying to steal anything. His girlfriend at that magazine you both write for assigned him a story. They're putting it together with whatever you get on your comedian."

I thought: rewind that. "His girlfriend?"

"Yeah, the chick at *The Betsey*."

I went from panic to economy-sized outrage. "Colin said he was going out with Daphne?"

Ben smiled. "It's not like you had a shot."

"What the hell does that mean?"

He held up his hands in defence. "Whoa. Don't lose it on me. I'm just your messenger."

"I'm not losing it," I said. I tapped on the glass. "If I'm losing it, then explain that." I tapped harder to emphasize my point, whatever it was. "That is not me losing it."

I watched the Thunderbolt for another minute before it turned down another street. I was too angry to think straight. Colin and Daphne had played me for a sucker. At least one of them had to know how I felt inside. And now they wanted to fuck over my story. I thought: do you even have a story? What I had were the unreliable recollections of a bunch of old Vegas weirdos, a few old photos, an incomplete paper trail, and trivia about some movies hardly anyone paid to see in the first place. I thought: you suck at this.

I hung back while Ben and the crew hung around the stage door to the Red Devil. Von walked out of the club wearing a brown blazer, a piano-key tie, a wig, and a porn-star moustache. He looked like a TV reporter who still believed it was 1975. Unrecognizable to the fans outside, Von interviewed them on camera as they entered the show or milled about, hoping for tickets. He asked questions in a gruff voice.

"Does listening to this music give you confusing urges?" he asked a pair of indignant teenage girls.

"You there!" he called out to a teenager whose hair shot up in tall red spikes. "Let me ask you: if you hate society so much, why don't you move to France?"

"I just spoke to your father," he said to one young dude, "and he wanted me to tell you that he's ashamed of you."

The kid looked hurt. "But he just dropped me off," he said in a trembling voice.

After the tomfoolery, I went inside, tagging along with the X types. The Red Devil was a converted fifties-era movie theatre decorated in red and black. The seats had been torn out but the old curtain was there. Though it was closed, the kids were still packed in tight at the front. They were pierced, pimply, and perspiring. I thought: no way am I getting laid tonight.

I looked for another kind of action, heading into the roped-off licensed area on the right side of the room. Ben was standing with a guy in a red T-shirt. He waved me over. "Hey, we gotta get a bunch more audience shots. Give Dean someone to talk to."

Dean worked at Network X in L.A. He was good company. I got my mind off Jimmy Wynn. We drank beer and talked about music, reminiscing about indie-rock shows we'd loved. When the band came on, we ignored them almost completely. (The exception: Von performed some lewd business with a vibrator and a Boston cream donut that struck me as quite inspired.)

I watched the door for Danielle's face. I thought: maybe she needs to pump me for more information. I thought: L.A.'s gotta have a few more surprises for me.

As the encore began, I left Dean and went to the bathroom at the back of the club. The noise from the PA rattled the porcelain. I was standing at the urinal when someone came in. Though the newcomer had the choice of three other urinals, he chose the one right next to me — a serious breach of etiquette. I hunched my shoulders and stared at the tiles above the urinal. I did my best to hurry up.

"Great show," said the guy.

I glanced sideways. He was staring into the tiles directly in front of him. He was about my height and maybe a decade older. His super-short buzzcut read "army" rather than "punk." Then he turned to me. I looked back at my tiles.

"I said it's a great show."

"Yeah."

"Great band." I felt his breath at the side of my head. He was close. Alarmingly close.

"Uh-huh." I shook quickly and zipped up. I walked out the door.

I was halfway back to where Dean was standing when I felt a hard tap on my shoulder blade. I turned and saw my guy. He wore a pressed black shirt covered in embroidered flames.

"Hey," he said. "That was disgusting."

"What?"

"Disgusting. You didn't wash your hands. Do you have any idea what kind of germs there are in there? It's a public bathroom."

A vein in his neck was visibly throbbing. Invisible waves of aggression poured from his body.

I spluttered the words "I washed my hands."

"No, you didn't. I was standing right there. You didn't even wet them. It's disgusting."

He reminded me of someone I encountered when I was fourteen. A friend of a friend took advantage of the regular absence of his parents by hosting hardcore-punk shows in his suburban basement. I got a charge from seeing the guys hitting each other. I was a lurker, a voyeur playing at being dangerous. At one show, I was standing at the edge of the mosh pit when a guy (greasy brown hair, shirtless, Iron Cross tattooed on his shoulder) bounded out of the thicket of bodies, landed in front of me, and punched the right side of my head. I felt like I'd been hit with a bag of nickels. When I was steady on my feet again, the guy got in my face, ready to go. I turned quickly and didn't look back until I was all the way home. I learned that some guys regarded gigs as a great place to hurt people. Maybe they figured that anyone willing to submit their ears to this abuse was begging for a beating.

I turned away from the bathroom guy. He grabbed my shoulder and turned me around.

"Get your hands off me," I said, tough as Nerf.

"Go back there and wash your hands."

"Leave me alone."

"Wash your goddamn hands."

Moving to the beat, he marched me by the shoulder back into the bathroom. Once inside, he shoved me toward the sink. "Go." Sensing serious bad mojo, two punk teens rushed past us out the door.

"This is ridiculous, man. What's your problem?"

"Shut up." He pointed at the soap dispenser. "Use it. If you don't use soap, you might as well be washing your hands in the toilet."

I tapped out some pink stuff and soaped up my hands.

"You've got to work up a lather for at least ten seconds."

I made eye contact with the dude in the mirror. "You're a total headcase."

"I don't hear you counting."

I rubbed my heads against each other. "One. Two. Three. I'm gonna call security. You can't do this. Four. Five. Six. You can't do this to me. Seven. Eight. Nine. Ten." Then I rinsed them again. "There," I said as I held up my palms to him. "Happy?"

And he was. He gave me a wide smile. "Yeah, that's great." His voice was suddenly calm. "Now keep up the good work."

He left me alone in the bathroom with nothing to dry my hands on — surely an oversight. I went to a stall and yanked out a handful of one-ply toilet paper that came apart in my fingers. By the time I came outside again, he was nowhere in sight.

Dean was at the bar nearest where we were standing. I tapped him on the shoulder. "Turn around very casually and tell me if you see a big guy with a buzzcut looking at us."

Dean turned around very casually. "I don't see any guy. Who was he?"

"I don't know."

"Did he do something?"

"He made me wash my hands."

"What?"

"He made me wash my . . . ah, forget it. It's nothing." I drank the beer quickly to quell my jitters, still scanning the crowd for any sign of my guy. Ten minutes later, the lights came on to signal the end of Stink's set. I looked for his face in the crowd. I saw only punk kids with dye jobs, Ben's stoic camera crew, and too-old record company staffers full of forced enthusiasm.

Dean bought me a shot of bourbon "for your nerves." It did indeed pacify me. I bought us two more while Ben and his crew packed up. The whole entourage went to an after-party at a warehouse club. The walls were covered in pieces of scrap metal. Suspended from the rafters were cages of go-go dancers wearing Mexican wrestler masks and dancing to techno. The light was Brylcreem blue. It was a scene of industrial-age Tex-Mex decadence. It smelled like old paint cans and sweat. I still smelled soap on my hand whenever I brought a beer bottle near my face.

We'd been there for about an hour when I noticed the dot. I was standing at the bar using up a drink ticket when I looked down and saw it. It was red and bright and positioned on the upper left side of my chest. I put my hand in front of it. I thought: it's like you can catch the light. It stayed steady on my palm. I thought: some jackass has a laser pointer. Then I thought: some jackass as a high-powered rifle with a laser targeting system. The situation suddenly seemed very uncool.

I panicked, albeit subtly. I ducked my head and hunched forward as I moved into a crowded patch of the club, watching the shoes of my fellow patrons. I thought: keep moving, it's nothing, someone's messing with you. But when I stopped to look at my chest, the red dot was still there. I thought: someone's tracking you. I looked for a source around me but saw only the writhing mob of L.A. scenesters. The source had to be above me. When I looked into the rafters, I saw only wrestler women. They mocked me with their demonic faces and flashing silver eyes.

I looked down at my red dot. My panic downshifted into dumb drunk bravado.

I thought: I've had it with the cloak and dagger shit tonight. "Let's finish this," I muttered, the words obliterated in the techno din. I stretched out my arms in patented martyr fashion. "C'mon," I yelled, "take me out!" I stared up into the ceiling and did a sloppy spin. Some girl gave me a disdainful look and turned her back to me. I thought: the dumb cow thinks I'm trying to pick her up. I snorted and spun again. "Take me out!"

But the shot didn't come. I looked down and saw the red dot trace a circle around my heart and vanish. I thought: huh? I put my arms down. I thought: stop being such a friggin' drama queen.

When I got back to where Ben and Dean were standing, I almost told them what happened. I almost told them how scared I was. I almost told them that I wanted nothing more than for all of this to end and for me to be able to go back to New York, to have the writer's life I'd been imagining for myself since I was eleven years old. But what could they do with that information?

I asked Ben if I could borrow his cell phone.

"You're not gonna drunk-call that chick at *The Betsey*, are you? Because that's a seriously fucked idea."

I assured him that I would not. I was going to call someone who could seriously sort all this out for me. Even in my inebriated and somewhat unhinged condition, I knew it was late to be calling but I felt that it was important.

I walked outside and found a place to stand near the entrance. I was fumbling with my wallet looking for Winston Sharpe's number when Ben's phone rang. I looked to see who the caller was but it was marked "private." There didn't seem to be any point to carrying it inside for Ben because it was too loud in there. I answered it.

"Yeah, Ben's phone."

"Nathan Grant." The voice was stilted and metallic, like it was being produced by some kind of synthesizer. I thought: oh great, now I've got robots after me.

"How'd you know?"

"Listen carefully. You are being followed. Your conversations are being monitored. Do not use telephones. Do not use e-mail communication. Take evasive action."

"Take what kind of action?"

The robot had already hung up. I thought: wha? I thought: behold the magical void. I looked up, half expecting to see someone right in front of me, a rifle pointed in my direction. There was only Von, smoking a cigarette ten feet away. He was wearing the brown blazer and fake moustache again, though the disguise now seemed more tragic than comic. He hadn't noticed me. His face was empty of expression. His presence calmed me so I stood there while he finished his smoke. I felt like we both wanted the same thing: to step out of our lives and let the circus carry on without us. Then he went back to his party and I went back to worrying.

The next afternoon, Ben drove me across town to meet David Maher. The Devendra Center for the Medical Arts was a seven-storey steel pyramid on Wilshire. Its gleaming brightness pained my bleary eyes.

"That supposed to be a hospital?" asked Ben, shielding his own eyes. "Not the most discreet place to get your lipo."

But it was perfect if you wanted to come out feeling like an Egyptian god. I felt more like I had shrapnel in my skull.

Ben dropped me near the entrance. "I've got a few meetings this afternoon, then I'll be back at the Chateau. Call me and maybe I can give you a ride back."

"I appreciate having a chauffeur."

"I like driving. I wouldn't mind living here."

It scared me that a friend of mine could ever say that.

I was about to shut the door when he spoke again.

"Hey, sorry about last night. I shouldn't have bugged you about Colin and that *Betsey* chick. I didn't know you liked her, bro."

"Don't worry about it."

I couldn't be angry. I was barely sentient. I hadn't slept the night before — the ill tidings weighed heavily on my soggy mind.

The world was closing in on me. I replayed that robotic voice in my mind again and again. I hadn't called or e-mailed anyone that day. In and of itself, the phone call was ridiculous, nothing to worry about. In tandem with the bathroom guy and the laser pointer, it felt like part of a conspiracy. Yet the whole thing seemed so amateur — maybe this was the only kind of conspiracy I deserved.

I attracted little attention from the stubble-faced photographers who lurked around the front of the Devendra Center. They must've been waiting for David Maher's girlfriend, the French singer. I couldn't remember her name.

I fished Sparkle's number out of my pocket and called her from the reception desk. She came through the heavy glass security doors a few minutes later with a hulking bodyguard who patted me down and opened my satchel. "Did you leave this bag unattended at any time since you packed it?" he asked in a deep bass voice.

"I don't believe so."

He removed my tape recorder and turned it over in his paw, checking every side. "What is this device?"

"A tape recorder?"

He regarded me with great suspicion. "You're not sure?"

"No, Tucker," said Sparkle. "That's just how he talks." She gave me a consoling look. "We have to take certain precautions."

I re-packed my satchel and followed Sparkle and Tucker through the glass security doors.

"Does David need so much security?"

"He's a very public figure," said Sparkle.

The hallways were bustling with important-looking medical professionals. I passed three doctors whose chins featured the same perfect cleft.

"He's bound to attract some negative attention," she continued. "That's absolutely to be expected. In Mr. Pantero's office, we began screening all the parcels because someone was sending us little boxes of soiled clothing. They'd been dipped in . . . something." Her face wrinkled in disgust. "People like Mr. Pantero or David become magnets for their diseased fantasies."

She led Tucker and me into the elevator and pressed the button for the sixth floor. We must've been in the centre of the pyramid. But what was at the apex — a sacrificial altar? A chin repository? "What makes me so sad," said Sparkle, "is that David's illusions give people the chance to dream. Do you know what I mean? They inspire hope and wonder in so many people. We've seen its effects again and again. People," her eyes were bright, "are inspired. David says our lives are where the true magic lies." She took on a troubled aspect again. "Other people see David's work . . . in a darker light." Her voice dropped to a whisper. "They think David likes to be hurt."

"Hurt?"

"Yes."

"And so these bad people, they want to hurt David?"

She nodded.

I remembered what Lenny Bruce had told me. I thought: David Maher is their horse.

The elevator doors opened and we walked out into another hallway. "David's very eager to talk with you," said Sparkle, "though I'm afraid he doesn't have much strength."

She opened the door to a room, which turned out to be an anteroom for the main suite. Another giant guard blocked the next door.

"We can go straight in," said Sparkle.

The guard opened the door. Inside, there were slanted windows on two sides of the room — we must've been in a corner of the pyramid. Horizontal slats blocked half of the light from outside and transformed the rest into long rectangular pieces. Maher lay in a queen-sized bed — the tubes on his left arm connected him to a hanging garden of IV equipment, the wires on his right arm to an imposing bank of medical machinery. He appeared to be sleeping.

"He lost sixty pounds in the cube," Sparkle whispered. "His situation is stable but we're not out of the woods yet."

Speaking of woods, Maher was still sporting his trademark black eyeliner, which gave him the look of a starving raccoon. The oddly outdoorsy vibe was enhanced by the sound of birds and running water inexplicably emerging from somewhere in the room.

She went to the bedside and touched David's hand. "David sweetie? Nathan Grant is here."

Suddenly he was alert, his blue eyes flickering open and focusing on me. "Good, good." He coughed. "Nathan, thank you for coming." He made a slight gesture to the chair at his right.

I sat down, opened my satchel, and reached for my tape recorder. But was this an interview? I wasn't sure.

"I'll be just outside the door." Sparkle touched me on the shoulder before leaving.

"You must be wondering why I asked you here." Maher's voice was mild and less pained than I expected.

"Sure. I mean, you must be very busy." I thought: was he really so busy? "I heard you were in a cube over a dam. That must've been . . . intense."

"That's right." His face was drawn but his eyes were soft and blue within the kohl circles.

"It's very restful here," I said.

"Yes. It is."

We soaked up the restfulness together.

The silence stretched on so long, I worried that David had gone back to sleep. Or maybe I had. Then he spoke again.

"You must have questions for me. You are a journalist. Asking questions must give you a feeling of purpose."

I nodded. "I guess that's true."

"You want to ask me how I knew you were looking for Jimmy Wynn."

"Okay."

"Sparkle told me. Sparkle likes to help me. She's been very kind."

I thought: maybe we can hurry this up a little. "So why did she tell you I was looking for Jimmy Wynn?"

He inhaled wheezily before speaking. "Because Jimmy Wynn is my father."

Though his words had little trouble traveling through my ears, they stumbled when they tried to burrow into my brain. They kicked hard to get themselves free of the muck. Then they stumbled forward again and landed right where they needed to go.

"Your father?!"

"Yes."

I wasn't sure what else to say so I made do with, "Huh."

"I will tell you what I know. He and my mother were married at the time though the union ended shortly after I was born. To tell you anything further would involve you in a deeply personal matter. I want to know whether this would be wise. I would like to know whether I can trust you." He looked right at me. "Can I trust you?"

I thought: how can I answer that? "Yes. Well, probably. I mean, you can probably trust me. I'm really not sure what you're asking of me or what you expect me to do with this information. This seems like a big deal. I mean, a father. That's a big thing. A private thing."

"I will be as explicit as I can, Nathan. I have not seen my father since I was one year old. Contact between us has been," he wheezed again, "more limited than I would have liked. I'm asking you to deliver a message to him if and when you find him. Do you think you'll find him?"

"Yes," I said. "Definitely. I feel real close."

"Good. When you do, his response to this message will determine the extent of my participation in your story."

This was another new wrinkle. "Your participation?"

"I'm sure you realize by telling you what I have just told you, I have already involved myself. To be frank, it would be embarrassing to me if my relationship to Jimmy Wynn came to light in a way that was damaging to my family. I expect a magazine with the reputation of *The Betsey* would be sensitive to this issue." He went quiet but I couldn't tell if he expected me to respond. He seemed to drift off for a few moments. "Nathan, do you have parents?"

The question, like the rest of this conversation, caught me off guard. "Yes." My answer was so faint, it was nearly drowned by the sounds of birds and water.

"Do they love you?"

"Sure. Yes."

"My parents love me, too. They have done all in their power to protect me. And even though the man who raised me is not my birth father, I love and respect him as if he were. My mother married this man because she believed he would be good to me. She believed my birth father would hurt me much as he had hurt her. She shielded me from him. She did this out of love. I understand this."

I was impressed by the clarity and precision with which he spoke. He'd evidently put a lot of thought into this. His voice was growing weaker.

"If I were to take any direct action to find him, it would be as if I betrayed my mother's love. I would like you to be my proxy."

"Um. All right." I sensed a catch was coming. "What do you want me to tell Jimmy Wynn?"

"Tell him I want him to see me."

I thought: I'm in over my head. I thought: do something. "How do you want me to handle this? I mean, in my story? This is probably a big deal, you being his, uh, birth son."

He smiled. "The irony is that I might be the best thing that could happen to your story. With my name attached, it becomes an event."

I couldn't imagine that would be a good thing. "Wouldn't you rather deal with this privately?"

He made a sound like a laugh except it didn't involve exhaling. "I have no private life, Nathan. I only have degrees of exposure. I hope that when the time comes, you and I can agree on how to proceed with this matter. For now, I want you to talk to him for me. Please get in touch when you've seen him. Take one of my cards."

He gestured toward the side table. There were several business cards on a silver tray. The cards had his name and a phone number printed in blue. I thought: this guy's mysterious and classy.

As I stared at the card, I began to work through the potential ramifications of this conversation. I felt oddly serene about the whole turn of events. On the hidden speakers, a brook continued to babble.

I slipped the card into my pocket and turned back to my host. His eyes were closed. "David?"

No answer.

"David?"

It was no good — he was asleep. I packed up my satchel and went to the door. Sparkle was waiting on the other side.

"Did you have a good interview?"

I did.

* * *

I assessed my situation in a coffee shop on the other side of Wilshire. My illusioneer was right. If David Maher was part of this story, it was an event. Jimmy Wynn's saga went from the back of the magazine to the cover. And yet I still had to worry whether there'd be any story at all. The harder I tried to bring Jimmy Wynn's life into focus, the less I was able to comprehend. Little of what I'd amassed could be arranged into a neat pattern. It would've been more convenient for me had Wynn's life ended along with his career in New Orleans. A stationary corpse would've been easier to find than a live has-been who displayed no shortage of tenacity as he achieved one failure after another.

If I were him, I don't think I could've survived the first two blows: the big death of Teddy Cannon and the little death of Katie Perry. Pantero called her a "bright, perky thing" — was she David Maher's mother? While waiting for Ben at the Books and Books a few days before, I had found Perry's picture in a book on dead celebrities. On the page with her entry was a pair of pictures: one featured a beautiful young woman with perfect Chiclet teeth; the other was her death site, all crumpled metal, broken glass, and blood-smeared asphalt. There was no mention of her having a baby. Besides, Maher was probably too young to be hers.

In any case, these two deaths should've been enough to finish Wynn — the universe had stuck a fork in his ass and said he was done.

I hailed a taxi outside and went to Sound and Vision to get *White Lines* so I could refresh my memory of it back in the hotel. At the counter was the same weaselly dude who had given me attitude before. He snorted when I passed him the tag.

"You don't have to do that every time I rent a movie," I said.

"I'm only exercising my right to free speech," he said smugly.

"Yeah, well . . ." I said. And that was all I had to say.

My eyes stung again when I walked outside the store. The sky was leached of all colour. I felt the sun on my neck. I felt impatient for that bullet.

I was within sight of the gated entrance of the Chateau Montpelier when I saw Dean. He moved briskly toward me.

"What's up?" I said.

He shook his head and waved his hand in front of his chest. "Shht. Not here." He directed me away from the hotel. I looked back over my shoulder to look at the rooftop, scanning for snipers. A blue Thunderbolt sedan was parked near the entrance.

"Don't look back," Dean hissed.

"What's going on?"

"Keep going. Try to look normal."

We marched briskly along the sidewalk in lock step, my body growing stiff with panic. Dean stopped me next to a red hatchback about thirty yards from the Montpelier's driveway. He pulled out his keys and opened the driver's door. Thrash metal blasted out of his car stereo when he turned on the ignition, jolting us both.

Dean abruptly turned off the stereo and looked back at the hotel entrance before pulling the car out of the spot. "Shit. I hope they didn't hear us. I don't think there was anybody looking."

"What is it?"

"There were some men at the hotel looking for you."

"Shit," I said, unsure of how else to express myself. "What did they look like?"

"Dark suits, dark sunglasses. Like detectives on TV." Dean spoke so quickly, I struggled to understand. "Ben and I came back to the hotel to get some tapes. I went to the gift shop to get a Fresca and when I came out, he was talking to two men. One of them had a picture of you. I thought they were from Immigration because you told me you were an illegal. I waited around the gate for you to come back. You can't go in there."

I gripped the dashboard, slumped forward, and groaned. "Damn. Damn, damn, damn."

"What did you do?" Dean was sweating like a professional wrestler.

"I haven't done anything. I told you already. I'm working on a story for *The Betsey*."

"But Ben told me you have no visa. They can arrest you for that."

"There are thousands of Canadian illegals in the States. None of us ever gets nailed unless we're trying to get in or out of the country. Nobody tracks down Canadians. There's too many of us."

"But if they're not Immigration, who are they? Oh, man.

You're so fucked." Dean checked his rear-view mirror. "Why were they waiting for you?" His breathing was fast and shallow. "I'm going to prison for this. I'm aiding and abetting."

"You're not abetting. You're driving."

"Where am I driving to?"

It was a good question. "Away from here." I rapped my knuckles on the dashboard.

"I'll take you to the airport."

"I don't have an ID card. If I try to get on a plane, they'll arrest me."

"Then how were you going to get back to New York?"

"I don't know. Could you calm the fuck down and let me think this through?"

I thought: it's all ending right now. I thought: you can get out of this.

"I'm going to prison," said Dean. He turned to me. "I'm not going to prison."

I looked ahead to the streetlight. "Red light!"

Dean had to hit the brakes hard. The screech of the tires pierced through my confusion.

"I have to keep working on the story." The steadiness of my voice surprised me.

He laughed. "That's insane. You're insane."

"If I get the story, then I have some leverage with *The Betsey*. They have the connections to fix this. Winston Sharpe can help me. Otherwise, I'll just be deported and that'll be the end of it."

"How can you get the story if Immigration's after you?"

"I'll keep moving. And I'll go somewhere they won't look for me. They think I could be in L.A. or New York or Vegas. I'll go somewhere else."

"We gotta go somewhere now. I can't keep driving around."

"How far can you drive me?"

"How far? I can't drive you. That's abetting."

"You're driving me right now."

"Yeah, but it's not abetting. I'm not actively abetting. I'm just picking you up and dropping you off." He rubbed his hand on his thigh. "You have to get out of my car."

"Take me to the bus station."

Dean nodded. "Yeah, that's good. I'll take you to the bus station. What happened was I was coming over to the hotel to get some tapes and then I ran into you and you asked me to take you to the bus station. I didn't see anybody at the hotel."

"That's right. You didn't see anybody at the hotel."

"And you didn't tell me which bus you're taking." He looked over at me again, his eyes teary. "Please don't tell me which bus."

I couldn't if I wanted to. As Dean tried to figure out how to get to the bus station, I silently assessed my situation. Judgment: dire, but not hopeless. My duffel bag and laptop were in Ben's room. As long as my gear wasn't confiscated for evidence, he could hang onto it, maybe send it to me later. Though I had been lamenting the weight of my bulging satchel all day, I was very glad that I hadn't cut my weight. It contained the majority of my story notes, a backup disc that contained many of the Vegas interview transcriptions, the freshly rented video of *White Lines*, and a few choice items from the Berman file. I pulled out Wynn's 8 x 10 glossy, hoping it had some kind of talismanic power. I thought: what next, Jimmy?

Dean pulled up to the bus station's passenger drop-off zone.

"Don't tell me where you're going."

"I won't," I said. "Thanks for the ride."

"That's right," he said. "It was a ride. Not escaping. Not abetting."

"Thank Ben for me." I shoved the 8 x 10 back into my satchel and pulled out the tape of *White Lines*. "Could you return this as one last favour? You can do it anonymously. It's not abetting that way."

The tires gave out a tiny squeal as Dean's hatchback sped away, leaving me standing there holding the tape.

Cars and buses came and went as I stood in the drop-off zone, waiting for my next idea. A crackly loudspeaker announced something in Spanish. Inside the concourse, a gang of children took turns pressing buttons on an ATM. I was running out of cash and wary of using my bank card — surely it could reveal my whereabouts to whoever wanted to find me. On the other hand, it was better to use my card here in Los Angeles than wherever I was about to go. The children scattered when I approached the ATM. I took out three hundred dollars, the daily maximum. That would have to pay my way to Jimmy.

I looked at the departures board. Cities and times were written in chalk. There were destinations in the Midwest, along both coasts, even in Canada and Mexico. I thought of my family in Fairview, Ontario. I could be there in four days. It would only take three to get to New York but I didn't know what awaited me there — maybe men in dark sunglasses and dark suits, or maybe a less dramatic form of failure.

I felt a rumble in my stomach — I hadn't eaten since before my encounter with David Maher. I went into the concourse snack shop. I scanned the wide selection of cheese popcorn and pemmican strips. I grabbed a bag of mesquite chips and a bottle of water. An old woman was fishing change out of her purse to buy a bag of mints so I went to the magazine section in order to kill time. It wasn't like I was in a hurry.

Among the smattering of right-wing newsmagazines, housekeeping titles, and biker porn, I found my way. It was inside *33RPM*, the British music magazine. Alongside the exhaustive articles on the rock gods of the sixties and seventies, it trumpeted the virtues of the unjustly forgotten and obscure. I read this issue's cover lines: "100 Greatest Guitar Solos Ever"; "Biscuits for Pleasure: Behind the Break-Up"; "Sisters in Arms: The Story of

Daisy." I flipped the pages until I saw something familiar: the cover of Daisy's record, *This Morning Is For You.*

"Sir!" It was an Asian man behind the cash register. "Not a library!" He waved an admonishing finger.

I bought my supplies, sat down in the lounge, and opened the magazine to read these words:

> Rosetta Pike serves a mean slice of brambleberry pie. No wonder it attracts folks from all over the Mojave to the Ambrosia, her ramshackle diner in the sleepy desert town of Carloff, California. They all know her as Rose. Like her sisters, she was named after a singer her father loved — in her case, it was Sister Rosetta Jenkins, the guitar-slinging gospel singer whose unbridled performances inspired many of the earliest rock 'n' rollers. Mitchell Pike believed his daughters had a future in music after a fortune teller told him they'd someday be pop's biggest sensations. That's not the way it turned out for the Pike sisters, otherwise known to their fervent cult of fans as Daisy. The music they created nearly thirty years ago didn't bear much resemblance to that of their storied forebears. In fact, it didn't sound much like anything at all. A lot of people thought Daisy was clumsy, tuneless, incompetent — maybe the worst band of all time. A few other folks thought their naivety made them very special.
>
> "Back then all we wanted was to sound like everybody else," says Rose Pike, sitting down to enjoy her signature pie. She tucks her long brown hair behind her ears before picking up her fork. "Nowadays, I'm happy we turned out to be originals.

Our old producer Jimmy Saddlecreek likes to tell me we sounded like angels with broken wings."

An hour after I read that name, I was on the bus to Carloff, California. I could try that pie for myself.

17

The window was cool against my forehead. I could feel the humidity drop and the smog dissipate as we headed further from the coast but it was probably just something in the air conditioning. A fragment to a song ran through my mind — *"Send lawyers, guns, and money, the shit has hit the fan."* I couldn't remember the singer.

As the bus ventured beyond San Bernardino, the scenery outside shifted from strip malls, gas stations, and bungalows with boarded windows to crowded freeway lanes, guardrails, and suburbs in brown and white. When the last housing developments receded, the desert tentatively emerged. I saw brush and cacti. With my head on the window, I dozily imagined the texture of the road under the wheels. After a while, I noticed a line of tiny eyes alongside the freeway. They belonged to creatures that looked like hares, except their ears were short and spiky. They lined the edge of the road, as if waiting for a show.

"Firejacks."

I turned to look through the space between the seats in front of me. The stranger had a rust-coloured cowboy hat. "Never seen firejacks before?" he asked, his voice a mix of grit and honey mustard.

I felt more sleepy than sociable so I ignored him.

"I asked you if you'd ever seen firejacks."

"No," I said. "I haven't."

He poked his head around the side of the seat, knocking his hat askew. "Their eyesight's sharpest at dusk. That's why you find them at the roadside at this time of night. Usually they can't run away from us fast enough. You're probably thinking that sounds like odd behaviour. And you'd be right. The problem is they don't belong here so they don't understand our ways. They're backward. They're from South America. Some wildlife expert introduced it as a food supply for the coyotes. Coyotes never got a taste for 'em, though. And the firejacks just keep breeding and breeding. There's nothing they like doing more than humping and watching the world roll by."

"Why are they called firejacks?"

"What, don't you like it?" he chuckled. "I find it poetical."

He went on to tell me everything else he knew about firejacks. Since there were so many, the state started an extermination program. Kids collected scalps and tails but even these toddler killing sprees didn't make much of an impact on the population. "They'll eat us out of house and home someday," he said.

I hoped I was only dreaming him. Every so often I'd get a whiff of his breath and be brought back to the here and now.

He asked me where I was going. I told him Carloff and he said, "Go, Coyotes! That's how people say hello in Carloff. 'Go, Coyotes!' They all say that. It's the football team. Almost made it to the state championship last two seasons. Good kids. I do a little this and that for 'em."

He reached into his shirt pocket and pulled out a tiny pillbox. "You wanna join me? I've got some good stuff. Real rockets."

He tipped his hat up and I saw his eyes. His pupils were the size of pinheads. There was a white crust at the edges of his mouth. His fingers tap-tap-tapped on his bouncing knee. I thought: my cowboy is totally wired.

"I'm fine."

"You know, your generation usually appreciates this kind of thing. They think I'm a real tamale."

He looked at me sullenly. He pointed out my window at something. "There. There. Walk ten miles and you know what you'll find? Do you know? A bona fide ghost town. My daddy showed it to me when I was a pup. Back then, there was still something left of the general store. Now it's all a bunch of old wood. Deadwood. The one out there's New Cardston. I don't know what happened to Old Cardston."

I looked out into the desert and saw no sign of either Cardston. "Anybody live out there now?"

"You got some tent folk. Young people." He grinned as he tapped the capsule in his pocket. "Desert walkers, too."

"Desert walkers?"

"Desert walkers. They go as far as their feet will carry 'em. They don't want to get too close to the cities or the bigger towns. They like it out here. They're all . . ." He pointed at his ear and made a circle. The finger was so jittery, the circle was more like a figure-eight. "As long as you're careful about not dying of thirst and you don't mind eating firejacks, you can stay out there as long as you like. Walking and walking and walking." He pointed at the window again. "Watch close and you might see one! Or a ghost. They say that if they die on their feet, the ghosts just keep on walking. That's why they all want to die on their feet."

I looked out the window and saw nothing but darkness.

"What do you see?" he asked.

"Nothing."

"Look harder, then." He cackled and turned around, apparently done with me. He got out at Crestberg, the town before Carloff.

It was a little after nine when I exited the bus, clutching my satchel. At the ticket counter inside the station, there was a sallow-faced man with inch-thick glasses.

"Excuse me, is there a motel near here?"

He pushed the glasses further up his nose. "You want somewhere cheap or nice?"

"Cheap."

"Try the Motel de Ville. Go out those doors and head right for about a quarter-mile."

I noticed a stack of T-shirts wrapped in plastic on the counter. "How much for one of those?"

"Ten dollars. Three of it goes to the Coyotes Stadium Fund."

I gave him a twenty. "I'll take a red one and a white one."

"That's the spirit." He put them in a paper bag. "Go, Coyotes."

"Uh-huh. Go, Coyotes."

Next to the bus station was a traffic light blinking yellow in all directions. Beyond the intersection was a collection of clapboard houses, a small set of storefronts, and a brick building with a clock tower. I heard cicadas and the sound of trucks back on the highway.

I was walking past the brick building when a truck rolled by slowly. In the back were three surly teenagers clutching cans of beer. "Hey," said one, his arm dropping back as he prepared to chuck the can.

I flinched and said, "Go, Coyotes?"

The teens looked at me then started to laugh. The kid with the can toasted me and screamed, "GO, COYOTES!"

The Motel de Ville was the only lighted structure on the far stretch of Main Street. The French name was deceptively fancy for such a dump. The office was a converted camper van. The sign outside said: "Press button for service." I heard a buzz on the other side of the door. Nothing else. I pressed the button again. This time I heard rustling and a bump.

A middle-aged woman in a baseball cap opened the door. She didn't say hello.

"I need a room for the night. For two nights?"

"You have a reservation?"

"No. Do I need one?"

She scowled. "It would have been the courteous thing. You traveling with your parents?"

The question threw me. "Uh, no. Just me."

She looked past me. "Where's your car?"

"I'm not driving."

"So did you walk here?"

"No, I was on the bus."

"I don't need your life story. A single's fifty dollars. You can pay me for both nights now. Fill this out." She handed me a clipboard.

I gave her my bogus last name and used the Mercury International Pictures office for my address. I handed over the clipboard and the cash. I didn't know how long I could last on the rest of my money.

"Room 7." She pointed down the length of the building.

"Is there anywhere I can get something to eat?"

"Near the highway."

"Anything closer?"

"No."

"What about the Ambrosia?"

She peered at me suspiciously. "One of her little admirers, huh? You some reporter here to talk about her godawful music? The real story is she's a man-stealing bitch." There was an uncomfortable silence as she glared at me.

"I'm gonna go now. Good night." Still no reaction. "Go, Coyotes?"

She replied with the same before shutting the door.

Once safely inside my room, I sat on the edge of the bed and made several wishes. First I wished that I had never left my East Village apartment. Then I wished that I was back in Las Vegas enjoying a Danny Pantero show. Finally I wished I had something

to eat. I tried to fill up on water. In between trips to the bathroom
— which, in keeping with the name of the establishment,
included a bidet — I thought about Jimmy and I thought about
what Rose Pike might be like.

* * *

When I woke up, I didn't know where I was. I itemized my immediate surroundings: wallpaper striped red and white like a candy
cane, an amateurish painting of a kitten, dirty green curtains, my
clothes in a pile at the side of the bed. The rabbit-eared TV and
Bakelite clock radio were so ancient, I couldn't even guess the year
with confidence.

Then I remembered the laser dot and the robot voice and the
men in black at the Montpelier. The fear sharpened my percep-
tions. I reached for the copy of *33RPM* on the nightstand. I
re-read the sentence that sent me into the Mojave Desert: "'Our
old producer Jimmy Saddlecreek likes to tell me we sounded like
angels with broken wings.'" It was the first time I'd encountered a
"Jimmy" Saddlecreek, not a James. All the L.A. types had called
him James. That was the name in the Mercury movie credits and
the Berman file. Jimmy Wynn seemed to like that distinction.

Pike's apparent mistake suggested a couple of possibilities.
One: Pike wanted to convey her own folksy-gal demeanor to the
journalist and, by extension, the reader. Two: Pike wanted to
indicate the warm feelings she felt for a musical mentor by using
the more casual form of his name. Three: Pike jumbled up the
names by mistake, an error that could be interpreted as knowledge of her producer's two identities. Four: At some point after
the seventies, the names converged into this meta-alias, which
indicated the creation of a new identity or a harmonization of the
two prior ones.

The other aspect of the sentence that compelled my trip to

Carloff was the use of present tense. According to Pike, Saddlecreek "likes to tell" her things. The phrase connoted that the action was part of a continuing rapport that she and Wynn/ Saddlecreek enjoyed. First inference: Wynn/Saddlecreek is alive. Second inference: There may be a whole series of things that Wynn/Saddlecreek likes to tell Rose, possibly while dining at the Ambrosia. Before Rose, only Danny Pantero had stated he'd spoken to Wynn (though not Saddlecreek) any time recently. Now I had some kind of verification.

My new confidence fought a pitched battle with the fear. Both of them ended up losing to hunger. I showered and put on my new white T-shirt. On the front was an illustration of an angry coyote with bared teeth. He wore a helmet and ill-fitting shoulder padding. His paws ended in long thin claws. A football was tucked in one of his armpits. I thought: how did he pick it up without puncturing the pigskin?

I picked up my satchel, walked out of the motel room, and headed back up Carloff's main drag. The town boasted more activity during the daylight hours. Cars were parked all around the brick building and leathery faced seniors and younger back-packer types milled in front of the strip of stores. A grey-haired man sat in an idling pickup truck. I stood at his open window. "Excuse me, sir, could you tell me —"

"Go, Coyotes!" he barked.

"Go, Coyotes!" I yelped back.

He grinned. The right incisor was missing. He reminded me of the cartoon on my T-shirt. "What can I do you for?"

"Can you tell me where the Ambrosia is?"

"Time for brambleberry pie!" he barked. He pointed at the last storefront on the main drag. "Have a slice for me!"

I thanked him kindly.

I had missed the Ambrosia when I had walked past the night before because it had so little signage. The name that had been painted above the door in red was mostly scraped away. An off-centred "Rest" was the only remnant. The menu was posted in the window — only there did I see the name of the place. I also found this line at the bottom: "Rose Pike, Proprietor."

Inside it was warm, bright, and busy. There was a row of red vinyl booths along one side of the restaurant. The rest was taken up by rustic wooden tables and mismatched chairs. A rectangular space in the back wall revealed the activity in the kitchen. I saw a college-aged white guy with a goatee and a middle-aged Mexican woman in a purple dress. There was a mariachi song on the stereo.

A young brunette in pigtails popped into my sightline. "For one?"

"Yeah. In a booth?"

"We usually reserve 'em for three or more. But," she smiled coyly, "since rush hour's over, that's fine."

She led me over and plunked down a menu. "The specials are on the board."

I had a look around. A man in a blazer and open-collared shirt gave me a thumbs up. I stared at him in confusion. He pointed at my chest.

"Oh," I said. "Go, Coyotes."

"That's enough of that," said the waitress as she put down a glass and poured out my water.

"Is Rose in this morning?"

"Nope. She left us holding down the fort. She'll be back in another hour." She studied me for a moment. "Let me guess. You're here to talk about her musical endeavours."

"Do I look that out of place?"

"The T-shirt's foolin' no one. They're all too polite to tell you."

The menu was full of diner staples gussied up to appeal to city-folk like myself. I ordered the poached eggs with mango salsa. Needing something to occupy my mind, I re-read the *33RPM* piece for the umpteenth time.

"Popular magazine," said the waitress as she put a coffee in front of me.

"I bet."

When my eggs came, I ate slowly. Eventually the place emptied out and the waitress took over the booth ahead of me to fold napkins around knives and forks. I looked at the Daisy pictures in *33RPM*. One was the official group shot, the girls smiling stiffly in front of a closed red curtain. The family resemblance was clear — they each had the same sharp blue eyes and long, narrow faces. Bessie was the bustiest of the bunch, Vera the homeliest. Rose, fifteen when the picture was taken, was a string bean. The other picture was a casual snapshot of the girls in the studio. The smiles seemed to be authentic this time. Bessie's mouth was frozen open in laughter as she sat behind her drum kit. Vera, the one with the guitar in her lap, would have been nearly twenty but she was every inch the gawky teenager as she sat behind the mike (she was also the lead singer). Gazing straight at the camera with her bass guitar slung low, Rose had something else going for her. With her long brown hair pooling at her shoulders, she was a Pre-Raphaelite rocker in a pink polka-dot shirt. She looked a little like Katie Perry, too.

The last picture was new. Rose sat in the booth where the waitress was now. It must have been late in the day because the front window faced west and there was sun streaming into the restaurant. The few grey strands in Rose's hair went silver in the light. She didn't hide the creases at the edges of her eyes and mouth, though her lipstick was visible. She seemed to look straight through the camera, as if she demanded to know who exactly would be looking back.

A bell rang. When I looked up, Rose was in the doorway. "Hello, Judy," she said to the waitress. "I trust you made it through a morning without me."

"It was heaven, Rose, it really was."

I hid my magazine and became inordinately focused on the dregs in my coffee cup. I heard Judy whispering.

"Mmm-hmm," said Rose. Then she came to the side of my booth.

"Have I kept you waiting? I have this terrible feeling that the nice girl at the record company neglected to tell me you were coming. I haven't checked my e-mail for a few nights."

"No, I . . . no."

She looked down at the place where I'd been staring. "Now that's a real tragedy, an empty coffee cup in the Ambrosia. Let me remedy that."

"No, that's fine. I had plenty."

"Is that so? I hope you're not like me. If I have more than one cup, I'm liable not to sleep for a week. The doctor says I have a tender constitution. He makes me sound like a real dainty one. Not like you. You look like a local. The shirt's a nice bit of camouflage."

"Go, Coyotes," I said. I thought: that felt strangely natural to say. I thought: damn, she's lovely, isn't she?

"So let me apologize again for making you wait." She slid into the booth opposite me. "What do they call you?"

"Nathan?"

"Aren't you sure, Nathan? People named Nathan should be sure about a lot of things. The name has a confident ring. And where do you call home, Nathan?"

"Toronto. No, I mean New York?"

"A jetsetter. What are you doing all the way out here? Did your friends in New York tell you this was the new international hotspot?"

"I, uh, came to talk about Daisy."

"Is that so?" She tucked a strand of her hair behind her ear. "It took quite a while for everyone to notice our unsung genius. We weren't trying for genius. All we wanted was to get Daddy to stop barking at us." Rose looked at her watch. "I wish I'd known you were coming today so I could've timed my day better. I'm gonna have to get to my lunch duties in a few minutes. I do apologize for making you wait but I —"

"I should be sorry," I said, interrupting. "You weren't really expecting me."

She cocked an eyebrow.

"I needed to talk to you about something. It couldn't wait."

"I can tell you're about to get straight to the point."

I looked into my empty coffee cup again, my nerves collapsing into a caffeinated jumble. The room went sour with silence.

"Straight to the point," said Rose, almost motherly. "You can get there, hon." She reached across the table to pat my hand.

"James Saddlecreek," I said. "I'm looking for James Saddle-creek."

Rose's brow narrowed for an instant. Then her features relaxed again. "Haven't heard that name in a while. You must be a real aficionado of my music."

"I'm trying to write a story about him. For a magazine. I talked to a lot of people about him already but I want to talk to him, too. You mentioned him. In the story." I picked up the issue of *33RPM* from the seat next to me and put it down on the table.

"He was a big part of Daisy. I'm sure you know that. But it's been a long time since I had any word of him."

"You talked about him as if you still knew him." I was no born interrogator so I mustered up all the courage I had. "I think you know where he is."

She began to shift along her seat. "If you'd like to talk about Daisy, we can have a chat. But you'll have to excuse me because I —"

"You called him Jimmy Saddlecreek."

Her whole body stiffened. "I called him what?"

"In the story. You called him Jimmy Saddlecreek."

"Well, that's his name, hon."

"No. No, it's not. I think you know both his names."

She paused again and looked at me with a mixture of suspicion and curiosity. "Is that right?" Her smile was sly. "You seem awfully insightful about the things I know and don't know, hon. I must be an open book to you." She patted me on the hand again as she slid along the rest of the seat. "You and I are going to have some things to talk about just as soon as I'm finished with the lunch crowd. We've got a busload of tourists arriving from Flagstaff in about half an hour. I sure could use your booth. Why don't you see what else there is to do in this town? I trust you can keep yourself out of trouble. I don't want to hear about some jetsetter chucking beer cans at firejacks."

I nodded. I thought: I got her, I can't believe I got her.

"That's a good boy. Now run along."

18

Rose was wiping down a table when I came back to the Ambrosia. Her hair was tied back, revealing the freckles on her neck. She was smiling to herself. A fragment of a Daisy song floated into my head. *"There is a boy in my class and I hope he takes the chance / to ask me to the dance / and I will say all right / because he is so nice / and it is so nice / to be a teenager in the world."*

On the original recording, Vera half-spoke, half-sung the lines, running them together as if she were trying to find rhymes at random and not having much luck. And yet its stream-of-consciousness quality was contradicted by the backup vocals from Bessie and Rose on "to be a teenager in the world." It was as if Vera committed her spontaneous ramblings to tape in one take and then someone else (Saddlecreek, most likely) had added many more tracks of instruments and voices later. It was a concrete tower of sound built on a foundation of marzipan. Somehow it didn't collapse. A lot of Daisy's songs left the same impression.

Rose saw me through the front window and signaled to me to stay where I was. She came out carrying two bottles of water. "I hope you didn't get yourself into too much trouble."

"How?"

"Oh, don't be a snob, New York. There's plenty for a young person to do around here. He can throw bottles at cars. He can learn to spit. He can even read a book. And if he's old enough, he can get one of the local girls in trouble with child."

"How old is that?"

"I'm not at liberty to say." She handed me one of the bottles of water. "Go ahead and open it — you look thirsty already. We're going for a walk. I think better when I'm moving."

She led me along Main Street, past the motel. Our goal was a hill situated just beyond the edge of town. "Ryder's Point," she said. "Don't worry, it's close."

Carloff was almost pretty in the daytime. The old-timey town centre was in the middle of an orderly grid of houses and businesses. Rose steered me onto a residential side street of small houses — most had "Go, Coyotes!" signs in their front windows.

We walked in silence for the first while. I fiddled with the tape recorder and pressed record. She looked over and saw the little red light. Instead of speaking, she whistled. The melody was ragged, more a series of notes that happened to find themselves in roughly the same place at roughly the same time. They regarded each other with nervousness and trepidation, like high schoolers at their first school dance.

I recognized the tune. "It's 'Teacher, Teach Me.'"

"Mmm-hmm." Rose began to sing. Her voice wasn't much, but then it never had been.

> You're sitting in the classroom but you're not really there
> Chewing on your pencil and twisting your hair
> Your future is now but you don't even care
> Listen to your teacher, she's got something to share

"It's the only verse I remember. I consider that something of a blessing."

"I really like Daisy's lyrics. There's a purity about them."

She laughed. "Aw, that's a crock. People throw all kinds of words around. Some university professor sent me something he'd written about that song. He was so deadly earnest, I thought it was hilarious. Most of the words in those songs were any old thing I could come up with."

"I didn't realize you wrote the lyrics until I read that article."

"Oh, yeah," she said without much pride. "Vera did her bit, too. She would extrapolate on what I'd heard. She's still a very imaginative lady. But when the band got going, Daddy figured I would be the songsmith because I already liked to write poems. He'd send me up to my room and not let me out until I wrote him a song. Some nights were real easy. I'd be in a good mood and thinking about my cat or how much I loved banana splits or how I felt when it was springtime and the words would pour out of me. Other nights I would be feeling mad about having to do so many music lessons and tired of hearing Daddy talk about all his plans. But Daddy wouldn't let me out until I slipped him something underneath the door. So I'd just write anything. The lyrics wouldn't even rhyme most of the time. Most of them were just dopey things that I wrote because I needed a laugh."

She got quiet again as we passed the last house and covered the ground between town and hill. Around me I saw pointy shrubs, little cacti, and short, tough grass that stuck out of the earth like facial stubble.

"Do you like meeting people, Nathan?"

The question threw me. "I suppose so."

"You strike me as one of those people who's happiest on his own."

"Why do you say that?"

"I'm very perceptive about people. When I used to travel with bands, I would meet folks from all walks of life." She drank from her water bottle. "It takes a lot out of you to be with people. You don't know who you are when you're around them."

I didn't like becoming the subject of this conversation. "Do you think we could talk about Jimmy?"

"You've had a lot of Jimmy on your mind, haven't you? What's that been like?"

"Fine. Interesting."

"So he's not just a paycheque to you?"

"No. I admire him."

"Why would a young man admire Jimmy?"

I thought: good question. There was a lot I wanted to tell her. "For one thing, he was smart. The comedy records were great and I really liked some of the movies. Mostly I admire his determination. He didn't stop trying even after he lost it all — *especially* after he did. Some people wanted him to stop so badly, they tried to hurt him. But I don't think they understood his mentality. I think he was like a lot of entertainers. Getting hurt was part of the process."

Rose looked at me very seriously. "Hmm." She took another draw of water. "I think you're getting ahead of yourself." She was silent for a few strides. The ground was becoming steep. "I must say it's interesting for me to hear somebody else's view of Jimmy. I've always had my own ideas."

"Really?"

"Yes, really." She turned to me with a smirk. "You must think I'm a great big tease about all this. Let's see if I can get to the point a little faster." She grabbed my hand and squeezed it. "I'm gonna tell you a story. Try to keep up."

We started up the hill.

## The Story of Daisy and Jimmy (Rose's version, abridged)

There once was a man named Mitchell Pike. He had one lovely wife and three lovely daughters. In 1965, Mrs. Pike died in a car accident, leaving Mitchell a forty-two-year-old widower with three girls to raise. Bereft and forlorn, Mitchell consulted a local medium and fortune teller to try to contact her spirit. Though his wife proved unavailable, the medium did relay a message from Mitchell's mother, who had died when he was very young. She said: my beautiful granddaughters will sing beautiful music.

After that, Mitchell poured all his energy and resources into fulfilling that prophecy, despite the fact that his daughters never evinced any interest in music. His eldest, Vera, was a shy, compliant girl who would rather have spent her time knitting than studying music. Her more extroverted sister Bessie resented her father for discouraging her from socializing with her peers and forcing her to practise drums. The youngest was Rose. Unlike her sisters, she believed in her late grandmother's prophecy, though her inability to master her bass guitar frustrated her to no end. She had begun to fantasize about life in places far from her home in Baker, California, a conservative town where the young people shunned the Pike sisters as "weirdos."

Mitchell organized concerts for the girls in a local church basement. Because there was so little entertainment going on in Baker, the shows attracted many local teens. They would ridicule the girls for their sloppy playing and inane songs. Cups would be thrown, though never bottles (the town was rough, but not that rough). "You've just got to try harder," Mitchell would tell his weeping daughters.

In 1970, Mitchell decided it was time to make a larger dent in the music business. He packed his daughters and their instruments in a camper van and drove them to Los Angeles. He had been in contact with a record producer who had many connections in the music industry and had his own studio. He said he would help the Pike sisters become successful. "Your daughters," he told Mitchell, "are unconventional. I can dig that."

His name was James Saddlecreek. Rose thought he was very strange. He wore a dark moustache and a jacket with fringes. He mumbled to himself when he thought he was alone. He rarely made eye contact. At the beginning, Rose said, "he was sorta try-ing to hide inside his own skin."

They all got to know each other. The girls played their songs for James in the studio, which was really only a shed in the back of the man's ranch house in San Lupe. There were songs about lis-tening closely to your teachers and giving good homes to puppies and how much grown-ups had to learn from children. Between each song, James would nod and say, "Good, good — do you have another?" When they had no more songs, he told them to go back to the main house while he went to think about some things.

When he came back, he smelled funny and he spoke slowly. He spoke about the purity of art, the divinity of youth, the sacred-ness of family, and all the other things that America was desperate for since the death of the president, an event that only Rose wasn't old enough to remember very clearly. Then James said he had a new name for the group, which had been known as the Pike Sisters. He wanted to call them Daisy because, as he said, "it's the most beautiful flower in all of creation."

Mitchell was impressed. This man seemed to know a lot about music and the young people of the day. James and the Pikes spent the rest of the summer working on the record. When September came around, Mitchell kept the girls from going back to school. Vera was very upset, being the most sensitive to disrup-tions. Bessie was thrilled. Mitchell told the girls it was make-it-or-break-it time. He was still convinced Daisy would become the most popular singing group in the world.

Their best song was called "Ageless Beauty." Rose wrote it, Vera sang it softly. James made the girls play it a lot. They got so good at it, they made hardly any mistakes.

As the fall wore on, Mitchell grew frustrated with James Saddlecreek. The producer insisted that the girls be available while he was mixing in case he needed them to play something. He kept them close by, especially Bessie, who laughed at everything he said. Mitchell and James had fights how some of Mitchell's money had been spent. They didn't talk to each other for a while — Bessie was their go-between. But the album was eventually finished. It was called *This Morning Is For You*. Rose came up with that — she was always an early riser.

While Mitchell returned to Baker and re-enrolled the girls in school, James went to record companies to shop around *This Morning Is For You*. Despite what he told Mitchell, James knew very few people. He had made a great deal of money for one company in the early 1960s, but no one there was interested in Daisy. Months passed. Mitchell and James had long arguments over the phone. Mitchell decided that he wanted the master tapes so he drove with the girls to Los Angeles. The arguments continued. Bessie joined in to defend James. In the course of doing so, she admitted that she and James were in love and going to get married. Mitchell slapped Bessie and James punched Mitchell. The elder Pike was unable to quell his middle daughter's rebellion. Vera hid in the car. Rose was at the door, unsure where she wanted to be.

Mitchell stormed out, swearing to come back with the police. But he also realized that the scandal would doom the band's chances. He consented to the marriage as long as the album came out and everyone kept quiet. "Daddy said he didn't want the press to get a hold of this," Rose said. "I'm not sure what kind of press he was talking about."

Bessie Pike and James Saddlecreek were married in a civil ceremony — Rose was the flower girl and sole guest. A small record company put out *This Morning Is For You* in the middle of 1971. It generated no attention, selling only a few hundred copies, mostly among relatives in the Baker area. Mitchell was apoplectic at the turn of events, calling Bessie to tell her how she ruined this opportunity for her sisters. A boy was born Christmas 1971. His name was Bud, like a flower bud.

Rose would take the bus from Baker to Los Angeles to go see

her sister and her brother-in-law. While Bessie was busy with Bud, she and James would talk in the shed. Now that he didn't smell so funny any more — he laid off for the baby — he had started to change. Another man emerged from behind the rough exterior. His behaviour was less erratic, his manner less moody. Even so, he talked a lot about being afraid. He had been through so much hurt in his life. Everything he ever wanted had been torn away from him. Worse yet, he knew a secret about an important man that he was never supposed to tell anybody, not even to Rose. "He acted so damn paranoid about it," she said, "I would've done anything to find out what it was."

Sometimes he talked about his mother. Sometimes he talked about being onstage. She'd laugh at his jokes, even when she didn't understand them. Rose called him Jimmy because that's what he called himself. She was careful not to do it when Bessie was around, so as not to seem too familiar with her brother-in-law.

After the school year ended, Rose spent the summer in Los Angeles. Mitchell, Bessie, and James fought constantly about the failure of the record, about the baby, about everything. Rose felt a whole lot older than fifteen. James got sad. He lost interest in recording and trying to get into the movie business again. He hardly laughed or told jokes anymore. Rose wanted to make him feel better.

Finally, Bessie caught her husband and her sister in a room together doing something they shouldn't have been doing. She bundled up Bud and told her sister that they were going back to Baker. When Rose refused to go with her, Bessie said that she would call the police and they would put him away for real this time. That was officially the end of the band, too, though they hadn't played together for ages.

Rose gave in and left with Bessie and Bud. James seemed resigned to it all. When Bessie called to say she and the baby were moving to her aunt's place in Minnesota, he only wanted to know where he could send money for Bud.

Whenever Rose called Los Angeles, he would say he couldn't talk and hang up the phone. She continued to call every couple of weeks, then every couple of months. Every so often, she would reach him. He told her about the movies he was working on. Sometimes he'd tell her that it was her fault he lost his wife and son.

He still had big plans. He was going to make a big movie. He was going to play Vegas again. He was owed favours. This talk surprised Rose. Even her daddy had given up his dreams. If Rose hadn't hid a box of LPs in her closet, then the Pikes wouldn't have a single copy.

She couldn't wait to get out of his house for good. She would have quit school if Jimmy hadn't encouraged her to stay. When she left, she was good and ready. She traveled, sometimes with a rock band, sometimes on her own. She prided herself on how well she had escaped. Every once in a while, whenever she was feeling low or uncertain or extra lonely, she would call the house in Los Angeles. If someone other than Jimmy answered, she hung up. If it was Jimmy but his voice was slurry or slow in the way that it got, she would hang up. She would sometimes call a dozen times before reaching the real Jimmy. Even then, she didn't feel like she'd really reached him.

"The story runs out of happy parts right about there," said Rose.

We were sitting on the mound that the people of Carloff called Ryder's Point. Rose took another drink of water and looked out over the town. "Everything looks so clean from here, so neat. I know it's not like that when I get close."

Some distance below me I heard the sound of a truck backing up. I slapped a mosquito on my arm. I didn't know what to say.

She touched my knee. "I've got to get back. They're helpless without me, they really are."

We talked some more on the way down the hill. I enjoyed that more than I can say.

She told me to come back at 8:30 and she'd fix me something. The intervening hours were not happy ones. I was too afraid to use the phone so I just walked the roads on the edge of town. The dry crunch of my footsteps was interrupted only by the occasional passing truck and the inevitable cry of "Go, Coyotes!" I tried to be hopeful about my story's fate. I knew if I could deliver Jimmy with some Nevada and a side of David Maher (a.k.a. poor little Bud Pike), Winston and Daphne would help me out of my mess. I thought: don't get negative, all I need now is Jimmy. And despite her pronouncements to the contrary, I believed Rose had a Jimmy to give.

I hung around my motel room until the evening. I tried the bidet but it didn't work. I only wanted to wash a shirt in it. I put the thing on anyway, figuring that the smell of fear had sufficiently faded since yesterday. Otherwise I only had the T-shirts to wear.

I walked very slowly back to the restaurant, arriving a few minutes before the appointed hour. I didn't see her anywhere. Judy was gone, too. The Mexican woman who had been in the kitchen that morning was now serving tables. I saw a slim Mexican man through the kitchen window. The customers were mostly hikers — I recognized them from the dirt on their boots and mussed-up hair. I sat at the same booth as I had that morning. The woman came over to me. "Miss Rose will be back to see you soon," she said in accented English.

I thanked her and ordered a beer. I was halfway through when Rose came in. "Dammit," she said in mock anger. "You're gonna ruin your palate." She showed me a bottle of wine. "I'd been saving this for a special moment and it's perfect with the catfish."

She took the beer off the table. "You're done with this."

She was right — the wine was perfect. She didn't stay for my meal. "My day's not done," she said. But when I'd finished and the hikers had gone, she returned to share the rest of the bottle. As her two employees — Flor and her husband Junior — cleaned up, Rose sipped her Muscadet and reminisced about her days on the road in the seventies.

"Even then, there was a certain amount of curiosity about Daisy," she said. "That tended to vanish as soon as people heard us. Still, we had our little cult. It was enough to get me some respect when I first hit the road looking for fun. The guys didn't treat me like some dumb chick. I wasn't very interested in playing music, though. I just liked the lifestyle. When I heard Crosby Campbell wanted a cook who would go on tour, I took the gig. I was really into slow cooking. Do you know much about slow cooking?"

I didn't, so she told me.

She asked me personal questions. She said straight out that she expected me to give up some more of myself in exchange for her earlier openness. I obliged as best I could. She wanted to know about my favourite places. I told her how excited I was the first time I got lost in the New York subway system and how my earliest memory of America was a visit to the Grand Ole Opry when I was five.

"Don't you think about your home more often?"

"New York?"

"No, Canada."

"I'm out of the habit. I feel like I'm a long way away."

"What's that place like? Where you grew up?"

I talked about the thickly wooded gully beyond the cul-de-sac on my street in Fairview. Because of its privacy, this site had hosted many milestones in the lives of kids I knew — first fights, first kisses, first cigarettes, first drunk-ups. Sometime around midnight, a pair of cops would usually stroll through, causing most of the teens to run away. I liked to run to a hiding spot halfway up the slope. I'd watch the cops' flashlights cut through the dark as I tried to stifle the sound of my breathing. I'd listen to them admonish the poor suckers who didn't get away in time.

"Did you ever go to Niagara Falls?" she asked.

I had, but only on a school trip when I was young.

"I like it a lot," she said. "The last time I went there I got drenched. You see, there are these tiny rain clouds that hover over the main lookout. It's because they built too many tall hotels near the Falls — they messed up the weather. Now there's a little patch of rain that never stops."

I said I liked that image. She gave me a thoughtful look, then inspected the bottle and found it empty. "I see that we are in need of more moisture." She slipped out of the booth and called out to the kitchen. "Flor, can you and Junior close up?"

She re-appeared at the side of the table. "The next bottle is at my place. I spend more than enough time here."

I slid across the seat. "Can we talk again tomorrow?"

"We can keep talking, hon. I just need a change of venue. Where are you staying?"

"The Motel de Ville."

She laughed. "The woman who runs that thinks I stole her husband."

"Did you?"

"No. The sad bastard only had eyes for Denny, my old sous-chef. They took off for the coast together. You never saw a rougher-looking couple. She should've had her suspicions about his inclinations when he tried to turn that dump into the palace of Versailles."

"That would explain the bidet."

Rose lived in a bungalow a few streets away. There was a big dreamcatcher in the front window, Japanese wind chimes over the porch. The screen door was missing a pane of glass. Inside, we drank white wine and vodka from the freezer. She untied her hair from its knot. We didn't talk very much about Jimmy.

When the hour was late, she got up out of her rattan chair and stood in the middle of the room. She leaned all the way forward from her waist.

"What are you doing?"

"Stretching out my back. Evening ritual."

Her shirt slid down her back and I saw the bottom vertebrae through her pale skin. The shirt slid down a little further and I saw a white bra strap. Her hair hung down to the rug. "Helps for circulation and respiration. Gives you good dreams. You try it."

"I —"

"No excuses."

She rolled back up and stood before me. Her face was pink and flushed.

I got up, gripping the arm rest so as not to wobble.

"Come and stand here next to me," she said.

I got into position. She put her hand on the small of my back.

"Get your spine nice and straight. Chin up. Bend your knees a little. Good. You can close your eyes if it helps you concentrate. Now breathe into the top of your chest and feel your ribs expand. Then as you exhale, tighten your abdominals and let yourself come forward one vertebra at a time."

For a moment, I thought I was losing my balance. My breath snagged on a piece of panic, then broke free. I felt clear. When I opened my eyes, I was looking at my knees. I felt her hands moving down my spine.

"Don't worry," she said softly. "I'm not going to push hard. I'm just going stretch you out a bit. Keep breathing. In."

In.

"And out."

Out.

I felt her hands spread over my shoulder blades. Her fingers graced the nape of my neck.

"Good," she said. "Good."

I felt her fingers at the back of my head, scratching my scalp. Her touch was rougher than I might have expected had I dared to expect. She pinched my right ear.

"Now on your next exhale, tighten your stomach and start coming up. Feel yourself stacking your vertebra."

I was vertical. I wobbled a little sideways but her arm was there to lean on. Her other hand was on the small of my back.

"There. Feeling steady?"

I exhaled in the affirmative.

"Good," she said. She came around and looked up into my face. She laughed. "Now that your spine's straight, you're too tall. Bend your knees a little." I followed her instruction. "Better." Then she kissed me, first on the centre of the lips, then in the right corner, then on the right cheek. She moved her mouth all the way to my ear. "No more sad things tonight, okay?"

I nodded, afraid that if I spoke, I would break the spell.

"It's settled," she said. She took my hand and led me out of the room.

* * *

My first thought in the morning was: score. My second was: hooray, an east-facing window. I hadn't been woken up by the sun for a long time. It reminded me of a place I'd go in the summertime. It was a cabin on Lake Huron on a patch of sandy beach owned by my father's uncle. My brother and I would sleep in the east-facing room and wake with the sun on our faces. Our heads would get so hot, we'd have to go swimming before breakfast. We didn't care how cold the water was.

I enjoyed the sun in Rose's bedroom. I got out of her bed and picked up my underwear — I felt proud to have a reason to leave them on someone else's floor. I saw a man's shirt hanging over the top of a chair. It hadn't been there last night so I presumed she'd put it out for me. I listened closely for a morning sound — a running shower, a radio, kitchen cabinets opening, the sizzle of bacon — but didn't find one. The silence spoiled my good mood and filled me with the usual anxiety. I thought of Danielle and the possibility of more sexy espionage. I opened the door and came back into the living room where we'd done our stretches. I was relieved to see my satchel — I didn't check the contents inside but the shape of the thing looked right. I moved on to the kitchen. The smell of fresh coffee was so reassuring, I could have cried for joy. On the table was a plate with a piece of toast. Underneath the plate I saw a note. "Good morning. I had an early errand but I'll be back soon. Coffee's hot. Wear the shirt."

After pouring myself a coffee and eating the toast, I puttered around the house. The only signs of Daisy's history were a copy of the new CD reissue and a brown-coloured record of *This Morning Is For You* in a frame. A little plaque on the latter read: "Commemorating sales in excess of five units." In a wooden bowl on a side table, I found a pair of men's watches. Neither was running. There was also a matchbook from a hotel in Niagara Falls, Canada. I thought: am I supposed to be looking for clues?

I dropped the matchbook when I heard the door open. Rose wore a black T-shirt with her hair tied back. "I like that shirt on you," she said. She opened a cabinet in the kitchen, pulled out a travel mug, and poured herself a coffee. "Get your shoes on. We're going for a ride."

"Where to?"

"We're seeing a friend."

"Who?"

When she turned to face me, her face was tense. "I think you know where we're going," she said in a cautious tone. "I'm warning you now, this isn't going to be easy. Not for anyone."

I grabbed my satchel, put on my shoes, and went straight out the door. We were heading for Jimmy.

"Is here okay?"

Jimmy hears his voice resound through the empty hall. Sound waves pound against the velveteen on the chairs and fake marble columns, then recede back at him from all directions — no bodies out there to soak it up. The voice is wrong — too scratchy from his morning ciga-rettes. He thinks of smoothing it out with some Cuban rum from his flask but he doesn't want to risk messing up his head this early in the day. Then again, it must not matter how he sounds because the tech guy's said nothing either way.

Jimmy tries again. "Is this where you want me? I can come, you know, further down the stage."

He shields his eyes with his mike hand and looks into the shadowy control booth. He thinks he can see somebody but it's so hard to tell with the spotlight shining straight into his eyes — at least the guy figured out how to switch that on. The producer told Jimmy he had to come in to sort out the blocking for his set. But when Jimmy showed up at the Empire, the only person there to meet him was some jerk-off tech who didn't even know Jimmy was coming. So he told Jimmy to get onstage and they'd work out the marks, get a few things straight for the lighting director whenever that limey fruitcake decided to grace them with his presence.

*Jimmy's used to people being unprofessional, but he expects more from Danny's people. Danny said he had the best in Vegas, the crème de la crème. They were gonna treat Jimmy like family because that's what he was. "Can you believe it's been twenty-five years since you and I got together?" He'd said that more than once since Jimmy got to town, like he was never gonna get over the fact. Danny liked to think he had a soft heart, when really it was just a shriveled piece of meat.*

*Jimmy squints into the light again. Should he say something? He feels like a chump — worse than that, an old chump. This whole show, it's not gonna be easy. When he did his last gig here with Pantero in '69, he was only in it for the cash — L.A. was his future then. Jimmy didn't know he would have a decade's worth of shit to eat. The food back home in Detroit wasn't much better — TV dinners washed down by whatever's handy. Every so often he'd stare at the wall and picture Jimmy Wynn's name on a Vegas marquee. Jimmy wasn't done with Jimmy Wynn. When Danny looked him up at his mom's old place and asked him to do some shows, Jimmy knew it was his moment. No more hiding, not behind Saddlecreek, not even behind Cannon. Past is past. Audiences want it tough now. It's a new era. Jimmy's not gonna be this shivering little nothing pissant anyone can take a shot at. He's not just gonna stand there and bleed. He's got the hide for it now. He's sure about it. Nothing's gonna get to him.*

*Jimmy grips the mike tightly and brings it to his mouth. "Hey." Nothing. "Helllooo. Buddy, you out there?" Nada. Maybe he's just being shy. Jimmy decides to have some fun. "Okay, I got one for ya. This guy's in a hospital bed. The nurse comes over so he puckers his lips and says, 'Gimme a kiss.' She says, 'No way, sir, don't be silly.' He puckers up and says, 'C'mon, just a little kiss.' She says, 'Remember where you are, this is a hospital.' He says, 'Please, just this once.' The nurse says, 'Look, for the last time, I'm not giving you a kiss. I shouldn't even be giving you a hand job.'"*

*Silence. I'm dying up here, he thinks. But he likes how it feels to be on a stage again. He likes it a lot. He gives it another shot. The joke isn't his but he doesn't want to waste an original on an empty room. You never know who's listening.*

*"Maybe you're gonna like this one better. A hunter's out in the woods and he sees this bear. He aims his shotgun and fires. Bang! When the smoke clears, the bear is gone. The guy says, 'Dammit, where'd he go?' Then he feels a tap on the shoulder. He turns around and the bear is standing right there. The bear says, 'Look, buddy. I can either rip your guts out right now or you can drop your pants and bend over.' The hunter thinks about it for a second and decides he doesn't want to die. The next day, he goes out and buys a real expensive high-powered rifle with a scope. He goes out looking for the bear. He lines him up in the scope and takes his shot. Blam! But the bear disappears again. Then the hunter feels a tap on his shoulder. The bear says, 'Okay, pal, you know the drill.' The next day the hunter goes to a military supply store and gets a bazooka. He goes back to the forest and finds the bear again. He lines up his shot and kablooie! The blast is big enough to knock him off his feet. The smoke clears — bear's not there. The hunter turns around and sees the bear leaning against a tree, filing his nails. The bear looks at him and says, 'You're not really out here for the hunting, are ya?'"*

*Jimmy likes hearing his voice all around him. It's so good, he can almost handle the silence that follows. But it's not quiet this time. Someone's out there, slapping their paws together to give Jimmy some respect. Jimmy sees a guy near the back of the hall. It's not the tech — this guy's wearing a suit. Sunglasses, too. Jimmy wishes he had a pair. Mr. Suit walks up the aisle. He calls out. "That's real good. You got a name, funnyman?"*

*Jimmy can't see the guy's face but he smiles in his direction. After all, Mr. Suit could be somebody important, not some Empire schmuck or Danny flunkie. He could be the one who puts his name in lights. "Jimmy Wynn."*

*"Just the man I want to talk to."*

19

I was standing at the passenger side of Rose's red Chevy Caprice when she came out of the house. She held a black bandana in her hand. "You have to wear this."

I imagined my new life as a cattle rustler. "Is he expecting outlaws?"

"What? No. I need to blindfold you."

"Why?"

"I got orders."

I would've weighed my options but I didn't really have any. "Okay."

Rose got into the car and I followed suit. I closed my eyes as she wrapped the bandana around my eyes and tied a knot in the back. She kissed my cheek and said, "That looks good on you, too."

The car rumbled to life with a sound like a bear chewing gravel.

"I hope nobody sees us," she said.

"Do you do this to a lot of young men?"

"Don't be smart. I'm liable to leave you hog-tied in the middle of the desert."

I heard the tick of the indicator and felt the car swerve left. As we picked up speed, the rumble was replaced by something more like a bear with asthma.

"Is the car going to make it?"

"Don't you worry about that."

"What should I worry about?"

She paused before responding, as if trying to figure out how to break it to me gently. "From the way you talked about him yesterday, I know you've got expectations about Jimmy. You hope he's the man he was thirty years ago, some slick Vegas type who's got a handle on everything. But you're too young to understand what time can do." She stopped talking. I listened to the car wheeze. "This is how a friend of mine explained it to me," she continued with a new tenderness in her voice. "Imagine that every person is an object hurtling through the universe, acting independently of all the other bodies. It can travel in only one direction, you can't change it. You can't change the speed, either. You're like a meteor, a piece of rock flying across the heavens. Meteors burn pretty hot to start with because of gases and whatnot. Then when you come into the atmosphere, you get so hot, you start to fall apart. You can't slow down so you break up. The thing you started with gets smaller and smaller as the rest splits away. Your meteor might have started off as a mountain but by the time you come to rest, you're the size of a marble and hard as a diamond." She paused. "That's a useful way of looking at the situation."

We were both quiet for a while. "Without being too specific," I said, "can you tell me what you see? I'm in the dark here."

"Why don't you tell me? Let's make a game out of it."

"Okay . . . the first thing you see is a road."

"Good guess."

"Thanks. And you see some trees."

"What kind?"

"Um . . . Joshua Tree?"

"Nope. Scenic choice, though wrong."

"A yucca?"

"Strictly speaking, that's a shrub. But I'll let you have that."

"And you see some firejacks."

"No, too early."

"I meant to say birds."

"You have to be more specific."

"Bald eagles. Fifty of them. One for every state in the union!"

She laughed. "Right you are! I hadn't noticed. Gosh, I thought they were endangered. But look here. They're flying in formation. Now they're doing figure eights and loop-de-loops. It's amazing. And would you look at that? Now they're flying backwards just a few feet ahead of the car. They're waving at us. Hi, there. Hi." She nudged me with her elbow. "C'mon, be polite."

"Where are they?"

"They're on your right side now."

I turned to my window and waved. "Hi," I said. "Hi, eagles." I knocked on the glass and laughed.

She thumped my knee. "How I wish you could see them, hon. They bring an all-American tear to my eye."

I desperately wanted to look at her. I tried to inhale her but smelled only vinyl, old coffee, and must. "I wish you'd been on my whole trip," I said. "We would've had a good time."

She squeezed my thigh. My worries about my imminent deportation, the end of my career, and laser-sighted rifles felt very far away. We were gonna have a good time with Jimmy.

I heard the indicator again and the car swerved right. Gravel churned underneath the wheels.

"We're nearly there. I'm going to give you his ground rules so listen closely. He's skittish about anything electrical so don't use your tape deck. Plus, daylight hurts his eyes so leave the shades alone. And sometimes his voice doesn't have a lot of strength but don't ask him to speak up. Like I said before, you're coming into this with expectations so watch yourself. Ask your questions clearly and I'm sure Jimmy'll do his best."

The car swerved left again then came to a sudden halt. Rose tugged at my bandana and suddenly it was very bright. I had to shield my eyes as I stepped out of the car. We were in some kind of ghost town. The ground was parched and brown. We'd parked near a cluster of buildings. Each had its own hitching post but not much else besides. The largest building was the most dilapidated — the roof was gone and the front wall looked like it was one stiff gale away from collapse. The outlines of what had been other buildings were marked by crumbling old wood.

But the building to the left was in pretty good shape. Its exterior had been patched up with newer scrap. The windows even had glass in them, though they were covered by something shiny on the inside.

"Where are we?"

"I can't tell you the name, but it was a mining town. Nobody's lived here for seventy years."

"Except for him, I guess."

"He's only here off and on for a while." She pointed at the intact building.

I stood there and thought: so this is where you ended up. It must've been very cold at night.

"Go on in," she said. "I'll be waiting."

I knocked on the door. There was no answer. I knocked again.

"Just go," said Rose. "No need to be polite."

The door didn't open easily. I shoved it and tumbled into the room. When I got my balance back, I shoved it closed again. There was just enough light to see what I was doing. All but the highest parts of the windows were blocked by aluminum foil, cut in large, neat sheets. The space was bare except for a cluster of furniture in the back corner and a tatty red sleeping bag on the floor. Chocolate bar wrappers and empty pop cans littered the place.

Facing away from me were two chairs: one was large and covered in dirty fabric, the other bare and wooden. I could just make out the thorny mess of curly hair poking over and around the back of the upholstered one. It suddenly flopped to one side.

"Somebody here?" The voice was low and raspy.

"Yes, sir? My name is Nathan — Rose told you I was coming?"

"Uh?"

"I'm a reporter, for a magazine?"

He didn't say anything. I stepped tentatively toward the empty chair, my eyes on the hair the whole time. As I reached the side of his chair, I glimpsed his side profile. I saw a man with a patchy beard. He wore dark sunglasses and a ratty suit jacket with no shirt underneath. He was half mad scientist, half homeless maitre d'. Without turning my way he shrieked. "Too close! Too close!"

I grabbed the chair and retreated to a space a few feet behind him.

"Better, that's better. Keep back. Gotta be polite." His voice was nothing like the one I'd heard on the records. He sounded like he'd been alive for a thousand years and guzzling battery acid for nearly as long.

"Can you tell me what your name is?"

"What kind of question is that?" he barked. "My name is James Davis Wynn. Born in the town of none of your goddamned business in the year of our Lord nineteen hunnerd and sevenny-five."

I kept my notepad on my knee and scrawled down what I could understand. I thought: how the hell do I do this? "Did you perform under the name of Jimmy Wynn?"

"Perform?! No performing. Only walking. I walked to Prescott. I walked to Mulholland. I walked to Low Gulch. I walked to Sweeney. I walked to Victorville, Palomas, Dante, Christchurch, Bridgeton, San Alomar. I have passed over every scrap of this desert. I know every inch of dirt." The coot on the bus had told me about desert walkers. I thought: so this is what one's like. His voice rumbled like Rose's Caprice. "I must've covered a thousand miles a day. Forward and back. All over it. The only nourishment I need is the sun. Water for sustenance, for survival. But the sun brings strength, courage, constancy." He trailed off. Then he roared with the force of a Southern evangelist. "Trust in the sun! Do you trust in the sun?"

I wasn't sure if I should answer.

"Well, do ya?!" He was shouting at the far wall.

"Oh . . . I *do* trust in the sun?"

"Good to hear!" He slapped his own knee, raising a cloud of dust. "Trust in the sun and it shall reward you. But you must fear it too. I fear it all the time. It wants too much. Do you hear me? It wants too much."

"Jimmy," I said in a tone I reserved for children and the elderly, "can I ask you some other questions?"

"Fire away!"

"Did you know the president?"

His tone turned stiff and clipped. "I served my country with honour, sir!"

"Do you remember your commander-in-chief?"

"I have served many fine commanders, sir!"

"Do you remember Theodore Ignatius Cannon? Teddy?"

"A great, great man." His voice slipped into a monotone, the pacing irregular. "Great man. A handsome man. His teeth were always very clean. He showed them to me once, from real close up. Every single one of those teeth was his own. Every other president I'd ever met — titanium. Awful stuff. But not Teddy's teeth. He took excellent care of them. He believed they were the source of a man's intelligence. Nothing can stay in a man's head if he doesn't have teeth to hold it in."

"Did you ever meet him?"

"Sure, I did. I remember he was out here not too long ago. I was walking from Oak Creek to Albertsville. I stopped and made a fire. He comes up to me and he says, 'You look tired, Jimmy.' I said, 'But I don't feel tired.' 'You look it.' I would've been mad at him but he had a way of saying things. Then he tells me, 'I like your jokes.' He passes me a cigar and we have a smoke by the fire. We watched the fire all night. Around the fire I could see the eyes of the little firejacks. Every so often one of them would get the courage to take a run and jump over the fire. One great big bounce. The president and I would laugh at that." Jimmy chuckled. "There was no sound like his laughter. Hearing that made you a richer man. I lean over and say, 'Commander, you've got a real swell voice, mind if I borrow it?' He says, 'Let 'er rip.' And I did that, I let 'er rip."

Somehow I didn't believe this was entirely accurate. I tried another tack. "Do you remember a night in Las Vegas when he told you something special?"

"Hmmph. I never been to Las Vegas. Only been here. I don't like Nevada. People are stuffy. I hit the border, I turn around. I like California. I walked all over it. I walked to Prescott. I walked to Mulholland. I walked to Low Gulch. I walked to . . ." He trailed off again.

"Jimmy?"

He was muttering something.

"Jimmy?"

"Hmmph."

"Do you remember Daisy?"

His rumble gave way to an eerie falsetto. *"Daisy, Daisy,"* he sang. *"She of the eyes of blue / My love will be forever true."* His tone turned suspicious. "Do you know that song? It's my song."

"Do you remember Rose and her sisters Bessie and Vera?"

"Hmmph."

"Do you remember Bud?"

He whistled.

"Do you remember making movies?"

"I saw a good one once. These guys, these guys, see, they're in jail and they smoke cigarettes, see, and they're real bad guys. What they do all day is walk back and forth across the prison yard. The prison yard is grey like it is outside. Some of them stay out in the sun because they know, they know what it's for. They get strong because they lift barbells and they trust in the sun. Then the day comes when they grab the guards and take back the whole prison. Blood runs down the stairs. You know that movie?"

"Yes, I remember it." I wasn't lying — his description did seem familiar.

"Good one, right?"

"Right."

He leaned back and jerked his thumb at the door. "They didn't get it. They never do. No taste. No class. Don't respect a professional."

"Jimmy, do you remember being a comedian?"

"Remember? I'm still a comedian. You like knock-knock jokes?"

"Sure, I —"

"Olive," he croaked. "Olive you. Nunya. Nunya business. Ben. Ben dover. Otto. Otto know I can't remember. Major. Major look. Ice cream. Ice cream if you don't let me in. Erma. Erma little teapot, short and stout. Figs. Figs the doorbell it's broken. Nobel. Nobel, that's why I knocked. Toby. Toby or not Toby, that is the question. Robin. Robin is against the law. Irish stew. Irish stew in the name of the law. Lettuce. Lettuce in, it's cold out here!"

He began speaking more quickly. I thought: is he even stopping for breath?

"Water. Water you doin' in my house? Dozen. Dozen anyone live here? Wire. Wire you asking? Kent. Kent you tell, I'm standing right here."

He started to look downright maniacal.

"Ida. Ida opened it myself if I had the key. Oh-say. Oh-say can you see, by the dawn's early light? Mary. Mary Christmas. Leaf. Leaf me alone!" He collapsed into cackles. "Leaf me alone! Leaf me alone!"

"Mr. Wynn, I —"

"Leaf me alone!" he laughed. "Leaf me alone!"

"I just wanted to ask if —"

He stopped laughing. He got up out of his chair and came toward me. I nearly tipped backward in my chair. "Leaf me alone!" He swung his arms like a crazed gorilla. Then I thought: he's doing this for show.

I got to my feet as soon as I could. When I heaved the door open, a stream of light entered the room. He cowered like a vampire. "Too bright! Too bright!" he shrieked. I got outside and dragged the door closed.

Rose was sitting on the hood of the car. She hopped back down to the gravel when she saw me. "Are you all right?" she asked. "It's not his best time of day."

"Will he be better if I come back another time?"

She thought about that. "No."

I couldn't hide how I felt: utterly defeated. All my hopes were dashed. Jimmy was too far gone. I had nothing to show for my efforts except for a mad geezer in a ghost town.

Rose took me in her arms. "I'm sorry, hon."

We drove home in silence. It didn't seem like much of a consolation but she forgot to put the bandana back on my eyes. I saw it on the floor of the back seat. Outside my window, I saw the plaque that said where we'd been: the original site of Old Cardston. What was left of the new one must've been further down the highway.

I didn't see how the "interview" had done me any good. I couldn't tell if anything I had learned was of value. And yet I felt compelled to at least tell David Maher what I had discovered at the end of my quest. Since Winston Sharpe only wanted a Jimmy who could still cough up his big Cannon secret, Maher might be the only person who cared about the sad little ex-meteor Rose had dug up for me.

"So what are you gonna do now?" asked Rose as we drove into Carloff.

"I don't know."

"Should I drop you off at my place? I have to go into the restaurant."

"Whatever."

"Are you gonna be okay?"

"Yeah," I said, trying to sound hopeful. "I need some time, you know, to sort out what to do."

"I understand." She squeezed my thigh.

"It's not so bad for me. I mean, I still have some kind of story. I'm not sure how happy the magazine will be with me. This is not the ending they wanted. I was so sure that he'd be . . . something other than he is."

"I know, hon."

Rose's house came into view.

"I just can't help feeling sad for David."

Rose slammed on the brakes. I smacked my head on the windshield.

"Sad for *who?*"

I was distracted by the pain. "What did you do that for?" I touched my forehead. "Ow." The fingers came back bloody. "I'm bleeding here."

"You should have worn your seatbelt. Now tell me again, you're sad for *who?*" Rose's eyes were real wide.

"I'm sad for David. David Maher. He's Bud, right? I know about him. You don't have to have a conniption about it." I touched my forehead again. "Shit, I'm totally bleeding here."

She leaned forward to look at my head. "How'd you know about David?"

"He told me. He found me in Los Angeles. He asked me to call him if I found Jimmy."

"He told you about Jimmy?"

"Yes," I said, "He did."

She pulled a napkin from her pocket, put it in my hand, and pressed both my hand and the napkin to my head. She was quiet as we drove the rest of the way to her place. When we were outside, she spoke again. "Look, hon. I have to go do some things that cannot wait. Keep pressure on that and wait for me inside the house. Whatever you do, do not call David yet. I'll explain later. This is a real sensitive matter. Family business. Understand?"

"But I —"

"No fussing. Just go inside."

I got out of the car and stood in Rose's driveway. As I watched the Caprice peel away, I felt as bewildered as a firejack.

20

I should have been thinking about all kinds of things but I was distracted by the blood. I applied direct pressure lest it all pour out of my head and leave my brain as parched as the land around me. I traded Rose's napkin for a handful of paper towel and — since I wasn't sure if I was dealing with a cut or a cut and a concussion — a bag of peas from the freezer. I was happy to have my hands busy since I welcomed any distraction from my failure. I thought: Winston Sharpe would not be impressed if he saw you like this. I thought: *no one* would be impressed.

I sat in the kitchen with my throbbing head in my hands, trying to sort through the details. Rose had flipped out when I mentioned David. Even I could tell there was something going on. When I felt well enough to stand, I looked around Rose's place for any evidence. I thought: how will I know if it's evidence? The dirty coffee cups weren't evidence. Scraps of torn-up paper in the garbage bag under the sink might have been evidence. I checked out her address book: it was open to the J page. Did Jimmy have a phone out in Old Cardston? I thought: if he had a cell phone, it would have to be a roaming number. Ha.

There was no entry for Jimmy. I scanned the rest of the page.

The other addresses and phone numbers were mostly attached to names I didn't recognize. The two names I did recognize were rock stars she used to cook for. I noticed that one entry was in the wrong place. Maple Leaf Theatre should have been under M. There was a phone number and an address for Niagara Falls, Ontario. Rose clearly had a thing for Niagara Falls — her story about the permanent rain cloud stayed with me. I wondered if she'd ever honeymooned there. I pictured quarters stacked on the headboard of a vibrating bed. I thought: what did she get me into?

The phone rang. Rose had never told me whether I should be answering her phone. I also didn't know if answering a call for someone else contravened the evil robot's "don't use the phone" rule — I hadn't touched one of the things in days. But how could anyone have tapped this one? No one was supposed to know where I was.

"Yes?"

"Oh, good. You're not asleep. If you have a concussion, you shouldn't fall asleep."

My voice soared up an octave in pitch. "You think I have a *concussion?!*"

"No, hon, I'm teasing. You had the tiniest bump."

"It felt pretty hard to me."

"Take a breath, Nathan."

I took a breath.

"You could try stretching, too."

"I'd lose the rest of my blood if I did that."

"Oh, you'll be fine. Can you come over to the café and give me some help? Everybody else is at the Coyotes game."

"I don't feel so hot."

"I'll borrow you for a few minutes then I'll fix you up properly and get you fed. Then you can sack out in a booth."

I agreed and went to the bathroom to sort myself out. Underneath the bag of peas and the wad of paper towel I found my injury free of fresh blood but red and tender. I attached an adhesive bandage. This one was higher and to the left (my left) of the Dazzle Cuts wound, still a skinny red line high on my cheek. The vinaigrette bruise on my other cheek was still discernible. I thought: would it be weird if I started wearing a goalie mask?

I was relieved that the streets of Carloff were so deserted — the whole place had decamped to Sweeney for the big game. When I got to the Ambrosia, the door was locked. I called out to Rose but didn't see anyone inside. Rose came around the side of the building. "Feeling better?"

"My head still hurts. And I look like I stopped a truck with my face."

She gave me a smile full of consolation. "You look just fine. I like the shirt. Now come with me to the back pantry. There's something too heavy for me and Junior's not here to give me a hand."

I followed her to the back of the restaurant. "I am so, so sorry about this morning," she said over her shoulder. "You must be so disappointed. I should have told you in the restaurant yesterday. But it's all a lot to take in and I wanted you to get a sense of Jimmy like I knew him, not like he is now."

She stopped at an open door on the other side of the building. "It's right in here." Inside the doorway, I saw a few steps leading down to a small space with cinderblock walls and a concrete floor. A single light bulb swung from the ceiling. I climbed down the steps. A set of pails on the floor looked like the heaviest items. The only label I could read said: Avedon Peaches. "Which one did you want?"

"Sorry, hon." She slammed the door shut behind me.

I rushed back, nearly tripping on the stairs. "Rose!" I pounded on the door.

No answer. I looked around and found nothing but cans, containers, and cinderblocks. There was no other way out. I turned and pounded on the door again. "What are you doing?" Nothing. "Let me out!" I thumped it one last time.

I thought: you're fucked. I thought: nice work. I sat down on the first step and put my head back in my hands.

My skull was a boiling cauldron of badness. I thought: oh fuck me, what-what-what, this is it, I'm dead, I'm dead, she trapped me, she trapped me so someone can get me, she's called someone and they're gonna get me, gonna kill me, I'm so screwed, what can I do, oh no, oh shit, aagh I hurt my hand on the goddamn door, that stings, my head still hurts, they're gonna kill me, they're gonna kill me like they killed Annette Newton and Ben Arnold and Nathaniel Fontainebleu, they'll make it look like an accident, maybe they'll drop a pail of peaches on my head, they'll pin me down and smash my head until my brains fall out, jeez, why did I come to California, I could've stayed in Vegas, I could've done all of this in Vegas, I could've done Colin's story about the fucking delegation and been done with it, I had the warnings, I didn't take the warnings, Winston asked me if I was up to the challenge and I said yes sir I'm your man and now I'm gonna die next to cans of corn and a bucket of green olives and two, no three canisters of okra, who eats that much okra? I'm gonna die here with okra.

And this is how I spent the first few hours of my captivity in the Ambrosia.

* * *

I was able to fall asleep and then wake up, which relieved me of one worry — I did not have a concussion. I was pleased to have foiled this part of Rose's plan, presuming she had intended to waylay me with a head injury. Maybe she wanted to make it look like I'd died of natural causes when Junior found me in the storeroom a week from now while grabbing supplies for the lunchtime special.

I didn't want to die there, on a concrete floor surrounded by sundries. Yet I almost preferred death to dishonour. For all this to be over would've been a great relief. What I wanted: to not face Winston Sharpe with my article in tatters, to not be trumped by Colin and Daphne, to not undergo the indignity of deportation, to not explain my American failure to my parents, to not send Jimmy Wynn back into the dustbin of history.

So when I heard the latch on the door, I almost — almost — hoped for my little red dot to be the first thing I saw. But when the door opened, my indifference was replaced by more primal instincts. I would not go out like this, amid canned food. My assailant was lit by the storeroom light bulb. Since I was expecting a black-suited heavy with a gun or Rose with an iron pipe at the ready, I was surprised by who I saw in the dusk outside. He was a tall man with short white hair and a bristly moustache. Like my adversaries back at the Chateau Montpelier, his eyes were concealed by sunglasses, but the lenses were blue, not black. Instead of a black suit, he wore a short-sleeved white shirt and chinos. He had no gun in his hand, only the keys for the door.

I grabbed a can of crushed tomatoes and charged with a battle cry of "Grrnnnahhg!" This time, one of my feet didn't clear the top stair. My target stepped left as I toppled right and landed in the dirt.

"Huh," he said. "That's gonna leave a bruise."

I tried to push myself up and my arms buckled. I rolled on to my side and tried to smash his shin with the tomato can. He jumped beyond my reach.

"Hold on there, pecker."

I swung again.

"Just settle down."

When I swung the third time, the can slipped out of my hand and flew into the darkness. The animal rage subsided, which was just as well considering how much good it did me.

"Are you done now?"

I knew his voice. When he bent down, I saw his face more clearly. I noted the weak chin, the hooded eyes, the hunch in his shoulders.

He helped me to my feet. "Damn," he said. "Did Rose do all this damage? I only told her to keep you in one place. She didn't have to kick your ass." He brushed the dirt from my shirt. "Remind me not to mess with that broad."

I'd swallowed some dirt so I had to cough to clear my throat. "Mr. Wynn?"

He stopped brushing. "Uh-huh. And you're Nathan? I'm presuming she's only got one of you locked up in there. There's nobody else, right?"

I nodded. "I'm happy to meet you." The words felt stupid coming out of my mouth but I was too shocked to say anything else.

"Yeah, yeah. Me, too." He shook his head. "Actually, naw, not at all. I was hoping this could've been avoided. But congratulations, sport, you got me. Now what do you want to do with me?"

I stared back.

"Wow," he said, "she really did a number on you. Did you get enough oxygen in there? Let's go in and eat. You hungry?"

I wasn't, actually — during my captivity, I had eaten three pounds of green olives.

Judy looked very serious as she led us to a booth. I guessed that she didn't approve of keeping me locked in the back storage space, though if she'd really felt strongly about it, she could have let me out. According to the clock in the Ambrosia, it was eight o'clock — I'd been locked away for six hours.

Jimmy Wynn ordered a grilled chicken sandwich straightaway. "Can you go light on the mayo?"

Judy looked at me expectantly but I didn't know what to say.

Jimmy ordered for me. "Get him some quesadillas."

Judy scribbled something on the pad and left us. There was no sign of Rose.

Jimmy took off his sunglasses and fiddled with them over the table. "Good sandwiches here. I can never finish them — I always end up taking half home. No sense in wasting them."

I studied his face. His complexion was lighter than anyone else around — this wasn't Californian skin, at least not anymore. There were deep creases around his eyes and at the sides of his mouth. The hair in his eyebrows and neatly trimmed moustache was a mixture of white and black. The thin layer of stubble on his cheeks indicated he hadn't shaved that day. The blue of his eyes was paler and milkier than I expected. If you showed me this man's picture and asked me what he did for a living, I would say he was the events coordinator at a retirement community. In other words, he was a whole lot more presentable than the Jimmy I met that morning.

The memory of the geezer in Old Cardston made my olive-filled guts roil.

"What in the fuck is going on here?" The question might have come out too loud.

Jimmy came back with a whisper, apparently hoping I'd follow suit. "No reason to get upset here, we're all reasonable folks."

"You could have killed me. Twice. Maybe three times today." I pointed at my latest head injury for emphasis.

Jimmy stuck with his whisper. "That's crazy talk, kid." He was nervous from all the eyes on us. He waved to his fellow patrons. "Go, Coyotes," he said and they went back to their business. From what I could gather, the Coyotes had lost the game. The citizens of Carloff were too busy wallowing to notice my dire straits.

"Now look," Jimmy continued, "I can understand you're upset but it does you no good to get your panties in a bunch. I apologize for the rough ride. I do. Let me get you a beer."

"Water," I said. "I need water first." The pressure in my head began to subside.

He waved Judy over and ordered some drinks. She looked worried I might explode again but I didn't have the energy.

She brought two waters, plus a coffee for Jimmy and a beer for me. I was desperately thirsty from the olives. The water helped, the beer more so. I felt well enough to brave my first official question. "So who was the guy in Old Cardston?"

He looked up from his sunglasses. "Where?"

"The ghost town."

"Right, him. I don't know who Rose got this time."

"You've done all this before? Put some crazy guy out in the desert and say it's you?"

"Only twice. Once for some movie-biz prick, another time for a fed. The problem this time is it was such a rush job. I should've been here to supervise but I had something going on. Rose did what she could. How was the guy?"

The question threw me. "How *was* he?"

"You know, was he convincing? I hate it when they overplay the crazy." Jimmy's voice conveyed his distaste. "Some guys you see on TV or movies, they just jump on the furniture and wave their hands all over the place and holler about receiving radio waves through their shoes and all this crap. They overdo it, right? Then there are the ones who try for creepy, like all that's missing is a wig and a dress from Mom's closet. That's just offensive. I like it when it's right on the edge, like sometimes he's way the hell out there in Nutsville then the next second he's as sane as you or me." He pointed at me with his glasses. "Rose found some guy in Albertsville, said he was a good actor and did his own makeup. So how was he?"

"You'd probably find him too close to the hollering, waving kind."

"Damn." Jimmy shook his head. "How was the bit about the fire?"

"Which part?"

"The dream. With the fire. And the . . . whaddya call 'em? Those rabbit things, the firejacks jumping over the fire."

"I couldn't really follow that part."

Jimmy thumped the table. "I gotta talk to Rose about this joker. He had plenty of time to look at the notes."

Amid my bewilderment, I tried to think of something positive. "He did seem very scared of the sun."

"Ah, I just threw that stuff in there because we needed to keep the room dark so you couldn't get a good look. I was worried Rose would get some Mexican — I don't know who's living out here these days. I wanted to do more with the desert-walker angle but I was afraid of selling it too hard."

"No, it was good." I thought: what am I, a theatre critic? "Getting the guy on the bus to tell me about it helped."

"What guy?"

"On the bus to Carloff. He told me about desert walkers."

"Really? No kidding?" Jimmy seemed genuinely incredulous. "That wasn't me, though I know people around here like to talk about those guys whenever they're not talking about football. Go, Coyotes, right?"

An old man in the next booth turned to us. "Go, Coyotes," he said mournfully.

Jimmy ignored him. "That meeting should've gone a helluva lot smoother. But you must've liked Rose's bit about the meteor."

"That was you, too?"

"The seed of the bit was mine, but she embellished a lot. I was impressed with what she came up with. She should kill with that."

"She almost did." I pointed to my head for emphasis. "Where is she now?"

"She didn't want to be around when I sprung you. She feels awkward. Kidnapping's not really her bag." He smiled. "Maybe assault and battery is more to her liking."

I pointed at the fresh bump. "She only did this one. The rest I got on my own." Jimmy raised his eyebrows.

Judy stopped to check up on us, clearly relieved that we were not about to make another scene. "Your food's coming up in just a minute," she said with a little more brightness than before. For his part, Jimmy seemed almost bashful toward her. He tapped the glasses on the table before giving me his attention again.

"So where are you from?"

"New York."

"You don't sound New York."

"I grew up in Canada."

"Ah! That I hear. You people love that nasal thing. It's 'aboot' the sonority. About, a boot, about, a *boot*." His voice was sing-songy. He smiled widely. "So why'd you go to New York?"

"I wanted to be a writer."

"Can't you write in Canada? I know guys who write in Canada. There was that guy who wrote the book about living with the wolves. That was a good one."

"I thought it would be better to write in New York."

"Everything feels better when you do it in New York. I was seventeen years old when I first went there. I remember eating my first hot dog in Central Park. I was in heaven chewing on lips and assholes. You get that feeling, don't you? Like the rest of the world's around the next block, just waiting to be conquered." His moustache crinkled when he smiled. "Is coming out here the way to conquer it these days?"

"I wanted to interview you."

"That so?"

"I found one of your records and I thought your story was interesting."

He laughed. "Interesting? That the extent of your vocabulary?"

I tried to think of another description. "Darkly compelling."

"Better. Here are the ones I don't like. I don't like tragicomic. It's got to be one of the other — using both just makes you seem wishy-washy. I don't like bittersweet, either — that's even worse. If I hear anything attached to the word 'ironic,' I blow my stack."

He wagged a finger at me. "Darkly compelling's not bad. Keep that."

I duly filed the phrase in my head.

Judy arrived with the food. I hoped Jimmy was buying because the little bit of money I still had was back at Rose's.

We ate in silence. I was too stunned to speak. I hurt all over, though mostly in the forehead and the right shoulder. I still believed this could be my last meal.

Jimmy finished the first half of his sandwich. "Nice," he said. "I'd offer you the other one but I should save it for the trip."

"Trip?"

"We gotta keep moving."

"We?"

Jimmy laughed. "Am I training a parrot here? Look, kid, once we're done fueling up, we're getting somewhere safe. Then I can tell you everything you want to hear." He turned serious again. "You haven't talked to Bud? I mean . . . David. You know."

"No."

"Good. It's a sensitive issue. Now eat up."

Dinner was finished in silence. Then he flagged over Judy and asked for the bill. He paid it and led me out of the Ambrosia. Rose's Caprice was idling outside. Jimmy opened the back door and ushered me in.

Rose reached over the seat and touched my forehead lightly. "I am so, so sorry," she said ruefully. "This has been a real struggle for me, you have to believe me." I turned away from her hand.

Jimmy got in next to her. "He said the meteor bit went real well."

"Did he?" She perked up. "I wasn't sure how that came off. It felt all right as I was saying it."

The Caprice pulled away. We headed in the direction of the highway.

"Where are we going?" I asked.

"Mignola Airfield," said Jimmy. "We're close."

Rose glanced over the seat again. "I really am sorry."

"She says a lot of nice things about you, Motown."

"Motown?" she asked.

"Yeah," said Jimmy. "I wanted to get a nickname for him because Nathan was too square. I was thinking, Nathan, Nathan, Nathan, then I remember Nathan Detroit. From that show, remember? And from Detroit I get Motown."

Rose seemed pleased. "Kinda ironic considering you're from Detroit, too."

Their banter reminded me of some old married couple. I couldn't stand it. "You two don't have to be so fucking casual about all this."

"Hey!" barked Jimmy.

Rose called out over her shoulder. "You okay, hon?"

"No," I said as steadily as I could. "No, I'm not okay. As far as I can tell, I'm getting kidnapped for the second time today. I'm tired of being pushed around and lied to."

"Please settle down," said Rose. "It's all gonna work out."

Jimmy looked over the seat. "You better cut the bitching, kid. By my estimation, whoever was making trouble for you in Los Angeles is about a day away from here. Events are in motion that you can't begin to understand."

I was defiant. "Try me."

Rose turned to him. "Ease up, Jimmy. He's been through a lot."

"Oh, so I'm supposed to feel sorry for the kid? Do you have any friggin' idea how much I'm at risk just by being here? This is not some vacation for me. And I don't exactly appreciate having to drop everything so I can play janitor."

"Don't get mad at me," said Rose. "None of this is my fault. Your situation with Bud couldn't go on forever and you were a fool to think otherwise."

"Things were fine between me and Bud."

Rose cackled. "Fine? You run away every time the poor boy comes calling."

"That's not true!"

"You've got to deal with him."

"It has to be on my terms. I don't know why you crazy Pike broads have so much trouble with that."

"That's rich." Rose muttered the words under her breath.

Jimmy made a "hmmph" sound like the fake Jimmy in Old Cardston. I thought: I wonder if Rose taught that to her actor. He folded his arms over his chest. "It's all a goddamned mess. Again."

"I don't mean to interrupt," I said in a tone that implied I was clearly meaning to interrupt, "but if this kidnapping is going to continue, can we at least get my stuff from your house? I left some things at the motel, too."

"All taken care of," said Rose.

I saw a sign for the Mignola Airfield. There was silence in the car until we got there. The fence was open for us. The length of the runway was lit up. Near a white building was a small jet. Its door opened as the Caprice came near. A man in a pilot's uniform came down the steps to the tarmac. Jimmy got out of the car, slammed the door, and walked toward him. The two men talked while I sat in the Caprice with Rose.

"This must have been one of the stranger days in your young life," she said.

"It's not easy keeping up with Jimmy."

She handed me a knapsack over the seat. "All your stuff's in there. I gave you some more shirts. There's some aspirin, too. I should've done more for that knock on your head. Does it still hurt?" Her guilt somehow enriched her beauty.

"It's all right."

She touched me on the cheek. "I don't want you thinking that I did what I did to trick you."

I made a "hmmph" like Jimmy.

She corrected herself. "I mean, I did some of that stuff to trick you, but not all of it. Not the nice stuff. I really did enjoy meeting you. I hope I can see you again. And I look forward to reading your story."

"You think there's going to be a story?"

"Why else do you think he came here? You're his comeback."

"He's got a funny way of showing it."

Before I could open the door, Rose reached over and took my hand. "Hey," she said. Her eyes were soft again. "Take it easy on him. On yourself, too." She gave my hand a squeeze and let me go. I left the Caprice without another word. I thought: avoid all dames from here on in.

Jimmy was on the top of the stairs, waving me up. "Get a move on, Motown. It's late."

Once I was inside the door, the man in the suit pressed a button and the stairs folded up into the plane. He shook my hand. "Welcome aboard. I'm Chet."

"We're in good hands," said Jimmy. "Chet knows this plane better than he knows the curve of his cock."

Chet had a chuckle at that before leaving us in the passenger cabin. I took a look at the cabin's décor and spotted several pictures of Danny Pantero. Jimmy noticed me notice. "This jalopy belongs to a friend," he said.

"I think I've met your friend. We had dinner. He didn't mention that he lets you borrow his plane."

Jimmy smiled. "We go way back."

Then I saw the notepad that Danielle had stolen from my hotel room on his seat. "Your friend let you borrow that, too?"

"Oh that?" He picked it up and handed it to me. "Your secrets are safe, Motown. I couldn't read a word of it. Someone should teach you how to use a pen."

I heard the plane's engine come to life. Chet announced

through the speakers that we should take our seats. We buckled ourselves in.

"So, where are we going?"

"Let me surprise you."

I fell asleep during takeoff — it had been a long day. When I came to, Jimmy was drinking a bottle of orange juice and leafing through a binder full of coloured pages. On the cover was a picture of showgirls in blue feathers.

"How long have we been in the air?"

Jimmy looked at his watch. "About six hours."

I pressed my nose to the window and peered down. Dawn was breaking. I saw the tops of wispy clouds and water far below.

"Are we over an ocean?"

"Nope. A lake."

"It's a big lake."

"That means we're close to home."

I thought of a place with big lakes that would have been six hours away by air. I hoped it was Minnesota and not . . . "Canada," I said.

"Don't look so disappointed. It's nice there. You should know."

"It's not that. If I leave the States, I can't get back in."

Jimmy waved away my concern. "I can take care of that. There's no other problem with you being in Canada, right? I want to make sure you haven't got any outstanding warrants for some big Canadian crime, like hunting beaver out of season or putting an extra man on the ice." He took a pen out of his pocket and flipped open the binder. "I should write that down. I'm always working on Canadian material. You know, anything to do with beavers, hockey, donuts, syrup, Labrador . . . is Labrador the island or the part that's attached?"

"Attached."

"Great. I had a bit about somebody digging a moat to keep the frogs out."

I thought: he's not really a comic in exile, is he? "You still perform?"

"I'm more of a behind-the-scenes guy. Writing, producing, directing. I'll show you my place — the Maple Leaf Theatre. We do a regular show. *Canad'eh?*"

"What?"

"It's like *Canada* and *eh?* except together. You say it *Canad'eh?* Like a question. It looks a little strange on the poster but it sounds all right when you say it."

"Oh."

"It's a musical tribute to your country."

"Oh."

"We do dinner, too." Jimmy's smile prepped me for a joke. "Michelin just gave us our third star. They liked us so much, they threw in a free pair of winter tires."

Chet's voice came on the PA. "We'll be landing in fifteen minutes, Mr. Howe."

"Mr. Howe?" I asked.

Jimmy chuckled. "My Canadian name. Everybody should have one. Of course you have one already. Grant — is that Irish?"

"Scottish."

"Aye," said Jimmy. "Aye."

He closed the binder and put it on his lap. "Before we touch down, we should hammer out some details about our little contra-taw."

"Our what?"

"Contra-taw. It's a French word. You should know it."

"You mean *contretemps*."

"Whatever. We just gotta talk about some conditions." He held up a single finger. "The reason I've taken you this far is Bud knows you're looking for me and probably has a good idea that you've found me. I ask you respect my wishes and not contact him until I say so." He held up another finger to mark the second condition. "It's better that nobody knows where we are. I ask that you don't contact anyone else." He held up a third finger. "In return for your discretion, I will help you with your article." He held up a fourth. "Because it's my life, I get last say in what goes in and what stays out. That's only fair."

"How is that fair? I —"

He silenced me with his thumb. "Five, in return for your co-operation, I will take you wherever you need to go. According to Rose, you've got no money and no way home. The only guy looking out for you right now is me." He reached across the aisle and patted my knee with his five fingers. "Let's make something good out of this screwjob, okay?"

I thought: don't trust him, he's making nice. I thought: what would Winston Sharpe do? Now that I had a story again, I didn't want to jeopardize it. Jimmy Wynn could hold onto the ball for now. Besides, I could make all the assurances he wanted, then turn around and write what I liked.

"Fine. But you've got to tell me everything I want to know."

"I am all yours."

"About Cannon and Delrocco and Saddlecreek — everything."

"I'm an open book."

I didn't believe him.

We arrived fifteen minutes later on another small rural airfield. After coming down the stairs, Jimmy led me to his car. We were not greeted by officials of any kind. "What about Canada Customs?"

"We've got private clearance. Danny comes up here every few months to play the casino. He gets better service than the Queen of England."

Jimmy drove a black Excelsior sedan — fancy, but not in the greatest shape. When I got in the passenger side, I pulled my recorder out of the satchel, put in a fresh tape, and started rolling.

Jimmy looked at me with some surprise. "You want to do this now?"

"I've been waiting long enough."

He chuckled. "I wonder if I remember how to do one of these."

"Just answer the questions."

Jimmy started the car and pulled out of the lot.

I thought: here goes. "Is Jimmy Wynn your real name?"

"I wanted to ask one more thing about the guy yesterday. How was his closer? The last thing he said?"

"It was gibberish."

"Couldn't you tell what he was saying?"

"Not really. He was mostly spewing crappy knock-knock jokes."

Jimmy liked to gesticulate as he talked, which meant he didn't spend a lot of time with his hands on the wheel. Luckily, the highway was quiet.

"I didn't know if the bit was going to work," he said. "I was trying to picture this guy who used to be a comic, except he goes nuts from too much sun. But even though he's nuts, he's still got a comic's instincts, right? So what kind of jokes does a nutbar tell? First, I thought, all set-up, no punchline. Like, two nuns and a pack mule walk into a bar where an Englishman and a Scotsman and an Irish fruitcake are drinking and then an astronaut comes out of the john and he says . . . you know where I'm going. Then I thought, too complicated. So what's the lowest form of comedy?"

"Political satire."

"Most people say puns, but no, something else."

"I don't know."

"Knock-knock jokes. No one ever laughs at 'em."

I thought: he put an awful lot of thought into this. "I see."

"Now what was your question about?"

"Your name."

"James Davis Wynn, Esquire."

"And how old are you?"

"Sixty-three. But my hair stylist swears I don't look a day over seventy."

"And when did you first meet President Cannon?"

He laughed. "Right to the Teddy questions, huh? I'm gonna put out, kid, but you gotta romance me a little. Take me out for dinner and dancing. We're not even off the highway yet. I want to get cleaned up. You don't smell too sweet either. That shirt makes you look like a migrant worker."

"Rose lent it to me." A note of hurt was in my voice.

"That explains it."

I felt suddenly chivalrous. "What's that supposed to mean?"

"Nothing, nothing. The lady is allowed to have a personal life. Who am I to disapprove?"

"What right do you have to say that? You took advantage of her when she was a minor."

"She was very mature for her age. In some parts of the country, she'd already be married off to a cousin long before I came around. Look, I don't want to talk about those crazy Pikes. I don't want the grief. I didn't even ask Rose for any piece of the Daisy record when she told me some company was putting out a CD. I don't even own it. I pawned off my last copy fifteen years ago. Guy gave me fifty cents for it. That's what I got for a year's aggravation.

I couldn't help myself from record-geeking him. "You should've held onto it. You could've gotten more. An original copy's worth five hundred dollars now."

The news was a little much for Jimmy. He shook his head. "That's the craziest thing I've ever heard. No offence to your good lady Rose but that record is a piece of shit. What are mine worth?"

"Which ones?"

"*Square Peg.*"

"Maybe fifteen."

He looked disappointed. "And *Who Does This Guy?*"

"I don't know. Maybe two. Or three. I couldn't find it."

"Oh," he said, suddenly thoughtful. "I worked real hard on that one. You should hear it some time."

The airfield must've been only a few miles from the Falls because we were already entering the periphery of the town, judging by the increasing density of houses, gas stations, and strip malls. As I'd told Rose, I hadn't been to Niagara Falls since a school trip when I was eleven. I was surprised that the edge of the Falls was curved — I expected the water to fall over a straight edge, like milk off the edge of a table. The Falls looked more like a toilet bowl stuck in the volatile early moments of a flush. I tried saying so to my classmates but I got tongue-tied and botched the joke.

We turned right before reaching the Falls and went north up the slope and through the main tourist drag. I saw a smattering of theme restaurants, indoor amusement parks, video arcades, haunted houses, and wax museums. At the very top of the hill was the new casino and the new skyrise hotels Rose had mentioned, the ones that left the Falls under a permanent rain cloud. I thought: Rose must know this place well. I didn't ask Jimmy how often she visited.

The Maple Leaf Theatre was on a less crowded stretch of road between the cheeseball tourism epicentre and the casino. The theatre was built to resemble an oversized log cabin. A giant fibre-glass beaver in a Mountie uniform stood at the door. A huge

Canadian flag flitted in the breeze. A sign on the flagpole read: TOUR GROUPS WELCOME, EH?

Jimmy stopped in front of the hotel across the street. "I booked you a room," he said. "Go get some rest and we'll meet in a couple of hours."

The woman at the front desk seemed authentically pleased to see me. We spoke to each other in questions — I saw no point in suppressing my accent. As Canadians, we knew how to relate to one another in a courteous and efficient fashion. She gave me a room on the ninth floor. Outside my window I could see the first tour buses arriving in the grey patch of rain at the Falls. I fell asleep in my clothes again.

My conversation with Jimmy Wynn resumed at noon in a pancake house. He wore a dark blue blazer and the same piano-key tie I'd seen on Von. I thought: was there a sale on? Jimmy was already tucking into an omelette when I arrived.

"There," he said between mouthfuls, "you look better. The Quasimodo vibe was getting to me."

I ordered coffee and banana pancakes and set the tape rolling again.

"When did you meet President Cannon?"

He laughed again. "You're just chomping at the bit, aren't you? I have lots to say about the president, believe me. We'll get around to it."

"So what do you want to talk about now?"

"I've got a Vegas story for you. A good one. It's about how I got past Teddy's doorman. You know, Sinatra. He was Teddy's lieutenant in our circles. This is late '61. This was still in the early days of the routine, when it was part of my show with Danny. I heard back from Izzy that Frankie had some 'concerns' about the act. Naturally, he hadn't even seen it, only heard about it from his flunkies. Luckily for me, Izzy was happy to tell Frank, 'Look, the act's completely respectful toward the president — you've got nothing to worry about. Plus, he's filling the room every night.' Frank's still got his so-called concerns. This is a big deal — if Sinatra didn't like your act, you didn't work. If he didn't like you personally, it could be real serious. Some singer refused to stop doing a song that Frank found a little too risqué for his gentle Catholic sensibilities, you know? Cops found this guy in a ditch with his tongue flopping through his neck. When some poor bastard turned up like that, we'd say he got a ring-a-ding-ding."

I thought: is he really telling me that . . . "Frank Sinatra cut another singer's throat?"

"Well, that's what he wanted you to believe, right? I always thought it was big talk. Everything to do with Vegas is ninety-nine per cent fancy lights and horseshit. But Frankie could still complicate your life. So he comes into the Sands one night. He sits close to the front so he knows I can see him. I'm sweating bullets but Izzy and I had a plan worked out for this particular eventuality. I come out there and go straight into it. I make it sound like I'm doing an official address to the whole community. So I say . . ."

Jimmy slipped into the Cannon voice. The technique was rusty but he quickly picked up the flow.

". . . I say, 'I extend my thanks to everyone who has graced us with their presence tonight — ladies and gentlemen of the press, local dignitaries, leaders of industry, the entertainment community of the great city of Las Vegas, which is not only the fastest growing city in the union but the, ah, loosest.' I can tell the crowd's edgy about Frank, waiting for a sign from the big man. I keep going, 'Connie and I very much appreciate the time you have taken out of your busy lives to join us here tonight. I'm sure there are many other demands on your time. Jack Hunter's doing two sold-out sets at the Dunes. Connie and I were hoping to make it over there once we finish up here. She was, ah, rather insistent about it. I only wish that she had made this request a little earlier. If you, ah, have any tickets that you are not using, please pass them on to one of my Secret Service men. They're posing as your waiters tonight. That's, uh, something I should not have mentioned. What's that? Oh yes. The boys want me to tell you that tips are appreciated.'"

"That's pretty funny." And I wasn't just saying that to blow smoke up his ass.

"So the room's warming up but around Frank's table, it's still a deep freeze. I start this spiel about the value of entertainers in America. I say that I've got a special announcement. I say, 'I would like to announce the creation of the Department of Cultural Directives and Applause Facilitation. Its objective will be to make sure the nation's entertainment industry has everything it needs to thrive — encouragement, promotion, highballs. It is my great honour to announce the name of the first secretary of the department. Please extend my warmest regards to Secretary Frank Sinatra.' We had a medal and a certificate ready for him. Now, Frank loved nothing more than getting a blow job onstage. Afterward, he pats me on the back and he says, 'Hey, punk, you're all right. I'm gonna talk to Teddy.' We were pals after that."

"And you were on your way to the White House."

Jimmy Wynn shook an egg-covered fork at me. "You bet."

The courteous Canadian waitress delivered my coffee and pancakes. I poured out the syrup and ventured forth.

"When did you first see the president?"

"In person, not for a while. On TV, that would've been '59. I didn't pay any attention to politics. I was a showbiz kid. Entertainers were the people I watched. When I was starting out, I was the worst busboy Eddie Prefontaine ever had. As soon as I got out of sight of the floor manager, I'd sneak into a seat and watch the show. I'd come back two hours later with a few dirty glasses in my hands and tell him, 'Slow night tonight, huh?' When there was somebody great onstage, not even an atom bomb could distract me."

"Is that why you were so good at impressions, this ability to focus?"

"You gotta pay attention to how somebody moves and how somebody talks but that's the easy part. You gotta get the aura, too. Do you know what I'm saying? A broad told me about it. It means the colours around something. Psychics see them around people — the different colours mean different things. If you're feeling down, you get dark. If you're happy, you're bright." Jimmy's manner became more uncertain. "It's more complicated than that, you know? I'm not explaining it too well. It just helped to think about him not as someone to be copied, more like a space I could get into. The aura thing was a way of getting a handle on what I wanted." He fidgeted with his hands. "When you write all this down, don't make me sound a nutjob who keeps tin foil under his hat. All this talk feels way too much like seeing my shrink."

I thought: is this a bit or does he mean it for real? So I asked him. "You see a shrink?"

He stared into his hands. "Yeah . . . sure. It's been a big help, the last couple years. I had issues, right?" He laughed. "Great big issues. A swimsuit issue." He trailed off as he tried to spin off the "issue" thing into another joke. But he gave up on the riff. "It's still early to be getting into this. Let's have a break. Finish your pancakes and I'll show you the Maple Leaf. Monday's usually my night off but we had a request from tour groups, so what the hey. Show will go on."

Jimmy told me that he had helped design the thing. He had spent a few years out west working on amusement-park stage shows in Alberta and British Columbia. Then a contact of his (they all knew him as Chester Howe) approached him about running a Canadian musical theatre to take advantage of the American tourist trade. The Maple Leaf was his pride and joy, even if the logs in his log cabin were made of fibreglass. Inside, the main hall space was more authentically rustic, with sawdust on the floor, some homey-looking gas fireplaces that never stopped running, and wooden tables and chairs arranged in two long lines facing the stage. On the walls, paintings of rustic landscapes were hung alongside cartoonish illustrations of woodland creatures dressed in Canadian-appropriate garb — a fisherman's yellow slicks, a lumberjack's plaid shirt, a miner's headlamp, a trapper's fur hat, a Habs jersey. The room smelled of cedar and rotisserie chicken.

When we walked in, there was a goateed man in track pants doing leg stretches on the stage. Another, much larger man sat on a piano bench with a newspaper section spread over the keys.

Jimmy tapped the side of his nose and whispered, "Canadian name only."

"Hey, guys," said Jimmy.

"Hi, Chester," said the piano player.

Jimmy pointed at me. "Guys, this is Dave. He's a reporter from New York. He's doing a story on me. He's gonna hang back and see how we do things, get a feel for the show. Dave, meet Barry and Sal."

Barry was the man in the track pants. He looked at me with avid curiosity. "From New York?"

"Yeah."

"I work a lot off-Broadway."

"Oh," I said.

"Not very far off-Broadway, though."

"Sal and Barry are trying out a new song I wrote for the show," said Jimmy. "I don't think it's ready for tonight but we're getting close, right?" He walked over to the piano and leafed through some sheet music. "You'd think that if I wrote the damn song, I'd know all the words."

"You write music?"

"I get by. I mostly handle what we call the libretto. Sal does most of the rest." He tapped Sal on the shoulder. "Whenever you're ready, guys."

Barry stood up on the stage. He held the page of lyrics in one hand and prepared to gesticulate with the other. Sal established a jaunty tempo on the piano.

Jimmy whispered to me. "Barry's missing his costume but you'll get the idea."

Barry's voice boomed through the empty theatre. His tone conveyed a heavy heart.

> *Some folks find me rather alarming*
> *My appearance fills them with dread*
> *Rest assured I am perfectly harmless*
> *As long as I've been recently fed*
>
> *My teeth and my claws might give you pause*
> *But I don't want you to cower or cry*
> *If I seem a little gruff, then please keep in mind*
> *It's no fun to wear a fur coat in July*
>
> *If you see me next to the highway*
> *Won't you spare a few moments for me?*
> *I'll pose for pictures and play with your cubs*
> *Bear hugs are my specialty*
>
> *Whoah-oah-oah*
> *Who loves the grumpy grizzly?*
> *Whoah-oah-oah*
> *I need someone to help fill my den*
> *Whoah-oah-oah*
> *Who loves the grumpy grizzly?*
> *Whoah-oah-oah*
> *I won't maul you if you'll be my friend*

Jimmy waved the men to a stop. "How's that?"

"Good," said Barry, after seriously considering the question. "I'll feel the character more when I'm wearing the costume."

Jimmy looked at me. "How about you?"

"Uh," I stammered. I too thought carefully about my position. "I'd love to see it in the context of the show."

"Context?" Jimmy looked flustered. "It's a bear song. It doesn't need a context. It's good anywhere. You can never go wrong with singing animals. In my career, I've done songs for singing dogs, singing cats, singing lions, singing giraffes, singing whales, singing wallabies — you name it. In this show, we've already got a singing beaver, a singing salmon, and a chorus of moose. Mooses?"

"Moose," said Sal.

"If I know anything about family entertainment," said Jimmy, "it's that you can never have too many singing animals."

Barry nodded sagely. Sal had already gone back to his newspaper.

"On the other hand," said Jimmy, "sometimes I wish I never had to know anything about themed family entertainment."

Jimmy and I went to his office while Barry and Sal rehearsed "The Winter's No Wonderland Without You" — what Jimmy called "the big Eskimo number."

We got to talking again. I was having so much trouble keeping him on topic that I thought I'd ease into the Cannon stuff this time.

"So what was your life like after the first record came out?"

He reclined back in his chair and folded his arms over his chest. "The only trouble with good times," he said, "is they move too fast. It was like a thousand miles an hour. City after city, night after night, then back to Vegas, then more TV, more radio. Teddy's a twenty-four-hour occupation. It's confusing for me. Other people, too — they start asking me what I think about world events, like I know about Africa or tax cuts. I wanted Teddy to give me some notes, you know, so I could make sure I had all the policies straight."

"When did you meet Teddy?"

"From across a crowded room our eyes met. It was love at first sight. Ain't that how it usually starts? He knew all about me already — I was flying into Washington just to use his tailor. This must've been in January or February of '62. Sinatra gave me the okay and I was doing a set in a suite up in the Flamingo."

I thought: bingo. "And this was the Nevada Delegation."

He gave me a look of surprise. "Huh. So much for the code of silence. Am I the only sucker who still believes in those? But if you wanna know, that name came later. All I know is it was a private party and I was expected to perform for the guests."

"And this was for the Delroccos?"

Jimmy turned taciturn. "I can't say."

"Do you mean you don't know?"

"No," Jimmy said slowly, "I mean I can't say."

"Are you saying you won't tell me about the Delroccos?" I didn't keep the frustration out of my voice.

"I prize discretion. Discretion is why I'm still here."

"You think you're alive because you never talked about the Delroccos?"

"No, kid, I'm alive because I'm smart. I kept my head down and kept moving. I'd advise you to do the same."

I thought: you said you'd give me everything.

He must've read it in my eyes. "Look, I know we're gonna get into all kinds of shit here. I'm gonna give you what I'm gonna give you and that's all I can do. Take it easy and enjoy the ride. I'm not such bad company, am I?"

I thought: he was polite enough to pick up the tab at the pancake house. I thought: and it's a nice hotel. I thought: and if I walk away from this right now, I'm so utterly screwed, I can hardly imagine how bad it'll be.

I nodded. "So what can you tell me about this private party for guests at the Flamingo?"

Jimmy brightened up again. "They got a little stage set up in the suite. This is basically the top floor of the hotel. Girls and cigars everywhere — just like you'd imagine it. There's even a statue of a little boy who pisses vodka. Just before I go on, Teddy comes in. The man knew how to enter a room. He had everyone in the place quivering like schoolgirls. And there's a lot of heavy-hitters in there — Frank, Jack, the Wald brothers, Chi Chi Montez. And I think, what am I doing here? These people will tear me to pieces when they see what I do to the guest of honour. All of a sudden, I'm on. The microphone feels like a limp dick in my hand. I'm ready to pass out. Then I ease into it. I stick to the softer stuff — the motorcade, the African diplomat routine, nothing about his kids. For the first few minutes, you can feel the chill, like with Sinatra. Everyone's waiting to see what Teddy does. But in no time, I've got him smiling, then chuckling, then big laughs. The motorcade one killed him. When I did that punchline about Washington drivers, he nearly hit the floor. God, it was a beautiful night. Afterwards, he comes and shakes my hand. He says, 'I think your show is tremendous.' That was his word: tremendous."

"Did you talk with him more at the party?"

"Everybody's fighting for his attention. I took off. It was the perfect night and I didn't want to ruin it by doing something stupid in front of all these big shots. Besides, I wasn't into the party scene. I didn't get a taste for it until later."

"Until California."

"I really, really don't want to talk about California."

Jimmy checked his watch and decided he needed a break. He left me in his office to stew. I wasn't sure how to steer the interview to where I wanted it to go. I wanted to know whatever it was that sent him running. I needed to know what sent Jimmy Wynn from the Sands to San Lupe to the Maple Leaf Theatre. I needed more than a geezer's stories about the good old days. I needed the very bad days.

When he came back, he brought donuts. That mollified me for

a few minutes. I picked out a Boston cream. Jimmy took a sour cream glazed.

"You got a favourite kind of donut? You can tell a lot about a guy from that. A Canadian guy, I mean."

"I don't eat donuts."

"But you're eating one now."

"Yeah, but I don't usually."

Then I remembered Danny Pantero asking me about my taste in women before sending Danielle to mess with my head and my loins. I worried that Jimmy would do something sneaky involving a box of Boston cream.

"I don't want to talk about donuts," I told him. "I want to get back to you meeting President Cannon. You saw him at the White House on . . ." I paused to flip through the notebook that I'd recovered from Danielle. ". . . November 18, 1962."

"That sounds about right."

"What did you discuss?"

"It was a social call."

"Which means?"

"We probably talked about my act. He had suggestions. He'd say things like, 'This windbag Congressman Peters is on my case. Maybe you could do a bit where I show him up.' Or else there'd be something about Connie, some anecdote that we would hash out. Maybe she bought a real expensive hat."

"You're telling me the president gave you *material?*"

"Not whole jokes. Nothing like that. It'd be like 'All people get is the negatives about the African situation — you can help them see the lighter side, Jimmy.' I was the lighter side."

"Was this the only time you discussed your act with the president?"

"There were a few other times. He called me sometimes."

"Just to talk about comedy."

"Yeah, usually."

"There were other things you talked about?"

He took a bite of his donut and shrugged.

"What were the other things, Jimmy?"

He wiped the crumbs from his lips with the back of his hand before speaking. "I want to get something straight here. If I give you certain pieces of information, I reserve the right to take them back. I need to know if I can trust you. What am I to you, anyway? Am I just some guy you're writing about? Like if you were going to write about some new movie star or a politician, it'd be the same deal."

I tried to contain myself. "No," I said. "That's not it."

"Well, then what?"

"You're obviously not just some guy." I kept my voice steady. "If you were just some guy, I wouldn't be scared to pick up a phone. I wouldn't be looking for snipers on every rooftop in case there really was some secret Cannon conspiracy squad after me. And I wouldn't be back in Canada with, like, twelve American dollars in my pocket." I let the words hang in the air before adding an emphatic "You know?"

"Jeez," said Jimmy. "You're in a real pickle, Motown."

"Yeah."

"I guess I am, too."

We sat there for a while in silence.

"It's getting close to showtime. We'll talk more afterward. We'll sort through this mess, make sure we're both taken care of, right?"

There was no chance in hell this was gonna work out.

Before he led me out of the office, he paused with his hand on the doorknob and turned to me. When he spoke, his voice was hesitant. "You don't know how careful I've had to be. The fact that you're here means it's starting all over again, all this shit I thought was over." He shrugged again. "But whatcha gonna do, right? Let's have a little fun while we're here. Do you want to stay for the show?"

As a matter of fact, I did.

22

Is there anything in the world lonelier than a table for one . . . in a dinner theatre . . . on a Monday? And I didn't even get a table for one. Since spectators at the Maple Leaf Theatre were arranged along two long banquet tables facing the stage, I sat on the furthest seat on the right side, separated from the nearest person by three seats. The audience was of a decent size for a Monday night. I counted a mixed group of French Canadians and a large contingent of pink-skinned women with broad Midwestern accents.

The servers talked more like me. They were all dressed in Mountie uniforms. The one who led me to my section called me Dave. I tried to think up a life for Dave but discovered my imaginative powers were at low ebb. Instead, I went to the buffet table and filled a plate with Canadian food. Inspired by some of my company that evening, I went for a Quebec theme: a hefty slice of tortière and two scoops of poutine. For a vegetable I had iceberg lettuce with Thousand Island dressing. I didn't eat like this very often. For dessert, I had a few spoonfuls of the chocolate mousse. Or chocolate moose. I'm not sure what a dairy dessert with antlers should be called.

As I ate, I leafed through a collection of press clippings about the theatre and *Canad'eh?*. "A great time!" said the *Niagara Reader*. "A laugh-a-minute tribute to our neighbors to the north!" declared the *Buffalo Ledger*. "See these hilarious hosers!" implored the *Rochester Telegram*. "The Great White North has never been greater!!" screamed the *North Tonawanda Buy and Sell* as it grabbed you by the lapels and pulled you so close, you felt the spray of its saliva.

If this had been any other night, I would have dreaded the show. It promised to be a parade of the signifiers that had always embarrassed me about my homeland. I hated that this was how the rest of the world saw my people: as singing lumberjacks, drunken fishermen, and redheads with pigtails. I despised these emblems so much, I tried to exile myself in another country before I'd even left this one.

But hate used up energy I didn't have. I was more curious to see what Jimmy Wynn would make of all this Canadiana I resented. But he didn't feel the same way about it. If I were to add my own blurb to the list, I (or rather, Dave) would have used a quintessential Canadian expression: pretty good. Catering to the sensibilities of both the Yankee tourists and the locals, Jimmy struck the right balance between reveling in the stereotypes and ridiculing the clichés for what they were. After an exuberant opening dance number, a young beaver named Gordie introduces himself to the audience. He ponders whether to leave his family and try his luck in the big pond to the south. "Will they think I'm worth a dam?" he croons. His Canadian friends (both beaver and otherwise) try to convince him his home has a lot to offer, performing songs and skits about the greatness of the nation. Of the many singing animals, my favourite was the salmon, played by a heart-faced young blonde with heaving gills — her cute jokes about spawning elicited gales of giggles from the Midwestern ladies. The lyrics were just as good in the Eskimo ballad, which ended with the refrain: "Please don't call us

Eskimos any more — you don't want to get into it with an Inuit."

Jimmy never did have a very good handle on the ethnic stuff. The audience still lapped it up when a girl in the cast strode across the stage wearing moccasins and a satin sash that said MISS FIRST NATIONS 1998. The actress looked Thai or Malaysian rather than native — not that there was any way to redeem the bit. I was just happy Jimmy didn't include any African jokes.

*Canad'eh?*'s only other serious flaw was Barry. He must've been hungry to get into Chester Howe's newspaper profile because he played the whole show straight at me. That night, I learned I don't like it when a Mountie sings me love songs.

Jimmy was here and there throughout the night, doing a little bit of everything in the Maple Leaf: leading customers to their seats, removing empty trays from the buffet table, conferring with the technical team, delivering drinks to Sal and his band of three bored-looking men in red berets. I caught him mouthing the words to the songs and the skits.

At the end of the show, he appeared at my end of the table. He was smiling but his eyes were teary.

"What's the matter?" I asked.

"Could be my last night. The clock's running. I wish Bud had been able to see it. It's not Carnegie Hall but it's a good little show. All original." He wiped his eyes roughly with his hand.

"I liked it."

"Ah, you don't have to say that." He had a bashful look that knocked half a century off his age. He patted me on the shoulder. "I'm gonna wrap up here. Then we'll go talk."

Fifteen minutes later, he found me again. We left the Maple Leaf and got into his Excelsior, but we only drove for a few blocks. Jimmy took me to a sports bar on the main tourist drag. The light inside was green and blue from all the neon beer signs blazing in the windows. All but one of the sixteen televisions featured a snooker tournament. The last was a weather channel.

Jimmy picked the table in front of it.

"I met Steve DaVinci in a place like this," I said.

"Oh yeah? How is Steve, anyway?"

"Good. He's a karaoke king."

Jimmy looked disgusted. "Karaoke is like a cancer. It was hard enough for a musician to make a living before that Jap shit came in. Steve oughta be ashamed of himself."

"He said he was the first one to call you the comedy com-mander-in-chief."

"Ah, that guy's got bullshit coming out his ears."

I decided to leave the topic of Steve DaVinci. A waitress came round. Jimmy ordered a gin and tonic. I asked for a Heineken.

"Vegas." Jimmy let the word sit in mid-air. "If the desert ever took it back, there'd be no one worth saving."

"Not even Danny?"

"Danny's different. We met in New York. He's Queens all the way. Loyal. Sure, he could be a glory hound when it came to who gets to headline but he'd lie down in front of a train if I asked him to."

"Did you ever ask him to?"

Jimmy chuckled. "There were times I should've."

"I wished I'd been able to see your show together."

"We did all right. Feels like a real long time ago."

We watched the weather until the drinks arrived.

"It's too bad you and Danny didn't do a movie."

"We were more of a live thing."

"I watched *Born Wild* the other night. I liked it."

"What's that?"

"You know, the movie you wrote for Don Kirby, about the band."

"I can't remember it. I was not in the best shape when I wrote those scripts. I'd load up on Mexican reds and write three in a weekend." He sipped his drink. "What happened in that one?"

I told him about the band and the orgies and the albino revolution.

"Jeez. I got pretty far out there sometimes. Did you see that movie they made about me a couple of years ago?"

"Yeah, I did."

"I wish I could've sued them. They really blew it. Me, I would've used the chance to do the real story about what happened in New Orleans. I had it mapped out. I was gonna play a Secret Service guy who conducts an independent investigation and busts the whole thing wide open. I worked like crazy on that thing. Then some things happened. I thought I was being watched. I got freaked out so I burned everything I'd written. Then I started all over again. Worked even harder. I burned that, too. I was so arrogant about it, you know, believing I had figured it all out." He took a sip of his gin and tonic. "I got stuck on the idea that I could fix things, for everybody."

"Is this because of what Cannon told you?"

"The reasons for this or that happening, they get hazy. You think you get something and it turns out you don't."

"I don't understand."

"Nah," he said wearily. "I don't suppose you could."

We watched some more weather. There was rain in Boston.

The conversation had run aground so I tried flattery again. "I really do love that Daisy record."

"So you said."

"I was wondering — did you name the band after Katie Perry's character on that TV show?"

Jimmy's face went tight. "I know I said everything was fair game but I'd rather not talk about her."

"We don't have to. I was curious."

"I was stupid doing that. Seemed like a red flag right around the time I needed to keep a low profile. I suppose more people might have picked up on it if the record had sold more than six copies."

"It's a nice little tribute to her."

"You're not here to talk about Katie, Motown. Katie's name doesn't sell magazines, it hasn't for a long time."

"No, you're right."

"What sells your magazine is Teddy."

"I can't imagine what it was like for you to lose him. Like, it must've been . . . huge." I thought: very profound, Nathan.

"Hmmph." Jimmy finished his drink. His mood continued to darken. "I had a look at your magazine. You know that guy who thinks he knows all that shit about New Orleans?"

I assumed he meant Colin. "Yeah, I know him."

"Smug prick thinks he knows all the angles. I was just like him. Right after it happened. Right after it all came apart. I was holed up in Los Angeles with no distractions. No Teddy, no gigs, no . . . no Katie. So I read all the papers. I start working it out. I talk to people like me, people who know things. Each of us felt like we had a tiny fragment and if we somehow got a look at all of the other fragments, we'd understand the big picture. I tracked down all kinds of people. We had a whole network. You probably know some of their names: Nathaniel Fontainebleu, Ben Arnold. They had pieces, too."

I was stunned to hear he knew these people, these witnesses to history. "They all died," I said. "They were killed because of what they knew."

He pointed a finger at me. "That's what I used to think. I used to think, 'They all died and someone's coming for me too.' It was just a matter of time for ol' Jimmy Wynn. I got so jumpy, I decided to get rid of him before somebody else did. Except what I didn't notice is they didn't *all* die. That's what took me so long to get straight. Let me give you a few more names. Fred Danilo. Troy Halberstrom. Bessie Manilow. You know these people?"

"Nope."

"They *didn't* die. Do you get it?"

Jimmy paused to order another round, leaving me flustered.

I squinted and pursed my lips. "I'm not sure I understand."

"Like me, they got to keep their pieces." Jimmy popped a piece of ice into his mouth with his fingers. "The point is, it's no good to look for some big conspiracy, to connect all these things. There is no pattern, Motown. There are suggestions of a pattern but no pattern. That's how they like to run things."

"What things?"

"Cannon. And everything after. It's like this song that you hear in little pieces. Maybe a few notes of the melody here or a few lyrics there. You think you can put the rest of it together in your head but you can't. You've only got these fragments that don't fit in the puzzle. So you try to get more pieces."

"I'm sorry, Jimmy but I —"

"When people die, you want there to be a reason for them to die. You want them to be part of a system." Jimmy put down his glass and pointed at me. "You keep them in a song. It sounds sweet. But then you make the mistake of listening too closely and you notice the pieces are all wrong. You think, 'This is all a god-damn mess, I didn't do anything right.'"

"Uh-huh." He was sounding more and more like the Saddle-creek I'd heard on the FBI recordings.

The waitress arrived with the drinks.

"Thanks, dearie," said Jimmy. He glanced at me long enough to sense my turmoil then turned back to her. "You better bring some scotch, too."

When the drinks came, Jimmy Wynn told me that he was a recovering addict. "I was sober for three whole years once. Then one night I decided I needed a drink."

"When was that?"

He smirked. "Tonight."

"Why stop now?"

"The show's over. It was a good run. A great run. But now you and I gotta pull up stakes and move on, say goodbye to Mr. Howe."

"I thought you said there was no pattern."

"I did say there was no pattern. What I didn't say is that there's no rules to the game. Someone is coming to kill me. I don't know about you. You're a big question mark."

He tilted the scotch at me at such a mean angle, a little bit sloshed out.

"Let me tell you what happened the last time I stuck my head above the foxhole."

## What Happened the Last Time Jimmy Wynn Stuck His Head Above the Foxhole

The year was 1982. Since fleeing the FBI sting operation, Jimmy Wynn had been living in his mother's house in Detroit. His mother was in a senior's residence. She had been left mentally incapacitated by a stroke. "Her light was out long before that happened." Even so, he went to visit her nearly every day. He thought a lot about the people he had lost — Katie and Teddy. He felt guilty about abandoning Bessie and Bud. He had not performed in many years. He nullified his feelings by smoking hash and drinking rum. "Chi Chi Montez taught me that. If you get the timing and the portions right, you don't need anything else in this world than decent smoke and Cuban rum."

Along with several other patients, Jimmy Wynn's mother died when a batch of spoiled eggs made it into a breakfast serving and caused an outbreak of salmonella. At the age of forty-seven, Jimmy Wynn found himself orphaned and bereft. Then, Danny called, inviting him back to Vegas. "It would have been so easy. Danny had out some video that got people excited about the old act. There was that big movie about Teddy, too [1982's *An Honorable Man*]. Finally, people could see Teddy's picture and not burst into tears. The whole era was back in style. Kids were dressing that way and everything. Danny was excited, I was excited."

Jimmy began to call himself Jimmy again, something he had not done for many years. He had changed his name to James Saddlecreek in 1969 not just because of security concerns but because so many people treated his name "as a licence to fuck with me." The new concerts with Danny were going to be classy affairs. First they would appear onstage together and do a brief set of highlights from old routines. Then Jimmy would do a solo set of new material. Some were straight jokes, some were impressions. Jimmy's plan was to eventually include some Cannon material, updated for the eighties. "Teddy would comment on current politics, like he'd been keeping up on things in heaven. These were solid bits." He didn't get the chance to try it.

Jimmy was doing a rehearsal when he had a visitor. He was a handsome young man in a dark suit with a blue handkerchief in the pocket. He told Jimmy that he had an important matter with him. He showed Jimmy a picture of a family. Jimmy didn't recognize the man or the boy, but he identified the frumpy smiling woman as Bessie Pike. Then he understood who the boy was. The handsome young visitor said Jimmy had a choice: either Jimmy Wynn disappeared or the family did. Though the man said he didn't really care the method by which Jimmy Wynn disappeared, he was quite specific about what would happen to the family, especially if they learned about this conversation. He left the picture with Jimmy. And that was what happened the last time Jimmy Wynn stuck his head above the foxhole.

Jimmy fished the photo out of his wallet and handed it to me. The colours had gone brown and the emulsion was worn down at the folds, but the family was still there. The woman looked like a Pike sister. The boy looked like he would grow up to be a famous magician who buried himself in New York Harbor and spent weeks in a shiny cube over the Wilson Dam.

"Wow," I said as I handed it back.

Two more drinks arrived.

"And that, Mr. Motown, was the beginning of Chester Howe's career in family entertainment. Danny was kind enough to throw me a few bones. I owe a lot to his kindness."

"And his private jet."

He raised his glass to toast me. "Here's to a smooth comfortable ride," said Jimmy. He shook his head. "They're gonna come after me again. I'm the loosest loose end they got."

"Maybe David can help. I mean Bud."

"Bud. Bud. He's good, ain't he? Smart. Smarter than I was. That thing with the cube — I was amazed by the thing with the cube. That took balls. When I read about how those assholes were disrespecting him down at the Dam, I wanted to go down there and bash their heads in with a pipe."

I imagined Jimmy Wynn clubbing the heads of Stink as if they were baby seals. Singing baby seals.

"I disappeared from his life, you know? No kid deserves that. No kid deserves to grow up wondering why his dad wasn't there when he could've been."

"Maybe that's why he became a magician. He wanted to make you reappear."

"Poof," said Jimmy Wynn as he stared at another weather report. "Big puff of smoke." He wasn't laughing.

I remembered David Maher's card was in my wallet. I fished it out of my pocket and slid it across the table.

Jimmy looked down at the card. "Yeah, well." He hesitated before picking it up and slipping it into his shirt pocket. He shook his shoulders to rouse himself and rubbed his eyes. "Ah, it's late. We gotta go." He flagged over the waitress and handed her a credit card. "Might as well use that while I still can."

I was pleased to see him pick up another tab. He might have been a lousy father but he was a good host.

When the waitress returned with the credit card receipt, Jimmy signed it with a theatrical flourish. "But," he said, "I'm not finished yet. We've got some things to do, some things that will really make your article sing. They won't forget the name of Jimmy Wynn." He laughed. "What the hell am I saying? What I mean is they won't forget it again. We're gonna make it real hard for them." He stood up and led me to the door. "Big plans, Motown. Big plans." He hugged me, pointed out my hotel, and sent me on my way.

Halfway back there, it occurred to me that I shouldn't have let him drive in his condition. But for Jimmy to drive into a lamp-post on the way home might have been best for all involved. I didn't want to be morbid. I was looking forward to these big plans. Besides, Jimmy had finagled his way out of telling me his piece of the puzzle. I still had to find out what he knew about Cannon that was so special and so dangerous. I pledged to myself that in the morning, I would be a better journalist.

Back in the hotel room, I needed more time to decompress so I turned on the TV. I channel-surfed until I saw two faces I recognized. It was John Sifredi and his wife Marla. They were smiling in front of Mt. Rushmore in a holiday photo. At the bottom of the photo were the words: DELROCCO ASSOCIATE SLAIN WITH WIFE. The TV announcer added a few more details. They were found in their suburban Las Vegas home. They had both been shot in the head. Local law enforcement officials decried the brutality of the crime.

I thought: holy shit. I thought: it's the clean-up operation — they're coming for me next. I put the chain on the door, a gesture that struck me as pathetic.

I didn't get very much sleep that night. What there was of it was fraught and restless. It didn't take much to wake me when I heard the pounding on the door. I figured my time had come. I looked to the window, hoping I could climb out. Then the phone rang. There was too much going on at once. I picked it up in case it was someone who could help me, who could come over and take care of the person banging on the door. It was a dim hope.

"Good morning, Mr. Grant."

I knew the voice. "Mr. Sharpe?"

"You should answer your door. We are on a tight schedule."

I put the phone down on the nightstand and went to open the door. On the other side was a man I immediately recognized. His buzzcut was still as brutal as his sneer. It was the man who'd made me wash my hands. He came forward into the room as I backed away. I retreated to the bedside and picked up the phone.

"Mr. Sharpe? There's a man here."

"I know this is very short notice but we need to have a conversation. Harris will take you where you need to go once you're presentable."

As I put the phone down, my heart sank all the way down to the lobby. Harris was still sneering. "Get in that bathroom and take a shower, you maggot. You're disgusting."

23

When Harris decided that I was clean — he made me brush my teeth for a full three minutes, clocking me with his watch — he took me up to the hotel's top floor. Looming over me in the close quarters of the elevator, his body radiated aggression, dominance, intimidation. It struck me that Winston Sharpe flaunted the same qualities, though his elegance and elocution diluted their effects. No such obstacles for Harris. He was pure uncut thug.

"Where'd you get that scratch on your face?" he asked, temporarily interrupting his sneer.

I touched the cut from my windshield encounter in Rose's Caprice. My repeated scrubbings had nearly caused it to bleed again. "Car accident," I said timidly.

"Wish I'd been there to see it."

Harris opened the door to the Skyway Suite on the 15th floor. The windows inside provided what would have been a spectacular view of the area around the Falls had they not been immersed in a soupy early-morning fog. The gloom outside permeated the room and seeped into my skin. I thought: get out, anyway you can. In my mind I saw the Sifredis begging for their lives from a sneering Harris. I pretty much wanted to piss myself.

Winston Sharpe sat on a divan facing the window. I thought he was talking to himself until I saw the bug in his ear. "That is unacceptable. No. You're not listening. Wait. Stop talking when I am talking. That is unacceptable. We will not go higher than five points. If the prime minister has any further objections, we will walk away from this deal. I'll move the entire project to Jakarta. This is not a hollow threat. This is my full intention. No. You are not listening. You cannot listen if you do not stop talking."

Harris crossed the room and stepped into his field of view. Sharpe ignored him. "If you do not stop, I will come to your office and personally supervise actions that will be detrimental to your physical ability to continue conducting affairs of state. That is also something other than a threat." He spoke calmly and without rancour. "Will you be quiet now? Good."

Sharpe finally acknowledged Harris with a nod. "That is all I want you to do. I want you to wait for my call. Only wait. When I call, I want you to be prepared to listen very carefully. I will repeat this so you have a complete understanding. In the moments after I terminate this call, I want you to sit quietly and begin preparing. You may start now."

Sharpe removed the bug and turned to face me. "Nathan," he said. I half-expected him to extend his hand but he didn't. Instead, he gestured to a glass table and directed me to sit down. I faced him and the window. The colour of the fog outside nearly matched Sharpe's hair.

"Let me explain my position as straightforwardly as I can," he began. "For the past two weeks, I have been supervising in two different capacities. The first, obviously, is as the editor of *The Betsey*. I hope that my advice and encouragement have been valuable. I am still very much looking forward to your article. The second capacity is as a member of a political action group whose name and precise function are not subjects for discussion. Nevertheless, I can say this organization has played an important role in forming the society we know and enjoy today. I understand if you have some questions." He looked at his watch. "Please be brief."

I instinctively looked down at my heart to check for a red dot. Nothing. "Have you been following me?" To my ears, my voice sounded gratingly shrill.

"Yes. You've kept a good pace and I must say that I have been impressed with your intuitive skills. I was initially concerned about leaving this task with a neophyte investigator, but you have far exceeded my expectations. I was banking on the hope your enthusiasm for the subject would carry you this far."

Exceeded his expectations? I was pleased at his compliments. I thought: don't listen to him, he's been fucking with you this whole time.

"Is someone trying to kill me?"

"The purpose of the tactics to which you refer was to keep you focused and motivated. There were certain time constraints, including the deadline for your story." He pointed to Harris, who glared at me like a wary predator. "Has Mr. Grant responded well to your strategy?"

"I would say very well," he said. He lowered his voice in imitation of my robot caller. "Do not use the phone," he growled in machine-like fashion. "Phone is forbidden." Then he laughed.

"You were just using me to flush out Jimmy Wynn." I couldn't hide my shock.

Sharpe's fingers drummed on the glass. "Mr. Wynn had been known to my organization for many years. Because he was in possession of certain pieces of information, he was a subject of some concern throughout the years after President Cannon passed on."

Passed on? I was confused by the delicacy of the phrase he chose considering *The Betsey*'s fetish for assassination lore. "Why didn't you kill him? That's what you do, right? You kill people?"

Out of my peripheral vision I saw Harris advance toward me.

Sharpe halted him with a movement in his hand. "Please, Nathan. Let's not get carried away. Our surveillance indicated that between his substance abuse and the state of his professional career, Wynn had neutralized himself far more efficiently than any action by us would have. His termination may well have attracted the sort of conspiracy talk that surrounds the likes of Nathaniel Fontainebleu, which is not something we want to encourage."

I thought: doesn't Colin's column encourage it? I thought: is he in on this, too?

"In the meantime," Sharpe continued, "the organization went through a period of reassessment. To be perfectly frank, I believe the organization suffered from a lack of strong leadership and needed to get back to the principles that inspired it in the first place. In any case, our Mr. Wynn did not get the attention he deserved. When Daphne informed me about your story idea, I realized that this was an excellent chance to deal with an overdue matter." He pointed at me. "What's more, it had the potential to be an excellent piece of journalism. I hope you're still on track."

"But what about —"

He held up his hand to stop me. "We need to talk seriously about your options. It was necessary to alert Immigration officials to your situation but they have been cooperative and, for the most part, non-intrusive."

"But the men at —"

"The hotel, yes. Nathan, please, no more interruptions. I am not going to ask you again. A team of agents was sent to the Chateau Montpelier. I also instructed Daphne to assign your colleague Colin to research the Nevada Delegation — I was counting on your competitive drive. Again, my sole objective was to get you on your way." He smiled slyly. "Congratulations on taking us so far."

I was gripping the edge of the table hard enough to hurt my fingers.

"The reason," he continued, "I called this meeting because we're moving on to the next stage of the assignment and you need to be aware of several factors. Wynn must suspect you've been followed. We believe he is making arrangements to flee the area and discard his current identity. You will persuade him to stay put, at least for another day. It shouldn't be difficult, considering his commitment to his theatrical endeavour. Harris purchased a compact disc for me featuring the music from his theatre. Atrocious. As a Canadian, you should be livid."

I thought: hey, it's not *that* bad.

"Persuade him to stay long enough to finish your interview. I expect that you both have much more to talk about. From the sounds of it, he's had a fascinating career. Most men endure only one or two major failures in their lives. Wynn has been subject to a rich variety of fascinating catastrophes. Failing could be his true forte."

I spoke without thinking. "You crypto-fascist bastard —"

Harris advanced forward to seize my throat. I immediately lamented the absence of a functioning windpipe as every vein in my head began to throb. "Mr. Sharpe told you not to interrupt." His breath was hot on my ear. Or else I was passing out. In any case, he held me for another long (very long) beat, then let go. I slumped forward against the table and the edge jabbed the middle of my heaving chest.

Sharpe gave me a sympathetic look as I spluttered. "Don't take this to mean that I am displeased with your performance. You have great promise as a journalist and I would be pleased to bring you aboard as a writer at the magazine. For the time being, you will continue with your conversations with Wynn while other matters come into alignment. Has he revealed what passed between the president and himself?"

I thought: should I be lying now? It couldn't have made much difference. I spat out a no.

"Then you have unfinished business." Sharpe brought his

hands together and triangulated his fingers under his chin. "This also presents an opportunity to develop an appropriate ending for your piece. It's not often that a writer finds himself in this position. Not only is this the kind of moment that forges a writer — here is a chance to craft history itself." He released his hands. "Not a defining moment in history, perhaps, but significant enough not to go unnoticed by the people who have seen behind the veil. When we first met, I told you that President Cannon created this world and that Wynn was that world's first citizen. Consider this next step the passing of an epoch."

Harris gave him a manila envelope. Sharpe opened it. "I trust you will be discreet. But if you do inform your comedian about this exchange or speak to anyone else about the matters we've discussed, there will be repercussions."

He emptied the envelope out on the table. There were several photographs. One featured my parents in front of a Christmas tree — it was the picture I kept on the refrigerator in my apartment. The next photo was of Ben standing outside the Network X van on the day of the Stink show in Los Angeles. In the third picture, Rose was coming out of the Ambrosia.

"I do not need to elaborate."

He collected the photographs and put them back in the envelope. Then he stood up and walked to the window. "To come all the way to Niagara Falls and see nothing but this." He shook his head. "Hopefully this will be the only disappointment I experience while I am here."

Harris pulled me to my feet. I felt soft in the knees.

"Oh yes," said Sharpe, turning to face me one last time. "Harris will return to you the notes, computer, and personal effects that you left behind in Los Angeles. I'm sure you'll want to get back to working on the article." He looked at me sagely. "Keep your pen at the ready, Nathan. You have the privilege of living in exciting times."

* * *

Ten minutes later I was standing next to the furry, buck-toothed Mountie in front of the Maple Leaf Theatre. There was no one there to let me in. I could have gone back across the street to the hotel, if only to sift through the stuff they returned, but I didn't want to be there. If I'd gone to my room, I would've faced the difficult decision: should I hide under the covers or hang myself with a bedsheet? Or, worst of all, work on the article as if everything was normal?

I walked down toward the Falls, feeling beaten and bewildered. The fog lent a mystical quality to the haunted houses and arcades on the tourist strip, as if Valhalla had been converted into a seaside resort. The gods were too busy enjoying the wax museums to aid me in my plight. I wondered if Harris had visited John and Marla Sifredi — I was scared to ask after he'd given my throat that hug.

There were positive repercussions from my unexpected morning meeting. Since the people who instructed me not to use the phone were the same people who were following me the whole time, I could finally disregard their advice. This was not very liberating news since I could jeopardize anyone who tried to help me. I still needed to talk to someone, if only to confirm that there was a rational world somewhere next to the one I was living in. I stopped at a pay phone and called my house collect. My mother answered on the third ring and promptly accepted the charges.

"This is a nice surprise."

"Yeah, I'm . . . uh, sorry I haven't called in a while. Things have been crazy."

"We were wondering what became of you."

"I'm fine. Just busy. With the writing." I thought: you and your glorious writing.

"Is everything all right at the magazine?"

My mother still believed I worked at *Hancock's*.

"Uh-huh. I've been working on an article about a comedian."

"A comedian? Somebody famous?"

"Not now. But yeah, he was pretty famous."

"That's terrific. I'm excited to hear that you're . . . oh, hold on." She held the phone away from her mouth. "It's Nathan." My dad's response was muffled. "He called collect." Dad said something else. "Yes, I know," she said. Then to me: "Your father wants to know why you're calling during peak hours."

"I don't know. It was convenient now. I don't get a lot of spare time, you know. The writing keeps me really busy?" I thought: even now you sound like a fake.

"What's that?" Then to me: "Dad said he'll call you back after 8 p.m."

"But I'm not in New York. I'm . . ." I thought: are you really going to explain this to them? "No, that's okay. I'll call you back."

"After eight."

A delivery truck roared past the corner and the rumble made the street shudder.

"What's that, honey?"

"Nothing," I said. "That wasn't me. It was a truck going past." I thought: bail out before you involve them any further. I thought: you're alone in this. "I should go."

"All right, Nathan. You'll have to catch us up on what you've been doing."

I hung up.

I hovered by the phone, wondering if there was someone I could call. Maybe I should've called Colin or Ben to tell them to run and hide. I couldn't see how my instructions would do them any good. For an instant I thought of calling Winston Sharpe. If I had been able to call him the day before, I would have told him about all the things that had gone right. I would have told him about having Jimmy Wynn in the bag. He might have even feigned surprise at the news.

I started walking toward the Falls again. The fog was beginning to dissipate. The neon in the window of a pizza place switched on while I passed by. The beer signs in the bar where I'd been with Jimmy were still off. The sidewalk sloped down toward the street that ran alongside the river. A black Excelsior sedan bounded up the hill toward me then stopped. The passenger side window descended.

"Hey, Motown."

I looked inside the car and found Jimmy. Despite the fog, he wore a pair of gold-rimmed sunglasses. New age piano music played loudly on the car stereo.

"Where you heading?" he asked.

I thought: be vague. "Nowhere in particular."

"Then get in."

I thought: you have to start this again, you have no choice. I thought: you are in the grip of forces far beyond your ken. "Um . . ."

"It's gonna be a big day," said Jimmy. "We gotta get moving."

I reached for the door handle. It was cool and slick with condensation. I paused. I felt fear and guilt and panic and loathing.

"You forget how that thing works?"

"No. It's just that . . ." I thought: there is nothing you can do to protect him, not right now at least. I played out my hand. "It's nothing. I'm a little hungover." I opened the door and got inside. "When can we start the interview?"

"Right now. Let's wrap it up. Chop, chop."

* * *

We went back to the waffle house. We both ordered cheesy scrambled eggs and coffee. I was surprised that I had an appetite. Then again, I wasn't lying about the hangover.

I fished my tape recorder out of my satchel. I realized I had no intention of fleeing until I was finished.

"What was the secret Teddy gave you?"

"Straight to it, right?"

"You said we didn't have much time."

"Fair enough. After this, I gotta keep my mind on tonight. Anyway, you can say in your story that Teddy asked me for a favour."

We were interrupted by the arrival of the coffee. Then some friend of Jimmy's spotted us in the window and came inside to talk. Jimmy introduced him as Al — he ran the wax museum that was devoted to famous crime scenes. Al had heard something about a special night at the Maple Leaf.

"Yeah," said Jimmy. "I'm hoping to get some folks out. What else are they gonna do on a Tuesday night?"

"I can think of a few things." Al had a lusty laugh at that.

Jimmy slapped him on the arm and Al bade us farewell.

"Good guy," said Jimmy to me. "Good guy. And yes, I do remember what we were talking about before he came in. Let me say one more thing about Teddy. I thought I understood him in a way that nobody else did. Did you know that your memory's not just stored in your brain? It's all over your body. I read that in a magazine. Think of the last time you got smacked with a baseball. Maybe it hit you right at the top of the chest. Maybe it hit you so hard, that spot on your chest never really healed. It hurts every time somebody touches it. And every time it hurts, you come back to that moment when you first felt it — wham." Jimmy loudly thumped himself on the chest. "That little spot stays in that moment for the rest of your life. Now think of all the other places where you store those hurts and you realize you've got memories all over. And they change the way you move, the way you place your body in a chair, when you're in a bed with a lady, when you're in front of a thousand people. I didn't just know the ways Teddy moved, I knew *why* he moved — I knew what was written on him. I built up that sense from the inside. Same with the voice. It was his voice all the way down to my guts. I made it that way. No one else could say they did that. No one else spent the time. And everything I got out of it — the gigs, the fame, the money — I earned that the hard way. I was never a leech. Never."

It took me a moment to take it all in. "And do you think he appreciated that?"

"He told me so. He said, 'We've got a special connection, Jimmy.' He told me that on the last night at the Flamingo. Then he asked me if I would change my face. I was surprised he asked because I thought I was his mirror image. But he was right. Onstage doing my thing, I was Teddy. If you compared us in a picture, the physical resemblance was not so hot."

"Why did he want you to change your face?"

"He said he needed to be in several places at once. He said, 'There are a lot of demands on my time.' There were safety issues, too. He told me I could still do gigs. The doctor could do it in steps so people wouldn't notice so much. Then Marco Delrocco — he was there at the meeting — he said, 'No, there's not enough time for that.' To be honest, I don't think they'd sorted out what they wanted to ask me. Or else they were out to confuse me, too. The bottom line is they were asking me to be Teddy's decoy."

I thought: wow. "This is what you believe he was asking?"

"Absolutely."

"Weren't you afraid of losing your career?"

"My commitment to Teddy was total."

"So why didn't you get the surgery?"

"What makes you think I didn't?"

We had a long moment before Jimmy busted up laughing. I was too shocked to join him.

"I'm just screwing around," he said. "But I wanted it. I wanted to show Teddy that I'd do it for him. I would have gone all the way. But months went by and I never heard from them. They were real specific about the 'don't call us, we'll call you' part of the instructions. In June, I was in the Flamingo and I came up to

Marco and asked, 'Hey, about that business we discussed.' And he looked at me real cold and said, 'It's taken care of.' That's all he said. 'It's taken care of.' First I thought: oh they don't need me after all. There's some other plan. Then I thought: they got some other guy. I was hurt they didn't want me. I was the best there was. No one knew Teddy like I did."

My head was spinning with the potential ramifications of this information. "Do you think a decoy was shot in New Orleans?"

"No. I've studied the Fontainebleu movie. I know the fucking thing forwards and backwards. The way he went down — pure Teddy. He seemed to be expecting the guy, though. You notice that, too — he looked straight at Martinez like he was looking for him in the crowd. Makes you think, don't it?"

I got out one last question before I thought my brain would shut down. "Did Teddy know the hit was coming?"

Jimmy's brow furrowed. "I spent a long time on this question. I believe Teddy knew someone was going to try something and he was taking steps to control the situation by talking to me. Maybe he knew about a plan, but only a plan. You see, it's all about the competing plans with these guys. You spend enough time looking at the hit and you'll see that. It's what I was trying to say last night: what looks like no pattern only looks like no pattern because there isn't one single pattern. What you've got is pattern on top of pattern on top of pattern. It looks like chaos but it's chaos that's been built up, right? I figure that Teddy had some idea about it, then the ground shifted again. It's hard to keep track of all the pieces. You hear a little bit of the song and you have to guess the rest."

Jimmy reached over and picked up my tape recorder. He brought the built-in condenser close to his mouth. "And that's all, folks." He clicked the recorder off and smiled as he put it down. "C'mon, kid. It's gonna be a big night."

24

In the hours before showtime for the quite-possibly-final per-formance of *Canad'eh?*, I was stuck between pattern and no pattern. Jimmy's piece didn't complete my puzzle. It made the shape and scope of the thing impossible to discern. It left a gap-ing wound in history that no Band-aid or hockey mask would ever cover.

And like he always did, Jimmy just wanted to get back onstage. The whole theatre was buzzing over the news that Chester Howe would perform in *Canad'eh?* before making some important announcement. They were probably expecting a tearful retirement speech. Maybe they would get one. In any case, it wasn't the first time he'd played in the show. Sal told me (told Dave, rather) Jimmy would occasionally contribute a dramatic monologue in the guise of an old Nova Scotian fisherman who was obsessed with catching the surly codfish that bit off his baby toe. "It got you right here," Sal said, indicating a space a little lower than his heart would be.

I asked Jimmy if it was wise to get onstage considering the run-ning of the clock and whatnot. "Wise is the last thing it is," he said, grinning. "But I'm tired of pulling the old disappearing trick. This time I'm gonna give them something to remember."

He spent the rest of the day bustling with the performers. He rearranged the show to accommodate new bits. Barry wouldn't stop complaining. He probably thought Jimmy was showboating for the benefit of the New York reporter who insisted on loitering around the theatre. I saw myself as I assumed they saw me: a disfigured young drip who behaved as if he was afraid of his own shadow.

Someone put a sign around the neck of the beaver Mountie that said: SPECIAL NIGHT TONIGHT! Lorna, the woman in charge of marketing the Maple Leaf, called radio stations to help get the word out. Lorna wasn't sure if they'd attract many newbies but she did have a tour group from Cincinnati already booked. "Chester's show has a great reputation all over the Northeast," she said. "People are very interested in Canada. They know they can have a really great time here."

I was not having a really great time. Again and again I fought the urge to take Jimmy aside and tell him to run. Like Cannon, he must have known what could happen, must have had some idea of a potential plan. I had forced him to stick his head above the foxhole again and I cursed myself for not realizing how I would endanger him.

To my amazement, Jimmy wasn't content to merely stick his head above the foxhole. He was going to climb all the way out and do the can-can. If there was going to be a target on his chest, he would paint it himself.

I hung back and watched him work. The singing-salmon girl was there. Jimmy was teaching her a few new gags. They seemed so familiar and comfortable with each other, I wondered if they could be an item. I hadn't asked Jimmy about women — were there any in his life?

Then he worked on the grumpy grizzly number with Sal and Barry, trying out different cadences on some of the lines. The wavering pitch in Jimmy's singing voice made his bear seem all the more poignant. I was standing at the back hearing the last "whoah-oah-oah" when I felt a hand grip my shoulder. I turned and saw Harris.

"Parking lot," he said.

I followed him out of the theatre. He opened the passenger door of a silver car and gestured me inside. He shut the door and began to walk back toward the hotel, leaving me alone in the car. There was a buzzing cell phone on the seat next to me. I switched it on.

"Nathan, it's Winston Sharpe. I want to . . ." His voice was consumed by crackle.

"Mr. Sharpe, I can barely hear you."

"I have been called away to business in Washington. The quality of the airplane telephone is far from ideal. But I wanted you to know everything is in place for tonight. We'll be recording the event, though I trust you'll be there as well."

"What's going to happen?" I thought: there must be a way out of this situation, there must.

"The element of surprise will keep your senses keen. This story has been going on for longer than you can imagine and I will not have the ending spoiled."

"But what am I supposed to —"

"Senses keen!" he shouted through the crackle.

The phone went dead. I looked outside and didn't see Harris. I left the car, pocketing the cell phone. My stomach was triple-pretzeled. Back inside the theatre, Jimmy was onstage. He wore a miner's headlamp and sang about a girl who was waiting for him somewhere bright and airy. His sense of good cheer in these rehearsals shocked me. He exhibited none of the tension that I felt. I thought: he has to know what's coming.

He climbed down the stairs from the stage and came up to me. There was a drink in his hand and it didn't look like apple juice. "Dave!" I was confused until I realized he was using my extra-Canadian name as cover. "I hope you're having a good time today."

I smiled weakly. The nervous anguish in my guts and smell of booze on his breath made me nauseous. "Sure."

"You must be bored watching me screw around. Why don't you go back to the hotel and take a breather? We can talk again while the customers are chowing down. Besides, I want to save you a few surprises for the show. Come back at 7:30."

I nodded and turned, bewildered by the amount of concern everyone expressed in my value as a spectator. I left the theatre, crossed the street, went up to my room, got into bed, and pulled the sheet over my head. People were going to die because of me. I thought: am I an idiot to believe I have any control over who those people will be?

\* \* \*

As I watched thousands of gallons of water plunge off the edge of the world, I tried not to be morbid — I failed. Gael Martinez, the man who fired the bullet that struck President Cannon in the right shoulder, was a former economics student at Emery College in Miami. According to his mother — who immigrated with her children to the U.S. in 1953 — Gael was a quiet, meticulous boy who was very good in school and caused no trouble. In 1959, he was one of a crowd of protesters peacefully demonstrating against American support for Cuba's repressive right-wing government. When police fired upon the demonstrators, two of Gael's closest friends were among the six dead activists. He was radicalized by the tragedy, becoming a central player in Accion Cubano, Miami's most militant left-wing group. He impressed many comrades with his devotion to the cause. In late 1962, he dropped out of Accion Cubano for unspecified reasons. His mother said that he loved to laugh.

Ernesto Cruz, the man who fired the bullet that struck President Cannon in the neck, was a first-generation Cuban-American. His parents had immigrated to Florida in the late

1930s. His father worked in a shoe factory. After dropping out of school, young Ernesto worked construction jobs throughout the American Southeast, establishing an itinerant lifestyle. In 1952, he took a clandestine trip to visit relatives in the province of Arragas and was appalled by the poverty there. Once back in the U.S., he wrote several supportive letters to Cuban communist leader Augustin Erice, then exiled in Venezuela. He trained with Erice loyalists living in a compound outside of Tallahassee, Florida. There was no record of his whereabouts between December of 1962 and two weeks prior to the assassination. According to his sister, Ernesto was outgoing and generous to a fault. He enjoyed the records of Chi Chi Montez, though vehemently disliked the singer himself for his support of the Cuban regime.

Despite the volume of literature about their actions on the day their names were immortalized, little has been determined about their motivations. All that was certain was that the Secret Service shot both men dead within minutes of the attack on Cannon. Some evidence suggests that they were recruited by a rogue CIA agent named Chuck Mercer, though the agency claimed to have never employed a man with that name. Others believe that they found each other through the loose network of Latin-American radicals living in the U.S. Perhaps each had his own assassination plan but detested the idea of being perceived as another disgruntled loner with a gun. Perhaps whoever orchestrated the operation felt that a two-man team implied the existence of a wider conspiracy less than a one-man team. One man cannot be expected to accomplish such an enormous task entirely on his own. As for two men, surely there's nothing they can't do together if they roll up their sleeves.

In comedy, an act consisting of two people assumed a familiar harmony of straight arrow and funny man, sensible Joe and hustler, smooth yin and nutty yang. None of the literature indicates which role belonged to Martinez and which to Cruz — their personalities remain frustratingly indistinct. What kind of chemistry did they have as partners? And how would they have gone over onstage at the Flamingo?

They must have believed in themselves as agents of history, as great men of destiny. I could only see them as actors who were cast in the play but had only been allowed to learn their own lines, not the whole script. They hit their marks but missed the real story.

I too had a walk-on part. Maybe, like Martinez and Cruz, Secret Service agents would acknowledge the completion of my performance with a barrage of bullets. Or maybe I would get my name on *The Betsey*'s masthead.

I tried to shake off my dread (and the omnipresent drizzle) as I walked back up to the Maple Leaf. I wanted my pen at the ready and my senses keen. I noticed two buses in the parking lot with Ohio licence plates. The cars were mostly from Ontario, Michigan, or New York State. I didn't see Harris's car. I still had the phone in my pocket. I should've used it to call back my parents but that wouldn't do me any good.

Recognizing me as Dave the reporter, a cheerful Mountie girl waved me past the ticket wicket. I looked in the theatre and saw the backs of the diners. A good two-thirds of the crowd looked like they hadn't seen a hot meal for at least half an hour. I thought: people from Ohio smell like hickory.

I scanned the room for men on their own, judging them to be the likeliest assassins. I wanted to spot them without being noticed myself. Since I had no confidence in my ability to do this, I didn't examine any of them very carefully. A man at the bar in the back right corner put film into a camera. He wore silver sunglasses and a brown leather jacket that looked two sizes too big. His face was obscured by the upturned collar. A pear-shaped middle-aged man in a blue hockey jacket stood facing the stage. A third man in a ball cap occupied my seat from the night before. From the back he had Harris's build. He had a video camera in his hand. My scan was interrupted by Al. He stopped to shake my hand and tell me how much he was looking forward to the show.

"Me, too," I said.

"Jimmy's got something up his sleeve," said Al. "You never know what he's gonna do."

I found Jimmy backstage. I noted there was no one guarding the door. I thought: I could be anyone, anyone with a gun. A curly haired blonde woman with a pair of cats on her T-shirt was applying black smudges to Jimmy's cheeks and forehead. Jimmy had shaved off his moustache. Resting on the table was a miner's head-lamp and a refreshed glass of scotch.

He spied me in the mirror. "Hey, Motown. Lorna says we're getting a full house tonight. *Ohio is my lady,*" he crooned in the fashion of the man he'd called "Teddy's doorman."

Ringed with black, his bright eyes and clean-shaven face gave him a youthful vigour that reminded me of the man on the cover of *A Square Peg in the Oval Office.* I thought: walk away right now, you don't have to see this. I thought: everyone's gonna die some time. I thought: get out of the theatre and go home. I thought: fuck the story. I thought: Sharpe's bluffing, he won't hurt Mom and Dad, he won't hurt Ben or Rose. I thought: he might do it anyway. I thought: Harris totally killed the Sifredis. I thought: keep it together if you don't want to die. I thought: how many people have to die so that Cannon can live? I thought: I should write that down. I thought: no, that's just melodramatic crap.

I felt the words rise up all the way from my diaphragm. They gave me a body to occupy. "You can't do the show."

Jimmy snorted. "Is that right?"

"Something's gonna happen tonight. To you. They told me they were gonna do it. The man who runs my magazine told me. Winston Sharpe. He's part of some secret group. He was here, in the hotel. Something's gonna happen but he didn't say what. They're getting ready to kill you. Just go. Disappear. I can go with you."

The makeup girl looked at us in confusion.

"Dana," said Jimmy, "that'll do just fine. Go take care of Barry."

She seemed scared. "Is something wrong, Chester?"

"What? Nah, nah. Dave's trying to make a joke. Evidently, it needs some work."

He patted her arm and she left us alone.

"Don't worry so much." His voice was soft. The smudges on his face reminded me of David Maher's pleading raccoon eyes — the family resemblance was clear for the first time. "It's gonna be a great show. Get out there and enjoy it."

"You don't understand."

"Ask yourself this question, Motown: how did Jimmy Wynn live this long?" He tapped his forehead, accidentally wiping makeup off the spot. "By *improvising*. The ability to read the moment, to see where the breaks are gonna roll. You gotta trust that. That moment is all you're gonna get. Beyond that," he spread his hands wide, "there's not a damn thing you can expect."

"Jimmy, listen to me. They're gonna kill you tonight."

He smiled at me as if I was an idiot. "Then you can do me the courtesy of getting a pretty girl to give me a big bunch of roses when I come offstage. That's always swell. Now go take your seat — I've gotta do my vocal exercises."

Jimmy Wynn and Winston Sharpe were in full agreement about the fact that the show would go on. My stomach couldn't take any more. I thought: it's not a joke, Jimmy, none of this is.

Jimmy rubbed his fingers with a Kleenex and stuck out his hand. "Wish me luck."

"Good luck," I said, returning the handshake. I had failed him.

"Whatever happens," he said, his smile impossibly wide, "remember this: I've had worse nights."

\* \* \*

The show was very different from the one I'd seen the night before
— Danny Pantero would've been shocked by the changes. Now
the Inuit ballad followed the beaver sequence, the soft-shoe tribute to the Confederation was cut in half, and the hockey fight was
dropped entirely. As usual, the singing animals went down a treat,
the Ohioans slapping away at their meaty thighs. Barry curbed his
showboating long enough to give the grumpy grizzly the right
pathos. Like everyone else there, I wished the bear could overcome
its feelings of loneliness yet I knew it would never be able to triumph over its own instinct to destroy.

The nice wide people from Ohio had every right to be enjoying themselves. I sat near the back left corner of the room with my
notepad and my pen. I was ready for everything and nothing.
During the breaks in the action onstage, I surveyed the crowd for
potential threats but it was too dark to see clearly. I saw the photographer but I lost track of the two other solitary men — my
former seat at the table was now empty. There was no Harris,
either.

Having no clear idea of what catastrophe to expect, I was distracted by the show — the bugger was designed to hold my
attention and that's what it did. The coal miner's love song was the
weaker of Jimmy's two solo bits — the tune and the lyrics were
unabashedly sentimental and lacked the humour of the other
songs. "*I hope someday you'll say you'll be true,*" sang Jimmy in a
raspy tone. "*My world is so cold and dark without you.*" For a
moment, all the lights in the house went down, leaving the headlamp as the room's only source of light. I thought: oh god, it's
gonna happen now. But it didn't.

Jimmy's fisherman routine was the big winner. It was basically
"The Old Man and the Sea" except with jokes about frozen fish
sticks and wet long johns. Jimmy played the character with a

weathered New England accent and a twitchy eye. As a temporary skin for Wynn, this one seemed good and sturdy. The brief monologue closed with the old man taunting a pan of fried kippers with the line: "The fight's gone out of ye, boys. I weeps at the sight." His words were a touch slurry — the scotch that bolstered his nerves made him sloppy but it worked for the character.

I tracked the photographer's movements. Every so often he would sally forth, crouch in front of the front tables, take a few shots, then retreat to the back right bar. He did photograph Jimmy, but not exclusively. As for the man with the video camera who'd been in my seat, he wore tinted glasses and had the same haircut as Harris — they could have been brothers. Or bunkmates in the same barracks. He moved less than the first cameraman, choosing to mostly stay close to the wall on my side of the room.

Then there were the perky servers in their not-quite-regulation Mountie suits. There were four in all. Loath to call attention away from the events onstage, they delivered the drink orders with the utmost stealth. I hoped that Jimmy would not meet his maker at the hand of an eighteen-year-old blonde from Queenston, Ontario, who agreed to do the deed for tips.

When it came time for the final production number, Jimmy was absent. The rest of the cast danced their way through the audience, happy to sing about Gordie the beaver's renewed belief in Canada's greatness, unaware that the man who wrote this patriotic libretto was about to be . . . what?

The lights went down again. The applause was enthusiastic. As the darkness persisted, it grew more tentative. Just as it began to fade out entirely, there was a single beam of light directed outward from the stage. The rest of the lights came up to reveal Jimmy and his headlamp. The miner's suit was replaced by something more formal, more presidential. He had the hunch. He had the walk. He had the smile. Yet it felt wrong — unlike Jimmy, Cannon never had the chance to age. With his white hair and creased face,

Jimmy's Pres was a Pres that never was. That begged the question: if the imitation outlasted the original, was it no longer just a facsimile?

Then I noticed Jimmy's neck. It looked like there was a piece missing out of the right side. The flesh looked wet and red, with pieces hanging off in loose, jagged flaps. The shoulder on the same side was also torn up, the fabric of the coat shredded, bloody and tattered. Something flipped inside my still-sensitive stomach when I realized why the phony wounds were where they were. I thought: oh no, Jimmy, you didn't.

It took most of the audience another beat to register that there was something odd about this friendly old guy in formalwear. Before they could react, the voice gave Jimmy the body again.

"Excuse the, ah, headgear," he said. He removed the headlamp and put it down on the stage. "I got a little lost there on the way in. They always say, 'Walk toward the light, walk toward the light.' But when you're coming the other direction, it's awful dark. Good evening there to you fine people. It's been far too long since we laid eyes on each other. I, ah, trust you've been feeling well. Me, I've been just fine. Don't worry about the mess. It only stings when the weather changes."

There were three distinct gasps during Jimmy's pause. One was mine.

"I got a few updates on your family from the folks who are already here, up in heaven. I heard Auntie Jean's sciatica was acting up. I hope that she's feeling better. And Sam's scholarship is good news — he's a bright kid. You know," he admonished us with a waving finger, "you could call more often."

The Maple Leaf Theatre was an abyss of merciless silence.

Driven by reasons I will never completely comprehend, Jimmy persevered. "Well, ah, enough with the chit-chat. We have a great deal of catching up to do. The Big Guy," Jimmy pointed to the roof, "made sure to brief me on current events. I expected there to be changes since I was, ah, suddenly removed from office. But what's going on now, gosh, these are troubles. Sounds like you could use me around. Lot of trouble with the *economy*." He punched the last word, apparently expecting the same collective grumble of sympathy a comic gets when he mentions taxes, Congress, or mothers-in-law. He heard none. "And I hear that things, ah, aren't so good on the dark continent." I thought: no, Jimmy, not the Africans, please not the Africans. "Back in my day, we had our troubles. Cuba was one. The people there said they wanted a workers' paradise. What they really wanted was a longer lunch break so they could finish their cigars."

The room didn't flinch.

"You might remember my wife Connie. She was a handful. She was born to redecorate. My first day in office, I show her where I work and she says, 'I can live with the place, but does it have to be white?'"

I could hear the movement of flatware fifty feet away.

"Sooo," said Jimmy, "a funny thing happened on the motorcade —"

"Hey," shouted a man in the audience. He rose from his seat.

"I wasn't taking any questions from the press."

"That's not funny," shouted the man.

"It's a state of the union address, sir. You can't interrupt unless you're my foreman."

"That's disrespectful," he said.

"The constitution does give every American the right to express his opinion, but I do hold veto power."

"It's sick!" It was a woman this time. "It's sick what you're doing, how you look. President Cannon was a great man."

"Thank you so much for saying so. You're liable to make me blush."

"Stop it!" she cried.

I thought: he's dying.

"I, ah, only wanted to have a little fun with you fine —"

"For God's sake!" she cried. Several Ohioans were weeping. The Canadians in the crowd were easy to spot from their gaping jaws and stricken expressions. Like them, I thought: stop, just stop before this gets completely out of hand. Confrontation was inevitable.

Jimmy held the mike in front of his mouth for a beat. "So what would you like me to do?" It was his own voice now — a little shaky but confident enough considering the hostile vibe in the Maple Leaf Theatre.

"We came here to hear some nice jokes about Canada," said the man who was the first to shout.

There were more "Yeah!"s and one distinct "please!"

Jimmy nodded. He shifted his shoulders out of the Cannon position. "You like the Canada stuff, *eh*?" He leaned on the eh real hard. "I thought you might have gotten enough of those already tonight, but I guess not. A guy from Newfoundland's driving to Toronto. He sees a sign on the highway that says, 'Toronto Left.' He says, 'Shit, why didn't nobody tell me?' He turns the car around and goes home."

Only a quarter of the room gave up any laughs. It was probably the Canadians. I don't think they really cared about the joke itself. They were just hoping that expressions of courtesy and good cheer would bring the room off the boil. Jimmy interpreted that as a good sign.

"Why do French-Canadian goalies wear face masks? So they don't wreck their makeup."

A little more laughter, this time from some Americans, too. I thought: he's pulling it out of the fire.

"What's the last line in Canada's national anthem? 'Can I get a cruller with that?'"

They were lapping it up. Jimmy didn't need the headlamp to beam.

"How do you tell a dozen Canadians to get out of your pool? 'Excuse me, could you please get out of my pool?'"

A little esoteric but it still went over gangbusters.

"How many Canadians does it take to change a light bulb? Two: one changes the bulb and the other won't shut the fuck up about how Canada invented basketball."

They loved it. I loved it. Our countries were united again. Jimmy reached up to his neck and peeled off the latex wound. I was happy to see the neck whole again. Things were looking up.

"So this Canadian girl goes out on her first date. The guy says he's gonna take her to the fanciest restaurant in town. She says, 'That's great, I'll wear my fur.' So when the guy comes to her door, she —"

No one got to hear the punchline. Launching himself from a few feet in front of me, the photographer in the leather coat bounded up to the edge of the stage. He pulled a gun from his pocket and raised it at Jimmy. I watched the scene like I'd seen it happen before. Jimmy must have felt the same because he turned ever so slightly to face the photographer before the gun was even raised.

The sound of the shot cleaved the air. The shot itself blasted through Jimmy's chest. There was a second shot. Blood splattered over the curtain behind him. Jimmy dropped to his knees and fell sideways. There was screaming, screaming, screaming. The photographer pocketed his gun and went through the fire exit at the right of the stage.

I was on my feet, ready to go help Jimmy. Then I got hit by the wave of people moving away from the stage. A man knocked me to the ground and kicked my arm as he charged past. Someone else kicked my notepad. A Mountie waiter cleared a space and picked me up. I resisted when he tried to pull me out of the room. "But what about Jimmy?"

"Get out!" he said. "Some American's got a gun!"

We poured out of the doors into the parking lot. There was a lot of shouting and crying from the people around me. I was panting like I'd just run a marathon. The parking lot filled with shocked fake Mounties, hysterical audience members, and weeping actors.

"Did someone call the police?" said someone.

An ambulance with screaming sirens came roaring up to the front of the theatre. Two paramedics pulled a stretcher out of the back and bolted into the building.

I thought: the gunman might still be in there. I thought: you could have stopped this, all this.

Less than a minute later the two paramedics carried out Jimmy on a stretcher. A third followed, carrying a box of gear. A few of the cast members trailed behind. I ran up to see Jimmy as they lifted him into the back of the ambulance. His eyes were half shut. I couldn't tell if he was breathing. The jacket of his suit was purple, his shirt red, his cheeks white.

"Is he going to be all right?" cried Barry, his eyes wide with horror.

"Stand back, sir."

The paramedics shut the doors and the ambulance sped away. I thought: I only saw two paramedics go in. I thought: where's the guy with the video camera? I thought: where's the photographer with the gun?

As the ambulance peeled out of the lot, two police cars arrived. All four cops came out at once. They herded people away from the doors of the building. They asked if anyone had seen the gunman. Other cops arrived. They sealed off the scene. I thought: I left my notepad inside. I saw the guy with the video camera. He was taking pictures of the crowd and the policemen, trying to be subtle about it. He must've been another of Sharpe's men. I wanted to punch him but I didn't want the attention. Cops moved through the crowd, collecting names and statements from the dozens of witnesses. I thought: I can't handle it if they question me. Everyone there knew me as Dave. I had no cover story. I slipped away from the throng of Ohioans and other American tourists, who mere minutes before had been laughing at the foibles of this country — so safe, so square, so dull. This sort of thing happened at home, not here. They would forever regard this place differently. I would too. I felt like I'd brought a terrible virus back with me on Danny Pantero's jet. I had infected this place of happy beavers and helpful Mounties. I was a harbinger of death and destruction. I was a horseman of the showbiz apocalypse.

Another ambulance arrived, its lights flashing. I thought: you're too late, you missed Jimmy.

25

The next fourteen hours were a mess and I was awake for a lot of them.

From the window of my hotel room, I watched police cars come and go. In the crowd, tourists and locals came and went, supplementing the audience who'd originally paid to be there and wanted to see if there'd be any resolution to the drama that night. The locals must've worried about what impact the event would have on their businesses. There was a killer in their midst. He could strike again. Or not. He established a pattern. Or none whatsoever. The newspapers and TV stations had yet to shape this into a narrative. The event was still a question, a rupture, a gap.

I found Sharpe's phone in my pocket. It was my phone now. I tried Rose. It was important for her to know. Besides Danny Pantero, she was the person with whom Jimmy shared the deepest connection. Her home phone rang until her machine answered. The time difference meant she would have still been at the Ambrosia. I didn't want to leave a message. As much I needed to talk to someone, to quell the chaos in my head, I didn't yet know who I could tell or what I could say. Everything was still so indeterminate, everything except for the blood I saw spray across that curtain.

I tried to call Winston Sharpe instead. I wanted to let him know how I enjoyed the little show he'd arranged. His office line went straight to voicemail. This time I left a message.

"It's Nathan. It's . . . 11:14 p.m. I just wanted to tell you I saw Jimmy Wynn die tonight. Good show. Bravo. We've made history. Bravo, you fascist dirtbag." I continued in this vein until the beep signaled that my time had run out.

I pulled the curtains closed and climbed into bed. I tried so hard to sleep, but my imaginary horror show of dead Sifredis and dead Mom and Dad and dead me was replaced by the bona fide snuff reel of Jimmy Wynn. I felt like most of me was still in the theatre, watching the photographer stride with remarkable grace to his position in front of the stage. I remember how Jimmy turned toward him, like he was expecting me to be there, like I was about to hand him that big bunch of roses he'd asked for.

I was not quite asleep and not quite awake when the cell phone trilled me back into the world. There was enough light creeping into the room around the edges of the curtains to suggest it was morning. I answered the phone. The voice was Sharpe's.

"Mr. Grant, we will begin this conversation after you have found a newspaper and read it carefully. When you call me back, I want you to tell me what you have read."

I took his order — a bad habit, I admit. On the elevator to the lobby, I thought: is this a ruse to send me into Harris's line of fire? This place was all right but I wanted to die in a nicer hotel. Down in the lobby there was a stack of the *Niagara Reader*. I grabbed one and sat down in a chair. There was a photograph of the Maple Leaf, the sky bright blue overhead. The headline underneath: Terror in Local Theatre. The first line of the piece stated what I already knew: "Chester Howe, a local performer and theatrical producer, was shot and injured by an unknown gunman last night while an audience watched Howe onstage in a popular Canadian musical."

The next few lines rehashed the events in more detail. Descriptions of the gunman were vague. Apparently, he was a shadowy presence to everyone in the room, devoid of any distinguishing characteristics besides his sunglasses and the general impression that he was wearing an oversized jacket. The interview subjects knew of no reason why anyone would attack Howe. A policeman said that judging by the gunman's careful preparations and stealthy getaway, it was likely that he'd specifically targeted Howe. Nevertheless, security would be bolstered at assorted Niagara area attractions for the time being.

Then came the wrinkle. "Officials could not confirm that Howe had been taken to a local hospital. Paramedics from nearby Prince Philip Hospital who arrived on the scene were informed that Howe had already been taken away by an ambulance that had not been officially dispatched. The origin of the ambulance that retrieved the injured Howe has yet to be determined. No emergency health care facilities in the Niagara region either in Canada or the U.S. have reported receiving the injured actor. Howe's whereabouts could not be discerned at press time, though witnesses at the scene described his injuries as critical."

I thought: it was a phony ambulance. I thought: you sneaky bastard, you're incredible.

I called back Sharpe. "He's gone, isn't he?"

"Apparently so. I am not at liberty to discuss more than generalities on this matter, Mr. Grant. What happened last night was not what we expected. I am still receiving information on the matter but it seems as if there was a competing project."

"I don't understand."

"Mine is not the only organization devoted to this particular cause. Others participate in these ongoing activities, though there are obviously differences in strategy and intent. For example, you are aware of the incident involving your contact John Sifredi and his wife. Our intelligence indicates the operation to remove him from play was Mafia-driven. Not that a centralized Mafia organization exists any more — we suspect a consortium of several cells. The cell is the new paradigm, Nathan. More cells mean more competition. But I believe competition strengthens us all."

This was clearly a load of crap. "You people can't even keep a conspiracy together."

"I don't like that word. It implies groupthink, conformity, conservative behaviour. I believe in the value of individuality. If not for individual action, this society would never advance. As the editor of *The Betsey* I believe this maxim more than ever. It has been more important for me to maintain my individual autonomy within the organization and allow my staff to function independently. Of course, as editor I have the opportunity to manage information as I see fit, but I prefer to let others act of their own accord rather than direct their actions. The whole operation runs much more efficiently that way."

I thought: is he telling me Daphne didn't know about all this? I thought: if that's the case, this guy really is as efficient as everyone says.

"If your friend Mr. Wynn was in fact acting alone and not in concert with another organization, then I admire his ingenuity. He's a fascinating character, isn't he? Frankly, he's provided you with a superior ending to your article than the one I had devised. Kudos. Of course, you'll have to obscure some of the details when you write the piece. Information will have to be managed."

"I'm not writing it."

There was silence on the line for once.

"I'm not," I repeated.

"Do we have an outstanding issue, Mr. Grant?"

"You said you were going to kill my family. And Jimmy. And me. And some other people. I can't begin to know how much damage and misery you and your people have caused. And for what? To cover for whichever one of you really killed the president? Or to make it so it doesn't matter who did it or why or —"

"If I could interrupt your lecture for a moment, I would like to tell you — what's that? Oh, right. Thank you, Alison. Nathan, I have to go into a meeting. I am very much looking forward to your draft."

"Don't you dare hang —"

Up. He hung up.

*  *  *

I checked out of the hotel and took a bus to Toronto. By that afternoon, I was home in Fairview. My parents were good about me staying over. I told them that my comedian story had led me back to Toronto but there'd been a problem with my immigration status and I wouldn't be able to get back to New York for a while — I didn't specify how long. What I'd told them wasn't exactly a lie so it was best to be vague.

Over the next week, I saw several stories in the local press about the terror in the theatre. Since Chester Howe's body never turned up, some people speculated that the first paramedics had conspired with the killer to cover up the crime by disposing of the corpse right away, perhaps by dumping it into the river. Several witnesses had noted, like I had, that an extra paramedic had left the theatre and this man was thought to be the gunman. Others thought that all this was crazy talk, arguing that Chester Howe had been collected by a team of legitimate paramedics but then been misidentified at the hospital. This line of reasoning inspired several earnest articles about how the misplacement of patients was a growing problem within Canada's overstressed health-care system. No one suggested that the paramedics were actors working in conjunction with a gunman who would have described the event as an act of illusioneering. Nor did anyone liken the event to a similar one that had taken place several years earlier during a

New York stage appearance by David Maher. I certainly would have, but none of the authors of these articles called me for my opinion.

Even though my period of living incommunicado was over, I maintained my low profile, mostly because my head continued to spin at an alarming velocity. I tried to write about where I'd been but didn't know how to begin. I was afraid to put it on paper. I distracted myself with other tasks, like checking my e-mail. I found several messages from Daphne marked high priority. They shifted in tone from concerned to frustrated, then onward to mollified. "Winston tells me there's something 'major' going on with your piece," she wrote in the last one. "I wish I'd been better informed about developments but everyone knows he likes surprises. I took it off the schedule for the September issue so the pressure's off but please let me know what's going on when you get the chance. Everything okay?" I thought: she cares about my welfare. I thought: well, she cares about my story, but she might care about my welfare, too.

There were two messages from Colin. The first said: "Missed you in Vegas. Waste of time — false lead. Sharpe wanted sidebar for your feature — he's v. excited." The second said: "Presume you heard about Sifredis. Back in NY on Sharpe's orders. Delegation story officially scrapped. Ben said Immigration nearly arrested you. All v. mysterious. Explain your adventure."

I didn't reply yet, unsure of what to say. However, I did get in touch with a few people. Lance was apparently under the misapprehension that I was already back in New York — along with the photograph of my parents that I had kept on the fridge, several batches of leftovers had also been removed. I presumed whoever had stolen the photograph had investigated the Tupperware situation. Not wanting to alarm Lance, I told him it had all been delicious.

Rose apologized for not coming clean about David's scheme

"This whole thing got to be such a mess. If Bud hadn't been around to clean it up, I don't know where we'd be."

I took her for sincere and asked her not to lie so much the next time she saw me.

"You have my word, hon."

After I hung up, I realized I still hadn't tried the brambleberry pie. I didn't remember seeing any brambleberries when I was locked in the storage room.

I let Ben know I was visiting my parents and would explain more at some unspecified later date. This would be the same date when I would be able to walk outside without scanning my neighbours' rooftops for snipers, when I would know what to do about Jimmy's story.

Then one morning the doorbell rang and my mother called me up from the basement. It was a courier asking for my signature. The package had come from Los Angeles. The first thing that fell out when I opened it was a greeting card. On the cover was a squiggly cartoon man with a forlorn expression sitting under a tiny raincloud. "Heard you're feeling under the weather," it said inside. "Get well soon!" It was signed by Sparkle. Ever helpful, the publicist had included another of David's business cards. "Please call him!" she'd written on the back.

And so I did. And we started talking about Jimmy and how it would be. I realized there were things we could do to win back the advantage from Winston Sharpe.

The next afternoon, I had a call from Ben. "How long does it take you to drive from your suburban hellhole to downtown Toronto?"

"About forty-five minutes. Why?"

"Stink's playing the Palladium. Meet me outside at eight."

I got there right on time. I knew the concert hall — it was a fancy old place just off the Danforth. The last band I saw there was Meat Locker three years before. There was a familiar throng of punk kids loitering outside. The Canadian variety looked much the same as the kind down south.

Ben and I hugged. For the first time I liked it when he called me bro.

"How's it going with the band?"

"Amazing," he said. "Dirk nearly attacked Von with a friggin' straight razor last night in Detroit. I think it might go all the way over the edge tonight."

"You mean kill him?"

"Well," Ben groaned, "not *kill* him. But something bad."

"And you have cameras at the ready."

"This is the reason why cameras were invented."

Ben ushered me past the security personnel into the back of the hall. He told me a friend of ours was holding a beer for me. I was just as pleased to see Colin but he wasn't a hugging kind of guy. We exchanged a manly handshake instead.

"Didn't expect to see you up here," I said.

"Ben told me you were in exile," he said dryly. "I wanted first-hand confirmation."

I thought: ask him what he knows. I thought: it can wait. Colin volunteered most of the information I wanted without me having to ask. The Nevada Delegation story had led nowhere. Besides Sifredi, none of the old-timers he'd found were willing to talk and that was before John and Marla were killed. He'd gotten the cold shoulder all over Vegas: "What is with these show business people?" he asked me. He'd only come out to Nevada because Sharpe said he wanted as much corroboration as possible and knew "Mr. Grant would be busy with other matters." Daphne cut the trip short, though even she had been unable to adequately explain why he'd been sent there in the first place. That was the last he'd heard about it all. He'd moved onto the column he planned in the first place, which included some sad new details about poor ol' Nathaniel Fontainebleu.

"You probably wanted to get back to Daphne, anyway."

"Why's that?"

"Aren't you seeing her?"

"Who told you this?"

"Ben."

Colin had an exasperated look. "Daphne and I went out for drinks twice before she decided we were both — and these are her words — 'too focused on our careers' to become involved romantically. I didn't like hearing it but I appreciated her straightforwardness. I'm relieved it hasn't had any detrimental effect on our working relationship."

"Oh." I did a poor job of concealing how pleased I was to hear this.

"Oh," repeated Colin. "I see." He smiled. "I can put in a word for you."

"Yeah. Maybe that would be good." I remembered the picture of Daphne that I'd cut out of the magazine so carefully. To my surprise, the image in my mind was suddenly supplanted by the *33RPM* photo of Rose in the Ambrosia. I would have to sort all this out at some later date.

"I hope you're not banking on a long-distance relationship," Colin added. "When are you coming back?"

"Soon. Real soon."

"So what happened with your comedian?"

The punishingly loud beginning of Stink's set allowed me to skirt Colin's question. It wasn't yet time to ask him to participate in what David and I were devising, though I expected that he would find the chance to help create a new conspiracy greatly appealing. Onstage, Von was in fine form, chugging champagne from a giant magnum and spewing it over the front rows. Dirk shot daggers at him (metaphorically speaking for now) from his side of the stage. Ben's camera crews stayed close to both men. I enjoyed this concert more than any of the others I'd seen. Maybe it was because I was not so distracted by sex-bomb operatives or sadistic clean freaks. Maybe it was because I had a newfound respect for the professionalism of these overgrown adolescents as they blasted through the same two-chord wonders they played with such enthusiasm night after night, regardless of how tired or sadistic or sad or bored they really felt. Maybe it was because this show ended with Dirk chasing Von around the stage with his guitar raised over his head, clearly ready to clobber the life out of the singer. After he snagged his foot on a cable, Dirk and the guitar crashed into an ugly heap. The audience took it for schtick and cheered for more but the band was done, and not only for the night.

As I drove home, I thought about the general contours of the article that David and I had discussed. David left it up to me to supply a lot of the finer details before Winston Sharpe came back into the picture. I would have to decide which version of Jimmy's story to tell and decide if it had a pattern or no pattern at all. David had even left it up to me whether to involve him in the story — the illusioneer's presence would create other ramifications. For days after I arrived back in Fairview, I would look at my notes, interview transcripts, and artifacts from the Berman files and wonder what it must've felt like for James Saddlecreek to watch his own pile of Cannon fodder burn. It couldn't have felt so bad if he had done it twice. But my way out of the situation couldn't be that simple or that drastic. I would need more finesse. That night, I dreamed about a Nathan with finesse and I woke up feeling hopeful for the first time in a while.

There was another courier in the morning. This time the package was larger, though the contents of the box were mostly Styrofoam packing. There was a record, too. On the cover, Jimmy Wynn participated in a frenzy of hat-related hilarity. In a quartet of pictures, he wore an Englishman's derby, a fireman's helmet, a gumshoe's fedora, and an Indian chief's headdress. Across the middle of the record, yellow letters said: *Who Does This Guy Think He Is, Anyways?*

There was no note attached and the only thing inside the sleeve was the vinyl disc. I took it over to my dad's stereo. I silently blessed him for keeping the record player in working order. I put the record on the turntable, clicked on the motor, and lowered the needle down on the first track. After the crackle came this:

"A guy walks into a bar. 'Ow,' he says, 'that hurt.'"

# ACKNOWLEDGEMENTS

Thanks to Jack David and Jen Hale at ECW, David Gee for the cover and his valuable comments, and Paul Quarrington, Richard Scrimger, Andre Mayer, and Kevin Connolly for their time, support, and encouragement. Large portions of this book were written at the Gibraltar Point Centre for the Arts on Toronto Island and in my friend Philip Tsui's apartment. Thanks also to the (mostly) anonymous people who first uttered a few of the jokes in these pages, like the one about the hunter who gets sodomized by the bear. That kills me.

JASON ANDERSON is a Calgary native who lives in Toronto. His arts journalism appears in *The Globe and Mail, Toro, Saturday Night, Toronto Life*, and *eye Weekly*. His fiction has appeared in *Taddle Creek* and *THIS* Magazine. The debut album by his band The Two Koreas — *Main Plates and Classic Pies* — was released in the spring of 2005. *Showbiz* is his first novel.